"Mary Jo Putney is a gifted writer with an intuitive understanding of what makes romance work."
—Jayne Ann Krentz

"Putney's writing is clear as crystal and smooth as silk."
—*Booklist*

PRAISE FOR
The Burning Point

"*The Burning Point* is sure to light a fire." —Debbie Macomber

"Passionate . . . The author has created a realistic, well-crafted story, laced with elements of suspense and mystery and featuring sympathetic protagonists whose biggest mistake was marrying too young."
—*Publishers Weekly*

"Powerhouse novelist Mary Jo Putney explodes on the contemporary scene with an emotionally wrenching and dramatically intense story. She tackles a very difficult subject with insight and compassion. Exceptionally powerful reading!" —*Romantic Times* (4$^{1}/_{2}$ stars, a Top Pick)

"Ms. Putney is one of the very best authors who excels at historical romances. Now she's crafted her first contemporary and fans of both genres will be delighted to learn that her incredible talent for compelling characterization and original premises comes through on every page. She takes a taboo issue not normally found in a romance and, with touching sensitivity, creates a poignant tale about forgiveness and the awesome power of love to heal all wounds. I could not put it down."
—*Rendezvous*

"Fascinating." —*The Romance Reader* (4 hearts)

"A winner." —Harriet Klausner

continued on next page . . .

Christmas Revels

Mary Jo Putney

BERKLEY BOOKS, NEW YORK

B

A Berkley Book
Published by The Berkley Publishing Group
A division of Penguin Putnam Inc.
375 Hudson Street
New York, New York 10014

PRINTING HISTORY
Berkley trade paperback edition / November 2002

Visit our website at
www.penguinputnam.com

Library of Congress Cataloging-in-Publication Data

Putney, Mary Jo.
Christmas revels / Mary Jo Putney.—Berkley trade paperback ed.
p.   cm.
Contents: A holiday fling—The Christmas cuckoo—Sunshine for Christmas—The
Christmas tart—The Black Beast of Belleterre.
ISBN 0-425-18621-0
1. Christmas stories, American.   2. Love stories, American.   I. Title.

PS3566.U83 C49   2002
813'.54—dc21
2002021563

PRINTED IN THE UNITED STATES OF AMERICA

10 9 8 7 6 5 4 3 2 1

To Gail Fortune,
an editor who does her best to make sure that
every day is a holiday for her authors.

Contents

A Holiday Fling

My full-length contemporary romance The Spiral Path *had a couple of appealing secondary characters who were single and a little lonely, so they immediately popped into my mind when I decided to do a contemporary Christmas story for this collection. Greg Marino and Jenny Lyme are both in show business, and they're both genuinely nice people who love their work. But he's American and she's English, he's behind the camera while she's in front, and when their paths had crossed a dozen years before, their careers swiftly took them away from each other. Can this time be different?*

One

The Tithe Barn Community Center
Upper Bassett
Gloucestershire, England

"THE Carthage Corporation wants *how* much?" Jenny Lyme blinked, thinking she must have misheard.

The head of the community center council, who happened to be her mother, Alice Lyme, repeated the figure. There were far too many zeros.

"Property costs the earth here in the Cotswolds, even in an out-of-the-way corner like Upper Bassett. Throw in the barn's age, and the price goes even higher." Patricia Holmes, third member of the council present—and Jenny's big sister—scribbled figures on a tablet. "Even if we sell every seat to every performance of the Revels, there is no possible way we can raise enough." She pushed the tablet away with a frown. "Resign yourself to the fact that some rich London stockbroker will buy the place and tart it up for use three or four weekends a year."

"No!" Jenny said vehemently. "The tithe barn is the heart and soul of Upper Bassett. Without it, our village identity will wither away."

"You're right. Many of my fondest memories occurred here." Her mother sighed. "But the lease is expiring, Carthage is determined to sell, and we simply don't have the money to meet their price."

"Do you think a bank would give us a loan using the property as collateral?" Jenny suggested without much hope.

"That might buy us some time, but even in a good year, the center only breaks even." Patricia pushed her glasses higher on her nose. She was a schoolteacher, and the gesture was very effective at convincing her classes that she meant business. "We will never be able to make enough money to pay off a loan, even assuming some bank officer is demented enough to give us one."

Jenny rose from the battered chair and crossed to the door of the small office. The ancient music ensemble was practicing on the stage at the far end of the barn. She had discovered her passion for acting on that stage, and she couldn't bear thinking that soon no more local children would have such an opportunity to perform, play, and build lifelong friendships. "If my career were in better shape, I'd donate the money myself."

"Your career is fine," Patricia said loyally. "You can't expect to go from one smashing series right to another, but you're still working."

"Even if you could afford it, that might not be the best thing for the village," Alice added. "This is a community center—it needs to be saved through collective action, not by one successful woman raiding her retirement savings."

Jenny supposed they were both right. Her career was having a slow spell but it wasn't dead yet, and her mother made a good point that the center belonged to all of them and should be saved by joint efforts. That was why Jenny had stepped in to produce and direct the upcoming Revels, combining the considerable local talent with her own skills and connections to create a professional-quality show. She was even performing as Lady Molly, the female lead.

But it wasn't enough. "The Revels are going to be marvelous. If only there was a way to use the production to generate more money—" She stopped as an idea struck.

"You've got that dangerous look in your eyes, Jennifer," Alice said warily. "Care to enlighten us?"

Jenny turned back to the office and leaned against the door frame as two identical pairs of blue eyes regarded her. The women of the Lyme family looked ridiculously alike, with dark hair, pale, flawless Welsh complexions, and deep blue eyes. She hoped that she and Patricia would age as gracefully as their mother was doing. "This isn't dangerous. It just occurred to me that we could film the Revels and sell videotapes of the performance. Get it reviewed or mentioned in some of the London papers.

If we do a really good job, maybe we could sell broadcast rights to the BBC for next Christmas."

There was a thoughtful silence while her mother and sister considered the suggestion. "We could set up a website and link with folklore and performing groups, but we'd have to sell a huge number of tapes to raise the kind of money we need, and we only have a few months," Patricia observed. "Selling broadcast rights would give us a larger chunk of money, but the production would have to be high quality, not just someone's husband with his video camera."

Alice said, "Perhaps Jenny has cameramen friends who could be persuaded to contribute their time to a good cause."

"It's very short notice." Jenny ran down the list of camera operators she knew well enough to impose on. Patricia was right that they needed someone who was first rate. Someone whose name would add value to the production.

Greg Marino.

With some reluctance, she accepted that he was far and away the best choice. Winner of the previous year's Oscar for best cinematography, he was a brilliant director of photography who brought texture and nuance into every film he shot. "I worked with Greg Marino once. He would be perfect, but he's an American and insanely busy. I doubt I'd be able to even locate him, much less persuade him to drop everything and come to England on a moment's notice."

"He shot *The Centurion*, didn't he? And that big fantasy movie that was such a hit last year?" With a sister in the film business, Patricia kept up with such things. "His work is wonderful. If he's a friend of yours, it's certainly worth asking."

Not a friend; a former lover. Would that be a plus or a minus? They hadn't seen each other in years, but they'd parted amiably and kept in touch, in a casual kind of way.

She pictured Greg, with his rangy American build and a smile that always made her smile in return. He'd helped her through a very bad time. If he could be persuaded to shoot their performance, he could transform the Revels from fun into Art, and maybe save the community center in the process. "I'll try to run him down when I return to London, but don't get your hopes up. He's very much in demand."

But her pulse quickened at the thought of having a reason to call him.

Two

GREG Marino emerged from his bed yawning. He was too groggy and disoriented to figure out what time it was in Australia, but his body sure thought it should still be there rather than in Los Angeles.

By the time he'd showered and shaved, a pot of steaming coffee had dripped through. He poured a mug full, sending silent thanks to the friend who had stocked his refrigerator with perishables the day before. People who made movies did a lot of coming and going, and he and his buddies took care of each other.

Yawning again, he rubbed the head of the shiny gold Academy Award that sat incongruously between the toaster and the drip coffeemaker. He liked keeping old Oscar there in a nice, visible spot. The statuette was his symbol of having made something of himself, contrary to the expectations of people who'd known him when he was a kid.

Taking his cell phone in case someone called, he stepped through the sliders onto his balcony. After swiping at the chair to remove the layer of urban dust, he sank into it and propped his feet on the railing. The view over the apartment complex courtyard wasn't thrilling, but it was home.

For the thousandth time, he told himself that he really needed to go house hunting. He could afford a house now, and it would be nice to have a larger place. One with a view. But house hunting took time, and it was easier to walk away from an apartment for months on end than it would be to walk away from a house.

Having reached his usual conclusions, he set the topic aside for another day. One when he wasn't so jet-lagged.

He slouched deeper in his chair and sipped at the scalding coffee, enjoying the pleasant coolness of the December air. It had been blazing hot in the Land Down Under, but the filming had gone well. The raw, primitive scenery had been a cameraman's dream. The images he'd captured had made up for the spoiled behavior of the movie's two stars. Actors. Couldn't live with them, couldn't live without 'em.

In mid-January he would be off to Argentina for the biggest budget, highest profile film of his career, but he had nothing booked before then. Maybe after he finished the coffee he'd call his manager to see if anyone wanted him to shoot a commercial or two. Such jobs kept him busy between feature films, paid well, and often provided opportunities to try exciting new techniques.

The cell phone played the first few notes of "Für Elise." Wondering if a commercial had come looking for him, he answered, suppressing another yawn. "H'lo."

"Greg—is that you?"

Not his manager. The female voice was deliciously British and familiar, but surely it couldn't be . . . "Yep, it's me. Sorry if I'm slow, but who is this?" With his luck, she was probably a high-class aluminum siding saleswoman.

"Jenny Lyme."

"Jenny!" He came awake fast, amazed that his caller really was Jenny. As if he could have forgotten her. Trying not to sound like a slavering idiot, he said, "Nice to hear from you. Are you in Los Angeles? If you are, let me take you out to lunch."

Smart, witty, and down to earth, Jenny was the kind of actor who made up for the prima donnas. She was also drop-dead gorgeous—a brunette stunner who stood out even in a business where beautiful women were a dime a dozen.

Strange things could happen on a movie set, and Greg's brief fling with Jenny was proof. Ordinarily their relationship would never have gone beyond casual chat, but she had been weeping her heart out over an actor boyfriend who'd thrown her over in favor of a high-profile affair with a famous French actress twenty years his senior.

Greg had been there with a sympathetic shoulder and a willingness to do anything that would make her feel better. Though he hadn't been able to cure Jenny's broken heart, he'd done his best, and even coaxed a few smiles from her. In return, he had acquired some indelible memories to warm his nights.

Her rich chuckle interrupted his reverie. "Sorry, no, I'm in London."

Damn. "What can I do for you?"

"I have a . . . a proposition for you."

He blinked, then ordered his libido to quit looking for double meanings. "Are you turning director and looking for a cinematographer?"

"Not exactly. But something like that."

"Yes?"

She drew a breath that could be heard a third of the way round the globe. "This is a charity project. I grew up in a village in the Cotswolds—that's west of London and very pretty—and I still have a home there. The parish tithe barn was turned into a community center just after the war, and it's a wonderful place for plays and music practice and yoga classes and pottery and all manner of amusements. It's the heart of Upper Bassett."

"Upper Bassett?" Hound visions came to mind.

"To distinguish it from Lower Bassett and Bassett on the Wold," she explained with a twinkle in her voice. "To make a long story as short as possible, the village owns only the lease on the barn. The actual owner is a big soulless corporation that wants to sell the property in six months when the lease expires. Property in Gloucestershire is staggeringly expensive, and the price they're asking is far beyond our means. If the village wants to keep it, we have to raise a lot of money fast."

He received more than his share of requests for his hard-earned money, but he was willing to oblige Jenny. "Where should I send the check?"

"That's awfully generous of you, Greg, but I'm not calling to ask for money." For an actress who made her living playing the sexy, good-hearted girl next door, Jenny sounded shy. "I'm on the community center board, so I decided to stage a Christmas mummers' play to raise money. I've persuaded some of my friends to lend a hand, and I think we'll draw a good audience for the performances."

"But not good enough?"

"I'm afraid not. We'll never make enough if we rely on ticket sales, so in six months Upper Bassett will have no community center. This may not sound very important, but community is what makes life worth living, and it can be very fragile. I don't want to see the fabric of my native village come unraveled."

He backtracked. "What's a mummers' play?"

"Oh, sorry. It's one of those British things. Medieval plays, usually a combination of religious themes grafted onto ancient fertility rites. Groups of mummers used to go around giving short performances for begging money. That's largely died out, but the plays are still performed on occasion. It's quite a jolly tradition."

A light dawned. "I saw a show like that in Boston once. Lots of singing and dancing and melodrama. It was a great evening."

"Ours will be, too. A couple of days ago, it occurred to me that the best way to make more money from our Revels is to film the show so we can sell videos and if we're lucky, license it to the telly."

"I think I see where you're going with this, but there are plenty of great cameramen in England. Can't you draft one of them?"

"Probably, but you're my first choice. You're known for being able to do marvelous work quickly, and your name will add value to the project." Her voice turned portentous. "The Upper Bassett Holiday Revels, filmed by Academy Award–winning cinematographer Gregory Marino."

"That's shameless flattery." He grinned. "Keep it up."

She had the sexiest chuckle in the Northern Hemisphere. "Very well. This production will be a bit of a hodgepodge, so we'll need your talent as well as your reputation. It won't be easy to make my Morris dancers and children's choir look dramatic instead of like amateur night. That's why I thought of you."

He toyed with the handle of his mug, thinking that it sounded like a hoot—the kind of wildly improvised project that he'd loved doing in his student days. But he hadn't been a student in almost two decades, and he was tired to the bone. "You're talking this Christmas, aren't you? Like, in the next week or so? I just got back from Australia yesterday and I'm in no mood to climb on another airplane and spend the holidays with strangers."

"You only just got home? Sorry—I thought you'd had more time to recover from the last job." She hesitated. "I know this is a lot to ask, but if you're willing, you could be the making of this project. What would it take to persuade you to come over?"

"Your fair white body," he muttered under his breath as he sipped some coffee.

"That's negotiable," she said without missing a beat.

He swallowed the wrong way and went into a coughing fit. When he could breathe again, he said, "Jeez, Jenny, you shouldn't make jokes like that when I'm drinking my first cup of coffee of the day."

"Sorry." She sounded stricken. "That was a silly comment. I'm serious about this project, but not to the point of giving my all for queen and country."

"Sleeping with a cameraman is a sacrifice no one would ask of you," he agreed. "How long do you think this would take? I assume you want the production to be magical and exciting and intimate, not just a static record of a stage show."

"Exactly." Sensing that he was weakening, she continued, "If you're willing, I'll buy you a plane ticket and you can stay in my guest room. This would only take a week or so. You can be home by Christmas, though if you'd like to try the holidays English style, it would be lovely to have you. You can borrow my family if you want marvelous people who will simultaneously make you feel welcome and drive you mad."

He chuckled. "Sounds just like my family." The sprawling Marino home in Ohio would be full of kids and food and relatives who thought of him as the beloved oddball. They were proud of him, but he was a goose out of water, and a target for his mother, aunts, and sisters, all of whom wanted him to marry a nice, normal girl, not a Hollywood type, and settle down. He spent every Christmas fending off their good intentions. Mostly it was fun.

But Jenny's job sounded like fun, too. How long had it been since he'd done any filming purely for the pleasure of it? He had been working like a lunatic for years, first taking any project he was offered to build up his credits, then, as his reputation grew, doing movies back to back to consolidate what he'd achieved.

It would be wonderfully relaxing to do a project where multimillion-dollar budgets weren't resting on his shoulders. On the minus side, working with Jenny would be a mixed blessing. He loved being around her, and unless she had changed—and she didn't seem to have—she didn't have a snobbish bone in her.

Unfortunately, he liked her a little too well. Prom queens—did they have them in English schools?—didn't pair off with oddball technogeeks like him no matter how many years had passed. Hell, she was a friend and former lover of Kenzie Scott, superstar and possibly the handsomest man alive, while Greg was Joe Average at best. Their brief affair had been a fluke. She had made it clear that he was being offered a guest room, nothing more. If he recalled his trade gossip correctly, she was currently involved with some rich international businessman. Unavailable.

But he was good at what he did, and quite capable of working with a woman he wanted and couldn't have. Shooting Morris dancers—what *were* Morris dancers?—and Christmas in England would be a nice change from his real life. Afterward he could fly home to Ohio. There was always leftover turkey when his mother was in charge of a kitchen. "Okay, Jenny, you've got a deal."

"Wonderful!" The enthusiasm in her voice was enough to banish his regrets over more jet lag. "Do you have personal video equipment you'd like to use, or shall I rent some here? And if so, what would you like?"

"I'll bring my digital camera, but are you sure you want to use video? Film is probably better from a commercial point of view."

"True, but we can't afford the extra time and money film would take."

"If I use 16mm instead of 35mm, the shooting time will be about the same as video. Don't worry about renting anything—I'll take care of getting the equipment. It's true that postproduction will take longer with film, but you'll have a finished product that will be easier to sell to TV, and will look good on DVD as well as video."

"I defer to your professional judgment. After all, that's why I wanted you." Her rich voice warmed. "Thank you so much, Greg. You shan't regret this."

He was sure she was right. To have regrets, there had to be a significant stake. This was just a little charity project. No consequences. Right?

Right.

JENNY hung up the phone. "I can't believe he agreed," she said to her companion.

"*Mrowrrrr.*"

"Don't look so smug, Plato. You may be a philosopher who always knows what's going to happen, but I'm not. It's a miracle Greg is even available, and I thought for sure he'd turn me down. He won an Oscar, for heaven's sake." Absently she stroked the gray cat's short plushy fur. "You think I'm idiotic. Right again. Why else would I be talking to a cat?"

Plato gave a lofty flick of his tail that said clearly that he was in perfect harmony with himself and simply couldn't understand human nerves.

Restlessly Jenny began to pace her living room. An actor's life was odd and irregular by normal standards. The good parts were very, very good. The bad parts were horrid. One of the worst bits was having many friends, yet too often being alone. She had achieved a fair amount of success as a television actress, and was generally considered by the British viewing public to be quite the glamour girl. Her appearance on a man's arm at a public event would enhance his reputation.

But being a famous man's wrist ornament didn't offer much for her. She stared out at the quiet West End street, where lights were beginning to shine mistily in the dusk. This near the winter solstice, days were short and nights were long. Very long, when one slept alone.

When had she begun to tire of glamour? Not during the first flush of success; she'd been giddily happy and made a fool of herself more than once. She had even believed men who said they loved her when what they really meant was that they wanted to bed her. There had been some good times, but usually she would care too much, and be left weeping.

Critically she studied her reflection in the darkened window. For an actress who was past her prime, she still looked rather well. A little rounder than her American counterparts, who tended to look like stick drawings, but few men minded that.

Though she had learned early that a pretty girl could usually get what she wanted, her no-nonsense mother made sure little Jenny didn't let that go to her head. Her looks were a gift in the genetic lottery for which she was grateful, but couldn't claim credit.

Talent was also a gift, source uncertain since everyone else in her family was normal. The only thing she could take personal credit for was the bloody hard work she'd put into her career, and the tenacity to keep going despite the chronic rejections that were part of a working actor's life.

"Do you think Greg and I might end up going to bed together? That would be rather nice."

Plato closed his golden eyes, bored. A bit of routine surgery in his youth had left him uninterested in gender politics.

Jenny drew heavy curtains against the encroaching night and crossed to the kitchen to make a pot of tea. She hadn't really been joking when she said that her "fair white body" was negotiable, and Greg's shock at her words was a little unflattering. Most men would have bantered with her, testing to see if she was serious, but Greg—Greg was different.

The American movie they'd worked on had been something of a disaster—her first and last foray into Hollywood. He had been a second assistant camera operator, while she was a nervous ingénue making her first feature film. The script was weak, the director was a bellowing sadist, and the leading lady hated sharing the screen with another female who was younger and prettier.

Jenny could have survived that, but she hadn't been able to handle the loss of a boyfriend she had hoped to marry. She had thought their relationship was rock solid, until the tabloids started running pictures of him and the French actress with whom he was having a torrid affair. The swine had been too much a coward to tell Jenny that he was tired of her, so he let the journalists do it for him. About the best thing that could be said of the experience was that her movie role called for her to cry a lot. That she had managed handily.

No, the best thing about that movie had been Greg. His sympathy and kindness had been achingly welcome at a time when she had been desperate for comfort.

Later she had felt guilty about using him to assuage the worst of her pain, but at the time she welcomed his lack of demands. He'd given her exactly what she wanted, with no strings attached. Just as their movie ended, she had received a heaven-sent BBC offer. Though she and Greg had planned to spend a quiet week at the beach recovering from the filming, instead he had cheerfully taken her to the airport and sent her off with a parting kiss and his best wishes. She flew home swearing never to return to Hollywood, and she hadn't. English show business had been much kinder to her.

The Christmas cards they exchanged always contained scrawled personal notes promising to get together when they were both in the same city and not too busy to socialize, but it never happened. Whenever she got his card—always a stunning photograph that he had taken himself— she would smile and wonder what might have happened if they had met when she wasn't suffering a broken heart. Greg was smart and funny and nice, with a rock solid steadiness that was increasingly attractive as the years—and the unreliable men—came and went.

But maybe there would never have been a right time. Not only did they live in different countries, but both were ambitious, committed to succeeding in a brutal industry. They had done well, particularly Greg, who had hit the top of his field while not yet forty. Good directors of photography could go on for decades, and Greg would.

Actresses had a much shorter shelf life. In the last year there had been two movie roles she had really wanted, but failed to win. Nor was she likely to find another television series as successful as *Still Talking,* since that had been one of the rare conjunctions of great writing, directing, and perfect casting. Her career had peaked, and the future held mostly playing character roles and mothers.

She wouldn't mind that, as long as she continued to work. Television offers still came in now and then, and she could do more theater work; stage makeup and distance from the audience could preserve the illusion of youth for years. But her days as a glamorous, sexy young thing were numbered.

Even if they hadn't been, she was tired of working so hard all the time. Eighteen-hour days, five A.M. calls, having to maintain her looks with the grim thoroughness of a pilot maintaining his airplane—sometimes she thought that digging ditches would be easier, though certainly less satisfying.

Plato twined around her ankles insinuatingly. "Are you saying it's supper time?" She bent and scratched his head. "If Greg and I decide to have a fling for old times' sake, you won't be able to sleep on the bed for a few nights."

The cat blinked his luminous golden eyes complacently. Even if he was briefly exiled from the bed, he would still be there after Greg left. "Mrrrowr?"

She smiled wryly and scooped him into her arms, carrying him toward the kitchen. Her career was in decline and her private life a desert, but feline hunger was eternal.

Three

GREG emerged wearily from customs at Heathrow. Rather than take Jenny up on her offer of a ticket, he had used his frequent flyer miles for a business-class seat that made the long flight from Los Angeles almost bearable. Since Jenny had said he'd be picked up, he glanced around, looking for a driver with a sign that said MARINO.

He was dodging around a woman when a familiar husky voice said, "Have I changed that much, Greg?"

Startled, he looked down and saw Jenny's vivid blue eyes under a stylish drooping hat. Her shining dark hair was pulled back and tied with a scarf that matched her blue and green sweater, and she wore little if any makeup. The effect was casually elegant, in an unobtrusive way that wouldn't draw unwanted attention.

Damn, he'd forgotten the power of those eyes at close range. Just looking at her made his heart accelerate and his palms cramp. Afraid he was staring like an idiot, he said, "You do incognito pretty well."

"I try." She took his arm with easy friendliness and began guiding them through the airport crowds. "When you got your Oscar, I saw that the beard was gone, but you've taken off quite a chunk of hair since then, haven't you? This is a nice length for you."

He fought down the impulse to run his fingers self-consciously through the expensive haircut he had acquired the day before. Though handsome was out of his range, he could manage presentable. "I got tired of being taken for a terrorist. With straight black hair, brown eyes, and dark skin, I attracted way too much attention at airports."

"I can see how that would be a nuisance. You do look rather Mediterranean, which makes sense if your ancestors are Italian."

They had never discussed family backgrounds all those years ago. "Only my great-grandfather was Italian. The rest of me is American mutt. The first Marino married an Irish girl, their son fell for a Lithuanian, my mother is Scottish and Norwegian, and there's some Cherokee in there somewhere, too."

"Americans are so *interesting*. I'm boring old English with a bit of Welsh."

"No woman who can talk to anyone about anything is ever boring."

She glanced up, pleased and surprised. "That's one of the nicest compliments I've ever received."

"I suppose being told you're gorgeous must get old."

She shrugged, some of her brightness dimmed. "Looking good is part of my business. A tool of the trade. Now let's escape from this hive."

Towing his wheeled suitcase, he followed Jenny into a chilly, overcast morning. Yup, he was in England, and Jenny's lush hand-knit sweater was not merely for decorative purposes.

Her car turned out to be a sleek, classy S-type Jaguar. He wondered if she'd picked the blue color to enhance her eyes.

After they stowed his luggage, she beeped the doors open. "Mind the dragon."

"I beg your pardon?" He bent to climb into the car, and found a huge, snarling dragon head glaring at him from the passenger seat. "You brought a chaperone?"

Jenny laughed as she knelt on the driver's seat and transferred the head to the backseat. "Sorry, I should have moved this earlier, but I was running late. I've been borrowing costumes for our production. Traditionally mummers wore disguises, often just strips of fabric or paper sewn all over regular clothing. Rather like a giant ragged chicken. Since we want spectacle, I drafted my friend Will, who's a set designer. He found all kinds of splendid costumes in theatrical attics."

Greg settled into the passenger seat, feeling weird to be on the left side of the car and not have a steering wheel in front of him. "You don't mind messing with the play's authenticity?"

"This is folk art, not Shakespeare. There are hundreds of regional variations, and they evolved over time. Upper Bassett has a very old tradition of mummers' plays, so I cobbled together some original scripts and tossed in whatever else I thought would make the production amusing." She settled into her seat, her legs shapely in well-tailored navy slacks. "I do hope you're not horribly allergic to cats. If you are, I'll have to book you into an inn instead of my cottage."

"I haven't an allergy to my name." For which Greg was grateful; the closer he stayed to Jenny, the better. "I love cats. There were more cats than kids in the house where I grew up. I'd have a couple now if I didn't travel so much."

"Oh, good. Since that's the case, would you mind if I let Plato out? He finds his carrier demeaning. He's a good fellow and won't cause trouble."

"By all means free the philosopher," Greg said cordially.

Jenny reached between the bucket seats to lift a padded carrier from the floor. When she opened it, a large gray cat oozed onto the console between the seats and regarded Greg balefully. He had a massive head and attitude to spare.

Since male cats could be possessive about female owners, Greg realized he had better try to make friends with this one. He held out his hand for the cat to sniff. "Pleased to meet you, Plato. If I'd known, I would have brought a piece of the salmon I had for dinner somewhere around Greenland."

A pink tongue ran over his fingertips, raspy as a wood file. Drawing on a childhood surrounded by felines, Greg began scratching Plato's head, adjusting tempo and pressure until the cat closed his eyes and began to purr. "He rumbles like a lawn mower."

Plato walked into his lap—heavily—turned three times, then lay down, his chin on Greg's knee. "I seem to have passed inspection."

"I'm impressed." Jenny snapped her seat belt shut. "Usually Plato sneers at passengers and sprawls across the backseat."

"He probably doesn't like sharing with dragons." Greg settled back, watching Jenny from the corner of his eye as she expertly maneuvered the car out of the airport and onto the motorway. He had a phenomenal memory for images, and one whole mental file folder was devoted to Jenny. The dimples that flashed when she smiled from the heart. The shadowed hollow above her collarbone. The arc of dark lashes against her cheek as she had slept beside him.

But he had filmed and met plenty of beautiful women, and could picture none of them so well. Though his photographer's eye had made him susceptible to beauty, it was Jenny's self that made her special. Direct, funny, and intelligent, she would have been irresistible no matter what she looked like.

Resist her. He was here to work and have fun, not try to seduce his hostess. Her tycoon boyfriend would probably be underfoot most of the time. Or maybe he was off on some business trip, from which he'd return in a Rolls-Royce filled with roses to shower on Jenny's beautiful head.

But a man could dream . . .

GREG awoke from his doze to find that the motorway had been replaced by a narrow two-lane road winding through picturesque hills. The landscape was quilted with fields, hedges, and dry stone walls, and veils of mist transformed the scene into the setting for a sword and sorcery fantasy. It was a perfect backdrop for the world's most beautiful driver and a philosopher cat that had him pinned down as thoroughly as his seat belt.

Moving carefully so as not to disturb Plato, he straightened and rolled kinks out of his shoulders. "Sheep," he said happily. "Plump, photogenic sheep munching their way across the meadows. So much nicer than freeways and road rage."

Jenny smiled. "Whenever I come to the cottage, I can feel the knots unwinding mile by mile. The Cotswolds are far too trendy these days, yet there's still something timeless and authentic about these hills. They're magical. Of course, I'm prejudiced, having grown up here."

He studied her elegant profile. The droopy hat had been tossed into the backseat, where it hung rakishly from one of the dragon's ears. Her sculpted cheekbones might have been designed to make a photographer weep. "Definitely magical."

Jenny slowed the Jaguar at a sign declaring that they were entering the village of Upper Bassett. Moving at a sedate pace, they passed cottages and shops of honey-gold stone. At the small town square, they turned right in to Church Street.

"Saint Michael's and All Angels," Jenny said as they drove by a beautifully proportioned church that appeared to have been standing there since the beginning of time. A quarter of a mile beyond, she turned into a narrow driveway. "Home, sweet home. Frightfully twee, isn't it?"

Greg caught his breath. Framed by trees and with the square church tower in the middle distance, the cottage belonged in a calendar of England. Despite the season, pansies and other hardy flowers bloomed lavishly, defying the overcast sky. Warm-toned local stone was roofed with immaculately groomed thatch, and a thatch goose raced whimsically along the ridgepole, just out of reach of a pursuing thatch fox. "If twee means so lovely it's unreal, this is twee. An American's dream of a perfect cottage."

Her voice softened. "Church Cottage is so candy box pretty that some of my oversophisticated friends tease me about it, but I love the place anyhow. The cottage was practically falling down when I bought it. Years of work were needed to fix everything the way I wanted."

"Beauty should never be sneered at merely because it's obvious. How many spectacular sunsets has the world known? They're still beautiful." Greg draped Plato over his shoulder while he undid the seat belt with one hand and climbed from the car. "Is the inside equal to the outside?"

"Better—the plumbing and heating actually work. It's the chief advantage of having to do major renovations." Jenny swung from the car and collected Plato so Greg could take his bags from the trunk. "I imagine you'll want to attend this afternoon's rehearsal, but do you want to rest for a couple of hours first?"

He smothered a yawn. "Good idea. Maybe then I'll be awake enough to figure out what I have to work with."

The front door opened into a large living area with a stone fireplace, a dining table at one end, and a kitchen beyond. Exposed beams and worn, lovingly polished floors gave a sense of great age, while country antiques, mellow oriental rugs, and overstuffed furniture provided a comfort that reflected Jenny's own hospitable nature.

Plato came alive and scrambled down from his mistress's arms to head for his food dish. After Jenny fed the cat, she led Greg up the narrow staircase and along the short upstairs hall to a bedroom decorated in soothing shades of blue and white.

"Here's the guest room. I managed to tuck a small private bathroom under the eaves, but mind your head when you use it—the ceiling isn't very high. Let me know if you need anything. I'll wake you in time for a bite to eat before the rehearsal." She hesitated, then added, "And Greg— thanks for coming."

After she left, Greg studied the church tower that rose above the trees. He felt as if he'd fallen into an English movie. Miss Marple would amble by any minute now.

Yawning again, he pulled off his boots, jacket, and sweater, then crawled under the blue duvet, glad he'd agreed to come. The perfect woman, a perfect cottage, and a project that was purely for fun. The only shortcoming was that he was in the guest room.

But it was a *nice* guest room.

"GREG?" Jenny tapped on the door, then called his name again. Still no answer. Cautiously she opened the door and peered into the bedroom. Her guest was sprawled across the bed on his stomach, his dark hair tousled and his chin bristling with whiskers.

She studied him thoughtfully, unprepared for the rush of affection she felt. He was everything she remembered, and more. When they had worked together all those years ago, his appearance had been pleasant but undistinguished. Maturity had carved lines of humor and authority in his face. Even asleep, he looked like a man who was good at what he did, and comfortable with that fact.

The duvet had slid to his waist, revealing his T-shirt–clad torso. He had filled out nicely over the last dozen years. In his early twenties he'd been gangly, but years of handling heavy equipment had added muscle. Altogether, he was quite delectable, and very dear.

Get a grip, Jenny! She raised her voice. "Greg, it's time to get up. Unless you'd rather sleep all day and stay awake all night, of course."

His eyes opened—really, it wasn't fair to waste those long dark lashes on a man—and gave her a rueful smile. "Frankly I'd rather sleep, but I'd better try to adjust to local time." He swung his jeans-clad legs from the bed, looking appealingly disheveled. "I'll wash up and be right down."

She retreated, a little unnerved by how attractive she found him. Though she had known there was a chance they might fall into bed together for old times' sake, this felt—different. And she really didn't need a dented heart for Christmas.

Four

GREG took advantage of the compact but admirably modern bathroom to have a quick shower and shave. Then he unearthed his professional-grade digital video camera and went downstairs, where Jenny efficiently produced a platter of sliced meats and cheeses along with a salad, warm bread, and a tasty rice pilaf.

Greg was finishing his meal when Plato strolled by with a black rod topped with fluffy red feathers clutched in his mouth. Greg blinked. "Did I imagine that?"

Jenny grinned. "That's his buggy whip toy. It turns up all over the house. The red feathers go rather nicely with his gray fur, don't you think?"

"Absolutely. And I think I've fallen through the rabbit hole into Wonderland." He swallowed the last of his coffee with a sigh of pleasure. "With a great cottage and food like this, I don't see how you ever get guests to leave."

"I turn off the heat. That sends them packing." Jenny rose to her feet. "Sorry to rush you, but we need to get moving."

Greg stood and put his plate and coffee mug on the counter. "What's a tithe barn? I figure I should know if I'm working to save this one."

"The tithe system goes back to the Middle Ages. Ten percent of all grain and livestock had to be given to the local rector to support him, the church, and the poor of the parish. A tithe barn was used to store the produce collected." They headed out to the car, leaving Plato to guard the cottage.

As she drove toward the village, Jenny continued her history lesson. "After Henry VIII dissolved the monasteries, a lot of the tithe rights went into private hands. Just after the war, the owner of the ninety-nine–year lease on the barn bequeathed the lease to the local council with the requirement that it be turned into a community center."

"You said you grew up here. Was the tithe barn part of your childhood?"

"It was my favorite place in the world. The family homestead is only a five-minute walk away, so I was always at the barn. It's where I learned that I wanted to act. I was five years old and playing an angel in a Christmas pageant. As soon as I set foot on the stage, I *knew*. At first my parents laughed and said I'd grow out of it." Jenny grinned. "Soon they started praying that I would. But I acted every chance I could, and after my A levels I won a place at the Royal Academy of Dramatic Art."

Though her comment was offhand, Greg knew that RADA was probably the world's best-known theater school, and entrance was fiercely competitive. Jenny was as talented as she was beautiful.

She turned down a side street, then into a driveway. "And here we are."

The barn was larger than Greg expected, with stone walls and a slate roof sloping down from a ridgepole that was rather less than straight. Double doors were set in the middle, and a handful of small windows marched along the side. "A nice building, but it's seen better days."

"If you'd started life in the fourteenth century, you'd be a little shabby, too."

Greg examined it with increased interest. "It's seven centuries old?"

"The oldest bit is." She parked the Jaguar among trees where scattered gravel produced solid parking without the ugliness of a regular lot. "It has been enlarged several times. There's an addition on the back that holds a pottery studio and a small shop where local craftsmen can sell their work."

As Jenny climbed from the car, a shaft of afternoon sunlight broke through the clouds and turned the stone walls of the tithe barn into shades of glowing honey. The sight of Jenny silhouetted against the structure went directly into Greg's permanent file.

She leaned into the backseat and removed the dragon head and the rest of the costume. Beauty and the beast, another image to remember. He wanted to engrave every one of her movements, every expression, on his brain forever.

He took the dragon costume from her and carried it toward the barn. "It must be pretty dark inside with those small windows."

"Wait and see." She opened one of the double doors and ushered Greg through.

He paused, surprised. Wide skylights on the opposite side of the roof filled the interior with soft light even on a gray day, while massive wooden pillars and beams arched overhead like trees. "This is terrific. It reeks of authenticity."

To the right was a sizable stage, while the other end of the barn had been subdivided into smaller rooms. The central area was open, suitable for dancing, games, or folding chairs for stage performances. Despite the damp chill, he could feel how this place was used and loved. He set the dragon costume in a safe corner, then laid a hand on the nearest rough-hewn pillar, feeling the silky texture of the ancient wood. "No wonder Upper Bassett is determined to save the place."

"The National Trust, which has custody of most historic sites, isn't impressed by our barn because so many modifications have been made." Jenny's gaze went to the skylights. "They prefer structures that are completely original. But our tithe barn is alive, still part of the world. I'd hate to see it turned into a weekend home for some rich Londoner, which is probably what will happen if it's sold."

The stage contained a rugged, evocatively designed set with several levels. He walked to the edge and squinted up at the rafters. "The lights look pretty primitive."

"They are. That's why we need a lighting genius like you."

He snorted. "Even genius can't get great results with bad equipment. We need to get something that doesn't date back to the reign of Victoria."

"Be grateful we don't make you use torches." She ran lightly up the steps onto the stage. "The Ad Hoc Upper Bassett Players have been rehearsing for weeks. We'll have performances starting this weekend, up through Christmas Eve. We'll do whatever you need for your filming. I hope you'll have enough time."

"Sounds fine." With radiant Jenny in front of him, he'd agree to anything. "I'll bet you were a cute little angel."

"All five-year-old angels are cute, just as all brides are beautiful. It's a law of nature. Did you get a chance to read the script I sent?"

"I skimmed it." He followed her onto the stage, evaluating the space and making mental notes about lighting and camera placement. "Dragons, knights, and resurrection."

"Plus a choir of adorable little children underfoot. With them in the production, naturally all their parents, grandparents, uncles, and aunts will come."

She dropped into a fencing posture, Errol Flynn style. A crisp lunge with an imaginary sword showed her lithe figure to advantage. "Traditionally a mummers' play had a resurrection plot, a wooing, a sword dance, or some combination of the above. Saint George slaying the dragon is popular, too. Our version has a romantic young knight, Sir George, before he became a saint, plus the dragon, a courtship, and a resurrection, interspersed with lots of music and dancing."

"Are you playing Sir George? You look qualified."

"No, I'm Lady Molly, the romantic object. I don't do much but look decorative." She laughed and thrust again with her imaginary sword. "Being in the tithe barn takes me back to the days when the only thing on my mind was acting. No worries about career or finances or where the next role is coming from. I once played D'Artagnan in an all-girl production of *The Three Musketeers,* and never had a qualm about the miscasting."

"Turning an obsession into a career is a mixed blessing. I love working the camera, but now that I've reached the exalted heights of director of photography, I'm supposed to let my camera operator have all the fun." He studied her face with professional thoroughness, thinking she looked hardly older than when they had first met. But now she was secure, comfortable in her own skin. Lovelier than ever.

He felt a curious duality. On the one hand, they'd been lovers, and very compatible ones, too. When they were in bed together, she wasn't crying over her treacherous boyfriend.

Yet they were near strangers as well. Though they worked within the same sprawling industry, their lives had touched only once for a handful of days. There was no reason for him to feel that they belonged together. . . . "Do you ever think about the time we spent together making that movie?"

Her imaginary sword stilled. "Often. You were so kind, and I was so . . . needy."

"Maybe. But that's not all I remember." He moved toward her, driven by an impulse stronger than common sense. Her chin was silky soft against his hand when he raised it so he could look into her eyes. She regarded him steadily, neither inviting nor retreating. Blue eyes so deep a man could drown . . .

Children's voices piped into the room, accompanied by the banging of small feet. Jenny jumped away from Greg like a scalded cat. Belatedly, he remembered that she had a boyfriend. He was in England for a little creative R & R and to help a good cause, not revive an old affair. No matter how much he might want to do just that.

"Miss Jenny's here!"

Swiftly composing her expression, Jenny turned toward the entrance and waved a greeting. "Hello!"

A gaggle of prepubescent children were skipping into the barn, cheeks rosy from the cold air. A dark-haired young woman followed the children at a more sedate pace. Her interested gaze went to Greg as she approached. "Is this Mr. Marino, Jenny?"

"It is indeed. Greg, meet my sister, Patricia Holmes, teacher and director of our children's choir. Patricia, here's our miracle worker." Jenny managed to introduce Greg without looking at him, confirming his suspicion that he'd embarrassed her.

Telling his libido to cool it, Greg studied Jenny's sister. He hadn't seen any teachers like Patricia Holmes when he was in grade school. Since she looked very like Jenny, she was a knockout. He guessed that she was two or three years older, and surely one of the little girl singers was hers—good looks ran in the family.

After they exchanged greetings, Greg gestured at the children ricocheting around the barn. "Your kids are photogenic, but will they stand still long enough to be filmed?"

Patricia put two fingers into her mouth and gave an ear-shattering whistle. The children instantly converged in lines in front of her, as demure as the angels they would be playing. "Sing your first song for Mr. Marino." She hummed a starting note.

"Oh, come, oh, come, Emaaa-a-an-uel . . ."

The children's pure, joyous voices carried Greg back to his boyhood. Children often sang, adults seldom. At what age did the singing stop? Except for the national anthem at sports events, Greg couldn't remember the last time he'd sung. Quietly he began humming along with the choir as his gaze drifted from face to face. He'd have to get plenty of close-ups—these kids were real crowd pleasers.

Patricia gave an order, and the children turned and marched up the steps onto the stage two by two, their voices ringing through the barn like a choir of bells. He turned on his video camera and shadowed them, thinking how he would handle this on film.

More people began to arrive, some carrying what looked like moose antlers, assuming that the things moose wore on their heads were called antlers. Most of the performers were local, Greg guessed, but he blinked at the sight of several famous faces. Jenny had obviously used her powers of persuasion on some of her London friends.

He returned to his camera, and mentally calculated the best way to light moose.

THE rehearsal was chaotic in the grand tradition. Since Jenny was performing as well as directing, she was run ragged putting the pieces together. Still, she was pleased with the results. The Ad Hoc Upper Bassett Players would not disgrace themselves.

Dusk was approaching and the dinner hour with it, so Jenny dismissed her troops and went in search of Greg. Though he had a talent for being unobtrusive, she'd been very aware of him moving quietly among the players, zooming in on faces, pulling back to catch a group of dancers. Very, *very* aware. A pity the children had arrived when they did. She had been quite in the mood for a kiss.

She found her quarry up among the catwalks, where he was examining the lights. "What do you think of our show, Greg?"

"You've done some interesting things with the material—the songs and dancing are really integral to the story. The filmed version will look great."

"You think so? I'm a little worried."

"No need. You have good performers, the barn and set have loads of atmosphere, and the costumes I spotted backstage will add plenty of color and excitement. Tomorrow I'll call a London camera house to borrow a camera package and some lights. We should be able to start shooting the next day."

One of the advantages of having an Oscar-winning cinematographer was that Greg could borrow any equipment he needed in exchange for a film credit. Persuading him to come was the cleverest thing she'd done on this project.

After they descended the narrow staircase to the stage, she checked to see that they were the only ones left, then locked the barn behind them. As they got into her car, she said, "My father was supposed to drop a Christmas tree and some greens by the cottage this afternoon. Would you like to help me do some decorating? Since I've been in London for the last fortnight, I have a lot of catching up to do."

"I'd love to help. It's been . . . Lord, at least a dozen years since I've so much as hung an ornament." Greg's voice was wistful. "Usually I rush home to Ohio at the last minute and the preparations have already been made."

They drove the short distance back to the cottage in silence. Jenny was looking forward to a companionable evening decorating the tree when Greg said abruptly, "Maybe I should move to a hotel."

Startled, she asked, "Why would you want to do that? There aren't any hotels that are convenient."

"Because if I stay in your guest room, I'm not sure I can keep my hands off you."

She found herself blushing. Good God, at her age! "There's no particular need to keep your hands to yourself," she stammered. "As I said when we first spoke, the fair white body part was negotiable."

He turned to look at her, his expression unreadable in the dusk. "I heard you were involved with some software tycoon."

"You mean Neil Carling? We're not really dating." She liked that Greg respected whether or not she was involved with someone else. She had always been punctilious about such things herself.

"No?"

"I'm his official facade." She parked by her house and climbed out. "He's courting a very sweet, reserved widow and he's afraid he'll lose her if she winds up in the tabloids. Neil and I are old friends, so he takes me to events where he needs a bit of arm candy. I coo and bat my eyelashes, and afterward he goes off to visit his Elizabeth."

Greg chuckled as he followed her to the house. "I've been in Hollywood long enough to understand why a man might want to hide his private life. But how will he ever get her to the altar if he's afraid to go public?"

"When and if she says yes, he plans to take her off to the Caribbean for a very quiet, private wedding. Once they're married, they'll be old news. There is nothing more boring than a faithfully married businessman. In the meantime, I have the chance to dress up and go out with someone who knew me when I was in pigtails."

Those chaste evenings with Neil were the most fun she'd had with a man in months. As she unlocked the cottage, her thoughtful gaze went to Greg again. Perhaps that was about to change.

Five

"IT'S a beautiful tree, if I do say so who shouldn't." Jenny stepped back and regarded their work with satisfaction. The gaily decorated spruce filled one corner of the living room, its gold filigree star touching a weathered ceiling beam.

"It's a fantastic tree." Greg hung a miniature Celtic harp on an upper branch. Jenny's ornaments varied from battered, beloved family heirlooms to delicate works of art. Just the way ornaments ought to be; he'd always hated flawless, overdecorated trees that made him think of department stores rather than homes.

Plato trotted up with his buggy whip and dropped it under the tree, then eyed a swinging angel ornament. "Behave yourself," Jenny ordered.

The cat gave her a flat stare to prove that he cared naught for her opinion, then curled up under the tree, an errant strand of silver tinsel accenting his gray fur. Greg smiled as he scratched Plato's neck. "A crackling fire on a cold night, a cat, good company, and decorating a Christmas tree. It doesn't get much better than this."

"I love Christmas." Jenny draped more tinsel in an under-sparkled spot. "A time to slow down and enjoy life and be with my family and friends. In busy years, it keeps me sane. In bad years, it makes me feel whole again."

"I've been doing the holidays on the express plan for too long. I'm lucky my family hasn't changed the locks to keep me out since I fly in a day or two before Christmas, and leave a day or two after." There was a long pause while he studied another ornament, a delicately made ceramic nest containing a pair of tiny bluebirds. He'd sent her the ornament the Christmas after their affair. Had he thought that the bluebirds of happiness nesting in the tree might bring them back together? Hard to remember after all these years. "I've spent so much time building my career that I forgot to build a life," he said quietly. "You seem to have done a better job of balancing it all."

"A rolling stone gathers no tinsel? Americans work too hard, I think. I'm lucky to spend half my time outside of London. In Upper Bassett, I'm Alice and the doctor's daughter, Patricia and Keith's sister, and a multiple aunt. The eccentric but amiable Lyme girl who's done rather well for herself. It keeps life in perspective."

Jenny flicked off the light switch so the room was illuminated only by dancing flames and the tiny colored tree lights. She had taken off her heavy sweater earlier, and the silk shirt she wore underneath skimmed her curves alluringly. The soft light gave her a haunting Renaissance beauty.

Greg's fingers tightened around the birds' nest. Though she had said he didn't have to keep his hands to himself, he still had trouble believing that she might be interested in him. Their romantic history had been a fluke of circumstances.

But maybe he wasn't the only one who had found those days magical. It was worth risking rejection, because he would never forgive himself if he didn't at least try. Carefully he hung the ornament out of Plato's reach. "Earlier today we were interrupted at an interesting moment."

Even though beauty was power, she looked vulnerable, almost fragile. "I didn't think you'd come to England," she said softly. "I'm glad you did. Even gladder than I thought I would be."

With one provocative motion, she pulled off the scarf that tied back her hair. Luxurious as ermine, the dark waves cascaded over her shoulders, catching auburn highlights from the fire. "I wouldn't mind a holiday fling. Shall we pick up where we left off all those years ago?"

Powerful awareness pulsed between them. For the first time he accepted that even though she was a glamorous actress, she was also the friend and lover he had never forgotten. "I hope we can, Jenny. The fact that we were together then is the greatest miracle I've ever known."

She came into his arms lightly. His first kiss was tentative, wondering, awed. How he'd longed for this mouth, these lips, the essence of Jenny.

Her head tilted back and she melted against him. Warm, curving, irresistible—and neither of them even tried to resist. He tangled his fingers in her glossy hair to bring her closer, jet lag forgotten as he came alive in every cell. "My God, Jenny . . ."

"How could I have forgotten this?" she whispered as she burrowed against him.

Doubts and time dissolved along with words as they tugged at each other's clothing. Jenny pulled a folded blanket from the sofa and tossed it in front of the fire. Giving thanks that he'd come prepared in case something wild and wonderful happened, he pulled her down beside him, craving the weight and feel of her intoxicating body.

Even that first time so many years before, they had come together with sweet harmony. Now there was harmony and more, as if they'd been waiting for years to set each other afire. He felt they had known each other forever as they remembered how to kiss, how to touch, how to laugh.

How to be in a perfect moment.

Afterward, shaking from reaction, he pulled her close and kissed her damp forehead. He had indeed fallen into Wonderland. In real life, it wasn't possible to be this happy. Perhaps this moment could only be perfect because it was so ephemeral. In less than a month he would be in Argentina.

But as he gazed into the embers of the fire, he mourned the knowledge of how soon such happiness must end.

NOT wanting to move ever again, Jenny rested her head on Greg's shoulder, pulling the blanket over them as she struggled for breath and composure. Never, even in her most heated dreams, had she imagined such a reunion. "It was good before, but not like this. Not so . . . so intense. Maybe because I was such a mess at the time."

"You were miserable then, but never a mess." He caught her hand and kissed her fingertips. "Did I tell you that I was entranced by your collarbones? When I shot that scene where you were half naked, I couldn't believe how lovely and subtle your shoulders were. At night I dreamed about them, sculpted by light and shadow."

She laughed a little wryly. "Don't look too closely. These shoulders are now thirty-five, not twenty-three."

"Still beautiful, though." He exhaled warmly into the hollow above her collarbone.

Her gaze went to the dancing flames. "You're an artist of light, Greg. You see beauty where others don't, and then you make them see it, too. It's a great gift."

"So is making people laugh and cry, the way you do. We're both lucky to be able to do what we love, and share it with others."

Yes, she'd been lucky, but not in all areas of life. "Have you achieved your dreams? Or have you reached them and now have others?"

She admired his face in the firelight while he considered her question. When he'd been twenty-five and bearded, she hadn't realized what a fine strong jaw he had. She liked his mouth, too. Not only the feel of his lips, but the humorous little quirk that made him always look on the verge of laughter.

"My greatest dream, which seemed impossible when I was a kid in Ohio, was to make movies," he said slowly. "Not the writing or acting or directing—that was for other people. The essence of movie making is images, and that's what I wanted to do: capture images that would delight and astonish and sometimes even terrify."

"Then you're successful."

"Professionally, yes. But maybe I didn't have enough different dreams." For a moment his eyes were shadowed. Shaking off the mood, he propped himself on one elbow and smiled down on her. "Have you achieved your greatest goals?"

"I was like you—wanting to act, not thinking it was possible to reach such heights, working hard to make it happen. The dream was to make movies—be an international star, you know." She shrugged philosophically. "I didn't achieve that and it's too late now, but television suits me and I've done better than most. Enough to feel good about my abilities, not so much that success has made my life difficult. Even though I'm past my prime, I'm lucky to be English. There's more room for aging actresses here. I should be able to grow old gracefully, moving between television and the theater, making enough money to live well and to spoil my nieces and nephews with Christmas presents."

He stared at her. "Where do you get this 'aging actress' nonsense?

You're a beautiful, desirable woman, and you always will be. Like Katharine Hepburn and the other great beauties, you're lovely in your bones, and in your spirit."

Her throat tightened at his palpable sincerity. "For a man of images, not words, you say wonderful things."

"Seeing is my business, and I see truth, Jenny."

Uncomfortable with the intensity of his eyes, she asked, "You said you need different dreams. What is the biggest thing that you don't have but would like?"

His brows furrowed. "Probably a house. I'm still living in that same two-bedroom apartment I had when we made *Almost Crazy*. Remember it?"

"I have fond memories of that apartment. In fact, your key is around here somewhere, since I forgot to give it back before I left." Actually, she'd kept it deliberately as a souvenir of their time together. "It was a nice apartment, but not the same as owning your own home."

"It's ironic. I've finally reached the point where I could afford a decent house, but when I come back from a location shoot I'm always too tired to call a real estate agent. The next thing I know, I'm off again." He smiled wryly. "I'm this big success, yet I live like a kid just out of college."

"California has wonderful houses. What would you like? A beach house?"

"I'd rather have a place up in the hills where you can see to forever. I love that kind of spaciousness. And I like modern architecture—airiness and lots of texture from natural materials."

"It sounds as if you've thought about this." She knew the kind of house he meant—she had visited one or two of that type when she was in California. "As dreams go, this shouldn't be too hard to achieve. Perhaps you should make a New Year's resolution to call an estate agent."

"Maybe I will." His gaze traveled around her living room. "Being here reminds me of what I'm missing."

Hearing more than he was saying, she said hesitantly, "It sounds as if you want not only a house, but a home. Real estate is easy. Homes are harder."

"I think you just put your finger on it." He gave a jaw-cracking yawn. "Sorry! Jet lag is mugging me again. I'd better go to bed while I can still manage the stairs."

He stood and offered her his hand, raising her easily. She skimmed her palm across his bare chest, thinking again how well he had filled out since they first met. He'd been an appealing youth. Now he was a rather splendid man. "My bedroom or yours?"

He gave her a slow smile. "Yours, if you don't mind having me there."

She closed the fireplace doors and turned out the lights, then slid her arm around his waist and they ambled toward the stairs. His height made her feel small and feminine. She tried to remember when she had felt so peaceful, but failed. Too long.

Greg hadn't been joking about his fatigue. After washing up and brushing his teeth, he hit her bed like a felled tree. She didn't mind, not when he drew her close against him. She gave a sigh of pure pleasure.

Plato jumped onto the bed, looking for an unoccupied corner. Jenny was about to shoo him off when Greg began absently scratching the cat's neck. Not bad for a man more asleep than awake.

As Plato settled down, purring, Greg murmured, "If I had asked you to stay after we finished shooting *Almost Crazy*—would you have?"

How had she felt then? Conflicted. "I don't think so," she said honestly. "I was desperate to go home. Being offered that Jane Austen role went a long way toward repairing my battered professional pride."

He exhaled, his soft breath stirring the hair at her temple. "That's what I figured."

His breathing became slow and steady, but it was a long time until Jenny slept. Probably she would have gone home no matter what Greg said then—but she wished she'd had the choice.

Six

GREG swiftly checked over the lights, reflectors, and other equipment. "Great," he said as he signed the manifest. "I really appreciate you guys lending me all this."

Sean, the young Londoner who had driven the borrowed equipment to Upper Bassett, said, "It's an honor, Mr. Marino." He hesitated. "Could I stay and help today? I'm a camera assistant, so I might be useful." Despite numerous piercings and hair that defied description, his gaze was as worshipful as a spaniel. "I really want to see you work."

Greg felt very old. How had he gone from being an eager kid like this one to an elder statesman? Trying not to think of the occasional gray hairs that were starting to appear, he said, "Sure, the help will be welcome. We'll start by rigging these lights."

They spent a long, sweaty day working on the catwalks above the stage, with Greg explaining the reasons for every equipment placement. His assistant nodded solemnly and jotted quick notes. With Sean's help, the installation was finished before the evening's dress rehearsal. Greg could never have managed that on his own.

Jenny flitted in and out, alluring in jeans and sweater as she attended to countless details. Whenever she appeared, all male activity temporarily ceased. She was pleasant to everyone, but for Greg she had a private smile that melted him in his tracks.

The three days since he'd arrived in England were the happiest he could remember. By day he and Jenny worked like maniacs to stage her production, sharing ideas and problems with easy camaraderie. The nights were even better as they talked and laughed and made love until they fell asleep in each other's arms. Usually with Plato sprawled against Greg's ankles. The three of them slept well together.

Greg was doing a lighting check when Jenny appeared. "My mother put together a buffet supper for family members involved in the show. The kids have finished, but the adults are eating now. Care to join us, or are you too busy?"

He suppressed a small twitch. Though the family members he'd met were great, he hadn't met her father yet, and Dr. Lyme might not approve of some ramshackle American hanging out with his youngest daughter. Reminding himself that he wasn't in high school, he said, "Sure. It would be nice to get out of here for a while."

He grabbed his coat and joined Jenny for the walk to her parents' house. The fresh air was welcome after the long day inside. Taking his hand, she led him along a path that edged a field and decanted them by a sprawling brick house. "This was called a villa when it was built in Edwardian times," Jenny explained. "My father wanted all the woodwork painted lime green in honor of the family name, but Mother wouldn't let him."

"Sounds like your father has a sense of humor."

"He has to, to put up with the rest of us," she said blithely as they walked inside through the unlocked front door.

The small front hall opened to reception rooms on both sides. The parlor on the right contained a tall Christmas tree, with the dining room visible beyond. High ceilings and handsome moldings gave a formal air to the house, but the furnishings were comfortable and just worn enough to be welcoming.

Jenny hung both their coats, then took Greg into the dining room, where platters and Crock-Pots were set on a sideboard so family members could help themselves to a quick meal. Alice Lyme wasn't present but Patricia Holmes and her husband, Ken, were already eating, and a white-haired man who had to be Dr. Lyme was nursing a cup of coffee at the head of the table.

Taking Greg's arm, Jenny led him into the dining room. "Hi, all. Dad, you haven't met my friend Greg Marino, have you?"

Dr. Lyme stood. Tall and angular, he had formidably bushy eyebrows. "No, but Jenny has talked of you a great deal."

"I was afraid of that," Greg said fatalistically. "I swear, practically none of it is true."

The doctor laughed and offered his hand. "It was good of you to come all this way to help out."

As they shook hands, Greg said, "I'm glad Jenny asked me—I'm having a wonderful time."

"You're from Ohio, I think? I once did a fellowship in Cincinnati." Dr. Lyme sighed nostalgically. "Cincinnati chili. Not like anything else I've ever eaten."

"That's because its ancestors are Greek, not Mexican." Greg made a mental note to send some Cincinnati chili spice packets to Dr. Lyme. "Our local specialty."

That started a lively discussion about regional foods while the new arrivals served themselves and sat down. Luckily, Greg managed not to step on the collie-ish dog that was snoozing peacefully under the sideboard. Given the way Jenny fussed over the elderly dog, he suspected that stepping on its tail would get him exiled permanently from the house.

Dr. Lyme replenished his coffee. "Is everything in hand for the rehearsal?"

"So far, so good," Jenny replied. "One of the horn dancers broke his right antler, but we were able to superglue the end on again."

Greg grinned, amused at the contrast of old and new. "I've been meaning to ask why moose antlers are worn for a dance."

"Not moose—red deer. The horned god is a pagan deity and tied up with fertility and nature," Patricia explained with schoolteacher precision.

"We included the horn dance because it's a specialty of this dance group, and it looks impressive," Jenny added. "Excuse me while I go change into my costume. Patricia, can you help?"

The two women disappeared, leaving Greg with the doctor and Ken Holmes. Ken, an engineer, was asking technical questions about film editing when the sisters reappeared. Jenny had traded her jeans for a flowing gown of burgundy velvet with gold embroidered borders, topped by a headdress with a diaphanous golden veil. The medieval finery gave her an otherworldly air at odds with the approachable woman who warmed his nights. "You take my breath away," Greg said honestly.

She dimpled and curtsied gracefully. " 'Tis honored I am to make your acquaintance, Sir Gregory of Ohio."

Their teasing was interrupted when Alice Lyme appeared. Greg had met her several times at the tithe barn, where she helped as needed. A silver fox version of her beautiful daughters, she usually had an unflappable quality that reminded Greg of his own mother, but this evening she was frowning. "Bad news, I'm afraid."

"What's wrong?" Jenny asked.

"I've just learned that the Carthage Corporation has changed its deadline. Originally we had until June thirtieth to meet their price. Now they say we must have the money by January first."

"They can do that?" Greg asked, startled. "Don't you have an option contract of some sort?"

Alice shrugged. "It was a gentlemen's agreement, which tends to be worthless when dealing with corporations. Last summer Carthage had the barn appraised and told us if we could raise the amount of the appraisal by the time the lease expired, the barn would be ours. But nothing was in writing."

"Probably they've received a higher offer," Patricia said cynically.

"They know the center can't raise so much money on such short notice." Jenny looked stricken. "When we fail, they accept the other contract. Come June, we're out."

Greg swore under his breath. Jenny had said once that the center had a good chance to raise the money, but it would take the six months they'd been counting on to edit and polish the Revels film and sell it to television.

Or would it? "Did they say in writing that they would let the village buy the barn if it raised the money by New Year's?"

Alice raised a paper she had brought in. "Yes; the cowards faxed me rather than telephoning. But what good does that do us?"

"The key is television sales," he replied. "Jenny has plenty of London contacts, and I know some people in American TV. If we can produce some good sample material quickly enough, maybe we can get commitments to buy the finished film for next year. With those in hand, it should be possible to get a bridge loan from a bank. I doubt the corporation would dare back out since you have their written promise to sell at the appraisal price. It would look nasty in the newspapers if they reneged, and corporations don't like looking like bad guys."

"Can that all be done in such a short time?" Alice asked doubtfully.

Jenny bit her lip, calculating. "It's possible. Barely. If Greg can pull together some fabulous footage in the next day or two. Can you?"

"I think so. I rigged the lights to give even illumination, which means I could shoot the dress rehearsal tonight in digital video. Sean has a similar camera, and he would love to act as second unit. Does anyone in Upper Bassett have a really good digital editing setup on his computer?"

"I do." Ken Holmes smiled self-deprecatingly. "We engineers love gadgets."

"He also has first-class recording equipment taking up far too much of the house." Patricia smiled at her husband affectionately. "He records music at our church and we sell the CDs. The sound is professional quality."

"Then let's go for it." Greg swallowed a last bite of supper and got to his feet. "We'll shoot and record the rehearsal, edit tonight, and by tomorrow morning we should have something that will convince the BBC that you deserve a piece of their budget."

Ken also stood. "I'll go home for my sound equipment and meet you at the barn."

After thanking the Lymes for their hospitality, Greg and Jenny collected their coats and left. By the time they reached the tithe barn, the building was teeming with cast members. A flock of cherubs, ridiculously cute in white robes and gilded wings, galloped by as Greg extricated young Sean from a group of dancers and enlisted him for the evening's shooting.

As Greg explained to Sean what was needed, Jenny marched up the steps onto the stage. "The tithe barn is on thin ice, my friends," she said in a carrying voice, "so tonight we have to do a cracking good job."

Swiftly she outlined the situation with a passion that would have inspired soldiers on the eve of battle. By the time she finished speaking, all of the actors, singers, dancers, and musicians were poised for their best work.

Within half an hour they were set to go, microphones in place and two cameras ready to record the performance. The next hours were a blur of motion and music. When possible, Greg loved to work fast and capture the spontaneity that was hard to maintain in multiple takes. In this case, he also wanted the action to be as uninterrupted as possible so that the performers could get the benefit of their dress rehearsal.

The show began with the children singing, "Oh, come, oh, come, Emmanuel," as they walked through the darkened theater, each carrying a candle and watched like a hawk by Patricia to see that they didn't set themselves on fire. The kids, as expected, were adorable, and they sang like crystal bells. With the lights low and the candles illuminating earnest young faces, the procession captured the eternal magic of the season.

As the story unfolded, the performers outdid themselves. The mixture of professionals and experienced amateurs put on a musical spectacular worthy of London's famous West End theaters. Sir George, the future saint, was played by an opera tenor, the Turkish physician was a famous Welsh stage actor, and Jenny as Lady Molly proved to be a first-rate singer with a rich voice that filled every corner of the barn.

Fiercely concentrating, Greg entered the altered state where he was no longer consciously aware of his movements, his whole body responding instinctively to what his eyes saw. A pan across the bright faces of the singing cherubs, *yes*. Pull back and up to capture the wild energy of the horn dancers. Descend to shoot the ponderous, glittering dragon as the beast slew the knight. A poignant shot of the fallen warrior.

And always Jenny, first as the saucy narrator who set the stage for the show, later as Lady Molly weeping over the body of her sweetheart. The camera loved her, caressing her expressive face and supple body as she became a woman of another time.

Enter the Turkish physician in his Eastern robes, and with a stage presence that had knocked London theatergoers dead for decades. The slain knight was revived, the lovers reunited, and the resurrection theme was expanded into a touching Nativity scene.

At the end, as Greg slowly pulled the camera back and up, the whole cast sang "Go, Tell It on the Mountain," the American spiritual somehow perfectly right. Adults, children, dancers, musicians, and even the dragon were united in peace and harmony. Damn, these people were good.

As the cast dissolved into postperformance chatter, relief, and analysis, Greg leaned against the wall, almost dizzy now that shooting was over. Having made her comments and compliments to her cast, Jenny slipped away to join him, her face flushed with a performer's high even though she had removed her makeup. "Was that as good as I thought it was?"

He nodded. "Better. More takes and angles and a wider range of zoom shots would have been nice, but we have what we need to shop the show."

Sean appeared, looking awed. "That was bloomin' marvelous! Better than a year's worth of course work."

"You were a great help, Sean. I'm glad you stayed," Greg said. "Maybe we can work together again someday."

After the young cameraman left, beaming, Jenny stood on her toes and gave Greg a swift kiss. "Thank you so much. There's still a long way to go, but if not for your wizardry, we wouldn't have a chance. First thing tomorrow I'll call my most influential BBC connection. With luck, we can have a meeting tomorrow afternoon."

Greg gave her a tired smile, the tanned skin crinkling around his dark eyes. "It's still early enough in the U.S. for me to call there tonight. If the editing goes well, tomorrow I'll be able to send a rough cut over."

He looked so huggable that it was an effort for Jenny to keep her hands to herself. Reminding herself that her mother and half her family were in the room, she behaved. Sort of. Linking an arm through Greg's, she said, "Before we go to Patricia and Ken's house to edit, let's stop by my place for a bite to eat and a pot of coffee to keep us awake. You can make your calls while my mother locks up here."

"Good idea; I'm ravenous. That kind of work really gives me an appetite."

Arm in arm, they said good-byes and left the barn. Jenny was still buzzing with exhilaration from the performance, where the sum of what they had done was so much more than the individual people. Yet underneath was a vein of melancholy, because in two or three days he'd be gone. She wondered if she would be able to kiss him good-bye at Heathrow without crying.

Even the best actress has her limits.

Seven

WHILE Jenny threw together a quick supper, Greg withdrew to his room and called a couple of people he knew in American television, plus a CBC friend in Toronto. All three wanted to see a rough cut of the performance.

He ended his final call, satisfied that everyone understood the need for a quick decision and money on the table if they were interested. If Jenny did as well in London, there was a fighting chance of raising the money by New Year's.

Plato trotted in carrying his buggy whip. After dropping it at the foot of the bed, he leaped onto Greg's lap. "I'm going to miss you, philosopher," Greg murmured as he scratched the furry neck. Though not as much as he'd miss the cat's mistress.

He didn't want to make a fool of himself by babbling to her what she meant to him—she probably got declarations of love from smitten males every week. But maybe he could find a special gift that would say what he meant without words. Not chocolate or jewelry—Jenny was quite capable of getting her own. What did she want most?

The dream was to make movies—be an international star, you know. Her flip tone hadn't concealed her underlying regrets. Despite Jenny's success at television, her one Hollywood movie had been a fiasco, and now she had the absurd notion that she was over the hill. Did he know anyone who might need a terrific English actress?

On impulse, he dialed the private number of Raine Marlowe, who had produced, directed, and starred in *The Centurion,* the movie that had given them both Oscars. Even though she and her family lived mostly on a ranch in northern New Mexico, she was well plugged in to the Holly-wood movers and shakers. In fact, she was one herself.

As the phone rang, he remembered that Jenny was a former girlfriend of Raine's husband, Kenzie Scott. Maybe she wasn't the best person to ask. Before he could decide, Raine picked up the phone, in the midst of baking Christmas cookies. After they offered each other best wishes for the season, he explained why he was calling. If something came of it, great. If not—well, no harm done.

As he hung up, Jenny called, "Supper's ready!"

"Coming." Greg stood, boosting Plato over his shoulder. "You're going to be mad if this works, big guy. Making a movie would take your mom away from you for months." Whistling softly, he went down the stairs. If he couldn't be with Jenny in person, he could watch her on the silver screen.

"DO all cinematographers know how to edit as well as you do?" Jenny asked as she watched Greg work on her brother-in-law's huge computer monitor.

He shrugged. "I like playing with video and I've hung out with a lot of first-class film editors. Editing is the critical step that pulls everything together."

Jenny smothered her yawn as they watched the final scene, a mar-velous image that young Sean had shot from the catwalk above the stage. Though an American spiritual was hardly traditional in a mummers' play, Jenny firmly believed that folk performances were a living tradition, and should evolve and grow and adopt new music.

The final frame dissolved into darkness. "Finis. It's a wonderful sam-ple video, Greg. Now all we need is for my telly people to bite."

"They're nuts if they don't." Greg saved the final version, then rose, yawning. His skill had made editing a pleasure. She had enjoyed dis-cussing the shots and trying different versions until they had captured the essence of the live performance. His competence was very sexy. If she weren't so tired, she'd jump him. There was privacy enough—Patricia and her family had long since retired.

When Jenny and Greg were outside the house, he slung an arm around her shoulders as they walked to the car. She loved such casual, affectionate gestures.

Starting the engine as quietly as possible, she headed through the empty village to her cottage. They were almost home when Greg asked, "It's well known that you and Kenzie Scott were an item at RADA. Were you in love with him?"

She guessed that he might not have asked such a personal question if he wasn't so tired, but she didn't mind answering. "Not really. I do love Kenzie—he's one of my dearest friends, and he's as kind as he is good-looking, which is saying a lot. But there was always something unknowable about him—an essence that I could never touch."

"I thought women liked mysterious men."

"Some might, but I think it's tedious to always be wondering what a man thinks. I'm afraid that I'm hopelessly middle class, Greg—I like a chap who's down to earth and knowable." Someone like Greg. She had dated her share of high-maintenance charmers, and they made her appreciate steadiness and good humor.

As they entered her cottage, she thought of his question from their first night together: Would she have stayed with him in California if he'd asked all those years earlier? She still didn't know what her response would have been—but looking back, she was pretty sure that she *should* have stayed.

SIMON Oxnard, Jenny's honcho friend at the BBC, clicked off the Revels recording. He had watched the first third straight through and skipped rapidly through the rest to get a sense of the whole. Greg sat and gloomily noted all the errors he'd made. Shots held too long, angles that could have been improved, lighting that wasn't quite right. He was beginning to wish he hadn't accompanied Jenny for this sales pitch.

Of course, it was always good to watch Jenny. She'd opted for the businesswoman look today rather than actress glamour or country casual. With hair swept up and a beautifully tailored suit, she looked ready to run the Bank of England.

"Very nice, Jenny. The script is a delightful blend of traditional and contemporary, and you've directed well." Simon glanced at Greg. "You took fine advantage of the intimacy and spontaneity of video, Mr. Marino. I felt that I was standing in the middle of the stage, immersed in celebration."

Greg thanked him, glad his errors weren't obvious to a noncameraman.

Simon continued, "I'll have to run this by some of our programming people before I can make a commitment. There's a good chance we'll want it, but it won't be anywhere near as much money as you need. Tight budgets, you know."

Greg sensed Jenny's disappointment, though she didn't let it show on her face. "I understand. Many thanks for making time for us today, Simon." She stood and offered her hand. "The Ad Hoc Upper Bassett Players thank you."

The executive smiled as he shook her hand. "Is that what you call yourselves? You have quite a lot of talent in your village. It's worth sharing with a wider audience."

After they were safely out of the bustling television center, Greg asked, "Was he really interested, or was he just giving us the local version of the Hollywood shuffle?"

"If Hollywood shuffle means what I think, no, Simon isn't like that. He really did like what he saw, which means he'll probably make an offer after he runs it by his programmers." She sighed. "Unfortunately, he's also being straight about the money. When one comes down to it, this is just glorified community theater. We'll be lucky to sell it at all. We won't get enough to buy the barn."

"There's a good chance of an American sale, and maybe a Canadian one as well."

"From what you told me, that won't be huge money either. At best, we'll have perhaps half the amount we need."

Much as Greg would have liked to disagree, she was right. Cable stations and public television weren't rich. "If you have contracts for half the money, you're in a better position to borrow the rest."

"Perhaps." Jenny shook off her mood. "We've done as much as we can on this front. Now it's time to start worrying about our performance tonight."

"You'll need your strength. Let me buy you lunch," he suggested.

"What a good idea. I know a lovely pub near the motorway. Beams, a fireplace, and lots of traditional English pub food like chicken curry."

"Chicken curry is a traditional English dish?"

"A legacy of empire." Her smile was rueful. "I've been working you hard ever since you arrived, and soon you'll be going home. I want you to see a bit of the real England—the way we actually live here, not England as a giant theme park for tourists."

He climbed into her car, depressed at the reminder of how soon he would be leaving. "You said when you first called that I could stay and experience a traditional English Christmas. Did you mean that? I don't want to intrude on your family."

"You'll stay? How absolutely fabulous!" Her expression brighter, she turned her car into the street. "It won't be an intrusion since everyone in my family knows you. Ken will talk your ear off about filmmaking, my father will go on about his garden, the children and pets will crawl all over you, Patricia will give orders like the bossy big sister she is, and my mother will feed you very, very well."

He grinned. "Sounds like fun. If you're sure you don't mind, I'll change my tickets to the day after Christmas."

"I'm so glad. I hope your family won't mind too much."

His mother would mind. It would be one thing if Greg was visiting a nice girl with daughter-in-law potential, but Jenny was not what his mother kept hoping for. "Not a problem. There will be such a crowd around the house no one will notice I'm missing."

"Liar. But we'll take good care of you."

And his holiday fling would end in a Christmas celebration he would never forget.

Eight

JENNY groaned as she set the phone back into its cradle. "Since the first three performances went smoothly, I actually dared hope that the show would finish its run tonight without real problems. I should have known better."

Greg glanced up from the coffeepot he was washing. Domesticity looked good on him. "What's happened?"

"Our dragon, Will Davies, has become violently ill and can't perform. His wife says it's food poisoning or some ghastly stomach virus—the phrase 'projectile vomiting' was mentioned." She bit her lip. "The part is a simple one, with no real dialogue, and the costume is designed so almost anyone can wear it. Patricia can do it, though she'll make a rather short dragon." Inspiration struck. "Greg, will you take over? You're impressively tall, and you've seen the performance often enough to know the part."

"Me? Appear onstage? No way!" he said, horrified. "My job is behind the camera. Even as a kid I was always a technogeek, never an actor. I'll make a hash of your whole show."

"No, you won't." She found his alarm rather endearing. He'd been as reliable as the Rock of Gibraltar ever since he'd arrived, and now he looked as if she had proposed to hang him by his thumbs. "You'll be completely covered up by the dragon costume. You don't even have to roar—the bellowing is prerecorded. All you have to do is flail about and kill Sir George."

"After all the work I put into filming the last few days, I was looking forward to loafing tonight."

"Think of George as the smug lad who was always captain of the football team," she said coaxingly. "Wouldn't you like to slay someone like that? This being England, most of the audience is on the side of the poor hunted dragon."

"Since you put it like that . . ." Greg's mouth quirked up. "The costume is pretty much the part, so I suppose I can manage. But are you sure? There must be others who could handle the role better."

"On one hour's notice? Not likely." She reached for her coat, glad they'd had an early supper. "Come along, my lad. You're about to make your stage debut!"

GREG stood rigid in the wings, thinking that tonight was karmic justice for all the times he'd silently scoffed at actors who were suffering from nerves. Will Davies didn't have stomach flu, he'd become sick because he couldn't stand to go onstage again. If Greg weren't swathed in dragon, he might lose his supper himself.

All the performances had been sellouts, but tonight's closing show was packed to the rafters, with every inch of standing room taken. The good news was that the community center would make more from ticket sales than anticipated; the bad news was that Greg would have to step out in front of all those staring eyes. Compared to the rest of the cast, he was a pathetic, terrified amateur. He would accidentally damage Sir George. He'd trip over his tail and George would accidentally kill him. He'd . . .

A hand came to rest on his scaly forearm. "You'll do fine, Greg," Jenny said soothingly. "Just go out with the dragon walk I showed you. Once you're onstage, you'll have fun. Pretend you're an egotistical actor."

In her flowing medieval gown, Jenny was hypnotically lovely. He would have kissed her if he wasn't wearing a dragon head. He settled for patting her shoulder clumsily with one rubber-clawed paw.

Sir George and five admiring village girls finished a dance. The owner of the local dance studio, a retired prima ballerina, had done a splendid job with the choreography. The ancient music group was equally impressive. Jenny and her neighbors were far more than "community theater."

The village dancers spun off the stage. Fortified by their admiration, the knight set out on his dragon quest, singing magnificently. All too soon the song was over, which was Greg's cue to enter.

He froze, unable to move until Jenny placed a hand on his spine and pushed him forward none too gently. Under the blazing lights, Greg was agonizingly aware of a packed audience of undifferentiated heads, all of them staring at him.

Sir George fell back, aghast. "The dragon comes!"

Pulling himself together, Greg swung into the dragon walk, a wide-legged stride that made him look massive and dangerous. A menacing growl rumbled through the theater. Barely in time he remembered to open his jaws as if he was the one roaring.

The knight drew his blunt sword and flourished it menacingly. They had done a quick practice fight earlier, so Greg had a general idea of how to proceed. He lunged forward, jaws open and tail lashing. The costume was complicated, and keeping its pieces straight required all his concentration.

The knight darted in and out, unable to plant a killing blow on the scaly dragon hide. Luckily, the tenor who played George was well trained in stage fighting, so Greg didn't have to do much but take fierce swipes at his paltry opponent. *Pretend you're an egotistical actor.* Beginning to enjoy himself, he lunged forward, lip-synching the roars as he moved in for the kill.

One last great bellow, a vicious slashing of rubber claws, and Sir George fell to the stage, mortally wounded. As a trained tenor, he could die and sing at the same time.

Greg swayed over his prey, slavering, before a hiss from the wings told him it was time to leave. He was tempted to raise both arms in a victory dance, but restrained himself. The dragon was supposed to be a metaphor for brute violence and the lower nature, not a comedian.

As he exited, Jenny blew him a kiss from the opposite wing, then darted onstage with a terrible cry. The crowd caught its breath, struck by her palpable grief as she began to sing an elegy.

Greg pulled off the dragon head so he could see and hear better. Though he had filmed her elegy twice, then he had been concentrating on his equipment. This time he was free to focus on her, and her haunting voice pierced him to the heart. Yes, she was a superb actress, but no one could sing with such a sense of loss unless she had a deeply loving spirit. What would it be like to be the beneficiary of such love?

The recognition that he was in love with Jenny struck like a sword through his gut. Though he had done his best to deny the knowledge, that was no longer possible. He had fallen head over heels for her when he was a gawky assistant cameraman, and never recovered.

For the first time ever, he wished that he were a handsome, successful actor. Or maybe a tycoon. The kind of man who could win the heart and hand of a great beauty.

A minor-key Middle Eastern theme announced the Turkish physician, and the character joined Jenny onstage to resurrect the fallen knight. Greg tucked his tail aside so no one would trip over it and kept his vantage point, his gaze on Jenny.

Patricia glided by and murmured, "You make a fine dragon," before she vanished to marshal her children's choir. After the knight was resurrected and had embraced Jenny—did old George have to hug her so hard?—ethereal children's voices heralded the shift from resurrection to Nativity. The show was almost over. Greg watched raptly, already nostalgic for these magical days when he was part of this group of people doing their best for a common goal.

The stage lights went off. There were several long beats before a pinpoint of light began to shine above center stage. It grew brighter and brighter until it became a blazing star that illuminated the stage. At the same time, performers began to move onstage singing, "Go, tell it on the mountain, Over the hills and far away." Softly at first, then louder and louder until the whole cast was singing the jubilant spiritual.

Jenny emerged from the group under the star and gestured for the audience to sing along. They were tentative at first, but more and more joined in until the massed voices reverberated through the walls and beams of the ancient building. People began to rise to their feet, compelled to show their exhilaration in one of the transcendent moments that occurred only at live performances. Jenny was right, the barn was a living structure that deserved to continue as a place of gathering and creativity.

The song ended, the curtains fell, and the show was over. Pounding waves of applause began, and the curtains obligingly opened again. Traditionally the least important players came on first, so Greg hastily donned the dragon head. He trotted out, getting laughter and applause when he bowed goofily before withdrawing to the back of the stage to make way for more important performers.

The dancers high-kicked their way onstage, men from the right wing, women from the left. After a swift set of turns, they stepped aside for the children's choir. The musicians were highlighted, then the Turkish physician, and last of all Sir George and Jenny. The ovation she received threatened to rip off the slate roof. She bowed again and again, her face flushed with excitement.

Finally she raised her arms for silence. "I want to thank all of you for coming. As many of you know, the Revels were conceived as our attempt to raise money to save the tithe barn as Upper Bassett's community center. I don't know yet if we'll be successful because time is running out, but win or lose, we've created something special here, something we're all proud of. And it has all been done with volunteers. I want to thank everyone who didn't appear onstage, starting with Alice Lyme, who as president of the community center council has been a tower of strength and wisdom."

She blew a kiss to her mother, then swiftly listed others who had been essential for producing the show. "Lastly, I want to give special thanks to Greg Marino, the only American involved in this show, one of the world's great cinematographers, and the man who filmed our production so those of you who wish to watch again at home will be able to. Not only is he an Academy Award winner but a good sport, willing to step in when our original dragon was laid low. Greg, stop hiding in back and come out to be thanked."

Aiee! He wanted to dive to the floor and disappear, but eager hands pulled him forward. Blue eyes glowing, Jenny kissed him on his dragon snout and whispered, "Take this off so people can see you!"

No way. Preferring to play the Beast to her Beauty, he dropped to his knees and laid his head against her waist, animal nature tamed by the lady. The crowd loved it.

The curtains closed for the final time. Jenny patted Greg's neck as if he were a large dog. "Will you come out from under there, my darling dragon?"

He stood and removed the head piece. "You did well, Jenny. Everyone did."

She grinned. "Even you looked as if you were having fun. Watch out, you may be hit by the acting bug."

"Once was enough." He suppressed the desire to give her a real kiss, since what he wanted was not something that could be done in public. Originally he had intended to fly back to the States the morning after this last performance. Changing his plans had given him three more days of Jenny's company.

Only three more days.

*   *   *

JENNY laughed and joked with people who came up to congratulate her, but the show's triumph was bittersweet. She hated to think this might be the last time she would ever perform in the tithe barn. They had yet to hear from any of the television networks, and time was rapidly running out. Next Christmas the barn might be hosting a fashionable cocktail party for a wealthy new owner who would hang angular modern paintings on the ancient walls.

The dragon was a popular character; Greg stood beside her, signing autographs for the under-twelve set. She hoped that the postshow party didn't run too late. She wanted to take Greg home and find out what it was like to bed a dragon.

A familiar figure emerged from the thinning crowd. "This is even better in person than on video, Jenny." It was her BBC friend, Simon Oxnard, and his wife.

"Simon, how lovely to see you," Jenny said, hoping his presence was a good sign. "Cassie, I'm glad you could come, too."

Cassie smiled. "So am I. It was a marvelous performance."

"If I'd known you were interested, I would have found tickets for you."

Simon waved off Jenny's regrets. "No matter. Standing in the rear took me back to our student days. We had a splendid time, and now I can tell you in person that we have an offer that might help you out."

She caught her breath, afraid to hope. "You want to broadcast the show?"

"Yes, and if you'll sign a contract for two more Christmas shows over the next two years, each with a different theme, we can offer you three times the money."

"What kind of themes would interest you?"

"Since this was a medieval-style mummers' play, perhaps next year you could do Victorian. Something different the year after that."

Her imagination caught fire. Glittering costumes, formal dancing, passionate creativity. "Elizabethan. They did spectacle so well."

"Excellent." Simon grinned. "We also want to broadcast the video sample you showed me next week, as well as the film version next year."

Greg, who had been listening with interest, exclaimed, "You're kidding! It's just a seat-of-the-pants video."

"The seat of some very professional pants," Simon replied. "We have a late-night BBC2 slot that isn't well filled, so I convinced the programming head that your Revels would be a refreshing change."

In other words, even more money. Jenny felt like turning cartwheels. "Wonderful! Let me introduce you to my mother—she's president of the community center board and in charge of all negotiations. I warn you, though, she drives a hard bargain." She signaled her mother, made the introductions, and then withdrew to circulate through the cast party.

Maybe the barn wouldn't be condemned to stockbroker hell after all.

Nine

KNOWING they might achieve their goal made the cast party riotous, but even so, Greg and Jenny left early. He had plans for the rest of the night.

At the cottage, he climbed from the car, then halted in amazement when he saw that the sky was starting to pulse with sheets and bands of colored light. "Good God, it's the northern lights, isn't it? I've never seen them before."

"Even though England is so far north, I've only seen them a time or two myself." Jenny came to his side. "How splendid. A perfect end for a magical night."

Greg opened his jacket and drew her inside, wrapping his arms around her waist so that she was snuggled cozily against his chest as they watched shimmering greenish rays that rippled like scarlet-edged draperies. "When I was a kid, I used to have dreams like this, where I saw moving pictures on the night sky. I think I was crossing drive-in movies with what I'd read about the aurora."

"So you saw movies in your dreams even when you were a child."

"I'm afraid so. I never dreamed of being a star. Just of filming them." In silence they watched one of nature's greatest shows. He supposed the aurora borealis was a good metaphor for their affair—lovely and evanescent, gone almost before it was identified.

The night was getting colder, but Greg wasn't. As the veils of light faded, he kissed the edge of her right ear. She turned toward him and lifted her face. The warmth where their bodies touched was a deeply sensual counterpoint to the winter night.

"You're just a little bit of a thing," he murmured affectionately. Catching her around the waist, he lifted her onto the rear end of the Jaguar, her long skirt falling over the dark finish in soft folds. He leaned forward to kiss her throat. "Perched here, you look like an advertisement for the good life. Buy a Jaguar and beautiful women will flock to you." Warm breath exhaled softly against her cleavage. "Except that this is the twenty-first century, and the beautiful woman bought her own luxury car."

She laughed, wondering why intimacy brought out the Tarzan/Jane instinct even in strong-minded females like herself. She adored knowing that he was bigger and stronger than she, capable of fighting off saber-toothed tigers while being tender with her. She drew him tightly against her. "You make a wonderfully sexy dragon, Greg. Shall we play Beauty and the Beast?"

Her words were sparks on tinder. Intoxicated by the performance and the exhilaration of success, he took advantage of the night's privacy to make swift, urgent love to her. Soft fabric, warm, intimate flesh, rapturous response. No wonder women used to wear long skirts in the past, because the sensual possibilities were entrancing.

She responded with feverish intensity, as hungry as he. With Greg, she felt young again, willing to open up and take risks and lose her heart.

"Jenny," he whispered, "Jenny, love . . ." Words failed, only touch and scent and passion were real. How could he let this intimacy end? They fit together too well, understood and enjoyed each other too much. . . .

Even when they were both panting with sated exhaustion, he didn't want to let her go. When had he ever known a woman who made him feel so alive, yet so at peace?

She stirred in his arms, murmuring, "I'm never going to think of this car quite the same way again."

"A vehicle fit for dragons." He lifted her from the car, dropping one last weightless kiss on her hair. As they headed indoors, arms around each other, he realized that he couldn't leave without at least trying to see if they had a future.

As they entered the cottage, Plato looked up from his seat on the sofa, gave a bored yawn, then tucked his nose under his tail again. As she peeled off her long coat, Jenny said, "Tomorrow will be time for cooking and shopping and wrapping presents, but first, ten hours' sleep. Agreed?"

Before he could reply, the phone began to ring. "I wonder who that could be at this hour? Perhaps Simon is calling to offer still more money." Jenny sank onto the sofa, avoiding Plato with the skill of long practice. "Upper Bassett 7533. Yes, this is Jenny Lyme. Yes? Oh! No, it's not too late, I just came in, actually."

Greg hung their coats and poured two glasses of merlot. Jenny was still on the phone, her posture vibrant but her end of the conversation unenlightening. "Yes, that's possible. No need to apologize—you obviously have no time to waste." She accepted her glass of wine with a nod of thanks, but took only a sip. "Yes, of course."

What the devil was going on? Greg sat in a chair at a right angle to Jenny, feeling a prickle of unease. The intimacy that had bound them dissipated now that normal life had intruded. He was no longer sure he had the courage to ask if she would visit him in Argentina. She had mentioned that she was between projects, and he'd been hoping she could come for a long stay. Maybe forever.

"Very well, I'll call back tomorrow and we'll finalize the arrangements after you've talked to my manager. I look forward to this." Her voice was buoyant but professional, until she put down the phone. Then she whooped with excitement and catapulted into Greg's arms. "I can't believe it! That was Marcus Gordon, the Hollywood producer. You worked with him on *The Centurion,* didn't you?"

"Yes, he's a great guy—an old-fashioned moviemaker who cares about quality and good stories." A sinking feeling in his midriff, Greg set her on the sofa beside him. "What did he have to say?"

"He's about to start shooting a movie that's a loose remake of *Auntie Mame,* and he lost his leading lady to the Betty Ford Clinic." Jenny was positively bouncing. "Then someone suggested I was available. He says I would have been his first choice—he and his wife are both huge fans of *Still Talking*—but the financial people wanted someone better known in

America. When their choice crashed, Mr. Gordon showed some clips of my work to the numbers crunchers, and got their agreement to make an offer. Oh, Greg, this is *wonderful*. It's what I've dreamed of—a great movie with a great moviemaker. I've always loved Mame, and now I'm going to be an updated version of her."

So the call Greg had made to Raine Marlowe had borne fruit. But he hadn't expected anything on this scale. "I've read the script—Marcus asked me to be director of photography, but the schedule turned out to conflict with this job in Argentina, which I'd already agreed to. You'll be fantastic as Mame—funny, madcap, and with a heart of gold. Anything from Marcus is first class, and the lead role is a real star maker."

Jenny's face fell. "To think we might have been working together! What's worse, because they're about ready to start shooting, Marcus wants me to fly to California day after tomorrow, on Christmas Eve."

Greg felt a weird sense of déjà vu—an offer that was too good to pass up had separated them the first time. "So we won't spend Christmas together after all. Well, that's show business. When this kind of opportunity shows up, we have to jump." It was an effort to keep his voice light when he could feel cracks forming in his heart. Down-to-earth Jenny, who put on a show in her hometown to save a local landmark, had seemed almost possible. Now she was heading for the horizon like a shooting star.

"If you want that English Christmas, I know my family would love to have you." Her blue eyes were stricken. "You could stay here. I'll even let you drive the Jaguar. Or . . . or you could come to Los Angeles with me, and I'll roast you a Christmas goose."

He thought wistfully of the holiday they'd planned in that rambling brick house. It would have been fun, with Jenny. "Thanks, but I'd rather go home to Ohio. If I can get a flight on the twenty-fourth, I'll be able to spend Christmas Eve with my family."

"Of course." She hesitated. "When you return to Los Angeles, might we be able to get together before you leave for Argentina?"

"You're going to be pretty busy." In his heart, he knew their affair was over. If they ran into each other in Los Angeles, Jenny would be friendly because that was her nature, but they would have nothing in common. Better to bow out now—and never reveal that he had ever had hopes of something more.

*   *   *

HEATHROW the day before Christmas was a madhouse. Jenny and Greg had flights to the U.S. that left within an hour of each other, but on different airlines. She clutched his hand during the limousine ride from the Cotswolds to the airport. He hadn't seemed to mind, but he didn't have much to say, either. Mentally, he'd already moved on. She suspected that he was already beyond Ohio and into Argentina.

Jenny, though, was firmly anchored in the present. She could feel the moments trickling away, one at a time, impossible to catch and hold. A phenomenal opportunity had fallen into her lap, but she was having trouble remembering that when her heart was numbed by their upcoming separation. How had daughters of Britannia kept a stiff upper lip when their husbands and sweethearts went off to India for years on end?

Inside the terminal, Greg stopped in the middle of the swirling crowd. "Time for us to go our separate ways. I have quite a hike to my gate."

"I know." She stared at him, trying to memorize that familiar, craggy face, not quite believing this was really the end. "I . . . I'm so glad you came and helped us out. You made all the difference. We should rename the barn the Marino Center."

"It was your inspiration and talent and leadership that saved it, Jenny. I'm just glad I was along for the ride."

She almost asked if he would shoot the Victorian Revels they would stage next year, but stopped herself. One didn't ask a favor of that magnitude twice. "Take care of yourself, Greg. Don't get caught in an Andes avalanche or anything."

"I won't." He touched her cheek, his brown eyes warm with affection. Then his expression became impersonal. "I'll eat popcorn and cheer for you when your turn comes on Oscar night."

He lifted his duffle and turned to walk away—tall, strong, self-contained. Unable to stop herself, she whispered, "Greg—can't we do a better good-bye scene than this?"

She thought he wouldn't hear her in the tumult of travelers, but his shoulders stiffened and he pivoted to face her again, his expression stark. Dropping her carry-on, she threw herself into his arms, not caring what anyone thought.

His lips were warm and dear, his embrace crushing as he kissed her. Passersby buffeted her, but she ignored them, all her focus on the man in her arms. She had come to know his body in passion and in tenderness, his mind in humor and in intelligence. Surely these feelings were mutual, they had to be. Surely . . .

Slowly he withdrew, his eyes dark with regret. "Good-bye, Jenny. Have a good life."

This time, there would be no curtain call. She took a deep breath, squared her shoulders, then turned and walked away.

Ten

Los Angeles

USUALLY the week between Christmas and New Year's was an odd, waiting time, when the real world was held at bay and a girl could catch up with friends, sleep, and shopping, if she was lucky.

Of course, mad preparations for a starring role in a movie were a different kind of luck. Jenny sprawled on the sofa in the living room of her hotel suite, sipping from a glass of white burgundy and toying with a key on a small brass ring. Marcus was taking very good care of his new leading lady. She had been working hard ever since she'd arrived in Los Angeles, but he made sure she was comfortable, and had even taken her home to his own warm, eclectic family for dinner on Christmas Day.

Jenny suppressed a yawn, knowing she should be studying her script. She loved this movie, and deep in her bones felt the rightness that came with having material that suited her. Whether the movie turned into box office gold or bust, she would never be sorry she had accepted the role.

But hotels were lonely. She would love to have Plato here, but that would mean six months of quarantine when she took him back to England, and that didn't bear thinking of. Instead, he was being spoiled rotten at her parents' house, where he stayed whenever she traveled.

A pity she couldn't call Patricia or another friend for a good gossip, but the hour was far too late in England, and she didn't have close friends on this side of the Atlantic. Former lovers like Greg didn't count. Even if she had his family's number in Ohio, she couldn't call. That nice cinematic farewell at Heathrow had been the end.

She spun the key ring on her finger. In a burst of sentimentality, she had dug out the apartment key Greg had given her so many years earlier. Not that she could use it, any more than she could call him at his parents' home, but it was a nice talisman for remembering the good times.

On the verge of bathos, she remembered that she did have one good friend on this side of the Atlantic, and he would be happy to learn of her lucky break. She found her address book and dialed Kenzie Scott's private number at his ranch in New Mexico.

"Hello?" The feminine voice was low and distinctive.

Belatedly Jenny realized that she should have anticipated that the phone might be answered by Kenzie's wife, Raine Marlowe. Though Raine had been civil the one time they had met, she might be less polite about a phone call to her husband from an old girlfriend. A little cautiously, Jenny said, "Hello, Raine, this is Jenny Lyme. I'm in Los Angeles and have some wonderful news that I wanted to tell Kenzie. Is he available?"

"We're having a lovely moonlight-on-snow night, so he took Faith for a walk," Raine explained.

Jenny did a quick mental calculation. "Faith is old enough to walk?"

The other woman laughed. "Actually, she's in a baby carrier across Kenzie's chest and probably sound asleep, but Kenzie likes taking her out. He should be back soon. If you give me your number, I can have him call you. Though if you don't mind sharing, I always love to hear good news, too."

Since Raine sounded friendly and interested, Jenny said, "Just before Christmas, Marcus Gordon called me out of the blue and asked me to step in as the female lead for his version of *Auntie Mame.*"

"So you got the role! Wonderful—it was made for you, and you'll look gorgeous in those 1920s costumes. Congratulations!"

This didn't sound like surprise. Putting two and two together, Jenny asked, "Did you or Kenzie suggest me to Marcus?"

"Yes, but Greg Marino was the one who set the ball rolling in the first place. Did he come back to Los Angeles with you?"

"No, he flew home to Ohio." Jenny's brow wrinkled. "How was he involved?"

"He called a couple of weeks ago and said that if any good parts turned up for a brilliant and beautiful English actress, we should think of you. A couple of days later Marcus told me his lead for the Mame movie had just gone to rehab, and did I have any suggestions? So I tossed him your name."

Jenny was silent for a long moment. "More was going on than I realized."

"There is no substitute for word of mouth. Since he knew your work, Marcus loved the idea of using you." Raine's voice softened. "Greg wanted to give you a very special Christmas present, and he succeeded."

Jenny blinked. "This was Greg's idea of a Christmas present?"

"What better than giving someone her heart's desire? The sign of a man in love. Some men give flowers or chocolate. Movie people give movies."

Jenny swallowed hard. "Greg isn't in love with me. He's just a really nice man."

"I'm sorry—maybe I misread the signals," the other woman said apologetically. "I thought the two of you were involved. He seemed rather gaga over you."

"Involved, yes, but only in passing." To her horror, Jenny heard a break in her voice. "It was just a . . . a holiday fling."

The phone wires hummed with silence until Raine said hesitantly, "Forgive me, this is none of my business, Jenny, but it sounds as if you need someone to talk to. Has something gone wrong between you?"

"Not really, we're just geographically challenged. Besides, he's wildly successful and always traveling and he certainly isn't going to settle down with an over-the-hill actress from another country." Jenny's voice came out brittle rather than casual.

After a long pause, Raine asked, "Are you sure that's how he feels about it? Maybe from his point of view, you're a gorgeous, successful actress and he's just a shy technician that you could never take seriously."

"Greg isn't just a technician! He's an incredibly gifted artist who can make us see the world in special new ways. He leaves his mark on every movie he does."

"It sounds as if he's left his mark on you, too. Perhaps you should rethink the question of whether or not you have a future together. Maybe it ended because you assumed it would end."

"A self-fulfilling prophecy?" Jenny frowned. "I . . . I need to think about that. Even if that's part of what happened, the geographical problems are real. My roots are firmly sunk into English soil, while Greg is wonderfully and deeply American."

"Marriage is never easy," Raine said seriously. "Our business has more than its share of conflicts and stresses that can fracture a marriage— my English husband and I almost divorced over such things. But we survived, after making a conscious decision to put the marriage first, always.

"And while there are downsides, the movie business has the advantage of flexibility. Why can't you have homes in two countries? It's a compromise, but one that makes your life richer, if a little more frantic. What matters is having enough love and commitment to find ways to build a life that will work for you both."

"You make a good agony aunt," Jenny said wryly. "Just what I needed tonight."

"Agony aunt? Oh, an advice columnist. Sorry, I've been speaking out of turn." A door closed in the background. "Kenzie just came in. Would you like to talk to him?"

"Please."

A minute passed before Kenzie's deep voice said, "Hello, Jenny. I hear that the gods have smiled and you're now getting the Hollywood star treatment."

She laughed, relaxing at the familiar warmth of his greeting. They'd been so young when they first met at RADA. Incredibly handsome and wrapped in aristocratic reserve, Kenzie had been promptly labeled a snob by some students. Jenny, as confident as a golden retriever, had made the effort to get acquainted and found that he was shy and surprisingly unsure of himself. Though they had sometimes been lovers, far more important had been this enduring friendship. "This is much nicer than my first visit to Hollywood. I'm half terrified and half over the moon."

"That sounds about right, but you'll do fine. You have the talent and the star quality, and now you have the right role." Kenzie's voice changed. "Faith just woke up. Faith, talk to Jenny, she's sort of an English aunt."

An infantile burble could be heard. Jenny's heart melted. As well as she knew Kenzie, she had never realized what a doting father he would be.

She made suitable remarks about Kenzie's precocious daughter when he came back on the line, asked him to give her thanks to Raine, then hung up, mind spinning.

A self-fulfilling prophecy. Yes, she had known from the beginning that any relationship between her and Greg would be short-lived, and that had governed her actions. Greg had shared the same belief. He was a rolling stone, too busy even to move from the apartment that served as not much more than a hotel room between projects.

But surely she hadn't imagined that there was something special between them? They blended together like whiskey and water. Of course, she had a history of thinking there was more to a relationship than the man did, but Greg wasn't like any of the other men she had dated. Though ambitious and hardworking, he wasn't a vain actor with an insatiable need for adulation, or a rich man looking for a trophy.

Maybe Raine was right that he had a kind of shyness under his easy confidence; he made more than his share of wry, self-deprecating comments. On some level, he must feel he was the behind-the-scenes technical whiz, the nice guy who didn't get the girl.

What an *idiot* he was! A woman would have to be mad not to appreciate a man as smart, sexy, and fun to be with as Greg. He had been splendid when he was just starting out on his career, and had only improved with age. He was . . .

He was the man she loved. Dear Lord, why had it taken her this long to realize something so profound and fundamental? Raine was right—their relationship had fallen victim to a self-fulfilling prophecy. They were *both* idiots.

When she first called Greg about the Revels, she had been feeling low, convinced her career was headed into permanent decline. Now that she thought about it, that had probably added to her obsessive need to fight for the tithe barn. She had been feeling the loss of her career, and couldn't bear losing the community center as well.

But the barn was going to be saved—an American television offer the day before had clinched it. And she had gone from fading actress to the lead in a major movie with one of Hollywood's most respected producers. Her career had changed in a finger snap—why not her relationship with Greg?

She stared at the key to his apartment. It was quite possible that she and Raine were both wrong and Greg had no desire to further their relationship. But she'd be a fool not to try for more. Greg was worth the risk of failure.

She sipped at her wine, now warm to room temperature. Greg had tried and succeeded in giving her a heart's desire. What could she give him of equal value?

Eleven

A New Year's Day flight swept Greg from icy Ohio to temperate Los Angeles. Home, sweet home. Wearily Greg bumped his suitcase up the steps to his apartment. Being enveloped by Clan Marino had soothed his frayed emotions, but now he was ready for peace and quiet. Preparing for Argentina should keep his mind off Jenny, at least some of the time. He hoped.

He wondered what she was doing now. Working on the script? Being introduced to Hollywood movers and shakers as the next hot new actress?

He unlocked his door, walked inside—and stopped dead at the sight of Jenny sprawled across his sofa, reading a book. Elegant long legs in casual black slacks, stunning figure draped in a shimmery blue tunic that matched her eyes, dark hair cascading over her shoulders. He wanted to cross the room and enfold her in his arms and never let her go. Instead, he said stupidly, "How did you get in here?"

Expression uncertain, she set the book aside and swung her feet to the floor. "I still have your key, remember? I thought you might not mind since I'm here to take you out for that Christmas dinner I owe you. Better late than never."

He dropped his bags by the door, almost angry at her presence. He had accepted that their affair was over. By the time he returned from Argentina, he would be able to run into her casually without making a fool of himself. But not now, when the pain of separation was still as raw as an amputated limb. "I suppose one of Marcus's gofers was able to run down my flight time."

She nodded. "Everyone is so helpful it's scary."

"They're grateful to have you. You're a better actress than the lady in rehab, and infinitely easier to get along with."

"All that, plus clean, straight, and sober. I sound like an alarming paragon." She moved toward him. "Can I have a hello kiss?"

He stepped back, banging into the door. Why did she have to be so damned adorable? "I may be coming down with a cold—I was exposed to several by my nieces and nephews—and you really can't afford to get sick if you're about to start shooting."

Her face fell. "I suppose you're right, but you're not getting out of dinner that easily. Come on, I'm driving."

He hesitated, torn between common sense and longing. "I've got work to do."

"It's New Year's Day, and even workaholics need to eat." She threw a flowing paisley shawl over her shoulders and gave him a smile that melted his resolve. "Please come. I need you to remind me which side of the road to drive on."

Surrendering, he followed her out the door. "How is the production going?"

"Very well, in an insane sort of way. I was in wardrobe for fittings about ten minutes after I landed. Everything is so exciting. I feel like a new woman."

He'd liked the old one just fine.

The car turned out to be a Jaguar much like her English car, though a rich shade of burgundy rather than blue. "Nice. You've settled in fast."

She shrugged as she started the car. "The studio leased this for me. I think they decided I'd be less likely to get into trouble driving a car like the one I'm used to. By the way, your calls to the American television people paid off—we have an offer for broadcasting the Revels here, and yesterday Canada came through, too. We've secured the financing we need for the tithe barn. The video version of the Revels got great reviews even though it ran very late at night, and advance orders for the tape are pouring in. In short—the Upper Bassett Community Center will soon be in the hands of those who use and love it."

"That's great!" He felt a surprising sense of satisfaction. Even though he wouldn't pass that way again, he liked knowing that the dancers and actors and potters—and dragons—would have a place to perform. "So the hard work paid off."

She smiled wickedly. "Yesterday my mother went to the Carthage people with financing in hand, and they had to accept her contract. I wish I'd been there to see it."

"Me, too."

A mile rolled by in companionable silence, until Jenny said unexpectedly, "Time for caroling. Shall we start with 'Oh, Come, All Ye Faithful'? Everyone knows that."

"I don't sing."

"Nonsense. If you can talk, you can sing."

"Not according to my junior high music teacher," he said dryly. "She ordered me to shut up and lip-synch at the annual Christmas concert so I wouldn't ruin everything. I pretty much gave up singing after that."

Jenny spared a quick glance from the road. "That teacher should have been whipped. Changing voices can be awkward, but singing carols isn't done for others, it's for oneself. Give it a try now. 'Oh, come, all ye faithful, Joyful and triumphant . . . '"

Her voice was so lovely that Greg automatically clamped his mouth shut. Then he remembered his thoughts at the tithe barn, how children often sang and adults didn't. He had liked singing when he was little. Voice tentative, he joined in toward the end of the first verse. Jenny knew all the verses—in English and Latin both.

When they finished, she gave a swift, approving smile. "Your voice is fine. A most pleasing baritone. Your turn to choose a carol."

He'd always had a fondness for the haunting melody of "What Child Is This?" Jenny knew the words to that, too, her knowledge carrying him through lines he couldn't remember. By the time they finished, his self-consciousness was gone. This was fun.

They were well into the hills and "Angels We Have Heard on High" before he noticed their route. "You found a restaurant up here? You've been busy."

"Not a restaurant." She turned in to a winding residential street, powering the car upward through well-kept contemporary houses that perched nonchalantly on the steep slope. The Jaguar crested the hill, then swung between a pair of massive eucalyptus trees that screened a sprawl-ing stucco house from the road.

The driveway ended in a wide garage that buffered the house from the rest of the world. Jenny hit a button on the dash and the right-hand door opened. As she pulled the car into the space, she said, "I've always wanted to have a garage with an automatic opener. It's so unbelievably deca-dent—at home, I don't even have a carport."

"You've bought a house already?" Greg asked, startled, as they climbed from the car. That was fast even by the standards of Tinseltown.

"No, it's a short-term rental. Another perk from the studio. They set me up with an estate agent who asked what I wanted, and brought me here the next day after I finished work. As soon as I walked inside, I asked the agent for the lease."

She opened the door into the house and ushered him through a gourmet kitchen and into a spacious living room floored with lustrous oak and magnificent carpets. A tall, handsomely decorated Christmas tree stood in the corner by the fireplace, but what made his breath catch was the opposite wall. Mostly glass, it showcased a spectacular view over Los Angeles. He opened a slider and walked onto the deck. The sun had just set, etching the western horizon with orange and indigo, while the vast city below was beginning to sparkle with scattered lights.

Bracing his hands on the railing, he inhaled the cool January air, enjoying the tang of eucalyptus. The hill fell away steeply here, and he guessed that the bedrooms were on the lower level with an equally spec-tacular view. In not much more than a week, Jenny had moved into the kind of house he had always wanted. While he vaguely dreamed, she got things done.

The thought produced an upwelling of sadness. Jenny was a star, twinkling high above, while he was irretrievably earthbound. She had magic, while he was a nuts-and-bolts creature of f-stops and lighting arrays.

"Do you like the house?" Voice shy, she came to stand beside him. "The owner was a bridge designer, of all things, so the house is con-structed in a way that he thinks should survive even a major earthquake."

"It's spectacular, Jenny." Schooling his face, he turned to her. "And it suits you. If you're going to be spending time here, maybe you should see if the owner will sell."

"Actually, he will—he and his wife have moved back east to be closer to their children." After a long pause, she continued hesitantly, "I was thinking—would you—might you be interested in buying the house with me?"

His jaw dropped. "What the hell . . . ?"

She turned on her heel and retreated into the living room. "Sorry, that was really clumsy of me. It was . . . just a thought. Never mind. Dinner is all prepared and will only require a few blasts in the microwave."

Talk about clumsy! Feeling like an idiot, he dashed after her. "Jenny, why did you suggest that?" Surely she didn't need the money.

She paused to contemplate the Christmas tree, a tall Fraser fir whose green and purple decorations were maybe a little too perfect. "I'm just suggesting that it would be nice to . . . to live with you. We seem to be getting along rather well."

The vulnerability in her posture produced a wave of tenderness. "I know Hollywood must seem a little scary now, especially since you had a bad experience here before, but it would be foolish to tie yourself down by buying a house with me just because we're . . . friendly. In a few months, you'll have plenty of friends and you won't need me." He tried to make his tone joking. "Or did you want to get a place with me because I'm never here? That is an advantage in a housemate."

She whirled around, eyes snapping. "Why the devil do you assume that I'm not going to want you for a friend six months from now? Do I seem that shallow? Or do you want to keep your distance in the future because actresses are so needy and demanding and you don't want to get sucked into my personal psychodramas?"

"Of course I don't think you're shallow! And you're certainly no drama queen." He made a helpless gesture with his hand. "But new worlds are opening up for you, Jenny. You're going to be meeting exciting, charismatic men who operate on the same level you do. Sure, you and I can be friends, but I'm just the guy next door. Not someone you should be buying a house with."

She made a feline sound of exasperation. "I'm thirty-five years old, Gregory Marino. Do you think I'm too dim to know what I want? I've dated more than my share of 'exciting, charismatic' men, and there isn't one of them I would want to buy a house with." Her face tightened. "The time we spent together was more than a holiday fling to me, Greg. In fact, it was very special. I . . . I thought it was worth finding out if you felt the same."

Her words rocked him back on his heels. How much courage had it taken for her to make herself so vulnerable? More courage than he had—but if there was to be any hope for them, he must try to match her honesty. "It was more than a fling for me, too. I . . . I've been in love with you since we first met, but I'm so much in the habit of thinking there was no future for us that I have trouble believing that . . . that you might want more."

For a moment, time seemed to stop. Then she stepped forward, clasped his head with both hands, and drew it down for a kiss sweeter than chocolate. "Believe it, Greg."

Heart pounding, he wrapped his arms around her as if she were a life preserver in a storm. "Please don't say this is a joke. I couldn't bear it."

"Do you think I'd joke about the rest of my life?" She walked him back into the low sofa and pushed him down, landing on top in a pile of tangled limbs and scented sensuality. "You must stop underestimating yourself—your talent and skill, not to mention your delicious self, make for a madly attractive whole," she said huskily. "Shall I demonstrate exactly how attractive I find you?"

Her words brought every cell in his body to urgent life, but even more desperately than he wanted to make love, he wanted to understand. "I'm still not quite believing this. What happened between last week when we said good-bye at Heathrow and now?"

"I called Kenzie Scott and ended up having a nice chat with Raine." Jenny wriggled into a more comfortable position on top of him. "Something she said made me recognize how our assumptions about having a brief fling had turned into a self-fulfilling prophecy, and that it was time to rewind and try for a new conclusion."

He slid his hands under her tunic and rested them on the warm, bare skin of her back, still incredulous that she was in his arms again. "I've always figured that my main qualification in your eyes was being available and more or less presentable when you wanted some company."

She rolled her eyes. "So I'm not only shallow and dim, but a slut. Trust me, I've never been so bored that I would sleep with a man merely because he was available."

He gave a crooked smile. "If I say anything more, I'm going to dig myself into a really deep hole, aren't I?"

She chuckled. "You're already halfway to Australia, but I'll forgive you because you're wonderful. You always were, even a dozen years ago. Now you're one of the best cinematographers in the world, while I'm just another actress who has good years and bad years. My confidence is up at the moment, which is why I have the nerve to chase you, but my career could vanish like a crocodile in a swamp if this movie bombs."

"It won't bomb."

"No way to tell yet." She gave him a level look. "You're not only successful and a great guy, but you've worked with some of the most beautiful women in the world. What about me is special enough to hold the attention of a man of substance?"

He began to laugh. "So while I've been busy worshiping you, you've been cherishing exaggerated ideas of my importance. I should have asked you to marry me on our first go-around. I wanted to, but you were so hung up on that idiot actor that I knew you'd say no."

"If you'd proposed I might have said yes, but that wasn't the right time, my love," she said seriously. "We were at the beginning of our careers. We needed to grow into our adult selves. In the last dozen years, I've met tons of men, dated a fair number, fancied myself in love a time or two. Now that I've looked over the field, I know the best when I see him. I'm ready to swim into deeper waters. Are you?"

He winced. Heaven was being offered, but not yet within reach. "I have to go to Argentina next week, and I'll be there for at least four months, probably longer."

"I'm going to be madly busy for the next few months as well. But if we dig out our appointment books, surely we can find a time to start living together."

For the first time, he really believed that she meant it. *She really meant it!* "No living together." He thought of his mother, who wanted him to marry a nice Ohio kind of girl. She'd freak at the sight of glamorous Jenny—then fall in love with her. "I'm from the Midwest, you know. If I'm going to take you home to meet the family, it will have to be marriage."

She bit one enchanting lip. "Are you sure you wouldn't rather live together for a year or two? We're both going to have to do some adjusting. I want to keep the cottage and spend a fair amount of the year in England. In fact, I'll have to for the future Revels productions. You might not want that. And we'll both have to cut back on our professional obligations if we're ever going to spend any time together."

These were serious issues, so he considered them for about three seconds. "All true, but doable. I love the idea of having a home in England and a home here. I love the idea of *this* home. I love your family, and having Plato trot around carrying his buggy whip. I love the idea of taking fewer jobs so I can spend lots and lots of time with you.

"Most of all, I love you." He caught her gaze with his. "I don't want to go into this with one hand on the doorknob so I can back out if we hit a few rough spots. I want the real thing, Jenny—an old-fashioned, till-death-do-us-part marriage."

Her shining smile could have lit up the whole London Underground. "How deliciously Neanderthal. Very well, we shall marry. My family will be over the moon—my mother and Patricia have been making pointed comments about how much they like you and how well you fit into Upper Bassett." She growled deep in her throat as she kissed him again. "But before we start looking for weddings dates, can we play Tarzan and Jane?"

"Sure," he said obligingly. "Which role do you want?"

Bubbling with laughter, she rolled off the sofa, taking him with her onto the thick carpet. "You can be Tarzan this time. Then it will be my turn."

Tenderly he cupped her face between his hands. "You're so beautiful, Jenny. So heart-stoppingly beautiful."

Some of her sparkle faded. "Appreciating beauty is a big part of what you do, Greg, but I hope to heaven you don't think you love me just because of the way I look. Will you leave me when I get gray and plump and wrinkled?"

Startled, he recognized the insecurity under her words. He studied her beloved face. She wasn't wearing a shred of makeup and fine lines showed at the corners of her eyes. It wasn't the face of a film icon, but a real woman—the one he wanted to spend the rest of his life with.

"I'll love every wrinkle and gray hair and soft curve, and give thanks for the chance to see them develop. If I were struck blind tomorrow, I'd still laugh at your jokes and rub your back when you're tired and talk to you long into every night because I love your ideas and humor and kindness and . . . and your general wonderfulness." He kissed her as if she were made of the finest porcelain. "I hate that we're not going to see each other for months. Maybe you can arrange your shooting schedule to come down for a few days? We can have a Groundhog's Day holiday fling."

"I'm sure Marcus will be able to arrange for me to have a few days with you, since it will improve my morale so much. But no more holiday flings, my love," she whispered. "Every day with you will be a holiday."

The Christmas Cuckoo

JACK Howard, late a major in the 51st Regiment, gave a depressed sigh as he folded his large frame into the chair nearest the fire. After eight weeks of nonstop travel, he was rumpled, tired, and in dire need of a haircut and a shave. He had looked forward to reaching the Red Duck Inn so he could eat, sleep the rest of the afternoon, eat again, then perhaps enjoy a spot of socializing in the taproom before retiring for the night. By morning he would have been sufficiently recovered from the rigors of travel to endure the ordeals ahead.

Instead, no sooner had Jack set foot from the stagecoach than he had been intercepted by a small gray clerk. The aptly named Mr. Weezle was secretary to the countess—everyone always called her "the countess," as if she were the only one in England—and he had been meeting the Portsmouth *Courier* every day for the last week. After the barest minimum of civil greetings, Mr. Weezle had swept Jack off to the coaching inn's private parlor, then pulled a paper from his pocket and begun reading through the items, ticking each off with a pencil. And the more the secretary talked, the more depressed Jack became.

Weezle punctuated his monologue by pulling a card case from his pocket and handing it to Jack. "The countess took the liberty of having new cards made for you."

"The countess has taken rather a lot of liberties," Jack said dryly as he glanced at the top card before slipping the flat gold case into the single piece of baggage by his feet. At least the spelling was correct. But then, it was hard to mistake a name as common as John Howard.

Ignoring Jack's ungracious remark, Weezle adjusted the spectacles on his nose and consulted his list again. "There are some people the countess wishes you to call on before you leave London, but of course you cannot do so until you are properly attired. After we leave here, we will stop at Weston's. Though this is a busy time of year, Mr. Weston has promised to produce some decent clothing for you overnight. Naturally, the garments won't be done to his usual standards, but at least you will be presentable. A more appropriate wardrobe will be sent to Hazelwood within a week."

"Obliging of Mr. Weston, but I have no intention of visiting any tailor this afternoon. When I do go to one, it will probably be Scott."

"The countess would not like that," the secretary stated, as if that settled the matter. For him it did. "Of course you need a valet, but it's impossible to hire decent servants at this time of year. A pity you didn't reach London last week, when you were supposed to. With Christmas just three days away, there simply isn't time to accomplish all that should be done before going to Hazelwood. One of the countess's cousins here in London has agreed to instruct you on how to get on in society, but there will be time for only a single lesson."

Among his friends Jack was famous for his imperturbable good nature, but Weezle's words triggered a slow burn of anger. "No," he said flatly. "My manners may be rough by her ladyship's standards, but I'm too old to learn new ones."

Weezle peered over his spectacles. "No one doubts that your manners are gentlemanlike," he said with a belated attempt at tact, "but since you've spent so many years in the army, the countess thought that a bit of polish would not go amiss. There will be a great deal of formal entertaining at Hazelwood."

Jack sighed, knowing that it was a waste of energy to be annoyed with the countess. She was his great-aunt by marriage and he had known her since he was in short coats. Usually he had been able to shrug off her domineering ways, so why was he so irritated today?

Perhaps because he'd had no chance to eat since hastily swallowing a slice of bread and a mouthful of ale at dawn. He stood and walked across the room to ring for a servant so he could order food and drink.

The secretary's gaze fell on Jack's shabby top boots. "Those boots will have to go."

Jack stopped in his tracks, once again terminally exasperated. "These are the most comfortable boots I have ever owned, and where they go, I go."

Ignoring the remark, Weezle said, "Perhaps Hoby can find time to fit you for new boots tomorrow morning."

"*No.*"

Belatedly noticing Jack's dangerous tone, the secretary said, "Would you prefer the afternoon? Perhaps before visiting the countess's cousin."

"No, and no, and no again. I have no desire to visit Hoby or Weston or any of the people on the countess's list, nor be drilled in etiquette like a raw lad up from the country. All I want is a meal and a hot bath and a decent night's sleep. Come back tomorrow morning and we can talk about your wretched list."

"Very well, if you insist," Weezle said stiffly. "I've reserved rooms for you at the Clarendon. I'll summon the carriage to take us there."

"What is wrong with staying here?" Jack glanced around the inn's clean and thoroughly comfortable private parlor.

"This is hardly a suitable place for you."

Jack laughed, his good humor restored. "There have been nights when I've haggled with a cow for the right to share her straw, and been grateful to have that much."

Weezle's nose twitched like one of the lesser rodents'. "You must be most grateful to be returning to Hazelwood."

"Not particularly." His brief amusement fading, Jack said, "I'm not sure that I want to spend Christmas at Hazelwood."

Weezle looked shocked. "But the countess expects you."

"She may expect me," Jack said recklessly, "but she is not my commanding officer and has no power to order my presence."

"The countess said you might prove recalcitrant," the secretary said with ill-concealed irritation. "But where could you possibly spend the holiday except at Hazelwood?"

Until now Jack had intended to fall in with the countess's plans, but

Weezle's remark was the last straw. "There is a whole world of possibilities out there"—he pulled his heavy greatcoat on, then stooped to pick up his bag—"and I'm going to discover what they are. Good-bye, Mr. Weezle. Tell the countess that I'll pay a call on her after the holidays."

Ignoring the secretary's outraged sputtering, Jack left the parlor and strode out into the courtyard. A fine, saturating rain was beginning to fall, and the bleak prospect made him hesitate while he considered what to do next. A pity he had no friends who would be in London this close to Christmas. Winter gales had blown his packet from Lisbon several days off-course, the journey up to London had been made interminable by muddy roads, and Jack was heartily sick of traveling. All he wanted was to enjoy a little peace and warmth after too many years away from his homeland.

His brief burst of temper cooled. He was about to return to the inn to make his peace with Mr. Weezle, when the secretary's sharp voice sounded from the doorway. "The countess will be *most* displeased if you don't come to Hazelwood."

Disapproval revived Jack's flagging resolve. He had no particular destination in mind, but he'd be damned if he would let himself be bullied by the countess and her minions. His gaze fell on a heavily loaded stagecoach that was preparing to leave. Impulsively he called to the guard, "Have you room for another passenger?"

The guard was busy stowing parcels in the front boot, but he paused to consult the waybill. "Aye, there's one outside place left." He shoved the waybill in his coat pocket and returned to his task. "But if you want it you'll have to move smartly, 'cause we're ready to roll."

As Jack turned toward the booking office, Mr. Weezle said, aghast, "You don't even know where that coach is going!"

"No, I don't," Jack said cheerfully. "But anywhere is bound to be better than the countess's demanding hospitality."

After hastily buying a ticket, Jack tossed his bag up to the guard, then began to ascend the ladder leading to the seats at the back of the carriage's roof. The vehicle lurched into motion, and Jack would have fallen if a helpful fellow passenger hadn't reached down to steady him. "Thanks," Jack gasped as he swung up to safety.

He turned and looked back. The last thing he saw as the coach left the yard was Mr. Weezle's slack-jawed face. The sight was almost worth the knowledge that Jack's grand gesture was going to cost him hours of cold, wet misery.

The seating consisted of two facing benches with room for three passengers in each. That is, there was room if one considered sixteen inches' width per passenger adequate, which it wasn't for most people, especially not men as large as Jack. As he squeezed into the middle place on the backward-facing seat, four of the other five passengers regarded him dourly, obviously regretting the amount of space the newcomer would occupy.

The fifth passenger, a rotund gentleman dressed as a farmer, was the one who had helped Jack up, and he offered the only friendly smile. "Going to be a cold ride to Bristol, brother."

"That it will," Jack agreed. So Bristol, where he didn't know a single soul, was his destination. He was going to spend hours in the freezing rain, squeezed as tight as a herring in a barrel, all for the dubious privilege of ending in another inn that would be no better than the Red Duck, and likely a good deal worse. It wasn't the first time his stubborn streak had gotten him into trouble, he thought philosophically, and it certainly wouldn't be the last.

Silence reigned as the coach rumbled through the crowded city streets, swaying like a ship at sea. Jack adjusted his hat in a vain attempt to keep rain from running down his neck. The raw cold bit to the bone. On the Continent, severe winters prevented coaches from having outside seats. Fortunate Britain, whose milder climate wouldn't kill outside passengers. At least, not quite.

An hour later Jack was thinking that he hadn't felt so cold since the retreat to Corunna when the rotund farmer reached inside his coat and pulled out a flask. "Me name's Jem," he said, addressing his words to all his companions. "Anyone care to join me in some Christmas cheer?"

Four of the passengers fastidiously ignored the offer, but Jack said, "Don't mind if I do." Though he knew that drinking on an empty stomach was a mistake, it was a little late in the day to start acting rationally. As he accepted the flask, he added, "My name is Jack."

Expecting brandy and water, Jack took a deep swig, then burst into strangled coughing as raw fire scalded his throat.

"Prime stuff, ain't it, Jack?" Jem said cheerfully.

"Quite unlike anything I've ever drunk before," Jack said with absolute truth. After a more cautious sip, he decided that the beverage was undiluted whiskey of a potency that should have dissolved the container. "Certainly takes the chill off."

Jem took a swig, then passed the whiskey back to Jack. "This is nothing compared to the winter of eighty-six. Why, I remember . . ."

Jack settled back contentedly. Cold and wet he might be, but Jem was certainly better company than Mr. Weezle.

THE striking of the kitchen clock informed Meg Lambert that she couldn't delay any longer. She glanced at the kitchen window, where rain had drummed relentlessly since midafternoon. Ordinarily Meg did not mind bad weather, for the contrast made her appreciate the comfort of her farmhouse even more. Tonight, however, when sensible people were staying by their fires, she must go out into the storm.

She drained the last of her tea and set the cup down, then ordered, "Out of the way, Ginger." When the calico cat ignored her, Meg unceremoniously jerked her brother's letter out from under the furry feline rump. Ginger raised her head and gave the mistress of the house an injured glance, then tucked her nose under her tail and returned to slumber.

Meg scanned the letter once more, wishing the contents might have magically changed, but no such luck. It still said:

Dear Meg,

Please excuse my hasty scrawl, but the courier is waiting for this and impatient to leave. I'm most dreadfully sorry to say that I will be delayed and won't be home in time to meet Jack Howard myself. The colonel has asked me to perform a commission for him, and one doesn't refuse one's colonel!

Jack will be arriving in Chippenham on December 22 on the evening coach from London. You won't have any trouble recognizing him—he's tall and dark and handsome and looks just as an officer ought. I expect Phoebe to be most impressed with him. (And vice versa, of course!) Jack is a great gun and will fit right in. I swear I will be home as soon as pos-

sible, though I fear it won't be until after Christmas. Save me some of
your special pudding and say all that is proper to Jack.

Love to all,
Jeremy

As Meg folded the single sheet again, her younger sister floated into the kitchen. Phoebe didn't walk like normal females; she had the drifting grace, ebony hair, and porcelain features of a woodland fairy.

"I'm going to take the gig into Chippenham now," Meg said. "I imagine the little girls are asleep, but you should probably look in on them later. And keep the fire up—I'm sure that Captain Howard and I will need it when we return."

Phoebe went to the window and peered out, her blue eyes concerned. "With a storm like this, perhaps Captain Howard has been delayed and won't arrive tonight."

"Perhaps not," Meg admitted, "but I still must go as long as there is any chance that he will be there."

Her sister frowned. "You shouldn't be driving alone on a night like this. Since Philip isn't home. I'll go with you."

"Thank you, darling, but there's no need. It's scarcely three miles, and Clover and I have made the trip hundreds of times. Besides, you're just recovering from one chill—it would be foolish to risk coming down with another one."

Phoebe started to protest, then stopped. "I expect you're right. But be careful."

Swaddled in cloak, bonnet, scarf, and gloves, Meg squashed her way to the barn, her pattens sinking into the mud as sheets of icy water swept across the farmyard and wind rattled the branches of nearby trees. She should have left earlier, for it would be a slow trip into town.

It took only a few minutes to harness Clover. Before climbing into the gig, Meg pulled a carrot from her pocket and gave it to the pony. "You'll get another when we're home again."

The pony flicked his ears back in acknowledgment of the bribe and they set off for Chippenham. Fortunately Meg knew the route well, for the slashing rain made it hard to see even the hedgerows that lined the lane.

The farmhouse stood on top of a large, gradually inclined hill with a brook winding around the base. Usually the water was scarcely more than a trickle, but now the ford was over a foot deep and a strong current rocked the gig as it splashed through the water. The lane beyond was soggy, and soon one wheel bogged down in the mud.

Meg sighed as she climbed down to push the vehicle free. Everything was going wrong, which was what always happened when one wanted matters to be exactly right. Even to herself, Meg hated to admit how much hope she had pinned on this visit of Jeremy's friend. Phoebe was twenty and it was high time she married, but it was hard for a girl to find a husband when she never met any suitable young men. Given the disastrous state of the family finances, Phoebe would never have the London Season she deserved. Meg had been deeply concerned about her sister's future. Then her brother wrote that he would be able to come home on leave at Christmas, and he had invited his best friend to join them.

Judging by Jeremy's letters, Captain Howard was the answer to Meg's prayers: honorable, good-tempered, and from a well-to-do family in the Midlands. Now, if the captain would just cooperate and fall in love with Phoebe. There was an excellent chance he would, for the girl was so beautiful and sweet-natured that any normal young man was bound to lose his heart to her.

Phoebe herself always greeted Jeremy's letters with an excitement that was more than sisterly fondness. Though the sisters had never discussed the matter, Meg suspected that the younger girl was halfway to being in love with her brother's friend. Yes, Meg had high hopes for Captain Howard's visit.

A branch slapped Meg's face, stinging her cheek and jerking her out of her reverie. As she batted the branch away, she thought wryly that Jack Howard had better be at the George, for she would feel most provoked if this journey proved fruitless.

"CHIPPENHAM! Twenny minutes fer dinner afore we go on to Bristol!" the guard bawled.

There was a stampede of passengers to reach the ground. Jack yawned and stayed where he was, grateful to have room to stretch his legs after hours of cramping. Not that he was feeling much discomfort. In fact, he felt nothing at all. Solemnly he pondered the question of whether he was numb with cold or paralyzed by his companion's whiskey. Probably both.

Before Jack could drift into full sleep, Jem tugged on his sleeve. "Come along, brother," the farmer said. "You shouldn't stay out here in the rain."

Obediently Jack stood and followed the older man down the ladder. The ground showed a distressing tendency to rise up to meet him, and he watched it with interest.

Jem grabbed Jack's arm and steered him into the inn. "You'll be better for some food in your belly."

Jack hiccuped. "Very likely."

The warmth of the inn hit him like a steaming blanket and he began wavering again. Tolerantly Jem steered Jack through the main taproom into a smaller room beyond, then deposited him on an inglenook bench by the fire. "I'll bring you something to eat."

"Much obliged." Jack hazily pulled a coin from his pocket and pressed it into the farmer's hand. Then he lay back on the bench and promptly fell asleep.

Jem took the silver crown and went to order food. More than ten minutes passed before he managed to purchase two hot meat pies from the busy hosts. Munching on one, Jem returned to his companion. "Here you go, lad, a nice pork pie."

Sublimely unaware, Jack slept on.

Next door the guard shouted, "Time to board the *Express*!"

Jem swallowed the rest of his pie and shook the sleeping man. "Look lively or you'll miss the coach."

Jack batted at the insistent hand, then subsided again.

Deciding stronger measures were needed, Jem tried to pull the other man off the bench, thinking that would wake him up.

Instead, Jack made a swift movement with his arm and Jem found himself polishing the floor with his breeches five feet away. Unhurt, he said admiringly, "Wish you were awake enough to teach me that trick, brother."

The guard yelled again, "Last call!"

Torn, Jem gazed at Jack and tried to decide what to do. Didn't look like the lad wanted to go anywhere, and Jem didn't want to learn what would happen to the next man who tried to wake him. Coming to a decision, Jem scrambled to his feet and dashed outside, where the coachman and guard were taking their seats.

"The gent who got on at the Red Duck at the last minute don't want to go no farther," Jem said breathlessly. "Toss down his bag. I'll take it inside and be right back."

The coachman growled, "Time we was leaving."

Knowing the infallible way to ensure cooperation, Jem gave each of the men a half-crown. "For your trouble."

The guard turned and rooted in the luggage, then handed the bag down to Jem. "Mind you hurry right back, or we'll leave without you."

Jem raced inside and tucked the bag under Jack's bench, then gave another half-crown to the landlord, who was regarding the sleeping man disapprovingly. "Let the lad spend the night here."

The landlord pocketed the coin. "Very well. I suppose there's no harm in it."

Jem still held the second pork pie, so he took a bite. "Have a happy Christmas, Jack," he said, his voice muffled with flaky pastry. Secure in the knowledge of his good deed, he dashed outside and boarded the coach that would return him to his own comfortable hearth before the night was over.

TIRED and splashed with mud, Meg tethered Clover inside the stable of the George. She guessed that the coach from London had already come and gone, and sure enough, inside the inn the landlord and his wife were clearing away plates left by hasty passengers. Meg removed her dripping bonnet and shook out her damp curls. "Good evening, Mr. Bragg."

The landlord glanced up, surprised. "What brings you here on such a nasty night, Miss Lambert?"

"A friend of Jeremy's was supposed to arrive on the London coach." Seeing only a handful of locals drinking ale by the fire, she asked, "Didn't any passengers get off here?"

"Well, there's a gent in the other room," Mr. Bragg said dubiously, "but I doubt he's the one you're looking for."

Hoping the landlord was wrong, Meg crossed the main taproom to the smaller chamber beyond. She halted in the doorway, wondering if the room's sole occupant could possibly be the right man, for her mental image of Jack Howard was quite different. Unconsciously she had assumed that Jeremy's friend would be in the same mold as her brother: slim and young and elegant.

Instead, the man sprawled along the bench was very large, very shaggy, and not at all elegant. Wisps of steam rose gently from his worn coat, and his hat had fallen to the flagged floor. Jeremy had mentioned that his friend was a bit older, but Meg had assumed Jack Howard would still be somewhere in his midtwenties. The man in front of her appeared to be at least a decade her brother's senior.

Systematically Meg compared the stranger against Jeremy's comments. Tall? Yes, definitely tall. Dark? She studied the long unruly hair. She would have called it brown rather than dark, but certainly it wasn't fair.

How about handsome? She examined the sleeping face, where several days' worth of beard darkened the long jaw. Even worn by fatigue it was a pleasant countenance, but "handsome" did seem rather an overstatement. Still, one tended to think one's friends were attractive, and Jeremy and Jack were very good friends. Meg just hoped that Phoebe wouldn't be disappointed.

Meg bent over the recumbent form. Then she stopped and wrinkled her nose. The gentleman smelled as if he had been held prisoner in a distillery. Not the most proper behavior for a man visiting friends, but fortunately Meg was not easily offended. Besides, on a night like this, spirits were a sensible way to counter the cold and damp. "Captain Howard?"

When there was no reply, she tried again, raising her voice. This time his lids fluttered open, revealing intensely blue eyes. Meg caught her breath, understanding why someone would describe this man as handsome. However, those gorgeous blue eyes were blank with incomprehension. "Are you Captain Howard?"

Hearing a military rank penetrated Jack's whiskey-aided exhaustion as nothing else would have, for a soldier who wanted to die in his bed learned to respond to emergencies no matter what his state. But what kind of emergency had a voice like spring flowers? "Not captain. Major."

The voice said with apparent pleasure, "I didn't know you had received a promotion. Congratulations, Major." Then, uncertainly, "You *are* Jack Howard?"

"I was last time I looked, but it's been rather a long day." Wanting to see the face that went with that delicious voice, Jack concentrated until her features came into focus one by one. A riot of bright brown curls. Thoughtful hazel eyes with green flecks. A scattering of freckles across cheeks rosy with good health. And an extremely kissable mouth. His gaze fixed on that last feature, he asked hopefully, "Do I know you?"

"I am Miss Lambert," she explained, as if that would instantly clarify his confusion.

Jack frowned, trying to recall the name. "Miss Lambert?"

"Margaret Lambert, Jeremy's older sister, though if he ever mentioned me, he would have called me Meg. Everyone does."

Margaret. Jeremy. Meg. Who were these people? He would never have forgotten this lady's face. For that matter, Jack thought as he raised a vague hand to his head, where the devil was he and how had he gotten here?

"Where is Jeremy?" He knew several men by that name. If he recognized Miss Lambert's Jeremy, this conversation might make more sense.

The mobile face above him showed regret. "Jeremy has been delayed for a few days and won't be home until after Christmas. He asked me to apologize for his absence."

Jack sighed; no enlightenment there. Doggedly he tried to recall what had happened. Ah, yes, the irritating interview with Mr. Weezle that had driven Jack to board the coach to Bristol. What then? With a faint shudder he remembered the friendly farmer with the lethal flask of spirits.

After a brief survey of his surroundings, Jack concluded that he was in a tavern. Either he had liked the place and decided to stay or he had been incapable of further travel. But none of that explained how this appealing lady knew him.

As Jack racked his brain, the lady said helpfully, "Were you expecting to be met by Phoebe? No doubt Jeremy spoke more of her, for she's the family beauty. I don't look at all like her or Jeremy, for I'm only a half-sister."

"You look quite whole to me." He surveyed her from muddy toes to curly hair, missing nothing in between. "Women like you are why men will fight and die to defend home and hearth."

Miss Lambert blushed prettily. "I can see why Jeremy said you were charming, but don't waste your flattery on me. Phoebe is a much more suitable object."

Jack started to shake his head, then stopped hastily when the world began spinning. "Not flattery. God's own truth." Belatedly recognizing his impropriety, he added, "Begging your pardon for the language, Miss Lambert."

"Quite all right. One can't expect a man who is foxed to have perfect control over his tongue."

"Not foxed." It occurred to Jack that a gentleman did not converse with a lady while lying on his back, so he sat up, exercising great care. "P'haps a trifle well-to-go." Being upright gave him a better view of the lady, and it was well worth it. She was of medium height and her cloaked figure was agreeably round in all the right places, not like one of those skinny fashionable wenches.

"If you're feeling more the thing, it is time we set off," Miss Lambert said briskly. "The weather is dreadful and it will be nearly midnight before we get home."

"Home?" Jack asked, startled. Was he dreaming? In normal life, well-bred, wholesome young ladies did not invite strange men home with them. Or perhaps she wasn't a lady? What a splendid thought.

"Of course." For the first time she showed a hint of impatience. "I certainly don't want to spend the night here. Can you manage to walk to the stables?"

Foxed he might be, but Jack knew a good offer when he heard one. "Be delighted to go home with you."

He stood, swaying slightly, then pulled his bag out from under the bench. Though she might not be quite a lady, she wasn't a tavern wench either. Her home would be much better. There was a danger that he would be in no shape to perform when he got there, but he would certainly try. He gave her a sweeping bow. "For the honor of the regiment!"

Meg laughed. "For the honor of the regiment." Though the major did not make much sense in his present condition, she couldn't help liking him.

Taking her guest's arm, Meg guided him through the inn. To her surprise, he put his arm around her shoulders when they stepped outside, but she guessed that he needed a bit of steadying. She didn't mind if he used her for a cane. He was good protection from the wind and rain.

However, even the most liberal of interpretations could not excuse what happened in the stables. Meg untethered the pony and sacrificed half of her remaining carrot to reward Clover for his earlier endeavors. After stroking his velvety nose and saying a few appreciative words, she turned to her guest, who had loaded his bag and was standing by the gig. "Will you open the doors so I can drive outside, Major?"

He nodded but made no move toward the entrance. Thinking he intended to help her into the gig, Meg put her hand in his. But instead of assisting her up as a gentleman should, Jack Howard gave a slight tug that pulled Meg against his broad chest.

Startled, she glanced up to find the major's face descending. When his warm mouth encompassed hers, Meg gasped, then began cooperating from sheer surprise. No one had stolen a kiss from practical Miss Lambert since her salad days. And none of the Chippenham lads had *ever* kissed like this.

The major's hands did interesting things that made Meg's knees weaken so that she had to cling to his large frame for support. She had forgotten just how pleasant a kiss could be. . . .

But how dare Jeremy invite such a dangerous man to stay under the same roof as his sisters! Immediately she realized that her brother would not knowingly have invited a rake home, so Jeremy must be ignorant of the major's disgraceful behavior. Well, if Jack Howard was a rake, Meg decided, he simply would not do for Phoebe.

Having reached that wise conclusion, she realized that all the time she had been weighing the major's scandalous misconduct, she had continued kissing him. In fact, her arms were twined around him like ivy.

Shocked more by herself than by him, she pulled her head back and exclaimed in freezing accents, *"Major Howard!"*

As an elder sister, Meg had developed an exceedingly peremptory voice. The major instantly released her and jumped back as if she were made of red-hot iron. "B-beg your pardon, Miss Lambert," he stammered. "Don't know what came over me."

He did not look at all rakish; in fact, his confused, guilty expression reminded Meg of a hound that had just been caught snatching food from the table.

Disarmed, she almost laughed. In truth, she was more flattered than angry. Men never noticed Meg when Phoebe was in the room, so she felt a secret guilty pleasure in the knowledge that the major had found her worth kissing. Suppressing her amusement, she said frostily, "We shall both forget that happened." She climbed into the gig—without help—and lifted the reins. "Please open the stable doors, Major Howard."

Hastily he complied. Meg drove outside, then waited while her guest closed and latched the doors behind her. Silently he climbed into the carriage and settled himself as far from her as possible, which wasn't very far in a gig.

The storm soon quenched Meg's amusement, for driving demanded all her attention. As she concentrated on avoiding the worst of the ruts, the major slouched beside her, so quiet that she might have thought he was sleeping or passed out from drink.

However, her passenger came alive whenever the gig bogged down in the mud, which happened about every ten minutes. No sooner would they shudder to a halt than the major jumped down, wordlessly freed the light vehicle from the rut, then climbed back in and returned to his torpor. Meg found it fascinating to watch him. Clearly a seasoned soldier could do whatever was necessary, even when half-seas-over.

The drive home seemed much longer than the trip to town, and by the time they reached the ford, Meg was tense with strain. Pulling Clover to a halt, she studied the rushing water, which was wider and deeper than it had been earlier. Briefly she considered returning to Chippenham, but she hated to give up when they were so close to home. Besides, Phoebe would worry if they didn't return. The water was a little high, but the streambed was firm and they should be able to cross safely.

Clover was less sure, and it took all Meg's powers of persuasion to convince him to move forward. As the gig entered the water, the current battered the wheels and the pony stopped, whickering nervously.

"Steady, Clover," Meg murmured, her hands firm on the reins. Clover started forward again and in another minute he reached the far bank and began scrambling out of the water.

Disaster struck with shocking suddenness. One moment Meg was holding the reins and in control of the gig. Then something smashed into the vehicle, knocking it over and pitching the passengers into the roiling stream.

Meg opened her mouth to cry out and found herself choking on icy water as her heavy cloak dragged her below the surface. There was a deep pool to the left of the ford, and the current tumbled her into it. Helpless, drowning in the pitiless depths, Meg succumbed to blind panic, striking out hysterically as she fought for air.

One of her flailing feet kicked a yielding object, and an instant later strong hands seized her and pulled her to the surface. The major was tall enough to stand on the bottom of the stream, and his powerful arms held her securely against his chest as dark water swirled around them.

Unable to touch bottom, Meg clutched her rescuer desperately as she coughed convulsively. Finally air reached her anguished lungs, but even though the danger was past, panic drummed through her with every beat of her pounding heart.

Then Major Howard murmured in her ear, his voice warm and amused, "That was quite fun. Shall we do it again?"

Meg choked in momentary outrage. Then laughter dissolved her terror. "You absurd man," she gasped, incongruously aware of the scent of wet wool and warm male. "If that is your idea of fun, perhaps I should take you back to the George."

"Don't do that. This is much more amusing." The major lifted Meg in his arms and carried her through the water to the bank. There he set her on her feet, keeping his arm around her waist until it was clear she could stand alone. "How much farther to your house?"

"J-just up the hill." Meg wrapped her arms around herself in a futile attempt to find warmth as the icy wind bit through her saturated clothing. "Do you know what caused the accident?"

"I think a tree trunk hit the gig and knocked it over. Your pony is over there, unhappy but unharmed."

Following the direction of his gesture, Meg saw Clover stamping about nervously, confused and distinctly disapproving. A tangle of harness attached him to the damaged carriage, which was snarled in a bush.

Major Howard guided Meg to the gig, then swiftly disconnected the harness and freed Clover. "Can you stay on the pony long enough to reach home?"

"I th-think so."

He put his hands around Meg's waist and lifted her to Clover's back, setting her sideways. Then he took off his greatcoat and draped it around her shoulders. "A pity this isn't dry, but at least it will block some of the wind."

The coat did help, but Meg protested, "You'll freeze!"

"Not as quickly as you will."

When Meg opened her mouth to argue further, the major barked, "No arguments, soldier!"

Stunned, Meg closed her mouth and obediently curled her numb fingers around the leather harness straps. Was her companion joking or so drunk that he wasn't quite sure where he was? No matter. He certainly knew what to do.

They began to climb the hill, the major guiding the pony with one hand and using the other to steady Meg. Eager to return to his own stall, Clover moved briskly, and in less than five minutes they reached the old farmhouse.

"This is it," Meg said, her voice a croak.

"Here?" he asked, a note of surprise in his voice.

Apparently Jeremy had not explained the family circumstances to his friend, and the major had expected something grander. Too drained to explain, Meg merely said, "Around the house to the left. We'll go in the back."

They circled the building and found light streaming through the kitchen windows. The major stopped at the door, then reached up and lifted Meg's shivering body from her perch. "You go inside and I'll stable the pony. I'll be along in a few minutes."

"But you're a guest," Meg protested through chattering teeth. "I'll take care of Clover."

He took her shoulders and turned her to the door. "Never disobey a superior officer. Now, *march.*"

Too cold to argue further, Meg fumbled with the latch. Almost immediately the door swung open and Phoebe was standing there, a lamp held high in one hand, her exquisite face warm with concern. With a small twinge, Meg knew that Jack Howard must be falling in love with her on the spot.

Oblivious of the dramatic picture she presented, Phoebe exclaimed, "Thank heaven you're home! I was getting worried. Don't just stand there, Meg, come inside—you're soaking wet." Then she looked over her sister's shoulder, her eyes narrowed as she peered into the darkness. "Welcome to Brook Farm, Captain Howard. Please, come in right away. You look as wet as Meg."

"He's a major now, Phoebe." Meg took off the greatcoat and handed it to her guest.

"This is not the time for formal introductions." The major draped the coat over his shoulders. "There was an accident and Miss Lambert is freezing. Put her next to the fire and warm her up. I'll be along as soon as the pony has been bedded down for the night."

Phoebe made a shocked sound and ushered her sister into the house. Once in the warm kitchen, Meg peeled off her cloak as she described the accident, then went to change into dry clothing while Phoebe set tea to brewing.

Still shivering, Meg returned to the kitchen and gratefully accepted a mug of tea fortified with brandy. "Major Howard hasn't come in yet?" she asked, wondering if some combination of drink, fatigue, and cold might have overcome him in the barn.

Before Phoebe could reply, the outside door swung open and their guest—large, unkempt, and gently dripping water from his soaking garments—appeared in the doorway between hall and kitchen. Now that the danger had passed, his decisiveness was gone and he had lapsed back into dazed confusion.

Meg stepped forward and handed him the other mug of fortified tea. "Drink this."

It took him a moment to comprehend her command. Then he took the mug and downed the contents in one long swallow that must have scorched his mouth and throat.

Phoebe took over, seating both orphans of the storm by the fire, then feeding them potato-cabbage soup hot from the hob. Warmed both inside and out, Meg felt considerably better. She assumed the major did, too, though he did not speak, simply ate his soup with clumsy hands and an unfocused gaze.

When he was done, Meg said, "Time for bed." Taking his hand, she led him upstairs as if he were a child. "Leave your wet clothes outside the door and we'll dry them tonight."

Reaching the bedroom that had been assigned to the guest, Meg opened the door and gave the major a gentle push. "Put your wet clothes outside," she repeated, hoping he understood.

Before Meg could leave, the major peeled off his blue coat and dropped it on the floor. It landed with a wet, squishy sound and was joined by his shirt a moment later.

Meg's mouth dropped open in astonishment. He really was a splendid specimen of masculinity. Her gaze riveted to her guest's muscular torso and the dark hair that patterned his broad chest.

Oblivious of his shocking impropriety, the major began to unbutton his trousers.

Released from her paralysis, Meg blushed scarlet and beat a hasty retreat. "There are towels on the washstand," she called over her shoulder before shutting the door. "And hot bricks in the bed."

Downstairs Phoebe waited, her expression doubtful. "He isn't at all what I expected. And . . . is it possible he has been drinking?"

"I'm afraid so," Meg admitted as she went to stand in front of the fire. "But in spite of that, he has been very gentlemanly. He also just saved me from drowning." Remembering how important it was for Phoebe to like their guest, Meg spent the next ten minutes giving a glowing description of the major's virtues.

All the while, she listened for the sound of the bedroom door, but upstairs there was only silence. Finally Meg sighed. "He must have fallen asleep right away. I'd better get his clothing so it can dry. Perhaps we can find his baggage in the daylight, but if not, the major has nothing to wear but what he had on. Jeremy's garments certainly aren't large enough."

"Let me get his things," Phoebe offered. "You should be in bed."

Meg was tired enough to be tempted to accept. Then a vivid memory of Major Howard unbuttoning his trousers made her shake her head. There was no telling what condition their guest was in, and Meg was not about to let her innocent young sister find out. "This will take just a moment. While I'm upstairs, will you make me another cup of tea?"

"Of course."

Meg was unsurprised when there was no answer to her knock. Steeling herself, she opened the door and was greatly relieved to find the major in bed and mostly covered.

The wet garments lay scattered across the room, but before collecting them, Meg found herself walking quietly to the bed and looking down at her guest. The blankets were drawn only to midchest, as if he had been too tired to finish covering himself, so Meg pulled them up around his throat. In spite of his ruffianly appearance, he looked exhausted and vulnerable.

With a surge of tenderness, she brushed back his thick brown hair, as she would have done with a slumbering child. "Sleep well, Jack Howard," she whispered.

As Meg made her way downstairs again, she thought that it would certainly be an interesting Christmas.

*   *   *

FOR a long time Jack hovered in the twilight area between sleep and waking, instinctively knowing that full awareness would not be a desirable state this morning. Then a bloodcurdling shriek shattered the last remnants of slumber.

Reflexively he opened his eyes and started to sit up. A wave of nausea swept over him. He fell back against the pillows, heart pounding and eyes closed against the sunlight streaming through the window. Though it had been at least a decade since he had experienced this particular kind of wretchedness, Jack recognized it immediately as the aftermath of a truly appalling carouse.

The shriek sounded from outside again, the noise stabbing his throbbing temples. After identifying the sound as avian and presumably harmless, Jack dismissed it from his mind.

Far more important was coming to terms with the events of the previous night, which he recalled with painful accuracy. London. The wet, freezing ride on the stage to Bristol. Jem. Then the coaching inn, where the delightful Miss Lambert had approached and greeted him. She had wanted a Jack Howard, and in his befuddled state he had been more than willing to oblige.

He winced as he remembered what had happened in the stable. Even three sheets to the wind, he should have known that a female so refined and well-spoken could only be a lady. Instead he had believed her a light-skirt and had lunged at her like a sailor just home from a year at sea. Though in fact she had not seemed to mind, at least not at first. . . .

Recalling that kiss in detail briefly mitigated Jack's misery. Then the faint sound of voices downstairs brought him back to the present.

Now that he was sober, Jack could hazard a guess about what had happened. Though the two men had never met, there was another officer named Jack Howard, a captain of the 45th Regiment. Probably there were half a dozen Jack Howards in the army; the name was common enough. And one of them was the friend of Miss Lambert's brother, but it wasn't the Jack Howard presently lying naked in bed in this pleasant farmhouse. That thought led him to offer a swift prayer that he had been conscious enough to undress himself, for the alternative did not bear thinking about.

Jack groaned as he considered the dreadful bind he had gotten himself into. How the devil was he going to tell Miss Lambert that he was an unintentional impostor? Last night she had been remarkably tolerant of his disgraceful condition, but the news that she had been misled would make those lovely hazel eyes flash with fury.

Immersed in his dilemma, Jack failed to hear the soft knock at the door, so Miss Lambert's entry into the bedroom caught him by surprise. He cast one horrified look at her, then behaved like any proper military hero would under such conditions. He dived under the covers and pulled a pillow over his head.

Unlike the shrieking bird that had awakened him, Miss Lambert's voice was gently soothing. "Forgive me for disturbing you, Major Howard, but are you feeling all right?"

"Better than I deserve," Jack said in a strangled voice.

"Sorry, I can't hear you clearly." The pillow was tugged from his clutching fingers. "Were you injured in the accident? Or did you take a chill from falling in the water?"

Turtle-style, Jack poked his head out from under the covers. Miss Lambert looked as bright and honest as a summer day. She was also remarkably self-possessed, given the fact that she was in the bedroom of a strange man. A man who was in fact considerably stranger than she knew. "The only thing wrong with me is just punishment for my sins."

"I thought you would be suffering the effects of intemperance." She motioned toward the tray she had set on the bedside table. "That's why I brought up a pot of coffee. Would you like some?"

"Miss Lambert," Jack said fervently as his head emerged from its cocoon, "you are a woman in a thousand. A million."

Though he would not be fully recovered before the next day, the large mug of steaming hot coffee went a long way toward restoring Jack's raveled nerves. It also reminded him of the impropriety of this situation. "Miss Lambert," he said, setting down the empty mug, "you should not be here. Have a care for your reputation."

She laughed and poured him more coffee. "I've been on the shelf far too long to need to worry about my reputation. At least, I won't worry when I am under my own roof with my brother's best friend." She gave him a sudden sharp look. "Of course, it's different with Phoebe, who is of marriageable age. I've always taken care to see that she is properly chaperoned."

Ah, yes, Phoebe, the very pretty, very young female who had let them in the night before. Jack dismissed Phoebe and her perfections without a thought. It was Miss Lambert's good graces he craved, and was about to lose. "Miss Lambert, I owe you a profound apology."

A hint of color showed in her face and her gaze flickered away from his. "Please, say no more about what happened. You were not yourself last night."

He *had* been himself—that was the whole problem.

While Jack tried to find the words to explain, Miss Lambert continued, "I assume that you imbibed a bit too much when warding off the cold. Consider the episode forgotten."

Once more Jack braced himself to confess his underlying crime, which was far worse than stealing a kiss. "There is something I must tell you, Miss Lambert."

"Call me Meg. I'd like to think of you as one of the family. By the way, do you remember my telling you that Jeremy won't be home until after Christmas?"

Jack nodded.

Meg gave him a rueful smile. "The household is at sixes and sevens just now. Besides Jeremy being delayed, Phoebe is recovering from a chill, Philip is visiting friends in Gloucester and won't be back until this afternoon, and my two goddaughters are here for Christmas because their older brothers have the measles and their mama asked me to take the girls until everyone is well again. And as if that weren't enough, our maid asked for a fortnight's holiday to visit her mother, who is ailing. I hope you'll forgive the disorganization."

"All soldiers become accustomed to disorganization."

Meg chuckled as she knelt on the hearth. "I imagine you'll want to bathe, since falling in a stream is not quite the same thing. I'll build a fire and bring up some hot water."

Jack sat up. "I'll do that. You shouldn't be acting as a servant for me."

"Major Howard!" she said, blushing. "If you don't stay where you are, I am going to be very embarrassed in a moment."

Abruptly remembering his nakedness, Jack slid down and pulled the covers to his chin. "I'm sorry. You are going to think me a complete lack-wit."

She smiled. "Having raised two younger brothers, I am not easily shocked by male impulsiveness."

"You raised your brothers?"

"To a large extent." His hostess struck a spark into the nest of twigs she had laid. Tiny flames began licking around the wood. "I don't suppose Jeremy ever explained the family situation?"

"He never told me a word," Jack said with perfect truth and a guilty pang. It was hardly the act of a gentleman to listen to her confidences, but he was curious to learn why people of obvious gentility were living in such reduced circumstances.

Meg sat back on her heel. "We lived at Peacock Hill, a manor about a mile west of here. The estate has been in the Lambert family for generations, and Jeremy expected to inherit it even though Lord Mason, our local *nobleman*"—her voice became heavily sarcastic—"tried to buy the property several times. Peacock Hill adjoins Lord Mason's estate, and his lordship has coveted it for years, but of course Papa never considered selling.

"Five years ago, my father died quite unexpectedly and I was left as guardian of the younger children. The day after the funeral, Lord Mason called and informed me that Papa had lost the manor to him in a card game several months earlier."

Jack sat up in the bed, remembering just in time to pull the blankets up to cover his bare chest. "Did Lord Mason have any proof of such an outrageous statement?"

"He had a deed, plus a vowel that he claimed Papa had written. It said that if Papa did not repay five thousand pounds to Lord Mason, Peacock Hill would go to his lordship on my father's death."

"You say 'claimed.' Were the documents false?"

"I think so, but I can't prove it, for the handwriting was very like my father's. When I told Lord Mason that I thought they were forgeries, he challenged me to produce a real deed. We searched through all of Papa's papers and everywhere else we could think of, but without success, so perhaps the deed he showed us is the real one."

"Was your father the sort of man who could have gambled away his children's inheritance?"

"It's not quite impossible," Meg said reluctantly. "Papa and Lord Mason were friends of sorts, and they did play cards occasionally. In a mad mood Papa might have wagered far beyond his means. If he did and lost, he would have been ashamed to tell anyone what he had done. Since he seemed to be in good health, he would have assumed there was time for him to repay the debt to Lord Mason, perhaps by taking out a mortgage."

Jack's mouth twisted. Miss Lambert had had to take responsibility for her family when she was not much more than a girl herself. "It's an infamous story. Since you thought the papers forged, did you consider taking the matter to law?"

"I hired a lawyer. Lord Mason hired three. What chance does a poor person have to win justice from a rich aristocrat?" Her hands, which had been lying quietly on her knees, suddenly clenched. "I despise the nobility."

Jack flinched back from her intensity, not that he blamed her for being angry. "Is this farm another family property?"

"No, Brook Farm belongs to me. My mother was the only child of an old yeoman family that has been here even longer than the Lamberts. Neither set of parents was enthralled when she and Papa fell in love, but the farm adjoins Peacock Hill and it made a decent dowry even though my mother's birth was inferior."

Using tongs, Meg laid several small pieces of coal on the fledgling fire. "My mother died when I was three, and two years later Papa married again. My stepmother was a wonderful woman and quite wellborn, but she was dowerless and left nothing to her children. So, when Lord Mason claimed Peacock Hill, Brook Farm was all we had left to keep us. A neighboring farmer works most of the land and the rent he pays is enough to support the family. Fortunately Papa had left enough money to buy Jeremy a commission. If Jeremy hadn't gone away, I think he would have gone mad with frustration."

"So you are devoting your life and your inheritance to caring for your family. You are very generous."

"It is not generous to perform what is both one's duty and one's pleasure." Meg's hazel eyes clouded. "Jeremy and Philip can make their own way, but I worry so about Phoebe. She deserves the opportunity to go to London, to see the world and find a man worthy of her."

"Even if the paragon proved to be a nobleman?"

"I doubt there are many worthy noblemen," Meg said dryly. "What I want for her is a man of character who will appreciate her sweet disposition as well as her beauty. He needn't be rich, just have sufficient fortune so that she will be cared for."

Jack was irresistibly reminded of a horse coper, though Phoebe was a much prettier piece of merchandise than a horse. It wasn't hard to deduce that Meg cherished hopes that her brother's friend might form a *tendre* for her sister.

Jack shifted uneasily under his blankets. He should have confessed earlier, before Meg Lambert had told him all the family secrets. Now he would have to wait a few hours, until a time when there wasn't such a feeling of closeness between the two of them. "Your concern for your family is admirable, but what do you want for yourself? A London Season? A husband and children of your own?"

"Heavens, no! No reasonable man would want me, for I'm the managing sort. As for a London Season . . ." She looked a little wistful. "Even if I could have made my come-out, I wouldn't have 'taken' in society. I'm not beautiful like Phoebe, nor as well-bred, and owning one small farm hardly qualifies me as an heiress. No, I'm plain and practical and opinionated, and I belong here."

"I think you underestimate the popularity you might have had," Jack said warmly. "Females who are attractive, charming, and intelligent are always in short supply."

Meg stood and brushed dust from her hands with quick, nervous movements. "I looked at the wrecked gig this morning, and for a wonder, your bag was still safely inside—it was only the passengers who went in the water. I'll bring the bag up, along with your clothes. They're a bit the worse for wear, I'm afraid, but at least everything is dry."

As she disappeared out the door, Jack folded his hands beneath his head and thoughtfully regarded the ceiling. What a splendid young woman she was, as pretty as she was kind and sensible. He envied the younger Lamberts for being the beneficiaries of her warmth and caring.

Jack sighed, knowing that he would have to leave Brook Farm as soon as he confessed that he was an impostor. A pity he had to reveal the truth, for a solitary holiday in an inn was not what he would have chosen for his first English Christmas in many years. It would be far more pleasant to stay right where he was.

Perhaps he shouldn't tell Meg that he was the wrong man.

Jack found that he was nowhere near as shocked by the thought as he should be. Too many years of military pragmatism had eroded his higher sensibilities. Having found a comfortable billet, he was loath to leave, even though his presence was based on a deception.

Even if he were shameless enough to conceal the truth, doing so was impractical, for Jeremy Lambert would be home in a few days. Worse, the real Captain Howard could walk in the door at any moment, and when that happened Jack would be in dire trouble.

Jack winced as he remembered how Meg Lambert had railed at the nobility. The lady had a temper, and she would feel hurt and betrayed by his abuse of her hospitality. At least if he confessed voluntarily, she might forgive his accidental transgression enough to let him call on her in the future.

He fervently hoped that she would.

AFTER washing, shaving, and rendering himself as presentable as possible, Jack went downstairs, prepared to confess all to his hostess and throw himself on her mercy. Unfortunately, the only person in the kitchen was Phoebe Lambert, who sat by the fire doing mending.

Jack paused in the doorway, struck by the room's welcoming warmth. The previous night he had been too exhausted to notice his surroundings, but now he saw that the old-fashioned kitchen was rich with the unpretentious beauty of utility. Delicious scents filled the air, clusters of dried herbs and onions hung from the beamed ceiling, and comfortable wooden chairs circled the scrubbed deal table.

Jack guessed that the Lamberts did most of their living and laughing here. No formal drawing room would ever be the heart of a home the way this kitchen was the heart of Brook Farm.

As he examined the room, he realized that Phoebe was not the only inhabitant. A tabby cat was curled on the girl's lap, a large black cat sprawled pantherlike on top of the cupboard, legs and long tail drooping over the edge, and a plump calico was tucked in on herself on a Windsor chair. Jack chuckled at the sight. Trust cats to find a snug spot. The kitchen made him want to curl up and purr too.

Hearing his sound of amusement, Phoebe looked up and became quite still for a moment. Then she set aside both cat and mending and came across the room to greet him, her eyes bright as the copper pans that hung on the walls. "I hope you have taken no harm from the accident, Major Howard. Meg told me how you risked your life to save her."

"I don't think the situation was quite that grave," Jack said uncomfortably. "While the water was over her head in that one spot, I think it likely that Miss Lambert would have been able to save herself if I hadn't been on the scene."

"You are too modest, Major. Would you like a cup of tea? Meg is outside feeding the animals, but when she returns we will have luncheon."

While Phoebe brewed the tea, Jack sat in a Windsor chair. The calico cat materialized at his feet with a speculative look, then sprang onto his lap. She landed with an impact that proved that she didn't miss any meals. Jack scratched her head, honored by her company.

As they chatted over their tea, Jack could not escape the feeling that Phoebe was disappointed in him, though her manner was entirely gracious. He suspected that she, too, had had hopes of Jack Howard, and was reluctantly letting go of them now that she was confronted with a real man rather than the image created by her brother's letters. If so, Jack was glad, for it would be a nuisance to have her become enamored of him simply because he was a new face—particularly since he was an impostor. Perhaps the real Captain Howard would please her more.

Jack had reached that point in his thinking when his hostess returned. She was accompanied by two miniature blond charmers and a shaggy dog of dubious breeding but noteworthy enthusiasm.

"I'm glad to see you so restored from the rigors of travel, Major." Meg deftly removed cloak and bonnet from the smaller child. "You haven't met my goddaughters yet, have you?" She gestured to the taller girl. "This is Tizzie." Then to the smaller: "And this is Lizzie. Girls, this is Major Howard."

Both girls curtsied gravely. While Tizzie shyly studied the stranger, Lizzie, a brazen little hussy, climbed into Jack's lap, which was vacated by the prudent calico.

Lizzie regarded him soulfully. "I been feeding the chickens with Miss Meg. She has the fanciest chickens in the world."

Not to be outdone, Tizzie piped up, " 'N I helped milk the cows."

"How clever of you. Miss Meg is very fortunate to have such good helpers," Jack said admiringly, thinking that it was quite pleasant to have a warm, trusting armful of little girl on his lap. Glancing up, he said, "If I am to call you Meg and Phoebe, you must both call me Jack."

"Fair enough. You'll have noticed that this is not a very formal household." Meg removed her bonnet and shook out bright chestnut curls. "The girls have been a wonderful help. They are going to help me with the Christmas baking."

Visions of nuts and fruit in his head, Jack said hopefully, "Can I help too?"

"Of course. The more the merrier. But I think I'll postpone the baking until this evening. There's a hint of snow in the air, so we had best take advantage of the good weather to gather the evergreens this afternoon."

As the dog trotted over to the visitor and rested his jaw on Jack's knee, Meg added, "That's Rugger. He's a variety hound."

Jack smiled at the description as he reached down to ruffle Rugger's ears. Snow? Surely that would delay Captain Howard. Perhaps it was safe to postpone his confession a bit longer.

The door opened again, and fickle Rugger bolted off to greet the handsome youth who entered. Meg welcomed the newcomer with an affectionate hug. "What wonderful timing, Philip! We were just about to eat. I suppose you were dreadfully underfed in Gloucester."

"Dreadfully," he agreed, laughing.

Taking her brother by the arm, Meg brought him over to Jack. "As you see, our guest has arrived, though Jeremy has been delayed for several days. Jack, I'm sure you could pick Philip out of a crowd as Jeremy's brother. They're as like as peas in a pod."

"A pleasure to meet you, Philip." Jack offered his hand without standing, since Lizzie showed no inclination to leave.

"It's a real privilege to have you here, sir." Philip accepted Jack's hand enthusiastically. He was a handsome youth of fourteen or fifteen, with Phoebe's dark good looks.

"It is I who am privileged. Your sisters have been making me feel very welcome."

Meg was pleased to hear the sincerity in Jack Howard's voice. She had worried that her brother's friend might be disconcerted by the modest way they lived, for she knew that he had been raised in much grander circumstances. But the tall major seemed perfectly at home. In fact, she thought with amusement as Tizzie came to lean against his knee, he seemed to attract children and animals like blossoms attract bees.

The major cleaned up exceedingly well. She hoped Phoebe was suitably impressed.

BUNDLED and basketed, the greens-gathering expedition set out. The weather was clear and cold, with only the softness of the earth as a reminder of the previous day's rain. Jack inhaled crisp fresh air and decided that Meg was right about the possibility of snow.

The party was passing the barn when another avian shriek rent the air. Jack jumped as a large, shimmeringly colorful bird, darted past. "Good Lord, is that a peacock?"

"It is indeed—one of what Lizzie calls my fancy chickens. The silly beast has escaped again," Meg said with resignation. "Philip, will you catch Lord Feathers and return him to his pen?"

"Yes, but it will take a few minutes," her brother replied. "Here, Phoebe, you carry my basket. I'll catch up with you once that imbecile bird is back where he belongs."

Minus Philip, the party proceeded. Phoebe walked ahead with Tizzie, Lizzie, and Rugger, while the older members of the party followed. Jack cocked an eye at his hostess. "Peacocks?"

"They came from Peacock Hill, of course," Meg explained. "Since they weren't technically part of the manor, we brought them with us. They're quite useless, but we thought that the least we could do was make Lord Mason buy his own peafowl." She glanced up at Jack, guilty amusement in her eyes. "The entrance to Peacock Hill has always been flanked by two magnificent topiary peacocks. The week after we removed to Brook Farm, someone cut off the tail feathers of both. I suspect that Jeremy and Philip did it, though I never dared ask."

"It was a relatively harmless way of expressing some of their anger. Topiary tail feathers will grow back."

"They have," Meg agreed. "It's more than Lord Mason deserves." They had been climbing steadily, and finally reached a summit that yielded a magnificent view of the rolling countryside. As the younger members of the party skipped ahead, Meg halted and pointed into the middle distance. "There is Peacock Hill. Since Lord Mason wanted only the land, the house is empty now. A pity, when it was always such a happy place."

Through the leafless winter trees Jack was able to distinguish the outlines of a lovely Cotswold stone manor. In the pale solstice sunshine, it seemed magical, a dream kingdom from which the Lamberts had been banished.

"I don't usually dwell on the past as I'm doing today," Meg said apologetically. "We're very fortunate we had Brook Farm to fall back on, and I'm proud of the way the younger ones adjusted to living in a farmhouse. After we moved in, there was never a complaint from any of them."

"Perhaps it was because you set them a good example."

As the major's gaze met hers, Meg found herself momentarily immobilized by the admiration in the dark blue depths of his eyes. He really shouldn't look at her like that, she thought weakly, as if she were as young and attractive as Phoebe. It was enough to make even a sober spinster lose her head.

Fortunately Philip chose that moment to catch up with them. As they resumed walking toward the clump of holly bushes, he said with shy eagerness, "Sir, Jeremy wrote us of what you did at the Battle of Vittoria—he said that he had never seen such courage in his life. If you don't mind speaking of it, we would greatly appreciate your describing the battle to us."

Jack Howard looked disconcerted. "I do mind, actually."

"Your modesty does you credit, sir, but I may never get another chance to meet a real hero," Philip said coaxingly. "I'd like to hear what happened in your own words."

Meg opened her mouth to reprove her brother for pestering their guest, but Jack's answer cut her off.

"War heroics are a sham, Philip," he said quietly. "Oh, sometimes soldiers act from great courage, but more often they do what they do because they have no choice—because it is safer to charge than to turn and run, or because they fear appearing cowardly, or because they are so tired of being afraid that death seems a welcome alternative. For real bravery, look at a widow struggling to raise her children alone or a doctor going into a plague-stricken city to treat the dying."

"Of course there are many kinds of courage," Philip said, taken aback, "but there is something splendid and glorious about risking death for one's country."

His voice edged, Jack replied, "Death may sometimes be necessary, but it is never glorious. For years my fondest ambition has been to die at home in my own bed."

Philip stared at their guest, shock and disillusion clearly visible on his handsome young face. Too polite to criticize the major for his unheroic attitude, he said stiffly, "I'd best retrieve my basket from Phoebe—the holly is just over there." Turning, he bolted off to join the others.

For several long moments there was silence between Meg and her guest. Then Jack said harshly, "Meg, I'm not the man you think I am."

Far more than her brother, Meg could guess at the bleak experience that lay behind his words. "Who of us is what others think? Certainly I am not the strong, generous woman you think I am, for I too have done what I have because I had no choice," she said softly. "Don't condemn yourself for not living up to a boy's ideal. Philip is too young to understand that nothing is simple, least of all courage."

"I know that, for I was no wiser at his age." The major drew a deep breath, his large frame rigid with tension. "But that is not all I meant— what I'm trying to say is that I am not Jeremy's heroic Jack Howard."

"Please, don't say anything more—words are never adequate for the deepest truths." Wanting to remove the shadows from Jack's anguished blue eyes, she laid a gloved hand on his arm. "My trials have been different from yours, but I have learned that heroism lies beyond despair. And while it is certainly admirable, it is never glorious."

"You say that words are inadequate, yet you have just said something vitally true far more clearly than I could have." He covered her hand with his, fingers gripping tightly. "But you are making confession very difficult."

For an instant, as their gazes met, Meg felt disoriented. The farm, the crisp winter day, her nearby family, all fell away, no longer important. Reality was the man in front of her, and the feeling of profound intimacy between them.

Shaken, she disengaged her hand. "Christmas is no time for confessions," she said, striving to keep her voice light. "This is the season for hope. Forget the past and your own imagined failings and simply enjoy the moment."

Jack opened his mouth, then closed it again without speaking. His tension disappeared as clearly as milk flowing from a spilled jug. "You make it easy for me to yield to my less admirable impulses, Meg. Please don't judge me too harshly when you find out what a weak, deceitful fellow I am."

"I'm sure that you are far too hard on yourself." She grinned remembering how he had barked at her after pulling her from the flooded brook. "You're under orders, soldier, to relax and enjoy the holiday."

Their laughter was interrupted by a distressed wail, so they hastened down to the holly bushes, where Lizzie was sucking fingers pricked by the spiky holly leaves. Meg quickly soothed her wounds, and the rest of the afternoon passed in simple pleasures. Working with leather-gloved care, they collected basketfuls of bright-berried holly, then added glossy ivy. Philip, his earlier discomfiture forgotten, scrambled up an oak tree and cut a large handful of mistletoe.

Lizzie tired on the walk home, so Jack transferred his evergreens to the others and carried her the rest of the way, her drowsy blond head nestled on his shoulder. He felt quite absurdly at peace. When Meg had commanded him to relax and enjoy the present, he had surrendered all common sense and scruples. Of course he was a fool to continue his pretense, for there would inevitably be a reckoning, but he refused to worry about it. For whatever reason, fate had sent him to this warm and welcoming place, and fate could jolly well help him cope with the inevitable explosion when the truth came out.

In the meantime, he intended to savor every glowing moment.

DUSK was falling fast when the party reached the house. Since it was unlucky to bring the evergreens inside before Christmas Eve, the prickly bounty was left in a shed before they proceeded into the kitchen.

After everyone had shared tea and currant cakes, Meg said, "Come along, girls, it's time for a nap."

"No!" her goddaughters said in chorus. Tizzie added, "We c'n help fix dinner, Miss Meg."

"It is very good of you to offer," Meg said seriously, "but if you don't nap now, I'm afraid you'll be too tired to help with the baking later, and I need your assistance for that more than I do for dinner."

The girls looked horrified, so Phoebe seized the moment and their hands and led them off to the small room they shared.

Jack watched them go fondly. "Is her name really Tizzie?"

"Actually it's Thomasina, but Lizzie couldn't pronounce that, and calling them Tizzie and Lizzie proved irresistible."

Philip interjected, "I'm going out to feed the animals now, before it becomes dark."

"Will you see if there are any fresh eggs?" Meg lifted an apron from a peg and tied it around her trim waist. "I'll be using a lot of them tonight, and we'll need more for breakfast."

Philip nodded as he lit a lantern to take outside.

Rather hesitantly Jack said, "Can I help with the chores?"

"Of course, sir, if you wish to," Philip said, his face expressionless.

Outside the temperature was dropping and a few errant flakes of snow drifted about aimlessly. As they crossed the yard, Jack said, "I'm sorry to prove such a disappointment, Philip."

The youth turned his head quickly to the visitor. "Please, sir, it is I who should be apologizing. Ever since you spoke to me, I've been thinking. Jeremy used to talk like I did, but when I remembered the letters he's written, I realized that they changed after he had been in Spain for a few months. He stopped writing about the war and mentioned fighting in only the briefest way, usually just to assure us that he was all right. Instead, his letters are about his friends, like you, and about amusing things that happen. I didn't really notice at the time, but now I think I understand better how war changes a man."

"That it does." Jack swung open the barn door and let his companion proceed in with the lantern. "Congratulations, Philip. You are learning wisdom much more quickly than I did. Is it your ambition to be a soldier?"

Philip hung the lantern on a hook so it illuminated stalls containing three horses and four cows. "I'll leave that to Jeremy. One of my father's cousins is in the East India Company, and he said he'll get me an apprenticeship when I reach sixteen. Someone in this family needs to make money if my sisters are going to be taken care of."

Clearly Meg wasn't the only practical Lambert, Jack thought, impressed by Philip's clear, unselfish thinking. "I imagine Phoebe will find a husband if she wants one. But why has Meg never married—have the men of Wiltshire no sense?"

Philip lifted a pitchfork and began transferring hay to the stalls. "An aunt offered to sponsor Meg for a London come-out. I was very small, but I remember how excited she was. Then my mother became ill and Meg canceled her plans. She's been taking care of us ever since, and now she's almost thirty." He shoved his pitchfork into the haystack with unnecessary force. "That's why I want to be in a position to look after her."

"Is it so unthinkable that Meg might still marry? She is hardly ancient."

There was nothing wrong with Philip's understanding. Resting the tines of the pitchfork on the plank floor, he regarded Jack with stern blue eyes. "Since Jeremy isn't here, it is my duty to ask if you have intentions toward my sister. And if so, whether they are honorable."

Perhaps it should have been humorous to see a boy so young challenging a man over twice his age, but Jack was moved rather than amused. He envied the Lamberts the love that bound them together. "Perhaps it is early to declare intentions, but if I develop any, I assure you they will be honorable."

Philip relaxed. "Good. I'd hate to have to put a pitchfork through you."

Jack chuckled. "Being a devout coward, I assure you that I won't risk such a fate. Meg is lucky to have such defenders."

"Even Tizzie and Lizzie would attack anyone who hurt Meg, and believe me, those two can bite when sufficiently provoked," Philip said with feeling. "Do you want to help me feed cabbage to the peafowl? Believe me, it's quite an experience."

In perfect charity they finished the chores in the stables, then went off together to the poultry shed.

MEG took the bubbling steak-and-kidney pie from the oven and set it on the wooden chopping block, regarding the crumbly golden crust with satisfaction. The pie was plain country food, but it did her no discredit. When Jeremy had first asked permission to bring his friend for Christmas, Meg had confronted the limitations of house and budget and decided that Jack Howard would have to take them as they were, or not at all. Fortunately, in spite of his privileged background, the major had accepted everything with cheerful goodwill. He looked like a man who would enjoy a good steak-and-kidney pie.

Across the kitchen Phoebe asked, "Is it time to start boiling the Brussels sprouts?"

"Wait until Philip and Jack come in." Meg gave the soup pot a stir. It was bean soup tonight, rich and savory. "There is nothing worse than gray, overcooked Brussels sprouts." Glancing up at her sister, she asked hopefully, "What do you think of Major Howard now that you've had time to become a little better acquainted?"

Phoebe made a rueful face. "I'm sorry, Meg, I know you were hoping that he and I might form an attachment, and I must admit that I had certain hopes in that direction myself. But I'm afraid it just won't do."

"Don't you like him?"

"I like him very well," Phoebe assured her. "The major is kind and good-natured and there's something wonderfully solid about him. But he's much older than I expected, and not at all dashing—more like a large shaggy bear. I just can't imagine falling in love with him, and he certainly shows no disposition to fall in love with me." She gave her sister a teasing smile. "I know that you're concerned about my future, but I'm not at my last prayers yet. Rather than casting lures to Major Howard, I'm prepared to wait and see if someone better comes along."

As Phoebe talked, Meg felt a surge of relief so intense that it shocked her. Could she possibly be yearning for the major herself? The idea was so nonsensical that she could feel color rise in her cheeks. To conceal her expression from Phoebe's interested gaze, Meg scooped up a spoonful of soup and sampled it, scorching her tongue. She gasped and waved her hand in a vain attempt to cool her mouth. "Needs more salt."

As she reached for a salt cellar, Meg decided that soup was really a safer subject than men, for a burned mouth would heal much faster than a burned heart. As she added a large pinch of salt to the pot, she reminded herself firmly that the fact Phoebe wasn't interested in the major did not mean he was available for her. Then she reminded herself again.

And again.

*　*　*

THE household Jack had grown up in had treated him with sufferance rather than affection, so he had never known the kind of holiday happiness he discovered that evening. Baking proved to be a family affair, with Philip and Phoebe chopping nuts and dried fruit, Jack assigned to grind lumps of sugar to powder fineness, and Tizzie and Lizzie aiding Meg in ways that seemed to involve squealing and covering all three of them with flour. The cats and Rugger made periodic patrols under the tables, hoping that all this activity would produce tangible benefits for them.

Under Meg's direction they made a vast quantity of tiny mince pies, enough so that everyone at Brook Farm could have one on each of the twelve days of Christmas, to ensure luck for the coming year. Then came gingerbread; Meg had everyone help her cut it into the shapes of stars before baking.

As the house filled with irresistibly spicy scents, Phoebe unexpectedly broke into song. To Jack's surprise, everyone else joined in, as if singing "Joy to the World" was the most natural thing in the world. For the Lamberts, it clearly was. Phoebe was a soprano, her voice a little weak because of her recent cold, but very sweet. Meg had a rich contralto and Philip a very passable tenor. Even Tizzie and Lizzie chimed in, their high clear voices like cherubim.

After the song was done, Meg looked up from the hazelnut-and-chocolate pudding she was mixing. "Do you sing, Jack?" she asked with a bewitching smile. "We could use a baritone."

As he looked into her warm hazel eyes, Jack felt something very strange happen deep in his chest. It wasn't the kitchen that was the heart of the Lambert household, it was Meg herself. And more than anything else on earth, he wanted to spend the rest of his life within the circle of her warmth. If they had been alone, he would have said as much.

Instead, Jack cleared his throat gruffly. "If you don't mind hearing a voice that has been described as capable of stopping a bull in its tracks, I'll be happy to join in."

This time it was Philip who started a song, choosing "The Holly and the Ivy," and for the next hour they sang all the Christmas carols they knew. Then Jack taught them a simple Spanish song that he had learned on the Peninsula.

The party broke up gradually, first the little girls being taken off to bed, then the adults yawning and conceding fatigue. As Jack drifted toward sleep with the calico cat sprawled on his stomach, he knew that he had never felt so much a part of a family in his life.

"YOU may enter the parlor now!" Phoebe announced grandly.

It was Christmas Eve, and Phoebe had insisted on total privacy while she decorated the kissing bough. Tizzie and Lizzie had been excited to near-speechlessness by the secrecy and would periodically peer into the parlor, attempting to steal a glimpse.

Caught up in the holiday mood, Jack had felt as much anticipation as the little girls. After doing the farm chores, he and Philip had brought in the Yule log. Then they all sat in the kitchen and turned the evergreens they had collected into yards and yards of garlands while Meg produced more delicacies for the Christmas feast.

Summoned by Phoebe, everyone solemnly entered the parlor to see the results of the girl's handiwork. Jack was prepared to admire whatever she had made, but it was quite unnecessary to counterfeit enthusiasm.

As Tizzie and Lizzie squealed rapturously, Meg lifted the kissing bough and exclaimed, "Oh, Phoebe! What a wonderful idea to use peacock feathers. I never thought of such a thing."

The kissing bough was a double hoop of dried vine, and traditionally it was decorated with evergreens, scarlet berries, candles, and mistletoe. That was quite enough to make it pretty, but bows of silver ribbon and the gleaming, colorful tips of peacock feathers made this one breathtaking.

"It was rather a stroke of genius, wasn't it?" Phoebe agreed. Clearly she was no believer in false modesty.

Taking the kissing bough from Meg, Philip gave his other sister a wicked grin. "Considering that you're as vain as a peacock, you should have thought of this years ago."

For a moment Phoebe teetered between behaving like a mature lady and giving in to her natural instincts. Instinct won and she threw a handful of feather scraps at her brother. "Beast! You should talk—it wasn't me who asked if I looked like that picture of Lord Byron."

"You don't have to—you look more like him than I do," Philip retorted, then retreated hastily across the parlor as Phoebe began stalking him with wrath in her eyes.

"Children, children," Meg said indulgently. "What will Major Howard think?"

Laughing, Jack replied, "Major Howard thinks that the Lamberts know how to have a good time."

Phoebe ceased chasing her brother and gave a wistful sigh. "I do so wish Jeremy was here. For weeks I've been looking forward to having him home for Christmas."

"We all have," Meg agreed, "but he'll be home soon, and that is almost as good." She smiled at their guest. "We're fortunate to have Jack here even though Jeremy was delayed."

Jack felt a massive stab of guilt at his deception, knowing that if Jeremy were here, Jack wouldn't be. "The good fortune is mine."

Meg scooped Lizzie into her arms. "It's time to put up the rest of the decorations. Shall we set this little angel on the mantelpiece?"

Lizzie shrieked with delight as Jack took her from Meg and perched her on the mantel, then put Tizzie by her side. With their bright blond hair, they made very fine angels for about one minute, after which the small sisters demanded to be taken down so they could help Phoebe weave bright bits of peacock feather into the garlands.

The mantel was decorated with candles and evergreens and ribbons, and the garlands were hung, filling the room with a tangy forest fragrance. Then Philip hung the kissing bough from the chandelier. As he lit the candles, all around the room feathers shimmered with iridescent blues and greens, and silver bows sparkled to life. There was a soft collective intake of breath as everyone admired the effect. Outside it was dark and a bitter wind rattled the windows, but the parlor glowed with warmth and color and love. Most of all, love.

Philip pulled Tizzie under the bough and gave her a smacking kiss on the cheek. "There!" he said with a grin. "That's what kissing boughs are for."

As Tizzie gazed at him adoringly, Lizzie moved in for her kiss, followed by Philip's smiling sisters.

A quick learner, Tizzie seized Jack's hand, tugged him under the mistletoe, then waited hopefully. He laughed and obliged her, thinking how much a child's delight added to the magic of the season. Of course Lizzie also had to be kissed, and after that Phoebe presented herself with as little self-consciousness as the girls.

After receiving Jack's playful kiss, Phoebe said gaily, "Your turn, Meg."

Jack gave Meg an appalled glance. As plainly as if it were written on the wall in letters of flame, he knew that they were both thinking of the kiss in the stable at Chippenham. So much for her comment that they should forget what had happened. Jack recalled with absolute precision how her soft body had molded against him, how she had tasted, and how she had responded. Remembering that, it was impossible to kiss her casually now.

Just before the silence became embarrassingly obvious, Meg stepped up and presented her cheek with a determined let's-get-this-over-with expression. Jack gave her a quick, awkward peck. Her creamy skin was silky smooth beneath his lips. Then the moment was over, to Jack's immense relief.

The evening's program was simple but rewarding for all ages. They dined, then danced as Meg and Phoebe took turns playing the old spinet. There was wassail for the adults and hot spiced cider for the little girls, and games like snapdragon and puss in the corner—once played with a real puss.

Eventually Tizzie and Lizzie curled up together in a ball, snoozing like kittens, and had to be carried off to bed. Then the adults relaxed around the fire, the Lamberts reminiscing about notable Christmases of the past. Jack said very little, though he several times compared this evening with what he would have had to endure at the countess's hands. As he sipped wassail, he gave thanks to the fate that had sent him here.

Finally Philip rose and clasped both of Phoebe's hands. "Time for bed, sleepyhead," he said, hauling his sister to her feet. "You'll have to walk because you're too heavy to carry."

"But I don't want to go to bed yet," she protested.

Her brother directed a meaningful glance from Meg to Jack. "Yes, you do."

Phoebe's eyes widened. Then she gave an exaggerated yawn. "For once you're right. I *am* rather tired."

As Philip tugged Phoebe from the room, he gave Jack a conspiratorial smile. Jack almost laughed; seemed to have acquired an ally.

As her brother and sister left the room, Meg murmured, "I should go to bed, too. It will be a busy day tomorrow. There's the goose to prepare in the morning, and church, and a thousand other things." But she made no move to rise.

Curled up on the sofa with two cats, a dreamy smile, and tousled curls that glowed in the firelight, Meg looked good enough to eat, even though Jack should not be hungry after all the food he had put away. If he had any sense, he would also go to bed and leave his hostess in safe solitude, but these moments of peaceful togetherness were too precious to end quickly.

Needing something to keep his hands busy and off his hostess, Jack put his glass down and wandered over to the large Black Forest clock that hung on the wall, sprigs of holly fastened on top. "I've always had a fondness for cuckoo clocks. Is this one broken or has it just run down because you've been too busy to tend it?"

"There is a story to that clock. My father bought it in Munich when he was on his grand tour. He was always very fond of the clock and kept it in his study at Peacock Hill." Meg raised her glass and drained the last of her wassail. "He died in that study. It was very sudden—the doctor said his heart failed. The clock stopped that day and never ran again."

Intrigued, Jack ran appreciative fingers over the silky, beautifully carved wood. The hands had stopped at 11:27. "Did you decide to leave it like this as a memorial to your father?"

"Not really. It was just that so much happened after my father died— losing Peacock Hill, having to move. There was neither time nor money to have the clock fixed." Meg smiled wryly. "I suppose that I should see to it. Jeremy won't have Peacock Hill, but at least he can have Papa's clock, and it will be much more useful to him if it works."

"Shall I take a look at it?" Jack offered. "I'm a fair hand with things mechanical. Even if I can't fix it, at least I should be able to find out what's wrong."

Since Meg looked doubtful, he said coaxingly, "Please? I didn't bring any real Christmas presents, so fixing the clock can be my gift to you. I promise I won't leave it in worse condition than I found it."

Meg smiled. "Very well, if you don't mind. I'm fond of the clock, though I've always thought cuckoos quite dishonorable for their habit of laying their eggs in the nests of other birds. The poor host birds become fagged to death raising the cuckoos' ravenous offspring."

Meg's words struck so unexpectedly close to the bone that Jack almost dropped the clock as he moved it to a table by the fire. What was he himself but a Christmas cuckoo who had ended up in the wrong nest? He uttered a brief prayer that Meg would prove more tolerant of him than of the despised cuckoo.

As he opened the clock, he remarked, "A cuckoo is not that different from aristocratic parents who give their children to nurses to raise."

"Another reason to despise the nobility," Meg retorted, "though at least nurses are paid, unlike the poor victims of the cuckoos' deceit."

Jack concentrated on the clock, uneasily aware that Meg was going to require a great deal of persuasion to see him as an acceptable suitor. Perhaps he should confess now, when she was mellow with contentment and wassail.

Resolved, he opened his mouth to speak, then frowned as his probing fingertips touched something unexpected inside the clock case. "There is some kind of obstruction—paper, I think. Could one of the children have stuffed something inside?"

"I suppose so," Meg said without much interest. "There were always children in and out of Peacock Hill. Be grateful if it's paper and not something dreadful like a petrified frog."

Jack managed to pull the paper out without ripping it. There was one large sheet, bulky and yellow-gray with age. Curious, he flattened the sheet on the table, then peered at the faded writing in the flickering firelight.

The words were in Latin and it took time to puzzle out the old legal phrases. Then he gasped, his heart speeding up like a galloping horse. "Meg, come look at this."

Startled by his tone, she set her glass aside and came to peer over his shoulder.

"I hope to God I'm not raising false hopes," Jack said in a choked voice, "but I think this is the deed to Peacock Hill."

Meg felt the blood drain from her face. Snatching the paper up, she tilted it toward the fire. "Merciful heaven," she whispered. "You're right, this *is* the deed. Not long before he died, Papa waved it at me when he said that Lord Mason would give a fortune to possess this piece of paper." She ran awestruck fingers over the old lettering. "How on earth do you think it came to be inside the clock?"

Jack considered. "You say that your father died in his study. When he was stricken, he may have become confused and felt that he had to put the deed somewhere safe, where Mason couldn't get it. The clock was right there and had always been special to him, so he shoved the deed inside, jamming the mechanism. We'll never know, of course, but that seems a plausible explanation."

"But how did Lord Mason know that we would be unable to find the deed?" she asked in bewilderment.

Jack thought some more. "Perhaps your father once told Mason that the deed was hidden safe away. Then, when he died so suddenly, Mason decided to gamble on the chance that no one would know where your father had left it."

"It's the sort of thing Lord Mason might do, for he is a famous gamester," Meg said thoughtfully. "He had little to lose by trying, and his gamble paid off spectacularly well. The despicable wretch."

"His gamester's luck has run out," Jack said with deep satisfaction. "Not only can you reclaim Peacock Hill, but you can file a suit for fraud against Lord Mason. He'll probably pay a handsome settlement to keep the case from going to court and becoming public knowledge. I doubt he will want to be known as someone who stole the inheritance of a family of orphans."

Meg was too happy to be concerned with retribution. "You know what this means?" she said, bubbling with joy. "Jeremy will be able to sell out and come back to Peacock Hill and marry his sweetheart, Anne Marshall. I'm sorry, Jack, I know you'll miss him, but we need him more here. And Phoebe will be able to make her come-out and Philip won't have to go to India unless he really wants to. . . ."

Distractedly she brushed her hair back as she tried to think of all the implications. "You've given us all a Christmas present beyond our wildest dreams. I know the words are feeble, but thank you, Jack, from the bottom of my heart. I must go tell Philip and Phoebe."

"Let them sleep. The deed has waited for five years, it can wait until morning." Jack stood and put a hand under her chin, lifting it so that her gaze met his. "You always say 'we' and 'us,' Meg. Isn't there anything that you want just for yourself?"

As Meg looked into Jack's intense blue eyes, she felt a shiver that started in her toes and tingled through her entire body. She made no protest when he drew her into an embrace under the kissing bough. His lips met hers in a warm, wise, leisurely exploration that bore no resemblance to the chaste kiss he had given her earlier.

Delirious with happiness and desire, Meg kissed him back. As Phoebe had said, there was something wonderfully solid about Jack Howard. But he was also the most intoxicatingly attractive man she had ever known. He made Meg feel as irresistible as Helen of Troy. She almost dropped the precious deed.

Abruptly Jack set Meg away from him, though fortunately he kept his hands firmly on her waist or she might have folded down to the floor. "Tomorrow, after breakfast and church and all the rest, I have something very important to say to you," he said huskily. "You—not Phoebe or Philip or Tizzie and Lizzie, but you. Then I'm going to ask you a question. You know what it will be, don't you, Meg?"

"Yes, Jack." On this magical night, Meg knew that anything was possible, even that this delicious man might fancy an old spinster like her.

"Good. Then think about your answer." He bent his head and gave her a quick, expert kiss in case she had forgotten in the last sixty seconds. "Just be sure that the answer is yes."

"Yes, Jack," Meg said obediently. She knew that her eyes must be shining like the Star of Bethlehem.

Turning her around, he gave her a gentle slap on the backside. "Now, go to bed, Miss Lambert, or tonight might end in a way that would make Philip feel honor-bound to put a pitchfork through me."

Meg floated across the room, then turned in the doorway. "Good night, Jack." She blew him a kiss. "I love you, Jack."

When he took a step toward her, his face glowing with joy, Meg whirled and dashed across the hall and through the kitchen to her room. The only thing that kept her from expiring with embarrassment was the knowledge that she had spoken the plain truth.

Her bedroom was freezing, so Meg set the deed on the table and quickly undressed. Then she moved the tabby cat, Striper, to the foot of the bed and slid under the covers. Wrapping her arms around a pillow, she whispered again, "I love you, Jack."

Life was perfect.

*   *   *

IT was very early when Meg woke, only the faintest hint of dawn coloring the eastern sky. She stretched luxuriously, feeling marvelous in spite of the short night's sleep. Could she possibly have dreamed the events of the previous night? No, on her table the deed was visible, a pale rectangle in the gloom.

Jack had said he had something to ask her, and that she should answer yes. Meg touched her lips, where the memory of his kiss lingered. The lovely, kind man upstairs actually wanted to marry her. When she was younger, she had twice refused suitors who wanted her but regarded her family as an unpleasant necessity. Jack was different, for he fitted into her family as if there had been a Jack-size vacancy just waiting for him. There would be no problem giving him the answer he wanted.

Meg was too full of energy to stay in bed, so she threw back the covers and dressed, then went into the kitchen and built up the fire. After stuffing the goose for roasting, she started readying potatoes, onions, bacon, and eggs for the hearty dish that was the traditional Lambert Christmas breakfast.

Breakfast preparations complete, Meg glanced out and saw that it was almost full light. A couple of inches of feathery snow had fallen in the night, enough to make snow cream. Tizzie and Lizzie would enjoy that. Jack probably would, too.

Thinking of Jack, Meg was gazing out the window with a foolish smile on her face when she heard the outside door open in the hall next to the kitchen. For a moment she was startled and a little alarmed. Then she realized that there could be only one person arriving so early on Christmas morning.

She raced across the kitchen. "Jeremy?" she called softly, not wanting to wake the others. "Is that you?"

A lean, snow-dusted figure appeared in the kitchen door. "It is indeed, Meg," said a familiar beloved voice. "Cold, hungry, and ready to be pampered."

With a squeal that would have done credit to Lizzie, Meg hurled herself into her brother's arms. As she did, footsteps sounded on the stairs and Philip appeared, dark hair wild and clothes hastily thrown on. "Jeremy—you finally made it!"

"Now, this is what I call a proper welcome!" Jeremy said, hugging his sister so hard that he lifted her from her feet. Setting her down, he added, "You've shrunk, big sister."

Turning, he wrapped an affectionate arm around his younger brother's shoulders. "And you've grown."

Meg studied Jeremy's tired but happy face. He looked older, of course, and stronger. Her little brother had become a man. Voice breaking, Meg said, "Oh, Jeremy, it only needed you to make Christmas perfect."

"Not quite." Smiling, Jeremy stepped back and motioned toward a tall black-haired young man who waited just inside the door. Meg had not noticed him, for the stranger had tactfully stayed in the background during the family greetings. "Look who else is here."

Meg was only momentarily off-balance. So Jeremy had brought another friend. Fortunately the goose was a large one. She gave the newcomer an approving glance. Like Jeremy, he, was travel-stained and bristle-chinned, but still very attractive.

"I'm very pleased to meet you. Do you mind if I call you Meg?" the newcomer said. "Jeremy has told me so much about his family that I feel as if I know you all."

"Please do. And what is your name?" Meg replied, thinking that the young man had a charming smile. Phoebe would like him.

Jeremy laughed. "This is Jack Howard, of course."

With a flourish, the newcomer kissed Meg's proffered hand. "I'm sorry that I was unable to notify you that I wouldn't reach Chippenham three days ago," he said apologetically. "My packet was blown off-course and I reached London about the same time Jeremy did. By the sheerest coincidence, we met at the coaching inn last night. The coach was full, so we hired a chaise and drove all night to be here for Christmas."

Meg gasped. "But you're not Jack Howard."

"I assure you that I am," he said, gray eyes twinkling. "No doubt you were expecting someone a bit more presentable, but Jeremy will vouch for me."

Meg felt as if she had been turned into a marble statue. Then her gaze turned to meet Philip's shocked stare.

It took her two tries to croak out the words, *"If you're Jack Howard, then who is the man sleeping upstairs in Jeremy's bed?"*

*   *   *

THE calico cat woke Jack, nuzzling his cheek in a bid for attention. Absently he scratched her furry head, his thoughts on Meg. He hoped she would agree to an early wedding date.

He heard sounds downstairs and guessed that it was Meg, up early and working. Quietly he rose and dressed, thinking that he could either help her in the kitchen or compromise her, whichever seemed most appropriate.

He went into the corridor to the top of the stairs and was just starting down when he heard the fatal words. "If you're Jack Howard, then who is the man sleeping upstairs in Jeremy's bed?"

Jack froze, one hand on the banister. He had become so convinced that fortune was favoring his cause that he had forgotten that the sword of Damocles hung over his head—and the supporting thread had just broken.

He almost bolted, but it was too late. A board shifted under his foot and the four people down in the hall turned to gaze up at him. There stood Philip and a frowning, older version of him, a tall black-haired young man with puzzlement on his face. And Meg—his darling Meg, who stared as if Jack were something she had just found under a dead leaf.

With a groan, Jack sank down onto the steps and buried his face in his hands, wondering how on earth to explain himself.

Before he had a chance to try, a white-faced Meg snapped, "Just who the devil are you?"

Jack looked up. "My name *is* Jack Howard," he said simply. "I'm just not the Jack Howard you were expecting."

Meg said icily, "Are you really a major?"

When Jack nodded, there was a soft murmur of surprise from below. Jeremy asked, "Are you Major Jack Howard of the 51st? 'Mad Jack' Howard, the hero of Badajoz?"

Jack winced. "For my sins, yes."

The black-haired man exclaimed, "Good God, Mad Jack Howard! It's a great pleasure to meet you, sir. I wish I had a guinea for every man who offered to buy me a drink, thinking I was you. I believe we are distantly related."

"Very likely," Jack agreed. "I have a great-aunt who would be able to explain the connection."

He saw that Philip had recovered quickly from his surprise and was now studying the fraudulent guest curiously, doubtless trying to reconcile Jack's diatribe on heroism with his ridiculous nickname. Meg, however, looked as if she had been stabbed through the heart.

Jeremy's brows drew together. "But I heard that you had sold out because you'd inherited the earldom of Winstoke?" he said, his rising tone making it a question.

Jack sighed. "You're well informed, Captain Lambert."

Jack's answer was the last straw for Meg. Face stricken, she whirled and fled down the hall.

"Meg!" Jack called out despairingly. "Please give me a chance to explain." Abandoning his efforts to make polite conversation, he bolted down the stairs, past the startled group of young men, and followed Meg into the parlor.

As the parlor door banged shut, Jeremy Lambert turned to his younger brother. "Would you kindly tell me what the devil has been going on here?"

Philip grinned wickedly. "Meg found him at the George in Chippenham. He followed her home and, if I'm not mistaken, she had just about decided that she wanted to keep him. Unfortunately, she's a bit disconcerted to discover that he may be a tiger rather than a tabby cat."

"You mean that Major Howard—sorry, Lord Winstoke—wants to marry our Meg?" Jeremy asked in amazement.

"I think so. Not that anyone tells me anything."

A clear voice sounded from above. "Jeremy, is that you?"

Phoebe scampered down the stairs, resplendent in a scarlet robe, her dark hair curling deliciously around her face. Just like her older sister, she leaped into her brother's arms. "Oh, marvelous, you made it home in time for Christmas!"

"Indeed." Jeremy laughed. "Though I'm beginning to wonder if I've landed in Bedlam instead." Taking Phoebe's arm, he turned her to his companion. "This is my friend Jack Howard. . . . *Captain* Howard of the 45th, not to be confused with *Major* Howard of the 51st, though apparently he was."

As she tried to sort out her brother's words, Phoebe automatically offered her hand, then gasped as she focused on the captain. "You—you look exactly as I thought Jeremy's friend would," she said stupidly.

The captain kissed her hand, then straightened without relinquishing his grip. "You are Phoebe. You couldn't be anyone else." He had the stupefied look of a man who has just hit a stone wall at high speed. "You can't imagine how much I've looked forward to meeting you."

Philip rolled his eyes. Fearing they would continue making sheep's eyes indefinitely, he gave his sister a light pinch on the rump. "Go put some decent clothes on, Pheebles—you are quite putting me to the blush."

It was Phoebe who blushed as she remembered her state of dishabille. She released the captain's hand, shooting Philip a dagger look and whispering under her breath, "Don't you dare use that appalling nickname again—Phippy."

"Pax!" He grinned. "No nicknames."

As the entranced captain's gaze followed Phoebe up the stairs, Philip decided that it was time to play the host. "Jeremy, Captain Howard, you must be cold and famished. Why not come into the kitchen for some hot tea and breakfast?"

The two travelers accepted with alacrity, and Philip ushered them into the kitchen with a philosophical sigh. It would be a bit confusing if they ended up with two brothers-in-law named Jack Howard, but no doubt they'd learn to cope.

THE fact that Jack had followed her into the parlor was the only thing that kept Meg from dissolving in tears. She retreated to the far corner of the room. "Your game is over, and I think it is time for you to leave, Lord . . . What was it, Winsmoke?"

"Winstoke, and I'm not leaving until I've said my piece." He looked at her pleadingly. "Later today I was going to tell you the truth—in fact, I tried to confess earlier, and you kept telling me not to say any more. I admit that I should not have left it at that, but I honestly did attempt to explain."

Meg gave a brittle laugh. "So you were being literal when you said you weren't the man I thought you were. Foolish me—I thought you meant something profound and mysterious. I didn't understand much, did I?"

"You understood a great deal more than I was able to say, Meg," he said quietly. "Please, try to understand now."

His words silenced Meg. As she thought back over the three days the major had been at Brook Farm, she realized that it was true that several times he had started to tell her something, but the conversation had always gone astray. And there had been other clues; he had never spoken of Jeremy or the regiment or any other aspect of his background. Thinking they knew who he was, the Lamberts had noticed nothing unusual in his behavior.

Meg's face burned as she realized how she had misunderstood him from beginning to end. Particularly last night; he couldn't possibly have meant that he wanted to marry her, not with him being an earl. God only knew what he had meant. Her hands clenched spasmodically. "Why did you come home with me?"

"I wouldn't have been so brazen if I was sober, but you seemed to know me, and you were so lovely and kind. I would have followed you anywhere," he said simply.

Meg shivered. He didn't look like an earl or a legendary war hero; he still looked like Jack, large and shaggy, with an unpredictable mixture of shyness and humor and those blue, blue eyes that were so misleadingly honest. "Why were you in the George at all? Surely the Earl of Winspoke had someplace better to be for Christmas."

"Winstoke. And no, I definitely did not have a better place to be." He gave a faint, humorless smile. "When you met me, I was running away from my great-aunt by marriage, the dowager Countess of Winstoke, the most terrifying old dragon you could ever hope not to meet." His voice softened. "You're freezing, Meg. I'll build a fire and you'll feel better."

Meg *was* freezing, but she maintained a wary distance while he knelt at the hearth and efficiently laid a new fire. "Why were you running away?"

He struck a spark, then sat back on his heels and watched as the tinder began to burn. "Do you want the short reason or the long reason?"

"The long one."

Still looking down, Jack said, "I was never supposed to inherit the earldom. I was an orphaned second cousin with half a dozen heirs between me and the title. With my parents dead, my great-uncle, the third earl, took responsibility for raising me. The dragon dowager was his wife. Just like you, they knew their duty to family and were quite punctilious about discharging their obligations. But, unlike you, they performed their duty with all the warmth and charm of a pair of testy hedgehogs."

He sighed and ran a hand through his brown hair, leaving it hopelessly disordered. "I don't mean that anyone was cruel to me. It was just that the Winstokes were very busy and I was very . . . insignificant, living in the margins of Hazelwood like a mouse in the larder. I was sent to school, though not Eton, of course. Eton was for heirs.

"I spent holidays at Hazelwood because there was nowhere else to go. I was given an allowance, a modest one, so I wouldn't get any ideas above my station, and a commission was purchased for me when I was old enough to be sent into the world. No one bothered to invite me to come back for a visit, although, to be fair, if I had visited, no one would have dreamed of asking me to leave. As a Howard, I had a right to be there. But that isn't quite the same thing as being welcome."

Reluctantly Meg felt a tug at her heart. There was no self-pity in Jack's voice. Just flat acceptance masking a sadness as large as all outdoors. She took a few steps toward the fire. "But now you're the master of Hazel-wood. Surely that will make a difference."

"I will be obeyed, of course, but hardly loved. There was never enough love to go around at Hazelwood, and my becoming the master won't instantly change that. I fell out of touch with the family and didn't realize how close I stood to the title. It was a shock to be summoned back to England to take up my responsibilities when my cousin, the fifth earl, died. I'm still not quite accustomed to the idea of being the head of the family." He smiled wryly. "The way you railed against the nobility made it even harder to confess my sins."

Meg bit her lip. She *had* sounded rather fishwifish. "You've only just arrived back in England from the Peninsula?"

"The very day I met you. The dowager countess arranged everything, but characteristically forgot to consult me about my wishes. Her secretary met me in London and presented me with a list of things I must do to avoid disgracing my new station. He couldn't bring himself to call me Lord Winstoke—in fact, he barely managed common civility. After half an hour of that, I succumbed to an attack of rebelliousness and walked out of the inn and got on the first coach I saw. It happened to be going to Bristol. The rest you know."

Meg perched on the edge of the sofa and held her hands toward the fire. She felt much warmer. "The countess sounds like a proper tartar."

"She is," Jack agreed. "Mind you, this is no easier for her than for me.

Her own son and grandson have died—seeing me in their place will be a bitter pill to swallow. But she will accept and help me because that is her duty. I've no doubt that she and I will learn to rub along tolerably, but it was not a bad thing to refuse to spend Christmas at Hazelwood. She needs to know that I won't let her bully me."

Meg shivered again; there must be a draft. "So Brook Farm was merely a convenient place to hide from the countess."

"When I reached the George, I was running away, and any inn would have done." His grave blue eyes met hers. "But as soon as I saw you, I had something to run *to*. As I said at the time, I knew you were everything men fight for: home, warmth, love."

Meg linked her hands tightly in her lap. "You weren't secretly laughing at our rural simplicity?"

"Good God, Meg, no! I was so moved, so grateful, for the way you and your family welcomed me. I felt as if I'd come home after a lifetime of wandering. Meeting you seemed like fate. Nothing else could explain my being at exactly the right place at the right time with the right name, and the correct Jack Howard *not* being here." He gave her a crooked smile. "If I had told you the truth, I would have had to leave, and I couldn't bear the thought of that. It would have been like expulsion from the Garden of Eden."

Meg gave an involuntary chuckle. "It was Adam and Eve who were expelled—the role you played was the serpent."

Jack's expression eased at her laughter. "Not the serpent—just a cuckoo who landed in the wrong nest and was too happy to want to be cast out into the cold, cruel world."

She bit her lip. "I wouldn't have cast you out if I'd known you had no place to go for Christmas."

"Then don't cast me out now, Meg." He held his hand out to her.

Hesitantly Meg accepted it, and Jack tugged her down onto the carpet next to him. This close to the fire, it was much warmer, quite cozy in fact.

He clasped both her hands in his. "Yesterday I said that I had something to say to you, and then a question to ask. Now you know what I was going to tell you. Have you been thinking about your answer to the question?"

"Just what was the question, Jack?" Meg asked.

His brows lifted. "Don't you know?"

"I thought I did, but perhaps I was wrong." The expression in his eyes made Meg feel rather breathless. It was really quite warm now, almost uncomfortably so. "You had better say exactly what you mean."

Jack smiled at her tenderly. "I want to marry you, of course."

"Is it because you want me to protect you from the dowager countess?"

"No." He grinned. "Or at least that's only a small part of the reason. I want to marry you because I love you and will certainly go into a decline if banished from your presence." He lifted her hands and kissed first one, then the other.

Meg's fingers curled around his. "I'm dreadfully managing, you know. I would torment you unmercifully."

He looked hopeful. "*Please* torment me, Meg. You can't imagine how much I look forward to that."

She could not stop herself from laughing. "Are you never serious, you absurd man?"

"I am when I say that I love you." Suddenly solemn, he met her gaze. "Were you serious last night, Meg?"

She blushed and nodded. "I've never been in love before. This morning I felt like a bit of a fool when I realized that I'd fallen in love with a cuckoo."

Jack laughed and drew her into his arms so that her head tucked under his chin. Meg relaxed against him, thinking how very large and comfortable he was.

He murmured into her ear, "You still haven't answered my question. Will you marry me?"

"I'll never make a proper countess."

"All it takes to be a proper countess is to marry an earl, and I'll take care of that part of it," he said, laughter in his voice. "With your warmth and wisdom, you'll make a countess such as Hazelwood has never known before."

Weakly she summoned the last argument she could think of. "We've known each other for only three days."

"But I've been looking for you all my life."

Meg caught her breath. It was easy to believe that he was a military hero, for he certainly knew how to destroy one's defenses. "Is it really that simple?"

"It is for me, Meg." He brushed her hair with one large hand. "And if you do love me, it should be simple for you too."

With a slow flowering of joy, Meg's hesitation dissolved. "It really is that simple, isn't it?" she said in a voice full of wonder. "Yes, Jack, I'll marry you."

He gave a whoop of delight and fell back onto the carpet, pulling her with him so that she was sprawled across his chest in a perfect position for serious kissing. For the next several minutes, guests and Christmas were utterly forgotten. Then came the faint squeaking sound of a tiny door opening, followed by a clear, "Cuckoo, cuckoo!"

They stopped kissing and counted. "Nine o'clock," Jack said with satisfaction. "The clock is working just as it ought. Do you think your father would be pleased?"

"Good Lord!" Meg clapped her hand over her mouth. "I had completely forgotten about the deed and Peacock Hill. We must go tell the others. What an unforgettable Christmas this will be!"

Jack stood, then assisted Meg to her feet. "It already is."

As she made a token attempt to restore her appearance to that of a decorous older sister, Meg said mischievously, "I never realized that the cuckoo and his foster family might become attached to each other in spite of their differences. But then, I never met a Christmas cuckoo before."

Laughing, Jack put his arm around his ladylove's shoulders and escorted her to the door of the parlor. But just before leaving the room he gave the cuckoo clock a salute—as a mark of respect between two birds of a feather.

Sunshine for Christmas

The very first novella I ever wrote, "Sunshine for Christmas," gave me the chance to settle a minor character from my Regency novel The Rake *(originally published as* The Rake and the Reformer*). Lord Randolph Lennox was a nice fellow who lost the woman he loved because of a single bit of foolishness when he was young, and I thought he deserved better than what he had. So I gave him a dash of seasonal affective disorder and packed him off to Italy, where, as everyone knows, magical things can happen. . . .*

IT was raining again. It had rained yesterday and the day before that. His hands clasped behind his back, Lord Randolph Lennox gazed out the window of his bedroom at the slick gray streets of Mayfair. "Burns, do you know how many days it has been raining?"

"No, my lord," his valet replied, glancing up from the wardrobe, where he was stacking precisely folded neckcloths.

"Thirty-four days. Rather biblical, don't you think? Perhaps it is time to order an ark."

"While the autumn has been a wet one," Burns said austerely, "it has not rained continuously day and night. Therefore, if I recall the scriptural precedent correctly, an ark should not be required."

Between amusement and depression, Lord Randolph considered the question of arks. Somewhere on Bond Street, among the tailors and boot-makers and jewelers, was there a shop that would supply an ark suitable for a gentleman? But that would never do, for arks were meant for pairs, and Randolph was alone. Had been alone for thirty-four years, save for one brief spell, and undoubtedly he would be alone for the rest of his life.

With disgust, Randolph realized that he was in danger of drowning in self-pity. Damn the rain. He was a healthy, wealthy man in the prime of his life, with friends and family and a variety of interests, and he had no right to complain of his lot. He knew that he should be grateful for the rain that kept "this scepter'd isle, this demi-paradise" green, but the thought did nothing to mitigate the bleakness outdoors, or in his soul.

He would have enjoyed snow, which was clean and pure and forgiving, but snow seldom fell in southern England. Farther north, in Scotland or Northumbria, soft white flakes might be floating silent from the sky. In London, the weather was merely miserable.

In a few weeks it would be Christmas, doubtless a drab, wet one, and Randolph was not sure which thought was more depressing: the rain or the holiday. As a boy growing up on the great estate of Dunbar, he had loved Christmas, had ached with excitement from the celebrations and the sense of magic in the air.

Randolph and his older brother, Edward, more formally known as Lord Westkirk, would burrow into the Dunbar kitchens with the glee of all small boys. There they stole currants and burned their fingers on hot pastries until chased out by the cook, who had a fondness for children except when a holiday feast was threatened.

Dunbar had been a happy house then. Indeed, it still was. Randolph's parents, the Marquess and Marchioness of Kinross, enjoyed robust good health and liked nothing better than having their family about them. Edward and his wife and three children would be at Dunbar for Christmas, as would numerous other Lennoxes. The great house would be drenched with love and laughter and happiness. It was expected that Randolph would be there as cherished son and brother, uncle and cousin.

He couldn't bear the thought.

It was only midafternoon, but the light was already failing because of the rain. Randolph studied his reflection in the darkening window glass with detachment. Above average height, dark gold hair, slate-blue eyes, regular features. During their courtship, his wife had said that he looked like a Greek god. It had been a sad disappointment to her when he had proved merely human, and not an especially dashing specimen at that.

He did not have to spend Christmas at Dunbar. There were other houses, other friends, more distant relations, who would welcome him for the holidays, but he no more wished to go to any of them than to his father's house. He did not want to be an outsider at the feast of other people's happiness. Neither did he want the good-hearted matchmakers of his acquaintance trying to find him another wife.

What did he want? Sunshine and anonymity. Bright skies, warm air, a place where no one knew or cared who he was.

An absurd idea. He could not just pack up and run off on impulse.

Why not?

Why not indeed? First with surprise, then excitement, Randolph realized that there was nothing to stop him from leaving England. Winter was a quiet time at his estate, and his presence was not required. Now that the long wars were done, the Continent awaited, beckoning staid Englishmen to sample its decadent charms. If he answered that siren call, his family would regret his absence, but he would not be missed—not really. His presence was essential to no one's happiness.

Quickly, before the impulse could dissipate, he turned from the window. "Burns, commence packing. Tomorrow we shall take ship to the Mediterranean."

The usually imperturbable valet so far forgot himself as to gape. "Surely you jest, my lord?"

"Not in the least," Randolph answered, a sparkle in his eyes. "I shall go into the City to book passage directly."

"But . . . but it isn't possible to arrange such a journey in twenty-four hours," Burns said feebly.

Randolph considered all that must be done, then nodded. "You're right. We shall leave the day after tomorrow instead." He grinned, feeling lighter than he had in months. "We're going to find some sunshine for Christmas."

WITH a lamentable lack of regard for his expensive coat, Lord Randolph crossed his arms and leaned against the brick wall, drinking in the grandeur of the scene before him. Even under damp gray skies, Naples was beautiful.

Having made the decision to leave London, he had booked passage on the next available Mediterranean-bound passenger ship. Its destination had seemed a good omen, for Naples was said to be one of the most sophisticated and enchanting of cities.

As further proof that his journey was blessed, Randolph had found lodgings at the best hotel in the city, with glorious prospects visible from every window. Naples seemed a magical place, and he had gone to bed the first night full of hope, sure that even a staid Englishman could find magic here.

The next morning he awoke to rain, and the local variety was every bit as dismal as the London kind. The hotel manager, heartbroken at being the bearer of bad news, admitted that December was the height of the rainy season, but hastened to add that the weather might well improve momentarily, if not even sooner.

Perhaps the sun would come out, perhaps not, but that morning the weather was exactly like a bad English November, which was what Randolph had tried to escape. His brief spark of hope flickered and died, leaving resignation. It had been foolish to think he could run away from either rain or loneliness. But, by God, he was here on the holiday of a lifetime, and he was going to enjoy himself if it killed him.

He hired a guide, and for three days he dutifully viewed churches and monuments. He bought antiquities and *objets d'art,* and an exquisite doll in native dress for his niece.

He had also admired the handsome Neapolitan women, had even been tempted by one or two of the sloe-eyed streetwalkers. But he did not succumb to temptation, for the price might be too high. It was said that the prostitutes of Naples often gave men souvenirs that could be neither forgotten nor forgiven.

Yesterday his guide had taken him to view a religious procession. For reasons incomprehensible to a northern Protestant, a statue of the Blessed Virgin was removed from its church and paraded through the streets. Men carrying fifteen-foot-tall torches had led the way, followed by musicians playing small tambourines, castanets, and enormous Italian bagpipes. Black-clad sweepers wielded brooms to clean the street for the Madonna, a most useful activity, and another confraternity strewed the cobbles with herbs and flowers.

The street and balconies were thronged with watchers, and at first Randolph had enjoyed the parade and the contagious enthusiasm of the crowd. Then came a troop of grim, barefoot penitents, with knotted cords around their necks and crowns of thorns seemingly spiked into their skulls. Behind them marched ominous beings dressed all in white, their heads covered by slant-eyed hoods. Most disturbing of all, six of the cowled figures were shirtless and they scourged themselves as they walked, rivulets of blood trickling down their shredded backs and arms to stain their white garments.

The whole concept of flagellation was repellent to a rational Englishman, and Randolph shuddered, his pleasure in the spectacle destroyed. Even through the general clamor, he heard the sickly thud of iron-tipped whips against raw flesh.

To his guide's mystification, Randolph turned and began elbowing his way through the crowd. He had been a fool to think he would be less lonely in an alien land. Quite the contrary, he had never felt more of an outsider. He was deeply different from the Neapolitans, and just as he would never understand that orgy of self-abusive piety, he would never be able to match their passion for living.

Seeking comfort among his own kind, that evening Randolph had attended a small gathering at the British ambassador's residence. The English community was a sizable one, and clearly eager to welcome a lord into their midst. There were numerous invitations for him to come to dinner on Christmas Day and have some proper plum pudding, not heathen food like the locals ate. But it was not authentic plum pudding that Randolph wanted. With the gracious vagueness of which he was a master, he had declined all invitations and returned to his hotel thoroughly depressed.

This morning had dawned overcast but no longer raining, and the sky hinted at possible clearing later in the day. Heartened by the prospect, Randolph dismissed the guide and set off on foot to explore the city himself. He marveled at the juxtaposition of magnificence and cramped poverty, at the fierce pulse of a city whose inhabitants insisted on living their joys and sorrows in public for all the world to see. His obvious foreignness attracted attention, and he had had to fend off small street boys whose innocence was dubious, no matter how young they were, but he had no serious problems.

In late morning his wandering brought him to a quiet residential square on one of the higher hills. Modest but respectable houses surrounded the piazza on three sides, while the fourth was bounded by a brick wall. The hill fell sharply away below the wall to reveal a splendid view of the bay. Pleased, Randolph crossed his arms on top of the wall and studied the city that sprawled so wantonly below.

The air smelled different from England, the breeze redolent with the rich, intriguing scents of unfamiliar vegetation and kitchens. The clouds were beginning to break up, and as he watched, the first shafts of sunlight touched the famous bay, changing the sullen gray waters to teal and turquoise.

On the far side of the bay loomed the indigo bulk of Vesuvius. This was the first day clear enough for Randolph to see the volcano, and he was intrigued by the small, ominous plume of smoke wafting from the top. What would it be like living by a volcano? Perhaps that constant, smoldering reminder of mortality was why Neapolitans lived life with such intensity.

The only other person visible was a bespectacled woman perched on a bench at the opposite end of the square. Oblivious to Randolph, she sketched in a pad balanced on her knees. Fair-skinned and soberly dressed, she must be another tourist. Randolph thought that it was rather adventurous of her to be walking out alone, then dismissed her from his mind.

One of the skinny Italian cats jumped up on the wall by Randolph, examined him with feral yellow eyes, then crept along the bricks, stalking a bird that flew away at the last minute. Several chickens wandered across the piazza, pecking hopefully at the ground, and somewhere nearby a dove cooed. It was the most peaceful spot he had found in Naples. He closed his eyes content to absorb the welcome warmth and brightness of the increasing sunshine.

A scraping sound caught his attention, and Randolph glanced over to see a young girl emerge from a house in the corner of the piazza, a bucket in one hand and a low ladder in the other. Paying no attention to the two tourists, she propped the ladder against the wall and scampered up, bucket in hand, to begin washing the windows.

The girl was very pretty, with olive skin, raven hair tied back with a scarlet ribbon, and a pair of trim ankles visible below her full skirts. Randolph watched her idly, enjoying the sight as he would any of Naples's other natural wonders.

After vigorously washing the nearest panes, the girl leaned over and began working on next window, the ladder swaying beneath her. Randolph frowned, thinking she would be wiser to move the ladder. But doubtless she had been washing windows that way for years. Even if she fell, the distance was not dangerously great.

Ready to resume his explorations, he started across the square. Before he had taken three steps, he heard a noisy clatter of falling objects, followed by a cry of pain. Cursing himself for not having attempted to caution the girl, Randolph hastened to where she lay in a dazed heap and knelt beside her.

"Signorina?" he said, gently touching her shoulder.

Long black lashes fluttered open to reveal melting dark eyes. The girl murmured something, probably an oath, then pushed herself to a sitting position and gave Randolph a shaky smile. She was very young, perhaps fifteen, and had the breathtaking Madonna face that seemed to be a Neapolitan specialty.

"I'm glad to see that you have survived your fall," he said, though he was sure that she would not understand. He started to rise so that he could help her up, but suddenly she swooned forward and he found himself with an armful of nubile young womanhood. From the feel of the lush curves pressed against Rudolph's chest, it was true that the females of the Mediterranean matured earlier than their northern sisters.

The girl tilted her head back dizzily, and this close, it was obvious that her mouth was the kind usually described as kissable. For a moment Randolph's arms tightened around her. It had been far too long since he had held a woman, and he was only human. But he was also a gentleman, and gentlemen did not take advantage of stunned children, be they ever so nubile.

He decided that the best plan was to lay her down on the street, then summon help from her house. Before he could do so, he heard hoarse masculine shouting behind him, followed by the sound of heavy pounding feet.

He looked up and saw two men racing across the piazza, a strikingly handsome youth and an older man. From their noisy concern, they must be family or neighbors of the injured girl. Hoping one might know some English or French, Randolph opened his mouth to speak as they skidded to a stop next to him.

Before he could say anything, the older man snatched the girl from his arms with an anguished howl, and the youth hurled a vicious punch at Randolph's jaw.

"What the devil!" The reflexes honed in Jackson's Salon took over. Randolph ducked his head and twisted away from the blow, his hat falling to the ground. As he scrambled to his feet, another fist connected solidly with his midriff.

As he doubled over, gasping for breath, Randolph realized that these two maniacs must think he had assaulted the girl. The wooden ladder had fallen nearby, and he grabbed it by two rungs and used it to hold his furious assailant at bay.

The situation was so ludicrous that Randolph almost laughed. Then he saw the wicked glitter of a knife in the young man's hand, and his amusement congealed. This was no longer a joke—it was entirely possible that he might be killed over a stupid misunderstanding. If that happened, doubtless the Kingdom of the Two Sicilies would express profound regret to the British authorities, but that would do Randolph no good.

Yelling, the youth swung the knife wildly. Randolph blocked the blow with the ladder and retreated to the wall of the house so that his back was protected. Amazing how noisy two Neapolitans could be. No, three, the girl had recovered her senses and was shrieking as she clung to the older man's arm, preventing him from joining the attack.

Then a smartly swung umbrella cracked across the young man's wrist, knocking the knife to the ground. The female tourist had entered the fray. Moving between Randolph and his assailants, she began speaking in fluent, staccato Italian. After a startled moment, the Neapolitans began addressing her, all three jabbering simultaneously.

Randolph had already noticed that Italians talked with their bodies as much as their voices, and he watched the pantomime with deep appreciation. The older man's impassioned gestures made it crystal clear that he had been struck to the heart by the sight of his treasured daughter lying lifeless in the arms of a foreigner. As Randolph recollected, the *signorina* had felt far from lifeless, but no matter.

Less clear was the young man's role, but he was equally distressed. Meanwhile, the girl, an angel of innocence, was apparently proclaiming that it was all a misunderstanding.

Since farce seemed to be prevailing over force, Randolph lowered the ladder and studied his defender. She was somewhere around the age of thirty, slim and quite tall. To his fascination, she combined the nononsense air associated with governesses with the lively body language of the Neapolitans. Perhaps she was also Italian? But she had the pale translucent complexion usually associated with England.

By sheer volume, the young man managed to shout down the other speakers. Arms waving, he made an impassioned diatribe, which he concluded by spitting at Randolph's feet.

The tall woman hesitated, took a quick glance at Randolph, then responded, a soulful quiver in her rich alto voice. She ended her address by gesturing toward him, then clasping her hands to her bosom as her eyes demurely fluttered shut behind her gold-rimmed spectacles.

Whether it was her action or her words, the two men looked at each other, then gave mutual shrugs of acceptance. The older man took the woman's hand and kissed it lingeringly, murmuring a baritone *"Bellissima."* The handsome youth, anger vanished as if it had never been, bobbed his head to Randolph, then offered a sunny smile.

The woman turned to Randolph. "Act as if you know me," she murmured in native-born English. "Smile graciously, bow to the young lady, and we can leave."

Randolph retrieved his hat and obeyed. Obviously recovered from her fall, the girl gave him a bewitching smile while her father beamed benevolently. Accompanied by a chorus of good wishes, the two Britons crossed the piazza. On the way, the woman collected the canvas bag that held her sketching materials, thrusting her umbrella into loops on the side. Taking Randolph's arm, she steered him into a street leading down the hill.

When they were out of sight of the square, he asked, "Would you care to explain what that was all about?"

The woman smiled and released his arm. "The two gentlemen are the father and betrothed of young Filomena, both of them stonemasons. They were returning home for lunch when they found Filomena in your arms. Being protective and volatile, they feared the worst.

"If it were just the father, he would probably have chastised Filomena for immodest behavior. But since her intended, Luigi, was present, her father could not admit that his daughter was a designing baggage. Hence, any fall from grace must have been your fault." She gave a gurgle of laughter. "It would not have been as serious if you were not so handsome, but I'm afraid that Luigi was expressing his regret for the fact that he will never look like Apollo."

Randolph found himself blushing. "Why should Luigi have regrets? He looks like Michaelangelo's *David*."

"Very true," the woman said with an unladylike amount of approval.

"But that kind of male beauty is not uncommon here, while you have the charm of novelty." Taking pity on his blushes, she continued, "Incidentally, I am Miss Elizabeth Walker."

"I'm Randolph Lennox, and very much in your debt." He gave her a rueful smile. "I was imagining the London headlines: 'English Tourist Accidentally Murdered in Naples.'"

"That's better than 'English Tourist Assaults Innocent Italian Miss and Is Executed on the Spot.'"

"Definitely. What did you say that convinced them of my harmlessness?"

A hint of color showed on Miss Walker's cheek. "Since they were unwilling to accept that you were motivated only by a spirit of helpfulness, I finally said that you were my husband, that we were on our honeymoon, and how could they possibly believe that a gentlemen like you would dishonor me by making improper advances to a young girl right in front of my face?" She held up her bare left hand. "Fortunate that Luigi and company were not close observers, or they might have doubted my story. I'm sorry, but strong measures were called for. Rational arguments weren't working."

"No harm done," Randolph said, amused. "You said that the girl was a designing baggage?"

"Oh, she is. I'm a governess, you see, and I'm up to all a young girl's tricks. Filomena watched you from an upstairs window for a while until she struck on a way to further her acquaintance. You should have seen her expression—like a cat watching a bird."

"Surely a girl so young would not behave in so forward a fashion!"

"You would not say that if you knew many young females," Miss Walker said feelingly. "But I doubt that she was interested in serious immorality—merely a bit of flirtation. My most recent charge was a girl much like Filomena, and let me tell you, getting Maria safely to the altar was a challenge to make Hannibal's crossing the Alps look like a stroll in Hyde Park."

Randolph remembered how Filomena had conveniently fainted into his arms, and how rapidly she had recovered when her menfolk appeared on the scene. "I thought that Italian girls were very modest and strictly brought up."

"They are, but human nature being what it is, some are modest while others are the most amazing flirts." She glanced at him. "Now I am shocking you. I have lived too long in Italy and quite forgotten proper English restraint. I could give you a lengthy dissertation on Italian behavior, but it is a rather warm lecture and, as I said, quite lengthy."

Randolph laughed out loud. It occurred to him that he had not laughed like this since . . . since September. Preferring to think of this refreshing female rather than the past, he said, "I should like to hear your dissertation some time. I know we have not been properly introduced, but if you are willing to overlook that, perhaps you will let me take you to lunch as a sign of appreciation for your most timely rescue? You can explain Italian behavior to me."

A wise woman would not casually accept a stranger's invitation, so she hesitated, studying his face as if looking for traces of dangerous derangement under his respectable appearance.

"I'm a very harmless fellow," he said reassuringly. "Besides, knowledge of local customs might save my life. Look at what almost happened."

"How can I refuse such a request? A luncheon would be very pleasant. Did you have a particular place in mind? If not, there is a *trattoria* near here that has good food." Her gaze flickered over Randolph's very expensive coat. "That is, if you are willing to eat as Neapolitans do."

It was easy to guess her thoughts. During his first days in Naples, Randolph's guide had insisted on taking him to boring establishments that specialized in English-style cooking. "Do I appear to be such a paltry fellow that I cannot survive on native fare?" He took her canvas bag. "I would be delighted to broaden my culinary horizons."

The *trattoria* was about ten minutes' walk away, on a market square. Unlike the residential square on top of the hill, this piazza bustled with activity. The *trattoria*'s proprietor greeted Miss Walker with enthusiastic recognition and hand-kissing, then seated them at an outdoor table.

After the proprietor had bustled off, Miss Walker said, "I trust you don't mind alfresco dining? Raffaello wants everyone to see that his establishment is frequented by discriminating foreigners. Also, while the day is rather cool by local standards, he assumes that it will seem warm to Englishfolk."

"A correct assumption," Randolph agreed. "It feels like a fine summer day in Scotland."

Miss Walker chuckled. Then the proprietor returned with two goblets and a carafe of red table wine. After pouring wine for both of them, he rattled off a spate of suggestions. Miss Walker responded in kind, with vivid hand gestures, before turning to her companion. "How adventurous are you feeling, Mr. Lennox?"

Randolph hesitated. He had never been the least adventurous, particularly where his stomach was concerned, but when in Naples . . . "I throw myself on your mercy. I will attempt anything that will not try to eat me first."

Eyes twinkling, she gave an order to the proprietor, who bowed and left. "Nothing so fearsome. What I ordered is a simple Neapolitan dish. Peasant food, really, but tasty."

For a few minutes they sipped their wine in silence. As he swallowed a mouthful, Randolph gazed over the piazza, enjoying the shifting throngs of people. Housewives, cassock-clad priests, costermongers, and workmen, all moved to a background of joyously conflicting street musicians. This was what he had come to Naples for: sunshine, exotic sights, enjoyable company.

His gaze drifted to Miss Walker, who was looking pensively across the square. Her appearance was unremarkable but pleasant, with nut-brown hair, a faint gold dusting of freckles, and spectacles that did not manage to conceal fine hazel eyes. She looked like the sort of woman who should be raising children and running a vicarage. She would counsel the villagers, help her husband with his sermons, and all would agree that the vicar was fortunate to have such a capable helpmeet. What had brought her so far from the English countryside? "I gather that you have lived in Italy for some time, Miss Walker."

She glanced at him. Very fine hazel eyes. "Over six years now. At first I lived in this area, but for the last two years I was entirely in Rome, teaching—or rather, standing guard over—the young lady whom I mentioned earlier."

"How did you come to Italy in the first place?" he asked. "That is, if you don't mind my asking."

"After my parents died, there was no reason to stay in England, so I jumped at the chance to become governess to a British diplomatic family that was coming to Italy. When they returned home, I decided to stay on. I am quite valuable here, you see. Aristocratic Italian families like having

English governesses, both as a mark of consequence and in the hopes that cold English temperaments will act favorably on hot-blooded daughters."

"Do you never miss England?"

Her gaze slid away from his. "A little," she admitted softly, taking off her spectacles and polishing them, a convenient excuse for looking down. "A sad consequence of travel is that the more one sees of the world, the more impossible it is to be satisfied with any one location. Sometimes— especially in the spring and summer—I long for England. Yet, if I were there, I should pine for Italy. Here at least I command a better salary than at home, and there is more sunshine." Then, almost inaudibly, she added, "And fewer memories."

It was a motive Randolph could understand. To change the subject, he said, "I envy your command of the language. I wish I had studied Italian, for I find it very strange to be unable to communicate. When someone addresses me, I find myself starting to reply in French, because that I do know."

Miss Walker replaced her spectacles and looked up, collected again. "The Italian taught in England would have been of limited value in Naples. Standard Italian is really the Tuscan dialect, for that was used by Dante and many of the other great writers. I knew Tuscan when I came here, but learning to communicate in Naples was almost like learning a new tongue."

"Not just tongue—also arms, torso, and facial expressions."

"Very true. One cannot stand still and speak properly. Italians are so expressive, so emotional." Absently she tucked an unruly brown curl behind her ear. "I suppose that is one reason why Italy fascinates the English."

"Fascinates, yet repels," Randolph said slowly, thinking of the flagellants in the religious procession. "I've seen more visible emotion in Naples than I have in a lifetime in England. Part of me envies such freedom of expression, but I would probably die on the rack before emulating it."

She regarded him gravely. "Is it that you could not, or would not, act in such a way?"

"Could not." Wryly Randolph thought that it was typical of his English reserve to find himself embarrassed at what he was revealing. Fortunately a waiter appeared and set plates in front of each of them. He studied the dish, which was some kind of salad consisting of vegetables, olives, and less definable substances. "This is the local specialty you warned me of?"

"No, this is *antipasto,* a first course consisting of bits of whatever is available. *Antipasti* are served throughout Italy."

The salad was lightly dressed with olive oil, herbs, and vinegar. After finishing, Randolph gave a happy sigh. "This is the best thing I've eaten since I arrived."

"Either you have been most unfortunate, or you are new to Naples." She neatly speared the last bite of her own salad. "The Italians, like the French, take food very seriously indeed. The main course will not appear for some time, for our hosts do not believe in rushing anything as important as a meal."

"I've only been here for four days," he explained. "I came on impulse, looking for some sunshine for Christmas, and felt sadly betrayed to arrive in Italy and find rain." As the plates were cleared away, his eye fell on her portfolio, which was peeping from the canvas bag. "Are your drawings for public view, or do you prefer to keep them for yourself?"

She eyed him doubtfully. "They are not private, but neither are they very interesting."

"If they are of Naples, I'm sure I will enjoy them."

"Very well." She pulled the portfolio out and handed it to him. "But remember, you have been warned."

Randolph smiled and opened the portfolio. The not-quite-finished drawing on top was the one she had been working on when the altercation broke out. Most of the sketch was devoted to a hazy, atmospheric rendering of the bay and the volcano beyond—how did she achieve such an effect with only pencil?—but what made it unusual was the skinny cat in the right foreground. The beast sat on the wall, sinuous tail curling down the weathered stone, its feral gaze fixed on the city below.

Randolph began leafing through the portfolio. It was amazing how much she could convey with a few deft lines, but far more remarkable was the imaginative way she viewed the world. Over a Roman ruin arched the gnarled, ancient trunk of an olive tree, fishing boats were seen through a veil of nets, and the massive medieval bulk of Castel Nuovo was framed by its Renaissance triumphal arch.

Most striking of all, Vesuvius was drawn from the point of view of a bird looking down on drifting smoke and stark craters, one powerful wing angling across the lower part of the picture. "You have great talent. It's extraordinary how the viewpoints you choose enhance and intensify the scenes."

Her cheeks colored becomingly. "Drawing is a common accomplishment, like embroidery or music."

"That does not mean it is always well done." He turned back to the first drawing, admiring how the thin, restless cat symbolized the passionate, demanding life of the city's slums. "But you have more than skill. You have a unique artist's eye."

Miss Walker opened her mouth to speak, then closed it. After a moment she said, "I was going to make a modest self-deprecating remark, but what I really want to say is 'Thank you.' That is a fine compliment you have given me, and I shall cherish it."

"Do you do watercolors or oils?" he asked as he closed and returned the portfolio.

"Watercolors sometimes. I would like to try oils, but I have little time." She made a face. "It would be more honest to say that I'm afraid that if I started serious painting, I would lose track of the world, and lose my situation along with it."

A pity she lacked the leisure to develop her gift. With his independent income, Randolph had the time to cultivate talent, but unfortunately he had none. Perhaps he should follow a fine old Italian custom and become her patron so that he could bask in reflected glory. But, alas, with a male patron and a female artist, the modern world would put a different construction on the arrangement, even though Miss Walker was an improbable choice for a mistress.

The waiter returned, this time placing a sizzling platter in the middle of the table. On it was a crispy circle of dough spread with herbs, sliced sausage, dried tomatoes, and hot bubbling cheese. Randolph regarded the dish doubtfully. "You are sure this fulfills my minimum condition of not attempting to eat me first?"

Miss Walker laughed. "I've never heard of anyone being assaulted by a *pizza*. I think you will be agreeably surprised."

And he was. The *pizza* was gooey, undignified, and delicious. Between the two of them, they managed to eat almost the entire platter, and he was eyeing the last slice speculatively when someone called, "Lord Randolph, what a pleasant surprise."

He looked up and saw a female detach herself from a group crossing the piazza. It was a woman whom he had met at the ambassador's dinner. As he stood, he ransacked his memory to identify her. Mrs. Bertram, that was her name. A lush blond widow with a roving eye, she lived with her wealthy merchant brother. Both were prominent in the local British community.

Ignoring Miss Walker, Mrs. Bertram cooed, "So lovely to see you again, Lord Randolph. Are you enjoying your visit?"

"Yes, particularly today. Mrs. Bertram, may I make you known to Miss Walker, or are you already acquainted?"

The widow gave Elizabeth Walker a sharp assessing glance, then dismissed her as possible competition. Randolph saw and understood that glance, and felt a small spurt of anger. So had his wife, Chloe, reacted whenever she met another woman. "Miss Walker and I are old friends," he said pleasantly, "and she has been kind enough to show me some of the sights of the city."

Mrs. Bertram's eyes narrowed in irritation. "I should have been delighted to perform that service. I have lived here long enough to know what—and who—is worthwhile." She looked at the last congealing section of *pizza* and gave a delicate shudder. "One cannot be too careful. There is a distressing lack of refinement in much of Neapolitan life."

Randolph's expression must have warned her that her cattiness was not being well received, for she went on, "I do hope you will be able to join us for Christmas dinner." There was a smudge on his sleeve from the earlier altercation, and she reached out and brushed at it, her fingers lingering. "One should not be alone at Christmas. You are very far from home. Let us stand as your family."

"You are most kind," he murmured, "but you need not be concerned for my welfare. I have other plans. Pray give my regards to your brother."

It was unquestionably a dismissal, and Mrs. Bertram was unable to ignore it. After a venomous glance at Randolph's companion, she rejoined her group, which was entering a jeweler's shop.

Relieved to be free of her, Randolph sat down again. Miss Walker regarded him thoughtfully. "Lord Randolph?"

He nodded. "My father is Marquess of Kinross." He wondered if she was going to be either awed or intimidated: those were the two most common reactions.

Instead, she planted one elbow on the table and rested her chin on her palm, her hazel eyes twinkling. "I presume that you did not use your title when you introduced yourself because you weary of being toad-eaten. It must be very tedious."

"It is," he said fervently. "And I have only a meaningless courtesy title. My father and brother must tolerate far worse."

"In fairness to Mrs. Bertram, I imagine that it is not only your title that interests her," Miss Walker said charitably. "By the way, am I an old friend on the basis of my advanced years, or the fact that we have known each other easily two hours?"

He pulled his watch from his pocket. "By my reckoning, it is closer to four."

"Good heavens, is it really so late?" She glanced over at the ornate clock suspended over the jewelry shop. "I must be on my way." She began to collect her belongings. "Lord Randolph, it has been an exceptional pleasure making your acquaintance. I hope you enjoy your stay in Naples."

He stared at her, disconcerted. She couldn't just disappear like this. She was the most congenial soul he had met since coming to Naples. No, far longer than that. He stood. "I should hate to think that I have endangered your livelihood. Let me escort you back. If necessary, I can explain that you are late because you saved me from grievous bodily injury."

She laughed. "Lord Randolph, can you think of anything more likely to be injurious to a governess's reputation than having a handsome man say it is all his fault?" When he looked sheepish, she continued, "You needn't worry. My livelihood is not threatened. I am between situations, gloriously free until I take up a new position after Epiphany." She wrinkled her nose. "Twins! The prettiest little vixens you can imagine. I don't know how I shall manage."

"Very well, I'm sure." The proprietor appeared, and Randolph settled the bill with a gratuity that put an ecstatic expression on the man's face. When the proprietor had left, Randolph continued, "Since it will not cost you your situation, will you accept my escort?"

She hesitated, and he felt a constriction somewhere in his middle. Probably the *pizza* fighting the *antipasto.*

Then she smiled. "That would be very nice. I am going back to my *pensione,* and it is not in the most elegant part of the city."

As they made their way through the piazza, Randolph carrying her canvas bag, she explained, "I am giving drawing lessons to my landlady, Sofia, who has been a good friend to me over the years. She is free for only an hour or so at the end of the afternoon, and if I am late, she will be deprived of her lesson."

Would Mrs. Bertram have abandoned the company of a man in order to fulfill a promise to a landlady? Randolph knew the question was so foolish as not to merit an answer.

As they threaded their way through increasingly narrow, crowded streets, Miss Walker gave an irreverent and amusing commentary on the sights. While she did not neglect splendors like the recently rebuilt San Carlo opera house, her real talent lay in identifying Neapolitan sights like the ribbons of wheat paste drying on backyard racks, and the ancient statue of a pagan goddess, now rechristened and worshiped as a Christian saint in spite of a distinctly impious expression.

All too soon they arrived at the *pensione,* a shabby town house on a noisy street. Miss Walker turned to make her farewell. "Thank you for the luncheon and escort, Lord Randolph. While you are in Italy, stay away from designing young baggages, no matter how dire their straits seem to be."

Impulsively Randolph said, "The discerning eye that makes you an artist also makes you a fine tour guide. Since you are at liberty now, would you consider acting as my guide? You could protect me from the designing baggages directly." When she frowned, he said coaxingly, "I would be happy to pay you for your time, at double the rate of the boring fellow who insisted that I eat only English food."

"It is not a matter of money," she said, uncertain in the face of his unusual offer. "Why do you want me for a guide?"

"Because I enjoy your company," he said simply.

For a moment her serene good humor was shadowed by vulnerability. Then she gave a smile different from her earlier expressions of amusement. This smile came from somewhere deeper, and it transformed her plain face to fleeting loveliness. "Then I will be very glad to be your guide."

ELIZABETH woke with a glow of anticipation, and at first she could not recollect why. Then she remembered. It was not yet time to rise, so she opened her eyes and gazed at the ancient fresco on the ceiling. In truth it was badly drawn, but without her spectacles, it looked splendid, a magical landscape inhabited by flawless lads and lasses. One golden lad looked rather like Lord Randolph Lennox must have at eighteen.

She tucked her arms under her head and reveled in the strange and wondrous chance that had brought them together. Perhaps heaven was giving her a special Christmas present as a reward for managing to keep Maria pure until her marriage? Elizabeth chuckled at the thought. The longer she lived in Italy, the more superstitious she became.

Eager to begin the day, she swung her legs over the edge of the bed and slid her feet into the waiting slippers. Then she began the slow process of brushing out her hair, which was thick and very curly. In the morning it tumbled over her shoulders in a wild mass and at least once a week she considered cutting it, but never did. A governess had little enough femininity.

Patiently she unsnarled a knot. He had said that he was harmless, but that was only partially true. Certainly he would not threaten her virtue, for he was a gentleman and she wasn't the kind of woman to rouse a man to unbridled lust. Heavens, not even bridled lust!

But that didn't mean Lord Randolph was harmless, because of course she would fall in love with him. Any lonely spinster worth her salt would do the same if thrown into the company of a man who was charming, kind, intelligent, and handsome as sin. And he would never even notice, which was as it should be.

After a day or two he would tire of sightseeing, or go north to Rome, or become involved in the glittering circle of court life for which he was so well qualified. And she would begin the task of taming the terrible twins, and tuck the image of Lord Randolph away in her heart, next to that of William.

She might cry a little when he was gone for good, if she wasn't too busy with the twins. But she wouldn't be sorry to have known him. Though magic must sometimes be paid for with pain, that was better than never knowing magic at all. When she was old and gray and dry, she would take his image out and dream a little. If anyone noticed, they would wonder why the old lady had such a cat-in-the-creampot smile on her withered lips.

Elizabeth glanced into the cracked mirror. With her glasses off and her hair curling madly around her face, she looked more like a blowsy baroque nymph than a governess.

For just a moment she let herself dream. Lord Randolph would fall in love with her beautiful soul and marry her out of hand. England would be home, but they would make long visits to Italy. They would have three children; she might be starting late, but she was healthy. She would paint, powerful unusual canvases that some people would love and others would loathe. His aristocratic family would be delighted that Lord Randolph had found a wife of such fine character and talent.

Her mouth thinned and she put her spectacles on and began tugging her hair back. As the nymph vanished into the governess, she knew that he would not fall in love with her, and that even if he did, she could not marry him. Even in her wildest flights of fancy, she could not escape the knowledge that her actions had put respectable marriage forever out of reach.

But that did not mean that Elizabeth could not enjoy this rare, magical interlude. And she did.

In Rome, she had been told of an Englishman who had decided that the main point of seeing sights was to say that one had seen them, so he had hired a carriage and crammed the Eternal City into two fevered days so he could devote the rest of his time to dissipation. Fortunately Lord Randolph proved to be a visitor of quite a different stamp, interested in everything and willing to take the time to absorb as well as see.

She began by taking him to all of Naples's famous sights, and when it became clear that he shared her taste for the unusual, she expanded the itinerary to include more eccentric amusements. Over the next week they explored Naples's narrow, teeming streets, ate fresh fruit, pasta, and ices purchased in the markets, and stopped to enjoy arias of heart-stopping purity that soared from the open windows of tenements.

When it rained they searched dark churches for neglected paintings by great masters, and smiled together at signs that offered, "Indulgences Plenary, daily and perpetual, for living and the dead, as often as wanted." As

Lord Randolph remarked, it was precisely the way a London draper would advertise.

Tactfully, Lord Randolph did not again suggest hiring her services; instead, he paid for all admissions, meals, and other expenses. On fair days he hired a carriage and driver and they went into the countryside. They visited Baia, which had been a fashionable Roman bathing resort, and speculated about the palaces that now lay beneath the sea. At Herculaneum they marveled at the city that had emerged after almost two thousand years beneath volcanic mud, and Elizabeth did sketches that populated the ruins with puzzled, ghostly Romans.

It was Lord Randolph who had suggested that Elizabeth bring her sketchbook. While she drew, he would sit quietly by, smoking his pipe, a man with a gift for stillness. It was not uncommon for rich tourists to hire artists to record what they saw, and Elizabeth quietly resolved to give Lord Randolph this set of drawings when they parted. When he looked at them to remember Naples, perhaps he would also think of her.

In the meantime, she utilized the governess's skill of watching unobtrusively, memorizing the angle of his eyebrows when he was amused, the way the winter sun shimmered across his dark gold hair, and a hundred other subtle details.

Alone in her *pensione* in the evenings, she tried to draw Lord Randolph from memory, with frustrating results. He would have been an easier subject if he were less handsome, because his regular features looked more like an idealized Greek statue than a real man. She did her best to capture the quiet humor in his eyes, the surprising hint of underlying wistfulness, but she was never satisfied with the results.

As an escort Lord Randolph was thoughtful and impeccably polite, and Elizabeth knew he enjoyed her company, but she also knew he was scarcely aware that she was a woman. Had he come to Italy because he was disappointed in love? Hard to imagine any woman turning him down. But she would never know the truth. Though their conversation flowed with ease and wit, they spoke only of impersonal things. Her companion kept his inner life to himself, as did Elizabeth.

The first few days they spent together, she was able to maintain a certain wry detachment about her growing infatuation with Lord Randolph. But the day that they visited the Fields of Fire, detachment dissolved as she fell blindly, helplessly, irrevocably in love with him.

The Campi Flegrei—Fields of Fire—lay north of Naples. The poetic name described an area of volcanic activity, a sight not to be missed by tourists. After spending the morning in the nearby town of Pozzuoli, they had driven to Solfatara, an oval crater where the earth was sometimes too hot to touch and noxious fumes oozed from the holes called fumaroles.

A local guide led half a dozen visitors into the crater, and as part of his tour he held a lighted brand over a boiling mud pot. Immediately the steam issuing from the mud pot flared furiously, as if about to explode. Even though Elizabeth had seen this before, she still flinched back.

Lord Randolph touched her elbow reassuringly. "That is just an illusion, isn't it?"

She nodded. "Yes, the fumarole doesn't really burn hotter, but whenever I see that, I can't help feeling that the sleeping volcano is lashing back at impudent humans who disturb its rest."

After tossing the brand into the fumarole, the guide stamped on the ground, sending a deep, ominous echo rolling through the hollow mountain under their feet. Then he led the group away.

Having had enough demonstrations, Elizabeth and her companion wandered off in another direction.

"It's an interesting place," Lord Randolph remarked as they picked their way through a field of steaming fumaroles. The pungent odor of sulfur hung heavy over the sterile white soil. "Rather like one of the outer circles of hell."

"Solfatara is a place every visitor to Naples should see, but I dislike it intensely." Elizabeth gestured around the barren crater. "When I come here, I always think it is the loneliest, most desolate spot on earth."

"No," her companion said softly, his voice as bleak as the dead earth crumbling beneath their feet. "The loneliest place on earth is a bad marriage."

That was when the fragile remnants of Elizabeth's detachment shattered, for in that instant she came to understand Randolph. It was not a shock to learn that he was married; she had never understood why a man so attractive and amiable did not have a wife. Nor did she feel betrayed that he had not mentioned his wife before, because she had always known there could be nothing between him and her but fleeting friendship.

What Elizabeth did feel was a disabling flood of love and tenderness.

It was tragic that a man so kind and decent should be so unhappy, that loneliness had driven him so far from home.

Even more than tenderness, she felt a sense of kinship. Impulsively she said, "You mustn't surrender to it."

"Surrender to what?" he asked, turning to face her, his slate eyes shadowed.

"To loneliness," she stammered, embarrassed at her own impertinence. "To give in to it is to dance with the devil and lose your very soul."

Under his grave gaze, she felt hot blood rise in her face. She looked away, bitterly sorry that she trespassed beyond the limits of friendship by alluding to intimate, solitary sorrows.

Quietly he said, "If you have danced with the devils of loneliness, you have escaped with your soul and learned wisdom into the bargain."

Elizabeth took a deep, steadying breath, grateful that he had forgiven her lapse. "I think I hear our guide calling. Come, it is time we went back, before he decides that we have fallen into a mud pot."

THE Via Toledo had been called the gayest and most populous street in the world, but Randolph paid little attention to the blithe people swirling around him as he strolled through the lamplit night. He had been walking for hours, his thoughts occupied by an alarming but deeply appealing idea.

He had enjoyed Elizabeth Walker's company from the moment they met, but he had thought her self-sufficient, completely comfortable with her life as it was. That belief had changed in an instant that afternoon at Solfatara. In a moment of weakness he had lowered his guard, and rather than ignoring or despising him for his lapse, Elizabeth had done the same. By the act of reaching out to him she had revealed a loneliness as great as his own, and her blend of warmth, generosity, and vulnerability was so potent that he had very nearly said that if they joined their lives, they might banish the worst of their mutual loneliness.

He kept silent, too skeptical, too wary, to propose marriage on impulse. Yet the idea had taken hold, and now he found himself wondering what kind of wife Elizabeth would make. And the more he thought, the more his conclusions agreed with his first impression of her. She would make an excellent wife.

He smiled wryly, thinking of Samuel Johnson's remark that a second marriage was the triumph of hope over experience. Randolph had thought that life had cured him first of love, then of marriage, and he had resigned himself to spending the rest of his life alone. Yet here he was, thinking that seeing Elizabeth Walker across a breakfast table would be a very pleasant sight indeed. Chloe had seldom risen in time for breakfast, and when she did, she was invariably irritable and self-absorbed.

Elizabeth was not a beauty, but one beauty was enough for a lifetime. Hard experience had taught Randolph that humor, honesty, and a tolerant mind were far more important in a marriage. And she was far from an antidote. While her face was unremarkable, it was engagingly expressive. He found frank pleasure in the supple grace of her slim body, and a mischievous whirl of wind had revealed that her long legs were truly outstanding.

Realizing that he was hungry, he stopped at a small café. The proprietor spoke enough French to take an order but not enough to carry on a conversation, leaving Randolph free to continue his thoughts over wine and *pollo alla cacciatora.* He was not in love with Elizabeth Walker, nor was he coxcomb enough to think that she loved him, but that didn't matter, for he was not convinced that love was an asset to a marriage.

What mattered was friendship, and in a short time they had become good friends. He knew that most people would think he was a fool to be considering marriage to a woman he had known only a week, but they had spent a great deal of time together, long enough that he felt he knew her better than either of the other women who had been important to him.

He thought the chances of her accepting him were excellent. She seemed to enjoy his company, he was presentable, and his wealth would allow her the time and money to paint. Yes, a marriage between them could work out very well. They were both old enough to know their own minds; if she were willing to marry him, there would be no reason for a long engagement.

Now he must find the courage to ask her.

THE morning air was cold but the sky was glass clear; December 24 promised to be the warmest day since Randolph had arrived in Naples. His driver and carriage showed up scarcely a quarter hour late, which was stunning punctuality by Neapolitan standards. Vanni was a cheerful fellow with a splendid baritone and villainous shaggy mustaches. His English was no better than Randolph's Neapolitan, but over the last several days he had learned to drive directly to Elizabeth Walker's *pensione*.

Elizabeth was ready when the carriage arrived, but punctuality was no surprise in her case. It was one of the things Randolph liked about her.

"Good morning," she said cheerfully. "Are you game for a drive in the country? My friend Sofia has a mission for us. It is the end of the olive harvest, and she has asked that we collect her year's supply of fresh oil. A respectable cook insists on knowing where her olive oil comes from, and Sofia swears that her cousin presses the best oil in Campania."

"Which means that it is the best in the world?" he asked with a smile.

"Exactly. You are beginning to understand the Neapolitan temperament, Lord Randolph." Elizabeth lifted a lavishly packed basket. "As reward for our efforts, Sofia has packed a most sumptuous picnic for us."

He helped her into the carriage, then he and Vanni stowed the basket of food and a large number of empty stone jugs behind the passenger seat. After a staccato exchange with Elizabeth, Vanni turned the vehicle and began threading his way through the crowded streets. Leaving the city, they headed south to the fertile farmlands near Vesuvius. To Randolph it seemed odd that lifeless volcanic ash eventually became rich soil, but lush fields confirmed the fact.

The ride through the hills was spectacularly lovely, and having someone to share the sights made them lovelier yet. After two hours of driving they reached their destination, an ancient rambling farmhouse surrounded by silvery olive trees. The two Britons were welcomed joyfully and given a tour, from the vineyards to the hand-operated olive press. As a farmer himself, Randolph enjoyed it thoroughly, and through Elizabeth, he and Sofia's cousin exchanged farmer comments.

After Sofia's jars were filled, Randolph and Elizabeth were offered oven-hot bread dipped in fresh-squeezed olive oil. Randolph accepted his in the spirit of being a good guest, but his first bite showed him that he had been honored with a matchless delicacy, the local equivalent of the first strawberries of spring. When he finished the first piece, he accepted a second, then a third, to the unconcealed satisfaction of his hosts.

As Elizabeth took a proper leave, a lengthy business, Randolph wondered how many members of the local English colony had experienced such simple pleasures. Probably very few. It was impossible to imagine the likes of Mrs. Bertram enjoying "unrefined" rural life. And had it not been for Elizabeth, he would have seen only the usual sights, met only socially prominent Neapolitans, and never known what he was missing.

Bread and oil takes the edge from an appetite, and after they left the farm, they decided to delay their midday meal and visit Balzano, a nearby hilltop town with a famous church. The inside of the church was dim after the bright sunshine, and Randolph paused in the door while his eyes adjusted. Vaguely aware that several people stood in front of the altar, he inhaled the scents of wax and incense.

"Look," Elizabeth murmured, "they've erected the *presepio*."

He followed her down the aisle and discovered that the figures he had assumed to be local worshipers were wooden statues, life-size, lovingly painted, and very old. The grouping formed a Nativity scene featuring Mary, Joseph, two shepherds, the Three Kings, and a family of sheep.

Softly his companion explained, "You see how the manger is empty? That is because the Child has not yet been born. During the service tonight, a real infant will be placed in the manger. They say it was St. Francis of Assisi who invented the *presepio*. He enacted it with a real mother and father and their babe, to remind people that Christmas was a season for holy celebration rather than profane pleasures."

"A most effective demonstration of the fact that the origin of the word 'holiday' is 'holy day,' " Randolph agreed. "Tonight, by candlelight, it will seem very real."

After viewing the rest of the church, they decided to stroll through the narrow medieval streets before leaving the town. As they neared the bustling market square, they were intercepted by an enterprising peddler who pulled a handful of small figurines from his basket and pressed them on Elizabeth, along with a torrent of enthusiastic words.

"These are *pastori*, figures for a Nativity scene," Elizabeth explained. She handed one to Randolph. "You might find them interesting. They are made of lapis solaris."

He accepted it from her, seeing only a rather crudely formed Madonna. "Stone of the sun?"

"Yes, the material holds light and will glow in the dark for hours. It was invented by an alchemist who was searching for the philosopher's stone. He never found that, but lapis solaris became very popular for rosaries and crucifixes and the like."

Randolph regarded the small figure thoughtfully. "I'm not sure if the basic idea is sublime or ridiculous."

"Both." Elizabeth's lovely hazel eyes danced. "Because he can see that we are *inglesi* of rare discernment, he will offer us a complete *presepio* of lapis solaris for a price so low that it will shame him before all of Balzano if we tell anyone."

Suddenly the ground moved beneath their feet, a subtle, disquieting shift that made the peddler's figurines chatter together in their basket. Randolph tensed, though this was not the first tremor he had experienced since his arrival. He doubted that he would ever get used to them, though Elizabeth and the peddler seemed unconcerned by the earth's betrayal.

As the tremor faded, the peddler spoke to Elizabeth with a smile and a triumphant lift of his hand. She burst out laughing. "He says that his price for the complete *presepio* is so low that God Himself was shocked, and that is why the earth moved."

Randolph joined her laughter. He had already observed that the local peddlers had an audacity that would make a gypsy horse coper blush. He decided that this peddler deserved to make a sale, but for the honor of the English, Randolph bargained over the price for the next quarter hour.

When they were done, the peddler wrapped the set in an old rag and presented it to Randolph with a flourish. As they walked away, Elizabeth said, "Well done. You brought him down to half the original asking price."

"Which I estimate is at least double what the things are worth," Randolph said with amusement. He removed the top figurine from the bundle. It was the Bambino. "Why do I have the feeling that this was made in Birmingham?"

"Cynic." Elizabeth chuckled. They had reached the market square, which was crowded with people buying the last ingredients for their holiday feasting. "I'm sure that it was made somewhere in Italy. Glowing religious artifacts are just not very English, are they?"

She stopped by a stall that featured marzipan shaped into exquisite imitation fruits and flowers. Knowing that the confections would be popular with the younger Lennoxes, Randolph bought a large number. While the marzipan was being wrapped in silver paper, Elizabeth suddenly jumped, at the same time giving a smothered squeak.

Alarmed, Randolph asked, "Is something wrong?"

"Just someone pinching me," she explained. "A little harder than usual, or I would scarcely have noticed."

"Someone pinched you? Outrageous!" Indignant, Randolph turned toward the square with the vague idea of calling such impertinence to book, but Elizabeth caught his arm.

"Don't be upset, it was not meant as an insult. Quite the contrary." She smiled at him. "It's one of the things I love about Italy. Even though I am much too thin and not at all in the local style, at least once a day someone will perjure himself by saying or implying that I am beautiful. I doubt there is another place in the world where a plain old spinster is made to feel so desirable."

Adding the marzipan fruit to his bundles, Randolph took her arm and began steering her through the crowd. "You do yourself an injustice, Miss Walker. You are not old, and what is thin to a Neapolitan is elegantly slim to an Englishman."

She gave him a startled glance. "Is that a compliment?"

He smiled down at her. "Yes, it is." She looked quite adorable in her astonishment. If they had not been surrounded by people, he would have proposed to her on the spot. What they needed was a place with a little privacy, which shouldn't be hard to arrange. "Shall we ask Vanni to find us a suitably scenic site for a late luncheon? I suspect that Sofia would be outraged if we returned her basket intact."

They had reached the carriage, and as Randolph put his purchases away, Elizabeth and Vanni conferred. Eventually she asked, "What say you to a ruined Roman temple, high on a hill, gloriously private, and possessing a matchless view of Vesuvius?"

"Perfect." Randolph helped her into the carriage, then swung up beside her. He was beginning to feel a little nervous. One would think that a man who had twice before proposed marriage would be a little calmer about the prospect, but that didn't seem to be the case. Still, his qualms did not run too deep. At heart he did not believe that Elizabeth would turn him down.

THE trail had been growing narrower and narrower, and finally Vanni pulled the horses to a halt and turned to speak to Elizabeth. She explained to her companion, "This is as close as a carriage can go. Vanni says the temple is a ten- or fifteen-minute walk along this path."

Lord Randolph nodded agreeably and took the picnic basket in hand. The condition of the path explained why the site was seldom visited. It was narrow and irregular, not much more than a goat track, and had been washed out and repaired more than once. The mountain face rose sheer on the right, then dropped lethally away to the left. Elizabeth went first, keeping close to the rock face and being very careful where she put her feet.

She rounded the last bend in the trail, then stopped, enchanted. The path widened into a large ledge, with a steep wall on the right and a sheer drop on the left. Perhaps a hundred yards long and fifty wide, the site had soil rich enough to support velvety grass and delicate trees. As Vanni had promised, the view of Vesuvius was spectacular. But all that was simply a setting for the temple, which looked as if it had floated down on temporary loan from fairyland.

Behind her, Lord Randolph said admiringly, "Anyone who ever built a false ruin would give his left arm to have this instead. It's the ultimate folly."

The small round shrine was built of white marble that held a hint of rose in its translucent depths. A curving wall formed the back half of the building, with dainty Ionic columns completing the front part of the circle. The roof was long gone and vines climbed the columns for an effect that was beautiful, wistful, and altogether romantic.

Elizabeth said, "Do you think we should invite Byron to visit? This deserves to be immortalized in poetry."

"Never," Lord Randolph said firmly as he set the picnic basket down. "If Byron wrote of it, the path would become so jammed with people coming to admire and languish that someone would surely fall down the mountain to his death, and it would be our fault. Much better to let it stay Vanni's secret."

The ruins of an old fire proved that the site was not precisely a secret, but certainly it was seldom visited, for the floor of the shrine was entirely covered with drifted leaves. Elizabeth knelt and carefully brushed them away, finding a charming mosaic of birds, flowers, and butterflies. "I wonder what god or goddess was worshiped here."

"A gentle one, I think."

Glancing up, she saw an odd, assessing look on Lord Randolph's face. Inexplicably she shivered, wondering if there was really tension in the air, or just another example of her overactive imagination.

Seeing her shiver, he offered his hand to help her up. "In spite of the sunshine, in the shade it is still December."

His hand was warm and strong as he lifted her effortlessly. Elizabeth released his clasp as soon as she was on her feet. Her awareness of Lord Randolph's strength and masculinity was acute and uncomfortable. She decided that it was because, in spite of a week of constant company, they had never been quite so alone.

She moved away from him quickly, knowing that her dignity depended on her ability to remain collected. She would rather throw herself from the cliff than let her companion know of her foolish, hopeless passion. Removing the folded lap rug that protected the contents of the basket, she asked, "Shall we see what Sofia has given us? I think we are going to benefit from her Christmas baking."

"There's enough food for an army, or at least a platoon." Randolph reached in the basket and removed the shallow oval bowl. After investigating the contents, he said, "Eel pie?"

"Very likely. The day before Christmas is meatless, and eels are a tradition," Elizabeth explained as she unpacked the basket. "We also have fresh fruit, two cheeses, braided bread, three kinds of Christmas cakes, *pizza rustica*—you'll like that, it's sort of a cheese pie with slivered ham, among other things—and enough red wine to wash it all down."

Randolph blinked. "If the laborers are worthy of their hire, I suppose this is an indication of how much she values her olive oil."

"That, plus the fact that she is continually trying to fatten me up. She thinks you are too thin also." Remembering what else Sofia had said about the English milord—all of it complimentary and some of it decidedly improper—Elizabeth concentrated on laying food out on the cloth. What was wrong with her? A simple picnic with a gentleman and she was behaving like one of her own hot-blooded, romantic charges, with every thought revolving around the man at her side.

The incredibly handsome, amiable, interested, courteous man at her side. Stop that! she scolded herself. She was glad to see that her hand did not tremble as she poured wine in the two stone cups provided.

The meal was a leisurely one. As they chatted amiably about the day,

Elizabeth's nervousness subsided. She considered asking Lord Randolph how much longer he intended to stay in Naples, then decided she would rather not know. Later would be soon enough.

After they had eaten, Elizabeth pulled out her tablet and began sketching the temple, though she despaired of doing justice to it. Having seated himself downwind of her, Randolph smoked his pipe in apparent contentment.

Eventually the lengthening shadows caught her attention and she glanced up. "Heavens, it's getting late. You should have stopped me earlier. I lose track of time when I'm drawing." She closed her tablet and slid it and her pencils into the picnic basket. "The weather is so warm that it's hard to remember that this is one of the shortest days of the year, but it will be dark by the time we reach the city."

"Miss Walker . . . Elizabeth . . . there is something I want to say before we start back."

Startled, she sat back on her heels and looked at Lord Randolph. Though he was still seated on the ground, his earlier ease was gone and his lean body was taut with tension. He looked down, fidgeting with his pipe, and she realized that he was using it as an excuse to avoid her eyes.

Taking out his penknife, he started carefully loosening the charred tobacco. "I have enjoyed this last week immensely." He gestured vaguely with his left hand, as if hunting for words, and instead spilled cinders on his fawn-colored breeches. Ruefully he brushed them away, then glanced up at her. "I'm sorry, I'm not very good at this. I had a speech memorized, but I've entirely forgotten it. Elizabeth, I am very partial to your company, and . . . and I would like to have more of it. Permanently."

If breathing was not automatic, Elizabeth would have expired on the spot. At first she just stared at him in disbelief. Then his eyes met hers, hope and uncertainty in the depths, and she realized that he meant what he said.

A stab of pain cut through her, anguish as intense as when she had heard of William's death. Amazingly, Lord Randolph wanted her to become his mistress. It was the best offer she would ever get—and she, Elizabeth acknowledged miserably, was too much a child of the vicarage to agree.

Tears started in her eyes and she blinked fiercely, refusing to let them overflow. Her voice a choked whisper, she said, "I'm sorry, my lord, but I couldn't possibly accept."

The hope in his eyes flickered and died, replaced first by hurt, then withdrawal. He had never worn the mask of the cool English gentleman with her before, but he donned it now. "No, of course you couldn't. My apologies, Miss Walker, it was just a foolish fancy."

He put his pipe and penknife in his pocket and stood, then lifted the basket. "Pray forgive me if I have embarrassed you. Come, it is time we left. The afternoon is almost over."

It wasn't just the afternoon that was over, but their friendship; Elizabeth knew from his expression that she would never see Lord Randolph after today. She scrambled to her feet unassisted, ignoring his proffered hand. Desiring him and racked with her own loneliness, she daren't touch him, for doing so would cause her to break down entirely.

Wordlessly she led the way back to the path, waging the battle of her life with her conscience. She was sure that his offer sprang not from casual immorality but from a lonely man's yearning for companionship. If he were free to marry, he would ask a younger, prettier woman, but she guessed that he was too honorable to destroy a marriageable girl's chance for respectability.

There was no risk of that with someone like Elizabeth, who had been on the shelf for years. Yet he must care a little for her as well, for he could have his choice of a thousand more likely mistresses.

She had known that she loved him, yet had not realized how much until now, when she found herself seriously considering abandoning the training of a lifetime so that she could give him the comfort he sought. But as Elizabeth picked her way along the narrow path, Lord Randolph silent behind her, she knew that her motives were only partly altruistic.

Yes, she wanted to ease his loneliness, but she also wanted to ease her own. She wanted his kindness and wry humor and beautiful body. And almost as much, she wanted to resurrect the Elizabeth Walker she had been before "the slings and arrows of outrageous fortune" had worn her hope away.

Intent on her despairing thoughts, she did not feel the first warning tremor, did not take the action that might have saved her. Her first awareness that something was wrong came when she staggered, almost losing her balance. For an instant she wondered if she had drunk too much wine, or whether her thoughts were making her light-headed.

Disaster unfolded with excruciating slowness. The ground heaved and a low, terrifying rumble filled the air, the vibrations so intense her skin tingled.

The path began to crumble beneath her feet. Elizabeth tried to scramble to safety, but it was too late, there was nothing left to cling to. She screamed as she pitched sideways from the cliff, falling helplessly. How far was it to the rocks below? And would she feel the shattering of her bones?

Randolph's deep voice shouted, "Elizabeth!" Between one heartbeat and the next, powerful arms seized her and dragged her back to solid ground. She slammed into the rocky path with rib-bruising force.

As she gasped for breath, Randolph pulled her farther from the edge, then threw himself over her, his body shielding her from a torrent of falling earth and gravel. In the midst of chaos and confusion, her sharpest awareness was of Randolph's closeness, the warmth and strength that enfolded her. If they were both going to die, she thought dizzily, she was glad that it would be in his arms.

The earth tremor was an eternity of fear that must have lasted less than a minute. When the ground had steadied and the last of the rumbling died away, Randolph lifted himself away, gravel showering from him. His voice ragged, he asked urgently, "Elizabeth, are you all right?"

Shakily she pushed herself to a sitting position and straightened her glasses, which by some miracle had not fallen off. "I think so. Thanks to you." She inhaled some dust and doubled over coughing. When she could speak again, she continued, "Thank you doesn't seem strong enough. I thought my hour had come. How are you?"

"A fairly sizable stone hit my shoulder, but nothing seems to be broken." He winced as he stood and brushed himself off, then examined a ripped sleeve ruefully. "However, my hat is gone forever and my coat seems unlikely to recover. My valet will be heartbroken—this coat is one of his favorites."

This time Elizabeth was grateful to accept his assistance in rising. "Is it one of your favorites as well?"

"I am not permitted to have opinions about matters that fall within Burns's purview, and that definitely includes coats." He looked beyond Elizabeth, then gave a soft whistle. "Fortunate that Sofia gave us so much food, for I fear that we may be here longer than we expected."

Still a little unsteady, Elizabeth turned cautiously, grateful when Lord

Randolph put a firm hand on her arm. She bit her lip in dismay at the sight behind. About ten feet of the path had disappeared completely, and it made her dizzy to look down, knowing how near an escape she had had. Beyond the gap, the path seemed intact but was covered with rubble until it curved out of sight around the hill. "I hope Vanni is all right," she said, "for both his sake and ours."

"I'm sure he is," Lord Randolph said. "He and the carriage were on solid, level ground."

Confirmation came almost immediately when the driver's voice shouted from around the corner, *"Signorina, signore!"*

Elizabeth called back, reassuring him that they were well, then explaining that part of the path had collapsed so they could not clear the rubble away themselves. After the driver replied, she translated for her companion. "Vanni say the path is clear and solid just around the corner, so it shouldn't be too hard to remove the fallen earth from that direction. He will go back to Balzano to get men to dig and planks to bridge the gap."

"What if the town has been badly hit by the earthquake?" Randolph asked grimly. "They may have more serious concerns than two stranded foreigners."

Elizabeth relayed his comment, then the driver's response. "Vanni says that this was only a little tremor. If the earth had not been soft from rain, there would be no problem here."

"Let us hope he is right. Tell him that I will pay the men he brings an exorbitant amount of money for their help, and double that if they can get us out this evening."

Another round of shouting and answer. Elizabeth shook her head at the reply. "Vanni says that it would be impossible to get anyone to come tonight since it's Christmas Eve, but he swears that tomorrow we will be free sometime between Mass and the midday meal."

Randolph sighed. "I suppose that will have to do." He turned and picked up the basket from where he had dropped it when the tremor hit. It had survived intact, if somewhat the worse for wear.

Elizabeth followed him back to the temple site. Still a little shaky from her escape, she was content to sit and watch while he explored the whole area, foot by foot. Eventually he returned to her. "If, God forbid, Vanni doesn't return, I think I could manage to climb over and around the landslide area, so we won't be trapped here indefinitely."

She looked at the steep rock face and shuddered. "Let us hope that it doesn't come to that."

"I don't think it will, but I am happier for knowing that there are alternatives." He looked at the sky and frowned. "The sun will be down in another hour, and it is going to be very cold here without any shelter. Fortunately I brought my flint and steel, so we can light a fire, but there is precious little fuel. I imagine that previous visitors used most of what was available. Still, we should find enough wood to keep from freezing tonight."

For the next half hour, the two of them gathered wood and stacked it by a shallow depression in the rocky cliff. It wasn't even remotely a cave, but it offered the best available protection from the weather. Elizabeth wrinkled her nose at the results. "It isn't a very impressive woodpile."

"No, but it should be enough." He retrieved the lap rug from the basket and handed it to her. "You had better wrap yourself in this."

She accepted the lap rug gratefully and wrapped it around her shoulders, wishing that it was twice as large and thrice as heavy. "Women's clothing is not designed for winter, just as men's clothing is usually too heavy for hot weather," she said philosophically, "but with this I will do well enough."

For lack of anything more productive to do, Elizabeth sat down with her back to the cliff, drawing her knees up and linking her arms around them. To the southwest, the massive black silhouette of Vesuvius dominated the horizon. The only signs of man were a few distant farm buildings. The scene could as easily have been Roman as in this civilized year of 1817.

Above the rugged hills, the sky was shot with gold and vermilion, while a nest of violet clouds hugged the horizon and welcomed the molten sun. Nodding toward the sunset, she said, "We may have a long, uncomfortable night ahead, but that is almost adequate compensation. How often do we take the time to enjoy a sunset?"

"Not often enough," Randolph agreed, settling down on the temple steps so he could admire nature's flamboyant artistry.

But in spite of the spectacular sky, Elizabeth found that more of her attention was on her companion, who sat less than a dozen feet away. Hatless and disheveled, his hair touched to liquid gold by the waning sun, he was no longer the impeccable English gentleman. Now the power that

underlay his gentle courtesy was visible, and she felt a faint sense of dis-
quiet. Might Lord Randolph decide to take advantage of their enforced
proximity to attempt seduction? If he did, she would be helpless before his
superior strength. . . .

With an appalled shock, Elizabeth realized that she wanted him to try
to seduce her. In fact, her devious lower nature was delighting in a situation that would allow her to submit with a clear conscience, absolved of
sin. Unfortunately, her vicarage morals were not so easily fooled.

Hugging her knees closer, she chastised herself for being a shameless,
disgusting creature. If Lord Randolph was the sort of man who would
take advantage of their situation to force his attentions on her, he was not
the man she had fallen in love with and she wouldn't want him. Besides,
she doubted that he had any such interest in her; he had said himself that
his offer was foolish fancy. By now, he was probably thanking his lucky
stars that she had refused.

But if he wasn't, this temporary captivity must be even more awkward
for him than for her. He was the one who had been rejected. He must be
hating the sight of her.

Oblivious to her lurid thoughts, Randolph said with a trace of wry
amusement, "I knew Christmas in Italy would be different from home,
but I never dreamed just how different."

"Yes," Elizabeth agreed somberly, "but at least we're alive. If we had
started down the path a few seconds sooner . . ."

"Very true," he said, his voice dry. "So I suppose there was some value
to my misbegotten proposal, since it delayed us."

"I know that being trapped here with me must be difficult for you. I'm
sorry," she said in a small voice.

He shrugged his broad shoulders. "Don't apologize—the fault is mine.
I should have known that one seldom gets a second chance where love
and marriage are concerned. For my sins of bad judgment, I must pay the
price."

His words cut too close to the bone, and she drew a shuddering
breath. "You are right. For whatever reason—bad judgment, bad luck—
most of us only get one chance for happiness. We think it will last an eternity, and then it vanishes like smoke in our hands."

He turned to face her, a silhouette against the bright sky. "What happened to your chance, Elizabeth? Why are you spending your life raising other women's children rather than your own?"

She sighed. "It's not a very dramatic story. William and I were childhood sweethearts. He was the younger son of the squire, I was the daughter of the vicar. Our families were not enthralled by the match, for neither of us had any prospects, but we were young, optimistic, willing to work hard. We had our whole lives planned. William's father bought him a pair of colors and off he went to the Peninsula. I was teaching and saving my salary. When he became a captain, we would marry and I would follow the drum."

"But that didn't happen."

"No," she whispered. "Within a year he was dead. Not even nobly, fighting the French, but of a fever."

"I'm sorry," he said gently. "That was a dreadful waste of a brave young life, and a tragic loss for you."

In her fragile mood, his compassion almost broke her. She made an effort to collect herself. "I feel fortunate for what little we had, even if it was much less than we had expected." She tried a smile, without complete success. "Really, it was a great stroke of luck that even one man wanted to marry me. I'm not the sort to inspire a grand passion, and without a portion I wasn't very marriageable. If William and I hadn't grown up together, I doubt he would have looked twice at me, but as it was, we . . . well, we were part of each other."

"I wish you would stop demeaning yourself," Randolph said sternly. "Beauty and fortune have their place, but they are not what make a good wife."

"As you learned to your cost?" she asked quietly.

"As I learned, to my cost." He stood abruptly. "I'd better start a fire while there is still a little light."

It was fortunate that Lord Randolph had flint and steel, and a penknife to whittle dry wood shavings from the inside of a branch. Soon a small fire was crackling away. He sat back on his heels, staying close enough to feed the blaze easily. "Having a fire brings civilization a little closer."

Elizabeth did not agree. Even with a fire, civilization seemed very distant, and she found herself speaking with a boldness that normally she would not have dared. "You said that you had committed the sin of bad judgment," she said tentatively. "If your sin was falling in love with a beautiful face, then finding that the lady's character was not so fine as her features, that is not such a great crime. Many young men do the same."

Lord Randolph must have felt the same lessening of civilized constraints, because he answered rather than giving her the set-down she deserved. "True, but that is not what I did. My crime was much worse. Like you, I fell in love young. Unlike you, our families were delighted. Lady Alyson was a great heiress, and I was a good match for her—of similar rank, wealthy enough so as not to be a fortune-hunter. And as a younger son, I would have ample time to devote to managing her property when she inherited."

Throwing the last shred of her manners to the winds, Elizabeth asked, "Was the problem that she did not love you?"

The muscles of his face went taut in the flickering light. "No, she did love me. And I, in one moment of foolish cowardice, hurt her unforgivably and wrecked both our lives."

The silence that followed was so long that finally Elizabeth said, "I realize that this is absolutely none of my business, but I am perishing of curiosity. Is what happened so unspeakable?"

His face eased. "Having said that much, I suppose I should tell the rest. I made the mistake of calling on Alyson with one of my more boisterous friends along. While we were waiting for her in the drawing room, my friend asked why I was marrying her. If Alyson had been a little golden nymph, he could have understood, but she wasn't at all in the common way."

Randolph sighed. "I should have hit him. Instead, because my feelings for Alyson were too private to expose to someone who might make sport of them, I said breezily that I was marrying her for her money. I knew that was a reason he would understand."

Elizabeth had a horrible feeling that she knew what happened next. "Alyson overheard and cried off?"

"Worse than that." Carefully he laid two larger pieces of wood on the fire. "I didn't learn the whole story until quite recently. She did overhear and told her father she wouldn't marry me if I were the last man on earth, but wouldn't explain why she had changed her mind. Thinking she was just being missish, her father became very gothic and locked her in her room, swearing that he would keep her there until she agreed to go through with the marriage. Feeling betrayed by both her father and me, Alyson ran away. She stayed away for twelve long years. Just this last September she returned and reconciled with her father."

"Good heavens," Elizabeth said blankly. "How did she survive so long on her own?"

"First she taught. Later, by chance, she became a land steward, quite a successful one. As I said, she was not in the common way. You remind me of her." Randolph glanced up from the fire, which he had been watching with unnecessary vigilance. "After Alyson vanished, I wondered if it was my fault, so when she returned I asked her. She confirmed that she had overheard me, and that was why she had run away." He gave a bitter laugh. "This story would be better told at Easter than Christmas. I felt like Peter must have when he realized that he had denied his Master three times before the cock crowed."

Elizabeth's heart ached for both of them—two young lovers shattered by a moment of foolishness. No wonder Randolph could not forgive himself. And the fact that Lady Alyson had run away from her whole life was vivid proof of the anguish she had felt at the apparent betrayal of the man she had loved and trusted.

Elizabeth tried to imagine what Randolph's meeting with his former love had been like, but imagination boggled. "Calling on her must have taken a great deal of courage."

"I decided that it was easier to know for sure than to continue to live with guilty uncertainty." The corner of his mouth twisted up in wry self-mockery. "In fact, Alyson was amazingly easy on me. I wouldn't have blamed her if she had greeted me with a dueling pistol, but instead she said that the fault lay as much with her and her father as with me, and that her life had not been ruined in the least."

"Your Alyson sounds like a remarkable woman."

"She is, but she's not my Alyson anymore. A few weeks after emerging from exile, she married one of the most notorious rakes in England, and I have it on the best authority that he is a reformed man: sober, responsible, and as besotted with her as she is with him. Alyson is happy now, and she deserves to be. She is one of those rare people who forged herself a second chance for happiness." Randolph linked his fingers together and stared into the fire. "I've been telling myself since September that it all worked out for the best. Her strength of character would have been wasted on me. I have no interesting vices to reform, and doubtless would have bored her very quickly."

"Do you still love her?"

He sighed, his face empty. "The young man I was loved the young woman she was. Neither of those people exists anymore."

It wasn't quite an answer, but at least now Elizabeth understood why he had offered her a *carte blanche:* it was because she resembled the woman he had loved. Where did his wife fit into the picture? In the lonely years after Lady Alyson disappeared, he must have married without love, and lived to regret it. Elizabeth did not dare ask about his marriage; she had already been unpardonably inquisitive. Sadly she said, "Perhaps it is only the young who are foolish enough, or brave enough, to fall in love, and that is the reason why there are few second chances."

Having let her hair down metaphorically, Elizabeth decided that it was time to do so literally as well, or she would have a headache before morning. After removing her hairpins and tucking them in the basket so they wouldn't get lost, she combed her tangled curls with her fingers in a futile attempt to restore order. When Randolph glanced over, she explained, "In case any wolves or other beasts find their way up here, I am letting my hair down so that I can play Medusa and turn them to stone."

He chuckled, his earlier melancholy broken. "You should wear your hair down more often—it becomes you."

Elizabeth rolled her eyes in comic disbelief, and he wondered if she ever believed compliments. In truth, by firelight and with her brown hair crackling with red and gold highlights, she looked very winsome. Perhaps not beautiful, but thoroughly delectable.

He hastily looked back at the fire, knowing that that was a dangerous train of thought under these circumstances, when she had made it clear that he did not fit into her plans for the future. Apparently, having loved well and truly, she did not want to marry without love. Perhaps she was wiser than he, for he had tried that once, with disastrous consequences. Nonetheless, the more he saw of Elizabeth Walker, the more he thought that they would deal very well together, if she were willing to lower her standards and accept him.

Perhaps speaking so openly of their pasts should have made them more awkward with each other, but the reverse was true. The evening drifted by in companionable silence, broken by occasional desultory conversation. They sat a couple of feet apart with their backs against the cliff wall, which offered some protection from the bitter December wind. Vesuvius was close enough for a faint glow to be visible against the night sky. It was a dramatic but disquieting sight. Fortunately the little fire offered cheery comfort as well as some warmth.

Eventually they made further inroads on the picnic basket and still had enough food for another meal or two. After they had eaten and drunk some of the wine, Randolph asked, "How are you managing? It's cold now, and it will be considerably colder by tomorrow morning."

"I'm fine, thank you."

Elizabeth's voice sounded a little stiff, and when Randolph looked more closely and saw how she was huddled into the lap rug, he understood why. "You're freezing, aren't you? And too practical to say so when we haven't enough wood to burn it at a faster rate."

"You said it, not I."

Randolph peeled his coat off and handed it to her. "Put this on."

"Don't be silly," she said, refusing to accept it and keeping her hands tucked under the lap rug. "That would just mean that you'd freeze, too. I will do very well." There was a suggestion of chattering teeth under her brave words.

"You don't appear to be doing well. Come, take my coat," he coaxed. "Cold has never bothered me much, while six years in Italy have probably thinned your blood to the point where you are more sensitive to cold than the average Englishwoman."

Elizabeth looked mulish; she definitely had much in common with Alyson. Why did tall, stubborn, independent females who were not in the common way appeal to him so much? He smiled a little, realizing that his question contained its own answer. "Very well, if you won't accept my coat, we will have to resort to a time-honored method of keeping warm."

He put his coat back on. Then, before she realized what he had in mind, he leaned over and scooped her into his arms. She squeaked in surprise, as she had when she was pinched in Balzano. It was a very endearing squeak.

"You really are freezing," he commented as she shivered against him. He arranged her across his lap and settled comfortably against the cliff wall as he began rubbing her back, shoulders, and arms, trying to get her blood moving again. She had a delicious scent of rosewater and oranges.

"This is most improper," she murmured into his lapel.

"Yes, but warmer for both of us. Think of your duty, Miss Walker," he admonished. "You may prefer to solidify into a block of ice yourself, but will you condemn me to the same fate?"

She pulled her head back and gave him a darkling look. "You're teasing me."

He grinned. "Making your blood boil should keep you warm."

Elizabeth knew that she really should not permit this, but she lacked the will to resist. It wasn't just his wonderful physical warmth, which was beginning to thaw her out; it was the intimacy of being in his arms. This was surely the most romantic thing that was ever going to happen to her, and she might as well enjoy it. She nestled closer, savoring the faint aroma of apple-scented tobacco that clung to his coat, but total comfort was prevented by a hard object pressing into her hip. She shifted her position. "If that is your pipe in your left pocket, I may be in danger of breaking it."

"Wrong pocket. I thought that one was empty, actually. Excuse me while I investigate." He removed his arm from around her and dug into the pocket, finally withdrawing an object in triumph. "Here it is."

His whole body stilled. Elizabeth twisted to see what had caught his attention, then sighed with delight. The lapis solaris figure of the Bambino had seemed crude by daylight, but now darkness transformed it. Cupped in Randolph's palm, the Holy Infant glowed with a soft, magical light, a miracle child come to bring hope to the hearts of men.

"I took it out of the *presepio* set earlier and must have slipped it into my pocket by accident," he murmured.

Elizabeth smiled and shook her head. "Not by accident. The Bambino came to remind us that tonight is a special night, the night of His birth. Remember that the Italian climate is similar to that of the Holy Land. It might have been just such a night as this in Bethlehem when the angels visited the shepherds." Quietly she began quoting from the book of Luke, beginning with the words, " 'And it came to pass in those days that there went out a decree from Caesar Augustus, that all the world should be taxed . . . ' " Not for nothing had she been raised in a vicarage; word-perfect, she retold the immortal story.

" 'For behold, I bring you tidings of great joy,' " Randolph repeated softly when she had finished. "Thank you, Elizabeth. You have just delivered the most moving Christmas service I've ever heard."

The only sounds were the crackle of the fire, the occasional distant bleat of a sheep, and the sighing of the wind. When the fire began to die down, Randolph asked, "Are you warm now?"

"Wonderfully so." She did not add that the heat that curled through her body was more than just temperature.

"Then it's time to make some adjustments. I don't suppose either of us will sleep much, but we might as well be as comfortable as possible."

To her regret, he removed her from his lap, so he could tend to the fire. When it was burning steadily again, he positioned the rest of the wood so that it could be easily added, a piece at a time. "If you lie down on your side between me and the fire, you should stay fairly warm, though I'll probably disturb you whenever I add wood to the fire."

She took off her spectacles and put them in the basket, then stretched out as he had suggested, the lap rug tucked around her. Randolph lay down behind her and wrapped his arm around her waist, pulling her close so that they were nestled together like two spoons. The ground was hard and cold and not very comfortable; Randolph was warm and firm and very comfortable indeed. Elizabeth gave a sigh of pleasure and relaxed in his embrace, thinking that this was even better than being on his lap.

"Merry Christmas, Randolph," she whispered. She had never been happier in her life.

RANDOLPH did not precisely sleep, but between bouts of tending the fire he dozed a little. Elizabeth was a delightful armful as she cuddled trustfully against him. Unlike him, she had slept soundly. The fruits of a clear conscience, no doubt.

As the sky began lightening in anticipation of dawn, he carefully lifted himself away and added the next-to-last piece of wood. The air was bitter cold, but fortunately the night had been dry and within an hour or so the temperature should start to rise.

Before he could settle back, Elizabeth stretched and rolled over on her back, then opened her eyes and blinked sleepily at him, her hair curling deliciously around her face. There was something very intimate about seeing her without her spectacles—rather as if she had removed her gown and greeted him in her shift. Thinking improper thoughts, he murmured, "Good morning."

She gave him a smile of shimmering, wondering sweetness, as if this morning were the dawn of the world and she were Eve greeting Adam for the first time.

It seemed the most natural thing in the world to lean forward and give her a gentle kiss. Elizabeth's mouth was soft and welcoming—and sweet, so sweet. He lay down beside her and drew her into his arms, wanting to feel the full length of her slim, supple body against him.

As the kiss deepened, her arms slid around his neck, and her responsiveness triggered a wave of fierce, demanding desire that brought Randolph to his senses. Knowing that if he did not stop soon, it would be impossible to stop at all, he pulled abruptly away from her. His breathing unsteady, he said, "I'm sorry, Elizabeth. You have a most extraordinary effect on me."

She stared at him, her eyes wide and stark. Then she sat up and grabbed her glasses from the basket, donning them hastily as if they were a suit of armor. Under her breath, she said, "The effect seems to be mutual."

Spectacles and propriety once more in place, she said, "Since the fire won't last much longer, shall we toast some of the cheese and spread it on the last of the bread? Hot food would be very welcome."

Randolph did not know whether to feel grateful or insulted that she was ignoring what had been a truly superior kiss. Dangerously superior, in fact; the idea of kissing her again was much more appealing than bread and cheese, and the results of that would warm them both through and through.

With difficulty, he turned his attention to practical considerations. "An excellent idea," he said, "though I think I would trade everything in the basket for a large pot of scalding hot tea."

"That is a cruel thing to say, Lord Randolph." Longing showed in her face. "Strong Italian coffee with hot milk would do equally well. And lots of sugar."

He laughed. "We shouldn't torture ourselves like this. Tomorrow morning we will be able to drink all the tea or coffee we want, and will appreciate it more for today's lack."

The melted cheese and toasted bread turned out to be an inspired choice for fortifying themselves for the rigors of the day. By the time the fire had flickered down to embers and the sun had risen over the horizon, Randolph felt ready to face the difficult conversation he had known was inevitable. "Elizabeth, there is something we must talk about."

Daintily she licked the last crumbs from her fingers. "Yes, my lord?"

"Since we have spent the night together, I'm afraid that you are now officially ruined," he said baldly. "There is really only one recourse, though I know it is not agreeable to you."

"Nonsense," she retorted. "I'm only ruined if people learn about last night, and probably not even then. I'm not an English girl making her come-out, you know. As a foreign woman of mature years, I exist outside the normal structure of Italian society and won't be judged by the same rules. Therefore I won't be ruined even if what happened becomes generally known." A glint of humor showed behind her spectacles. "Indeed, most Italian women would envy me the experience of being 'ruined' by you."

Ignoring her levity, he said, "Do you think the family of the terrible twins, who want a cold-blooded Englishwoman to govern their hot-blooded daughters, will be so tolerant? Or other potential employers?"

Uncertainty flickered across her face as his words struck home. "There could be problems if last night became generally known," she admitted, "but I still think that is unlikely. I am not really part of the Neapolitan English community. Who would bother to gossip about me?"

"You think that everyone in this part of Campania hasn't already heard that there were two *inglesi* trapped up here on Christmas Eve? If the story hasn't already reached Naples, it will today." Randolph grimaced. "Unfortunately, I was engaged to dine at the British Embassy last night, and my absence will have been noted. The local gossips know we have been spending time together. How long will it take someone to guess who the marooned *inglesi* are? Your reputation will be in shreds and you will be unemployable, at least as a governess."

Her face pale, she said, "Shouldn't we wait and see before assuming the worst?"

"Perhaps my anxiety is premature, but I don't think so." His mouth twisted. "I know you don't want to marry me, Elizabeth, but if there is the least hint of scandal, I swear I will drag you off to the nearest Protestant clergyman. Even if you have no concern for your reputation, I'll be damned if I want to be known as a man who refused to do the right thing by you."

Elizabeth was staring at him, her shock palpable. Cursing inwardly for having upset her, Randolph said in a softer voice, "I swear that I won't force you to live with me, or to do anything else you don't want to do. I will settle an income on you and you can live wherever you choose and paint until you lose track of what year it is. But I will *not* let you be injured by an accident that would never have happened if you had not been acting as my friend and guide."

She swallowed hard. "But how can you marry me? What about your wife?"

"My wife?" he asked, startled. "Where did you get the idea that I was married?"

"When we were at Solfatara," she faltered, "you said that the loneliest place on earth was a bad marriage. You sounded so much as if you were speaking from experience that I was sure you must be married. It seemed to explain so much about you."

Randolph was silent as he thought back. "You're very perceptive, Elizabeth. I *was* speaking from personal experience, but my wife died three years ago, after not much more than a year of marriage."

He remembered the day before and frowned. "Good God, did you refuse my offer yesterday because you thought I was setting up to be a bigamist, or lying in order to seduce you?"

She was so surprised that she let go of the lap rug and it slid from her shoulders. "You were asking me to *marry* you?"

"Of course. What did you think I was doing, offering you a *carte blanche?*" He said it as a joke, and was appalled to see her nod. "I would never have offered you such an insult, and I think I should be angry that you believed me capable of it."

Her face flamed and she looked down. In a choked whisper, she said, "I didn't feel insulted, I felt flattered. I was just too cowardly to accept."

Seeing the humor in the situation, Randolph began laughing. "I certainly bungled that proposal, didn't I?" He stood and crossed the half-dozen feet to where she sat regarding him uncertainly. Going down on one knee, he caught her hands between his. "I will try again and see if I can get this right. Elizabeth, will you marry me? Not to save anyone's reputation, but a real marriage, because we want to be together?"

Her cold hands clenched convulsively on his. Behind her spectacles, her eyes were huge and transparent as silent tears began welling up. "Randolph, I can't."

She tried to pull away, but he kept a firm grip on her hands. Yesterday he had accepted rejection too quickly, and that was not a mistake he would make again. "Why not? Is it that you can't abide the thought of having me for a husband?"

"I can think of nothing I would like more."

He smiled; they were making progress. Patiently he asked, "Do you have a husband somewhere so you aren't free to marry?"

"Of course not!"

"Then, why won't you say yes? I warn you, I will not let you go until you either accept me or offer a good reason for refusing."

She turned her head away, her face scarlet with mortification. "Because . . . because I could not come to you as a bride should."

He thought about that for a minute. "Could you be more specific? I want to be sure I understand."

"Before William went into the army"—her breath was coming in ragged gulps, and she could not meet his eyes—"we . . . we gave ourselves to each other."

"I see." Profound tenderness welled up inside him, and another emotion too unfamiliar to name. Releasing Elizabeth's hands, he wrapped his arms around her and pulled her close so that her head was tucked under his chin. She was trembling. Gently he stroked her unruly curls, trying to soothe away the unhappiness he had caused. "Because you gave yourself in love to the man you were going to marry, you think that you are unfit to be a wife? Quite the contrary. I can think of no better qualification for marriage. Will you marry me, Elizabeth? Please?"

She pulled back and stared at him. Her glasses had steamed from her tears and she took them off so she could study his face better. "Do you really mean that, Randolph? Or would you have second thoughts later and feel cheated?"

"Yes, I mean it." He stood and drifted over to the steps of the shrine, searching for the best way to explain his feelings so that in the future she would never doubt him. "As you guessed, my marriage was not a happy one," he said haltingly. "I wasn't really in love with Chloe, but I had given up hope that Alyson would ever return and I wanted to marry. Chloe was well-bred and very beautiful, and she made it clear that she would welcome an offer from me. Everyone said what a 'good match' it was. She was very proper and reserved, but I thought that was just shyness, which would quickly pass once we were married.

"I was wrong." He turned to face Elizabeth, who stood a half-dozen feet away in grave silence. "I had thought her desire for matrimony meant that she cared for me, but soon I realized that though Chloe wanted the status of wife, she did not want a husband. Perhaps it was me in particular that she couldn't bear, but I don't think so."

He looked away, swallowing hard, thinking that it was simple justice that he must speak of something that was as painful for him as Elizabeth's confession had been for her. "She did not like to be touched, ever. Nor did she ever touch me, except in public sometimes she would take my arm, to show other women that I belonged to her.

"I don't mean just that she disliked marital relations, though she did. As soon as she had done her duty and conceived, she told me not to come near her again. Being denied her bed did not bother me half so much as her total lack of interest in giving or receiving any kind of affection. Perhaps the need for warmth and affection is deeper than physical desire. Even when she was dying, she would not take my hand. There was nothing she ever wanted from me except my name and fortune."

He caught Elizabeth's gaze. "Do you understand now why I welcome the knowledge that you are a warm and caring woman? If you could give me even half as much warmth as you had for William, I would think myself the luckiest man alive."

"Unfortunate Chloe, to be unable to accept any love or affection," Elizabeth said with deep compassion. In a few swift steps she closed the distance between them and flowed into his arms. "And unfortunate Randolph, to have so much to give and no one to value the gift or the giver."

Her embrace was more than passionate, it was loving. And as he crushed her to him, Randolph identified the emotion that had been growing inside him. "I was wrong," he said softly. "There are second chances. I thought I wanted to marry you for companionship, but my heart must have known before my head did. I love you, Elizabeth. I came to Italy for sunshine, and I found it when I met you, for your smile lights up the world."

"Truly?" She tilted her head back. "You hardly know me."

"Wrong." He rubbed his cheek against Elizabeth's curly hair. She was a very convenient height. "We may not have known each other long, but I know you better than I knew Alyson, and infinitely better than I knew Chloe." He gave her a teasing smile. "Is it safe to interpret your shameless behavior as a willingness to wed?"

"It is. You were quite right, Randolph, I *am* ruined, so hopelessly, madly, passionately in love with you that I shall be good for nothing unless you marry me." Elizabeth gave him the heart-deep smile that made her incomparably lovely. "Just as Lady Alyson is your past, William is mine. I loved him and part of my heart died when he did, but the woman I am now, plain middle-aged spinster that I am, is yours, body, heart, and soul. Will that do?"

"You are going to have to stop talking such nonsense about how plain and middle-aged you are. Just how old are you?"

"Thirty."

"A wonderful age. Thirty-one will be better, and fifty better yet."

Randolph kissed her with rich deliberation, working his way from her lips to a sensitive spot below her ear. She gasped, thinking her knees had turned to butter.

He murmured, "Do you think I would want you this much if I thought you were plain?"

Elizabeth was twined around him so closely that she had no doubts about just how much he did want her. "I think that you need spectacles more than I do," she said breathlessly, "but since beauty is in the eye of the beholder, your opinion is inarguable."

"Good. I can think of much better things to do than argue." Randolph was about to start kissing her again when a shout sounded from the direction of the path.

Elizabeth called out an answer. After a lengthy exchange, she reported, "Vanni says they will have us out within two hours, so we can be in Naples for Christmas dinner."

"Tell them not to rush," Randolph murmured. His slate-blue eyes warm with love and mischief, he removed her spectacles and tucked them in his pocket. "We don't want your glasses to steam up while we wait, do we?"

Her heart expanding with joy, Elizabeth lifted her face to his, and as the Christmas sun rose in the sky, they celebrated the season of hope. Together.

The Christmas Tart

IT began with a ring. One day late in November 1809, the irritable Lady Guthrie was careless when she searched through her lacquered jewelry case for the best ornaments to adorn her scrawny person. The heirloom diamond ring that had come from her husband's family was valuable but ugly, and she brushed it aside impatiently as she searched for more attractive treasures.

Amidst the clinking of baubles, she didn't notice when the ring tumbled from the case, rolled unevenly across the lace-covered surface of the dressing table, then dropped into the narrow gap between table and wall. Halfway to the floor, the heavy ring hooked over a wooden peg that had worked loose until it projected from the back of the table.

And there the ring stayed, suspended, not to be found until the next year's spring cleaning. But by then Christmas had come and gone, and so had the young French seamstress.

A cold, heavy sky made the afternoon seem more like dusk, and it was difficult for Nicole Chambord to see the riding jacket that she was trimming. Closing her eyes for a moment, she laid the jacket down and straightened up, stretching her arms in an effort to relieve the strain on her back and neck. *Sacre bleu!* but she would be glad when Christmas was over.

During the month that Nicole had been sewing for Lady Guthrie, she had not had a single afternoon off, and every night she had worked late by candlelight to complete everything her ladyship deemed necessary for the holidays. While Lady Guthrie's important clothing was done by an expensive modiste, there were many lesser items, such as chemises and undergowns, that could be made by a household seamstress. And of course there was always mending, refurbishing older garments, and making shirts and cravats for Sir Wilfrid, the master of the house. Nicole had sewed so much that she wore white cotton gloves to prevent her sore, pricked fingers from bleeding onto valuable fabric.

Still, food in the Guthrie establishment was abundant, if bland, and most of the other servants were pleasant. Best of all, Nicole was now living in London, closer to her goal than she had been in Bristol, where she had lived for fourteen years. Come spring, she would look for a situation with a fashionable dressmaker who would be willing to take advantage of an assistant's design skills. Someday, after much hard work and saving of money, Nicole would open a shop of her own called Nicole's, or perhaps Madame Chambord's.

She luxuriated in the thought for a moment, then sighed and returned to her work. The happy day when she would be self-employed was many years away. Just now, her task was to use her nearly invisible stitches to attach military-style braid to the jacket in her lap.

She was just finishing the job when the butler, Furbes, swept into the small workroom without knocking. "Her ladyship wishes to speak with you, Chambord," he snapped. "Immediately."

"Of course," Nicole murmured, unalarmed by his manner, for Furbes was always rude to his inferiors, and Lady Guthrie was always in a hurry. Likely her ladyship had decided that a project she had wanted completed tomorrow must instead be done today. It would not be the first time.

But instead of normal impatience, Nicole found disaster. As the French girl entered Lady Guthrie's bedroom, her mistress spun around to glare at her. "You stole the Guthrie diamond ring," she said furiously. "What have you done with it?"

Nicole was so shocked that for a moment her usually nimble tongue was paralyzed. "But no, my lady, I have never seen your ring, nor have I taken even a candle stub from your room. Could the ring have been misplaced?"

"It's gone." Lady Guthrie gestured at her abigail, who wore a distressed expression. "Merkle has searched everywhere, including all the drawers and the floor under the dressing table. And tonight we dine with my husband's family, and his mother will want to know why I don't wear it!"

Still not quite believing the accusation, Nicole said in bewilderment, "I am sorry if your mother-in-law will be upset, but why are you accusing me? There are a dozen servants in this house, or a thief could have broken in and robbed you. I swear on my mother's grave that I have stolen nothing from you."

"Any thief who broke in would have taken the whole case, not just the ring, and all my other servants have been with me for years. You've been here less than a month, and you're clever—I saw that right away. You probably thought I wouldn't notice if only a single piece of jewelry was missing, especially one I almost never wear, and you've had ample opportunity, because you often work alone in this room," Lady Guthrie retorted. "As soon as I thought of you, I had your room searched, and Furbes found the proof hidden under your mattress."

She lifted a leather pouch from her dressing table, then dropped it again, the coins inside clinking as the pouch hit the tabletop. "Over fifty pounds! Where could you get such a sum except by theft?"

Nicole stared in horror at the bag that contained her life savings. "For years I have spent nothing on myself so I could save every shilling possible." All of it dedicated to the dream of a future. "Surely if I had stolen your precious diamond ring, I would have more money than that."

"Stolen goods go for only a fraction of their true value." Lady Guthrie's faded blue eyes narrowed triumphantly. "And just how did you know that the ring was a diamond?"

"Because you said so yourself!" Nicole exclaimed, feeling as if she had wandered into Bedlam. "*Mon Dieu,* your ladyship, if you have been robbed, call a magistrate. I am not afraid to be questioned, for I am innocent."

Before Lady Guthrie could respond, her maid Merkle said hesitantly, "Perhaps the chit is telling the truth, my lady. Her references were splendid, and she has always done her work well, with not a shred of complaint from anyone. There is no proof that she took the ring."

Nicole could have kissed the other servant for her bravery in speaking up, but it did no good.

Her employer's mouth tightened to a harsh line. "Bah, she belongs in Newgate, but if she blinks those big brown eyes at the magistrate, I don't suppose she'll get what she deserves, so there's no point in turning her over to the law." Lady Guthrie scowled at the seamstress as she decided what to do. "You're dismissed right now, girl, without a reference."

She lifted the pouch again, her bony fingers digging into the thin leather. "This I will keep as compensation for your theft."

Appalled, Nicole gasped, "How dare you! That is my money and if you take it, it is you who are the thief!"

"Don't speak to her ladyship like that, you little slut," Furbes ordered. The butler had been a silent witness to the exchange, but now he grasped Nicole's shoulder with cruel pressure. "Shall I allow her to gather her belongings, my lady, or put her out on the street as she is?"

"Let her gather her things, but watch to see that she doesn't try to take anything else," Lady Guthrie decided. Turning back to Nicole, she said viciously, "You can thank the fact that it's almost Christmas for my mercy, girl."

And that was that. Ten minutes later, still dazed by the swiftness of events, Nicole was standing in the alley behind the house, having been escorted out the kitchen door by Furbes. Everything she owned in the world was in a canvas bag slung over her shoulder.

She shivered, and not just because a cold, misty rain was saturating her threadbare cloak. She had never been so frightened in her life, even when her family had fled France to escape the Reign of Terror. Only six years old, she had seen that as a grand adventure, serene in her trust that no harm could befall her when she was with her parents.

But now both parents were dead and she was utterly alone, without a situation, money, or references to help her find another job. If she had been in Bristol, she could have found shelter with friends, but not in London, where Nicole knew no one but the servants in the Guthrie household. To make matters worse, it was Saturday afternoon and within a couple of hours all of the modistes' shops would be closed until Monday morning.

She set her chin and began marching down the street. There was nothing she could do to prove her innocence or recover her savings from Lady Guthrie, so there was no point in wasting time on regrets or curses at life's unfairness. All of her energy must go toward survival.

She had just reached the street when the kitchen door opened and a low voice called her name. She glanced back and saw Merkle standing in the door and beckoning. Nicole obeyed the summons, but as she approached the maid, she said bitterly, "Has Lady Guthrie decided I cannot take my own clothing? I should think my things would be too poor for her taste."

"She hasn't changed her mind about anything," Merkle said sadly. "I'm sorry, Nicole, I don't believe you stole the ring, but there's nothing to be done with the old besom when she's in a mood like this. She knows her husband and his family will be furious with her for losing the ring, and she had to take it out on someone. A pity it was you. And to discharge you so close to Christmas!"

The maid had a mass of scarlet fabric draped over her arm, and now she raised it for Nicole's inspection. "Take this cloak. It was one of her ladyship's mistakes in judgment so she gave it to me after one season. Too gaudy for my taste, so I've never worn it, but it's warmer than that old thing you're wearing. Here, put it on."

Nicole's first reaction was to refuse to take anything that had been Lady Guthrie's, but practicality overcame her principles. Accepting the scarlet cloak, she draped it over her own thin garments. Immediately she felt warmer, though considering the color and the vulgar feather trimming, she understood why neither Lady Guthrie nor Merkle wanted it.

Next Merkle offered a greasy packet wrapped in newspaper. "Here's a meat pie. It's all I could take without Cook noticing. And here's five shillings. For that, you should be able to rent a room for a few nights if you know where to look."

"Where might I find such a place?" Nicole asked. "In the month I've been in London, I have learned nothing of the city."

The maid thought for a moment. "Around Covent Garden might be best. There are plenty of lodgings, and when the market is open you should be able to get damaged produce at a good price. But be careful, child. London streets aren't safe at night, and sometimes not even in the day, leastwise not for a girl as pretty as you." She sighed. "I only wish I could have convinced her ladyship not to blame you for the ring's disappearance. Lord only knows what happened to the blasted thing."

Trying to sound confident, Nicole said, "Don't worry about me. I'm on my way now to seek employment. The money and food you have provided will keep me until I can start work." On impulse, she rose on her toes and kissed the other servant on the cheek. "Thank you, Miss Merkle. You are a good woman."

Then Nicole turned and set off without looking back.

FOR a gentleman about town, there was no more desirable residence than the Rochester. The rooms were elegant and the discreet staff always ready to provide any service required. That was convenient for Sir Philip Selbourne, since his valet had a cold and had been left home in Northamptonshire. At the moment, however, Philip was not reflecting on his good fortune. In fact, as he climbed the front steps of the Rochester, head bent and mind absorbed in calculations, he was so abstracted that he quite literally ran into his best friends.

The baronet was murmuring an absent apology when a familiar voice said, "Philip! You've just arrived in town?"

Brought back to the present, Philip raised his head to discover the Honorable James Kirby and Francis, Lord Masterson, another close friend. After greeting both men and shaking their hands, Philip said, "I've been here for two days. This is only a quick trip to take care of some business."

"And you didn't let either of us know?" Kirby said reproachfully. At twenty-five he was the same age as Philip, but his round face and flaming red hair made him seem younger. "With all three of us living in the same building, you can't say that it was too much effort to call! It's been months since we've seen you in town—surely not since March." Abruptly he stopped speaking as he remembered why his friend had left London then.

Philip grimaced. "I've been deucedly busy since my father died. Having grown up at Winstead Hall, I thought I knew something about farming, but it turns out that I knew a good deal less than I believed. His death has caused a number of unexpected complications."

Lord Masterson's cool voice said, "Problems? That surprises me. I would have thought Sir Charles the last man on earth to mismanage his affairs."

"He didn't," Philip said, quick to defend his father. "One of the difficulties is the unexpected number of investments he left, none of which I knew anything about." He gave a wry smile. "In the last six months, I've worked harder at educating myself than all the years at Winchester and Cambridge put together."

"Come along and tell us all about it while we dine," Kirby urged. "It's too cold to converse here on the steps."

"Sorry, I can't accept," Philip said regretfully. "In a few minutes my solicitor is coming, and we're going to spend the afternoon finishing the business that brought me to London. I want to return to Winstead tomorrow morning."

"Stay an extra day," Masterson suggested. "So many people have left to spend the holiday in the country that town is rather thin of company." He gave a faint, charming smile. "Under the circumstances, even you offer welcome diversion."

Philip returned the smile, but shook his head. "I really must get back. This Christmas will be hard for my mother."

"Then join us for dinner in my rooms," Kirby said, undeterred. "With the three of us together, it will be like old times at Winchester."

Philip hesitated, tempted, then shook his head again. "I really can't. The solicitor will leave mountains of documents, and it will take me all evening to go over them."

"Surely your fusty documents can wait another day," Kirby said, his wide blue eyes showing hurt.

Before Philip could answer, Masterson raised his dark, elegant brows. "You must remember to take time for your friends, Philip, or someday when you need them, you may find that you have none."

Philip felt color rising in his cheeks. "You still know the best place to strike, Masterson. No wonder you were so good at fencing."

He sighed ruefully. "You are both absolutely correct. In the last six months I've spent so much time running in circles and feeling incompetent that I've half forgotten why life is worth living. I'd be delighted to join you for dinner. Seven o'clock in your rooms, Jamie?" After the time was confirmed, he touched his hat in farewell and swiftly climbed the last steps into the Rochester.

Frowning, Kirby watched until his friend disappeared into the building. Then he turned and fell into step with Masterson as the two young men walked toward St. James, where they would be able to find a hack. "Philip's not looking at all well. He's been working too hard."

"Very likely," Masterson agreed. "It was quite a shock for him when his father died so unexpectedly—they always got on amazingly well. Being the responsible sort, Philip's obviously feeling the weight of being head of the family."

"He really needs to relax a bit before he goes dashing back to the country," Kirby mused. "Now, what's most relaxing?"

Recognizing the tone, Masterson eyed his companion with misgiving, for Kirby's innocent face masked the devil's own capacity for mischief. "Dinner with friends is relaxing, and just to make sure, I'll send down half a dozen bottles of my best claret. That will relax all of us."

Ignoring the comment, Kirby said with an air of great enlightenment, "*Females* are relaxing. That's it—what Philip needs is a girl." Turning his wide blue eyes to his companion, he said, "Let's find one and put her in his bed tonight."

Masterson stopped dead in the street. "You've finally lost your mind," he said flatly. "The first day you showed up to fag for me at Winchester and I saw that shade of red hair, I knew your sanity was precarious. Granted, females are sometimes relaxing, but just as often they play the very devil with one's sanity. Besides, Philip is quite capable of finding a girl of his own if he wants one, but at the moment, he has other things on his mind besides dalliance."

"Which is why he needs a girl to cheer him up," Kirby said. "A nice jolly one will make a perfect Christmas present. While Philip's dining with us, your valet can spirit her into his rooms. Now, where can we find one?" He pondered. "You can ask Michelle if she has a friend who's free tonight."

"Neither Michelle nor her friends come free," Masterson said dryly. "And as it happens, she and I came to a parting of the ways last week. If I went to her house and asked her to find another female, she'd likely drop a chamber pot on my head."

Undeterred, Kirby said, "Then we'll have to find a girl somewhere else."

The two men were still arguing as they hailed a hack and set off to lunch, but already Masterson was resigning himself to the inevitable. Kirby was bound and determined on his plan, so Masterson had better cooperate to make sure that the thing was done right.

AFTER more than twenty-four hours without eating, Nicole was so cold, hungry, and tired that she was unsteady on her feet. It was time to eat the meat pie Merkle had given her, so she turned into a small, cluttered alley and sank wearily onto a stone step. Then she pulled out the cold pie and held it, wanting to postpone the moment when it would be gone.

Her spirits were as low as they had ever been in her life, for her determined efforts to find a situation the day before had come to nothing. Two modistes had refused to talk to her since she had no London references. Three more had said that they weren't hiring and wouldn't be for months, for the Christmas rush was over and business would be slack until spring, when the ton returned to London to prepare for the Season. Nicole had not expected that, and had been frightened to realize that it might be months before she might find a position as a seamstress.

Not wanting to spend her five shillings before she had to, Nicole had slept rough the night before, shivering in a deserted corner of a stable yard behind an unoccupied house in Kensington. The night was dry and she was protected from the wind, but even so she had been numb with cold by morning. Because it was Sunday, she had gone to church, partly to be under a roof, and partly because prayer seemed in order. The vicar had read the Christmas story, and Nicole had found herself with new empathy for Mary and Joseph, who had found no room at the inn. Closing her eyes, she uttered a silent prayer that she, too, would find the shelter she so desperately needed.

She considered asking the vicar for help, but when she timidly approached him after the service, he gave her a glance so contemptuous that she left without speaking. That had been hours ago, and ever since she had been drifting through the London streets while she planned how best to eke out her money and what kinds of employment she should seek.

The onset of more bone-chilling rain brought her to a reluctant decision; since she might not survive another night sleeping rough in this weather, she must spend some of her limited funds to rent a room. Remembering that Miss Merkle had said there were cheap lodgings near Covent Garden, she had asked directions, then set off to find it.

A plaintive meow brought her back to the present. She glanced down to find a scraggly, half-grown cat sitting on the step beside her, its gaze fixed on the cold meat pie in her hands. The little creature's splotchy calico fur was matted with rain, and its huge green eyes were a mixture of hope and wariness. "Sorry, *ma petite*," Nicole said apologetically. "This is all I have to eat, and the good Lord only knows where my next meal will come from."

She bit into the pie, so ravenous she wanted to stuff the whole thing in her mouth at once. Instead, she forced herself to take a small mouthful, then chew slowly, so it would last as long as possible. Even cold, it tasted wonderful. After she swallowed the first bite, she took another. It wasn't easy to ignore the pleading green feline eyes.

With a small, *mrrp*ing sound, the cat jumped onto her lap and began rubbing its head against her chest. "Your manners leave much to be desired, my patchy friend," Nicole scolded as she held the pie out of reach. "But you are not as wild as most street cats. Did you also have a home until someone cruelly evicted you?"

The dangerous thought made it impossible to ignore the cat's yearning expression. "Very well, *ma petite*," Nicole said. "Perhaps it will bring me luck if I am generous to one less fortunate than I." She took a morsel of meat and offered it to the calico.

Her companion did not wait for a second invitation. The fragment disappeared instantly; then, with dainty gluttony, a warm, raspy pink tongue licked Nicole's fingers. For the first time since the day before, she found herself smiling. From then on, each bite she took herself was followed by a shred for the cat.

When Nicole was done, she stood and brushed the crumbs from her hands. "*Au revoir,* my little friend, and good hunting."

Refusing to be dismissed, the cat stropped her ankles. Unable to resist such friendliness, Nicole lifted the calico and cradled the skinny little body in her arms. Immediately it began to purr so strongly that Nicole felt the vibration through her layers of cloaks. Severely she said, "Don't try to turn me up sweet, *ma petite*. The last thing I need at the moment is someone to take care of."

The cat tilted its head up and offered what looked very much like a coaxing feline smile. "Oh, very well, you silly beast," Nicole said with resignation. "If you are willing to travel in my pocket, we will give it a try. But mind you behave."

To her surprise, the cat settled happily into the right pocket of Nicole's cloak, its small body creating a spot of warmth against her side. Feeling unreasonably cheered, Nicole continued on her way to Covent Garden.

"WHO would have thought that whores would be so thin on the ground?" James Kirby grumbled as he surveyed the wet, dismal intersection at Covent Garden.

"This weather would drive anyone indoors," Masterson said dryly. "Besides, even ladies of pleasure are entitled to take a few days off at Christmas." They had seen several raddled, gin-soaked streetwalkers, but Masterson had flatly refused to let Kirby approach them, on the grounds that the object was to give Philip a night's pleasure, not the French pox and God knew what else. "Time to give the idea up, James. Let's go back to my rooms and make a bowl of hot punch."

"Wait!" Kirby pointed across the street. "She's perfect."

Masterson examined the object of Kirby's interest, a slim girl who stood in front of the new opera house. She was dressed in a voluminous and much-bedraggled scarlet cloak, and it was easy to see why she had caught Kirby's eye. What was visible of her face under the hood was very lovely—and also very innocent. "She's attractive," Masterson agreed, "but I'm not sure she's available. Doesn't quite have the look of a doxy."

"Who but a whore would wear a cloak like that? And she has exactly the right look for Philip—he's never liked the brazen sort. Come on, let's ask her. If she's respectable, she'll give us a flea in the ear quick enough, and we'll be no worse off than we are now." Kirby started across the street.

Masterson had to admit that the garment in question was unlikely to be worn by anyone but a prostitute or a dashing society lady. Decent females didn't wear such violent, expensive shades of red, nor did they have masses of ostrich feather trim drooping about them, and they certainly did not wander alone in Covent Garden. Resignedly he followed his friend.

As soon as Nicole realized that the two young men were heading straight for her, she started to hasten away, for a day on London's meaner streets had already taught her caution. Then one of the men called out, "Wait, miss, we want to talk to you."

The voice was polite and seemed sober, so warily she stopped and turned to face them.

The redheaded young man who had called gave her an ingenuous smile. "We're looking for someone to keep a friend company tonight. Would"—he considered—"five pounds be sufficient?"

As soon as she realized his meaning, she gasped in shock. How dare he! What kind of girl did he think she was?

Misinterpreting her gasp, he said, "Very well, ten."

Nicole realized that it was quite obvious what kind of girl he thought she was. She opened her mouth to give him an icy set-down, then slowly closed it when a shocking but practical thought occurred to her. Ten pounds was a substantial amount of money, enough to support her for weeks if she was careful. Enough to make the difference between surviving or starving.

Though part of her was appalled that she would even consider such a proposition, she found herself coolly evaluating the risks. She would lose her virtue, of course, but virtue would be of precious little use if she starved to death. There was also the disastrous chance of pregnancy, but from what she had heard, that was unlikely to happen after a single night.

Her hasty calculations suggested that the benefits of being ruined would outweigh the risks. Nonetheless, the idea of allowing a total stranger such intimacy was abhorrent; the man might be revolting or even vicious. Stalling for time to make up her mind, she said, "Is your friend such a monster that he cannot find a woman for himself, so he sends you to pimp for him?"

"He's a perfectly pleasant fellow," the redhead assured her. "We are doing this as a surprise Christmas present, since he's been working too hard."

Taking a deep breath, Nicole decided to put herself into the hands of fate. "Twenty pounds," she said firmly. If they would pay such a great amount of money, she would take it as a sign that letting herself be ruined was the right thing to do.

"Twenty pounds?" the redhead said dubiously. "That seems a trifle steep."

With a mixture of regret and relief, Nicole said, "It is my price, monsieur. If it is more than you wish to pay, so be it."

"Wait." For the first time the dark-haired man spoke. He pushed Nicole's hood back onto her shoulders. Then, while the cold rain spattered her cheeks, he took her chin in one hand and studied her with a detached gaze. "She's very pretty. A sweet face. I think Philip would like her."

Nicole's companion chose this moment to stick its head out of her pocket and give a piercing yowl. Both men gave the furry, triangular head a startled glance.

"My cat," Nicole said, rather unnecessarily. "Where I go, she goes."

The corners of the dark-haired man's mouth twitched with amusement. "James, does Philip like cats?"

"Of course. Don't you remember that great ugly ginger tom he smuggled into our rooms at Winchester?"

The dark man gave a faint shudder. "Good God, how could I possibly have forgotten Thomas Aquinas and his unnatural attachment to my boots?" He smiled at Nicole. "Clearly you are singularly well qualified to please this particular gentleman. Come, let us adjourn to more comfortable quarters."

For a moment Nicole teetered on the verge of flight, but the streets offered nothing but cold and damp and danger. At least tonight she would be warm, and probably well fed. In return for a few hours of endurance, she would have the money she needed to survive. Face set, she pulled her hood over her dark hair and followed the two young men to their carriage.

PHILIP had not spent such an enjoyable evening since his father died. It was good to laugh with friends, to remember that he was still young and that worrying himself into a decline would do no one any good. When Kirby's clock begin to chime midnight, he got to his feet with reluctance. "A pity to leave so soon, but I must if I want to be off at dawn tomorrow morning."

He expected Kirby to insist that he stay, but his host said only, "You're right. I need some rest myself if I'm to make it to the ancestral home tomorrow." He gave Philip a bright-eyed smile. "When will you be in town again?"

"I'm thinking of hiring a house and bringing my mother up for the Season. She'll be out of mourning soon, and I think some gaiety will be good for her." Philip made a face. "Unfortunately, she's been hinting that it's time I looked for a wife. If I bring her here, she'll throw every suitable miss in the Marriage Mart at me. She's already introduced me to every eligible female in Northamptonshire."

Horrified, Kirby exclaimed, "That's a dashed dangerous business, Philip. It's all very well to be a dutiful son, but if you aren't careful, you could end up leg-shackled."

"Believe me, I'm aware of the perils. I trust that forewarned will be forearmed." The baronet collected his hat, shook hands, and wished his friends a happy Christmas, then went into the hall to climb the two flights of stairs to his own rooms. So convenient to live in the same building.

But that wouldn't be true much longer. Regretfully Philip realized that he really must let go of his rooms. He'd had them since leaving Cambridge, but he was unlikely to be spending lengthy periods of time in London again, so it was far more reasonable to stay in a hotel for his brief visits.

He sighed. One after another, the realities of adulthood were catching up with him. He had obligations to his family and his name that could not be neglected. Which brought him back to the depressing topic of marriage.

In an attempt to preserve his good spirits, Philip counted his blessings as he ascended the shadowy steps. Though he had initially been intimidated by his new responsibilities, he now had them well in hand. He very much enjoyed being master of Winstead, for there was something elementally satisfying about working the land and seeing to his tenants' welfare. Though he did miss London friends like Kirby and Masterson, he had other friends in Northamptonshire, and family as well, so he certainly wasn't lonely. Nor did he mind bearing his mother company, for she was the most delightful of women.

As he pulled out his key and opened the door to his rooms, he realized why marriage was such a depressing prospect: he'd never met an eligible girl who was half so amusing as his mother or his sister, Marguerite. It wasn't just bias on his part; they both really were exceptionally charming, intelligent females. It must be the French blood. A pity that the Continent was closed to Britons; perhaps in Paris it would be possible to find a bride who wouldn't bore him, but with Britain and France at war he was unable to put that theory to the test.

His sitting room was warm, and he saw a glow of lamplight coming from the corridor that led to the bedroom. A member of the staff must have come in to build a fire and leave a light for him. It was like being in his own home and explained why there was always a waiting list for rooms in the Rochester.

Whistling softly, Philip hung up his hat and walked down the short passage to his bedroom. He was starting to untie his cravat when his gaze came to rest on his bed.

He stopped dead in his tracks. Kneeling in the middle of the blue counterpane was a dark-haired young female, a delicious-looking creature who wore nothing but a provocative white negligee and an enormous red silk bow tied around her slender neck.

"What the devil?" Thinking that he must have drunk more than he'd realized, Philip gave his head a sharp shake, but the nymph was still there. "Who are you, and how did you get in here?"

"My name is Nicole, Sir Philip," she said in a soft voice that contained a charming hint of accent. "I am a present from your friends downstairs. They said you have been working too hard, so they hired me to . . . to entertain you for the night."

For a moment Philip felt pure exasperation at such high-handedness. Tonight he had wanted to get a good night's sleep to prepare him for the long drive home. If he had been in the mood, he would have found a girl himself.

But as he examined his visitor, he realized that he could easily get into the mood. She was very lovely, with delicate features and huge brown eyes, and her sheer white gown revealed as much as it concealed. His fascinated gaze came to rest on the spot where the trailing ends of the red bow curved over her left breast.

His pleasant languor vanished under a surge of vivid anticipation. Apparently his friends knew what he needed better than he did.

"Nicole is certainly an appropriate name for the season." He peeled off his coat and waistcoat and tossed them aside, not bothering to watch whether they hit chair or floor. "But I've never seen a St. Nicholas who was half so appealing."

After tugging off his boots, Philip sat down on the edge of the bed facing the girl. She was even prettier close up, her wide eyes like dark velvet pansies. Seeing green leaves twined in her hair, he leaned forward for a closer look, then chuckled.

"You really are a perfectly wrapped Christmas present." Touching one of the waxy berries, he added, "Mistletoe is my favorite holiday tradition."

Enjoying the moment, he let his fingers drift down through her silky tresses and along her graceful neck. Then he moved his hand to the back of her head and pulled her close for a kiss. He closed his eyes, the better to revel in the soft warmth of her lips and the tantalizing invitation of her spicy scent.

But even as his breath and blood quickened, he realized that something was wrong. Under his hands, her shoulders were rigid, and he felt a touch of moisture against his upper lip.

He opened his eyes and found that huge tears were silently flowing down her pale cheeks. It was an unnerving sight. While he was no gazetted rake, he'd never had a girl cry when he kissed her. "What's wrong?"

Her own eyes flew open, and he saw alarm in the dark depths. "Nothing, monsieur." Raising one hand, she wiped at the tears with the back of her wrist. "Please, just go ahead and do—whatever it is you are going to do."

As Philip mentally reexamined the last few minutes, a horrible suspicion occurred to him. "Surely this isn't your first time!"

She nodded, her expression a heartrending mixture of misery and valor.

For Philip the effect was similar to having a bucket of cold water poured over his head. While there were men who delighted in deflowering virgins, he and his friends had always preferred the practiced embraces of skilled demireps. But now that he examined the girl more closely, he saw that she was definitely not of that company; in fact, her demeanor more nearly resembled that of an early Christian trying to appear brave while lions entered the Coliseum. "Why on earth did those idiots choose you?"

"I was in Covent Garden and wearing a truly vulgar cloak, so they assumed I was the kind of female they were looking for," Nicole replied. "Does it matter that I am inexperienced?"

"Yes, it matters," he said shortly.

"I see—my ignorance will reduce your pleasure. I'm sorry—I did not mean to cheat them. Or you." Distressed tears trembled in her eyes again. While she had steeled herself to accept passively whatever was done to her, she was unprepared for talk or explanations.

With some violence, the baronet slid off the bed and stalked across the room. Tall and powerfully built with the breadth of his shoulders emphasized by his white shirt, he was a daunting sight. Still, there was no denying that he was a fine figure of a man. In spite of what the redhead had said, Nicole had expected someone repulsive.

After muttering something under his breath, Sir Philip turned and leaned back against the fireplace mantel with his arms folded across his chest. His voice overcontrolled, he said, "Why did you agree to do this?"

Perhaps there was a protocol for such a situation, but if so, it was not one Nicole's mother had ever explained. Well, when in doubt, use the truth. "For the money, of course," she said in a small voice. "I am a seamstress, but I lost my situation, and since I've been in London for only a month, I had no one to turn to. Even so, it did not occur to me to . . . to sell myself, but when your friends made the offer . . ." She shrugged expressively. "It seemed like providence."

His brows drew together. "So it was a choice between me or starvation?"

"Well, yes," she said uneasily, hoping he would not take offense.

"How wonderfully flattering," Sir Philip said caustically. "Are you planning to take this up as a career?"

"Most assuredly *not,*" she retorted. "I will find another situation before the money runs out."

He studied her face for a long moment, then sighed and ran one hand through his thick, light brown hair. "Taking advantage of desperate virgins is really not a habit of mine. Perhaps it's best if you go now."

He didn't find her attractive. It was an oddly disconcerting thought, even though at the same time Nicole was so relieved that her knees were shaky when she slipped off the bed and went to the neat pile of possessions she had tucked in a corner.

She was sorely tempted to change into her own clothing and leave without saying more, but unfortunately honor insisted that she could not do that. She knelt and fumbled with her cloak until she found the bank notes in the pocket, then rose and walked to Sir Philip. "Here," she said, her voice bleak. "Please return this to Lord Masterson, for I did not earn it."

After a still moment, his hand closed around hers, locking the notes in her hand. "Keep the money," he said gently. "Neither he nor Kirby would expect to be repaid, and your need is greater than theirs."

Nicole bit her lip, wanting to cry again because of his kindness. Before she could become maudlin, the baronet said testily, "Now for God's sake, put on something more opaque before I forget to be noble."

Glancing up, she saw frank desire in his gray eyes. Warm color flooded her face, but there was satisfaction in knowing that he did admire her.

After collecting her clothes, she went to the dressing room so that she could change away from his intense gaze. However, she had forgotten who was closed inside. As soon as she opened the door, small furry feet roared across her bare toes and headed straight for the man by the fireplace.

After a squeak of surprise, Nicole raced after the cat and managed to scoop it up before it could assault Sir Philip.

"I'm sorry, sir," she stammered as she clutched the cat to her chest. "I forgot my cat was in the dressing room."

Luckily he was amused rather than offended. "So it was to be a ménage à trois. What's her name?"

Nicole hadn't chosen one yet, so she made an instant decision. "Merkle."

"Merkle? An unusual choice for a cat." He reached out to scratch the cat's chin. As the little calico began to purr under his ministrations, Nicole was very aware that the baronet's fingers were within an inch of her breasts, and that she wore only the sheer negligee that Masterson had provided. How would it feel if those knowing fingers caressed her with the same gentle strength that was enrapturing the cat?

Scandalized by the direction of her thoughts, Nicole stiffened and moved away. "Miss Merkle was very kind to me when I lost my position, and I wanted to honor her. Though I suspect she mightn't be flattered to be remembered this way."

"How did you lose your situation?"

Nicole stared down at the cat, not wanting to say, but unable to lie. "I was accused of stealing."

"Were you guilty?"

She raised her head and looked the baronet right in the eye. "No, I was not. My mistress suspected me because I was new in the household. She had my belongings searched, and when my savings were discovered, she became convinced that I was a thief. So she stole my money and threw me out onto the street with no references."

She wanted him to believe her, and was unreasonably disappointed when he frowned. Reminding herself that his opinion didn't matter, she said, "You do not believe me, but then, why should you? I am just a failed doxy." She gave him a slightly mocking curtsy. "I shall be gone in a few minutes, monsieur. You may search my belongings before I leave to assure yourself that I have taken nothing."

Philip raised his brows. "I didn't say that I didn't believe you. I doubt that a girl who so conscientiously tried to return money that she hadn't earned would be a thief. What bothers me is the unfairness of what happened to you, but I suppose nothing can be done."

He was rewarded by a faint, sweet smile. With dark curls tumbling around her shoulders and her oversized negligee half off one shoulder, Nicole was a tantalizing sight. What a pity she was an innocent, for if she had been what his friends thought, the two of them could have spent a delightful night.

Instead, she looked as fragile as she was gallant, and he realized that he could not possibly send her into the December night. "You'd best stay here until morning. I don't want to be responsible for you catching lung fever."

"You are very kind, Sir Philip." She glanced at the window, where icy raindrops were drumming, and shivered. "It is not a night fit for man, nor beast, nor pelican. Do you have a blanket? I will sleep on the sofa in the drawing room."

Pelican? Philip smiled at her turn of phrase as he took blankets from the top shelf of his wardrobe. She had an interesting mind. Among other things. But what would happen to her tomorrow, after he went home and she was left to her own devices? "How much did Masterson pay you?"

"We agreed on twenty pounds, but only half was paid in advance. I was to receive the other half in the morning, in return for the night's work." Unexpectedly her eyes twinkled. "Alas, I have not earned that, but the ten pounds you said I could keep is still a considerable sum."

Philip bit his lip as he calculated how far ten pounds would go. It wasn't much of a cushion against disaster. "You're French, aren't you?"

"By birth, but I have lived in England since I was six."

Philip switched to speaking French. "My mother was born and raised in France, near Toulouse. Her family name was Deauville."

Nicole smiled with pleasure. "Then we are countrymen of a sort," she replied, answering in the same language. "Unfortunately I have never seen Toulouse, but my mother often said it was a lovely city."

Yes, the girl was definitely French, and she spoke with as refined an accent as Philip's mother. Returning to English, he said, "Are you from one of the aristocratic families who escaped the French Revolution with little more than their lives?"

She shook her head. "My family name is Chambord, and while of decent rank, we were not noble. More like one of your English gentry, for my father had a single estate of moderate size." She added conscientiously, "My mother had a cousin who was a count, but the connection was not a close one."

Philip suppressed a smile. The girl was nothing if not honest; it was not uncommon for émigrés to exaggerate the status they had had in the Old Country. Still, Nicole was clearly wellborn, and her coloring and gestures reminded him a little of his own sister. A brilliant idea struck him. "Are you willing to work outside of London?"

She looked hopeful. "Of course. Without references, I cannot afford to be too particular in my tastes. Do you know of a position for a seamstress?"

"Not for a seamstress, but a companion," he replied. "My only sister married last winter, and my father died only a month later, so my mother has had a lonely year. Several times I've suggested that she hire a companion, but she always said that was unnecessary. However, if I present her with a fait accompli, I think she would be delighted to have you."

Nicole looked shocked. "Monsieur, I am an accused thief and obviously no better than I should be, or I wouldn't be here. You cannot possibly take me into your home, much less introduce me to your mother!"

He raised his eyebrows. "Of course I can. In fact, I have every intention of doing so. For over twenty years I've been bringing home stray dogs, cats, birds with broken wings, even the odd injured hedgehog now and then. If my mother can tolerate them, she can certainly deal with you."

"I am considerably odder than a hedgehog," she said severely. "Surely you can see the difference."

Philip was forced to admit that Nicole was right. It was no small thing to introduce a complete stranger into one's home, and even the most broad-minded mother was apt to look askance at a fledgling lightskirt. However, his judgment of people was usually good, and he was willing to swear that the French girl was as honest and well-bred as she appeared. "There is no need to mention how you and I became acquainted. I will just say that you are a distant connection of Masterson's who needs a situation. My mother won't question that."

As Nicole frowned, the cat batted at the red bow, causing the white negligee to dip even more precariously. "I do not want you to perjure yourself on my behalf."

Philip realized that he was getting new insight into the expression "honest to a fault," as well as a highly distracting view of his guest's pleasing person.

After swallowing hard, he said, "Allow me to worry about that. My conscience will be a good deal more troubled if I leave you here to starve." Seeing that Nicole looked unconvinced, he decided that it would be good strategy to imply that she would be doing him a favor. "If you and my mother get on well, you'll save me from a terrible fate. She's been plotting to marry me off—if she has you to fuss over, she might leave me alone, at least for a while."

Nicole smiled a little. "Clearly it is my duty to save you from disaster." Her eyes began filling with tears again. "This morning I prayed for a miracle and *le bon Dieu* has sent me one, for your generosity is truly miraculous. Thank you, monsieur."

With effort, Philip wrenched his gaze away. There was no denying that Miss Chambord was something of a watering pot—nor that she looked dangerously fetching with tears in her great dark eyes. "You stay here, and I'll sleep on the sofa tonight. Time we both get some rest, for I want to be off at dawn tomorrow."

Then he beat a hasty retreat, before he found himself trying to kiss her tears away.

PHILIP was awakened by the faint sounds of someone building up the drawing room fire a dozen feet away. It was still dark, and it took him a moment to remember just why he was sleeping fully dressed and in such an uncomfortable position. Then he remembered and sat up, sore muscles protesting at having been laid to rest on a sofa that was hard and far too short.

He vaguely expected to find Stephens, the Rochester servant who had been looking after him for the last few days, but instead he saw a slight feminine figure kneeling by the hearth and using tongs to set lumps of coal on the embers of last night's banked fire. So the gift-wrapped girl on the bed hadn't been a dream. This morning she was fully dressed in a severe but well-cut gown whose color he couldn't determine in the predawn darkness.

Merkle was curled up in front of the hearth, a pointy-eared silhouette against the increasing glow of the fire. Both girl and cat looked very much at home.

Hearing his movement, Nicole glanced up with a shy smile. "Good morning, Sir Philip. I trust you slept well?"

"Well enough." He raised one hand to cover a yawn, then pushed aside the blanket and got to his feet. As the clock began striking six, he said, "Any moment now, two of the Rochester's staff will arrive with hot water and breakfast. You'd better retreat to the bedroom. Quite apart from the fact that female visitors are frowned on, the less people who know about last night, the better for your reputation."

"Why should it matter?" she asked, puzzled. "I am of no account to anyone."

"As my mother's companion, you might be coming to London for the Season. Your reputation will matter then, to her and to yourself." He stretched to loosen his knotted muscles. "In fact, after breakfast, I'll pay a brief call on Masterson, thank him for the unexpected gift, then tell him to muzzle James so this little episode doesn't become common knowledge."

"Isn't it too early to call on a gentleman like him?" she said doubtfully as she stood and hung up the fire tongs.

"If I wake him, so be it," Philip said callously. "However, in spite of Masterson's air of languor, he's an early riser. Kirby, on the other hand, hasn't had firsthand experience of dawn since he came down from Cambridge."

"When you visit Lord Masterson, will you return the negligee he lent me?"

"So that's why the thing was so large on you," Philip said, amused.

"His last mistress was a strapping wench." Then he frowned. "Sorry. I really shouldn't speak of such things in front of you."

Her eyes danced. "Last night I was a fallen woman and this morning I am respectable, but in truth I feel little different."

They were sharing a companionable smile when the servants' door at the back of the apartment swung open with a gloomy creak. Nicole immediately darted into the bedroom and pulled the door shut before the footmen could see her.

While the senior footman, Stephens, set a large tray with covered dishes on a side table, the younger servant headed for the bedroom door with the copper of hot water. Philip hastily interposed himself between the footman and the door. "Set the water down on the hearth."

The young man gave him a curious look, but obeyed. As he set down the copper, Merkle decided to dash across the room in a flash of calico lightning. Stephens blinked at the cat. "Sir Philip, there is a Feline Creature here."

"Indeed there is." Philip watched uneasily as the cat took position by the bedroom door and began to cry for her mistress. "I saw a mouse here yesterday, so I enlisted expert help."

Stephens looked scandalized. "Mice are not permitted in the Rochester. In fact, it is against the rules to have any sort of Lower Creature here."

The younger footman said helpfully, "The way that puss is carrying on, maybe there's a mouse in the bedroom now." He started across the drawing room to open the door.

Once more Philip took several hasty steps to block the way to the bedroom. "I think the cat is just interested in finding its food dish." Anxious to get rid of the servants, he continued smoothly, "I know you must both be about your duties now, but before you leave, allow me to offer my best wishes for the season, and to express my appreciation for your fine service over the last several days."

Substantial vails, augmented by a generous Christmas bonus, served to distract the two footmen from the question of what might be in the bedroom. As Philip ushered them from his rooms, he said piously, "I will take the Feline Creature back to the country this morning, so it shan't cause any trouble." Then he closed the door before anything more untoward could occur.

After the footmen were safely gone, he returned to the drawing room to find that Merkle had leapt onto the side table and was now sniffing enthusiastically around the aromatic covered dishes. Before Philip could intervene, Nicole cautiously opened the bedroom door, then scurried across the drawing room and removed the cat from the table. "I'm sorry," she said apologetically as the little calico protested with a heartrending wail. "The Feline Creature's manners aren't very good."

"Hunger will raise havoc with manners." Philip lifted dish covers until he found a platter of ham. "Give her a few slivers of this so we can eat in peace."

After Merkle had been fed and both humans had washed up, they sat down to break their fast. Nicole's interest in the food was as great as the cat's, though her manners were considerably better. In fact, with her pleasant expression and disinclination to chatter, she made an ideal breakfast companion. Philip had a brief, unpleasant mental image of her starving on the streets and gave thanks that fate had put her in his path.

After he finished eating, Philip went into his bedroom and packed the few possessions he had brought with him, plus the Christmas presents he had purchased on Bond Street. Most of the gifts were easily stowed in a leather portmanteau, but the music box he'd bought for his mother began to play when he lifted it. The box was a pretty trifle, its circular base surmounted by a delicate porcelain angel that rotated to the melody of "The First Noel."

As the sweet notes filled the room, Nicole came to investigate, then gave a soft admiring exclamation. "How lovely! A present for your mother or sister?"

He nodded and handed the music box to her. "My mother collects music boxes. I think she'll like this one because of the Christmas theme."

When the movement slowed, Nicole turned the key on the bottom again. Her small face glowed as the angel pirouetted, its gilded wings and trumpet shining in the lamplight as the carol played. "I think your mother is blessed to have a son who is not only considerate, but who has such good taste."

"I'm fortunate to have her and my sister. Losing my father so suddenly has made me aware of how fatally easy it is to take those we care about for granted." Then, more to himself than his companion, Philip added, "I never told my father that I loved him. Now it's too late."

Nicole said gravely, "I'm sure that he knew. Love needn't be spoken to be understood."

Philip found a surprising amount of comfort in her words. He had known that his father loved him, though it had never been said aloud; it made sense that his father had been equally aware of his son's regard. "I hope you're right."

Uncomfortable with the extent to which he'd revealed his emotions, he took the music box from Nicole, carefully wrapped it in a heavy towel, and wedged it securely into the leather portmanteau. "My curricle will be brought around in a few minutes, so I'll go down and speak to Masterson now. Can you be ready to go in ten minutes?"

"Oh, yes." She smiled. "I've little to pack."

Philip collected the neatly folded white negligee, then took a lamp to light his way down the Rochester's dark stairs to his friend's rooms. Hair tousled and suppressing a yawn, Masterson himself answered Philip's knock.

After identifying his visitor, Masterson smiled lazily and gestured for Philip to come into the narrow vestibule. "I'm surprised you aren't still enjoying your warm bed."

"That warm bed is why I'm here," Philip said dryly as he handed over the negligee. "While I must thank you and Kirby for your generous gift, a mistake was made. Miss Chambord is a lady, not a lightskirt." Then he succinctly described Nicole's background and his decision to take her to Winstead Hall.

Leaning against the wall with his arms folded across his chest, Masterson listened with amused interest. "So the chit batted those long lashes and said she's a distressed gentlewoman. You actually believe her?"

Not liking the tone, Philip said shortly, "Yes, I do."

The other man shook his head cynically. "Be careful the little tart doesn't rob you the moment you turn your back."

"She's not a tart." When Masterson gave him a skeptical glance, Philip's eyes narrowed. "You may have catastrophic judgment about women, but not all men are such fools."

The other man's brows shot up. "A low blow, Philip," he said without rancor. "But no doubt you're right. If the girl is an innocent, it would explain why yesterday she gave me a set-down worthy of an Almack's patroness when I told her I was in need of a mistress and asked if she was interested in the position."

So Masterson had offered the girl a *carte blanche*. Philip teetered between satisfaction that Nicole had turned him down and a strong desire to plant a fist on his friend's jaw. He settled for saying, "Time will tell which of us is right, but until Miss Chambord's honesty, or lack thereof, is established, I'd thank you not to say anything that might ruin her reputation."

"I shall be a model of discretion," Masterson assured him. "And I guarantee that Jamie will be the same. If she is a decent girl fallen on hard times, she deserves a chance."

Satisfied, Philip offered his hand, then took his leave.

Masterson grinned as he returned to the comfort of his bed. Philip was obviously taken by the girl. If pretty little Nicole was what she claimed to be, she might turn out to be a more lasting Christmas gift than they had intended.

IN spite of his defense of Nicole's integrity, Philip found himself troubled by doubts as he made his way up the dim stairwell. He had believed without question everything the girl had said, but perhaps he'd been naive to do so. The fact that she had an air of refinement and spoke excellent French didn't mean she was honest; perhaps she was a deceitful little vixen who had been stealing his purse while he was talking to Masterson.

Frowning, he entered his rooms and glanced around, but saw no sign of his guest. He crossed the drawing room in half a dozen steps and entered his bedroom, but there was no sign of her there, or of his luggage, either. Cursing himself for a gullible fool, he spun on his heel and barked, "Nicole, where are you?"

He was so sure that she had fled that it was a shock to hear her voice floating from the narrow hall that led to the servants' entrance. "I am here, monsieur." She trotted into sight carrying a battered wicker basket in one hand. "I found this in a closet. May I use it to carry Merkle in?" Her expression became anxious. "You don't mind if I take her with me? I couldn't bear to abandon her to starve."

Her gaze was so transparently honest that Philip felt like six kinds of idiot for doubting her. "Of course she can come. Put a towel in the basket to keep her warm—it's going to be a long, cold drive."

Back in the drawing room he saw that Nicole had neatly stacked all of the luggage beside the front entrance. He'd been in such a hurry when he came in that he'd rushed right by it.

He was just congratulating himself that Nicole knew nothing of his doubts when her gentle voice asked, "Did you think I had robbed you and run, Sir Philip?"

He could feel hot color rising in his face. "The thought had occurred to me."

She nodded with apparent approval, then laid a folded towel in the bottom of the basket. "That is only natural. What do you know of me, after all?"

Deciding to cast his lot with instinct over logic, Philip said, "I know that you are entirely too perceptive, and you have honest eyes. That's quite enough for me. How do you know that I am not a murderer, or going to sell you to a slaver who will ship you to a harem in Arabia?"

She looked up at him and laughed. "Because you are *not*. I knew you were honorable as soon as I saw you." After which placid statement, she scooped up Merkle and put the cat in the basket, making soothing noises to allay feline protests.

After staring at her dark head for a moment, Philip decided that the girl was either a genius or a lunatic, possibly both, but amiable in either case. Hearing the sound of hooves and wheels outside, he went to the window and saw that the livery groom had brought his curricle right on schedule and now waited in the street below. "The carriage is here. Don't you have a cloak? If not, you'd better wear something of mine, though you'll be lost in it."

In answer, Nicole lifted a garishly scarlet garment that had been draped over the back of the sofa. Philip blinked in disbelief as she wrapped the voluminous folds around her. Eyeing the fluffy ostrich trim, he said, "I can see why Masterson and Kirby thought you were no better than you should be."

"It's a most vulgar garment, *n'est-ce pas?* But warm." Then, less confident than she pretended, she set out to meet her fate, cat basket in one hand, canvas bag in the other, and ostrich feathers trailing behind.

*   *   *

RELUCTANTLY Nicole left the warmth of the Saracen's Head Inn for the damp, bitter chill of the stable yard, where the curricle waited with a fresh pair of horses. As he held the door for her, Philip said, "It's getting colder. Do you think you'll be all right? I know this is not the season for a long trip in an open carriage, but this is the last stage—Towcester is less than fifteen miles from Winstead."

Nicole ached with weariness, but knew that Philip must be far more tired than she, for it took strength, skill, and continuous concentration to drive safely over the winter-rutted roads. "I'm fine," she assured him. "You have made the trip such a comfortable one. Fresh hot bricks every time the horses are changed—*quelle* luxury! And this is the third time we've stopped to eat."

"You need fattening up." Philip gave Nicole a teasing smile as he helped her into the curricle, then tucked a heavy blanket across her and the cat basket she carried on her lap.

As he climbed into his own seat, Nicole reflected that when he decided to marry, the girl he chose would be very fortunate, for his consideration made one feel cherished. She slanted a glance out of the corner of her eye. He was also kind, amusing, intelligent, good-natured, and handsome. Yes, when he was ready to marry, his chosen bride would be a very lucky woman.

A mile beyond Towcester, Philip swung the carriage from the main road onto a narrower track that led east. "This is a shortcut to Winstead. We should be home just before dark."

Nicole hoped he was right, for it was already midafternoon and the lowering clouds threatened to drop something unpleasant on the hapless travelers. *Eh bien*; there was no point in worrying about it, she decided philosophically as the curricle lurched into an unusually large rut. She wrapped her right arm around the cat basket and gripped the carriage rail with her left hand. "Will there be hot mulled wine when we reach Winstead?"

"If not that, something equally warming." The road was getting progressively rougher so Philip slowed the team's pace. "How did you come to England, or is that something you would rather not discuss?"

"It's not a dramatic tale. We had been in Paris and were returning to Brittany. A few miles from home, one of my father's peasants, who had been watching for our return, stopped our carriage to warn us that Guards were waiting at the manor to arrest the whole family. We abandoned the carriage, and the peasant drove us to the coast in his cart. Then a fisherman took us across the Channel to England with no more than the luggage we had brought from Paris.

"I was only six, and everything happened so quickly that I didn't understand that I would never again see my playmates on the estate, or the nurse who raised me, or my pony. But we were fortunate—we had our lives. Others were not so lucky."

"Did you come to London?"

"Only for a few days. My mother had a cousin in Bristol, so we went there. Because there was hardly any money, my father found work driving a coach between Bristol and Birmingham, which paid enough to keep us in modest comfort for the next few years." Her voice wavered. "Then Papa's back was broken in a coach accident, and he never walked again. Since he could not work, my mother took in sewing. I was almost eleven then, so I helped her."

Philip hauled back on the reins to let a small group of homeward-bound cows amble across the road. "What a pity. It almost seems like your family was cursed."

"It sounds dreadful, and in many ways it was," Nicole said slowly. "Yet the next five years were the happiest of my life. The three of us were very close. Papa became my teacher, for he said that an informed mind was the true mark of gentility. A gentleman who lived nearby let us borrow any book in his library, so I learned Latin and some Greek, read the classics, debated the ideas of the great philosophers. Then Papa died of lung fever, and my mother's heart died with him."

Nicole used the icy rain as an excuse to brush at her eyes, which were disgracefully moist. "Maman survived another three years, mostly from a sense of duty to me, I think. Then when I was eighteen and she knew I was capable of taking care of myself, she just . . . faded away."

"And ever since, you've faced the world alone."

"It hasn't been so bad. I have friends in Bristol, and I had a good position there. But I was ambitious and wanted to work in London and someday have a shop of my own. That is how I came to Lady Guthrie's household." She made a face. "Going to work for her was the worst mistake of my life, but it seemed like a good opportunity at the time."

He gave her a quick, warm smile. "You are a remarkable young lady, Mademoiselle Chambord."

She laughed. "There is nothing remarkable about making the best of one's lot, Sir Philip. Not when one considers the alternative."

After that conversation flagged, for the weather was steadily worsening. The mizzling rain froze wherever it touched, and the muddy ruts began to solidify to iron-hard ridges that rattled the curricle and its occupants to the bone. Earlier there had been a steady trickle of traffic in both directions, but now they were alone on the road.

The Northamptonshire terrain consisted of wide rolling hills that took a long time to climb. It was at the top of one such ridge that the curricle's wheels got trapped in a deep, icy set of ruts that ran at a tangent to the main direction of the road. Caught between the pull of the horses and the ruts, the curricle pitched heavily, almost spilling both passengers out.

"Damnation!" Using all of the strength of his powerful arms, Sir Philip managed to bring the carriage to a safe halt. "I'm sorry, Nicole. In a heavier carriage we could manage, but the curricle is just too light for these conditions. We've scarcely eight miles to go, and I'd hoped to make it home, but it's dangerous to continue. There's a small inn about a mile ahead. We can stop there for the night."

Struggling to keep her teeth from chattering, Nicole nodded with relief. "Whatever you think best, monsieur."

He urged the nervous horses forward again. "What a polite answer when you would probably rather curse me for risking your neck."

"I'm in no position to complain. Two days ago I was this cold, but then I had no prospect of finding a warm fire at the end of the day."

The road down the hill was steep and dangerous, so icy the horses sometimes slipped. The light was failing and visibility was only a few yards, but with Philip's firm hands on the reins, they made it almost to the bottom without incident.

Then they reached a bare spot where the wind had turned a wide puddle into a treacherous glaze of ice. As soon as the curricle's wheels struck the slick surface, the vehicle slewed wildly across the road.

The horses screamed, and one reared in its harness. Philip fought for control, and Nicole clung to railing and cat basket for dear life, but to no avail. The curricle tipped over, pitching both occupants onto the verge. Nicole struck the ground hard and rolled over several times, coming to rest in an ice-filmed puddle, too stunned to speak.

While she struggled for breath, a piercing cry split the air. Immediately Philip shouted, "Nicole, where are you? Are you hurt?"

Another shriek came from the vicinity of Nicole's chest and she wondered dizzily if that was her own voice and she was too numb to know what she was doing. Then she realized she was still clutching the cat basket in her arms. Poor Merkle had been tossed and rolled as much as her mistress and was now protesting in fierce feline fashion.

As she pushed herself to a sitting position, Nicole gasped, "I'm all right. At least, I think I am. Merkle is the one carrying on."

"Thank heaven!" Sir Philip emerged from the gloom and dropped to his knees beside Nicole, then pulled her into his arms, basket and all. She burrowed against him, grateful for his solid warmth.

"You're sure you're not hurt?" he asked anxiously, one hand skimming over her head and back, searching for injuries.

Nicole took careful stock. "Just bruised. A moment while I check on Merkle."

She would have been happy to stay in Philip's embrace, but conscience made her sit up and lift the lid of the basket. Merkle darted out and swarmed up her mistress's arm, crying piteously until she found a secure position on Nicole's shoulder, claws digging like tiny needles.

"Merkle can't have taken any injury either or she'd not be able to move so quickly," Sir Philip observed as he got to his feet. He helped Nicole up. "Just a moment while I see if the curricle is damaged."

Nicole tried to brush away mud and crushed weeds with one hand while soothing the cat with the other. The puddle had finished the job of saturating her cloak, and the bitter wind threatened to freeze her into a solid block of ice.

Sir Philip muttered an oath under his breath. "The horses seem to be all right, but the curricle's left wheel is broken."

"Surely it can't be much farther to the inn you mentioned," Nicole said through numb lips. "We can walk."

"Up one long hill and down another," he said grimly. "That's too far on a night like this. Luckily there's an old cottage just a few hundred yards from here. I don't know who lives there, but it's always well kept so I'm sure it's occupied. Just a moment while I get the curricle off the road and unharness the team."

To reduce her exposure to the wind, Nicole hunkered down beside the road and returned an indignant Merkle to the basket. The baronet undid the leather harness straps, tending the job horses as carefully as if they were his own. Nicole's father would have approved; he always said that how a man treated his beasts was a good guide to his character.

When Philip had freed the team from its harness, Nicole stood and joined him, the basket handle slung over one arm. "Which way, monsieur?" she said with a hint of chattering teeth.

"Just along here." Taking the reins in his right hand, Philip put his left arm around his companion, wanting to warm her. He felt her slim body shaking under her damp cloak, but she did not complain. She really was the gamest little creature.

The lane had a surprisingly smooth surface, which meant that it was now treacherous with sheet ice. Even with Philip's arm to support her, Nicole was skidding with every step. After she had barely survived several near-falls, he turned and scooped her up in his arms, cat basket and all.

When Nicole gave a little squeak of surprise, he explained, "Like the curricle, you are too light for these conditions."

She gave a gurgle of laughter, then relaxed trustingly against him. Between carrying her and leading the placid horses, progress was slow, but ten minutes of trudging through the dark brought them to the cottage, which was a small thatched building of undoubted antiquity.

Fortunately a light was visible inside. Philip set Nicole on her feet and looped the reins around the gatepost, then guided his companion to the cottage's front door. A knock produced no results, so after a moment's hesitation he tried the knob.

The door swung open with a creak, and Philip ushered Nicole into the cottage's large main room. A fire burned in the hearth, and the air was warm and rich with the scent of simmering soup, but there was no one in sight.

As he looked around uneasily, a soft female voice with only a trace of country accent came from the chamber behind the main room. "Emmy, what kept you? I've been expecting you all day."

A moment later the owner of the voice appeared. A small, elderly woman with straying white hair, she was dressed plainly, but with neat propriety. Seeing the unexpected visitors, she stopped still, her eyes widening with alarm.

Nicole said reassuringly, "Your pardon, madame, but we are travelers who had a carriage accident on the road outside. The wheel is broken, and to walk to the next village in this weather would be dangerous. I know this is a great imposition, but may we spend the night here?"

The woman went to a window and pulled the curtain aside with one gnarled hand, knitting her brows at the sight of the icy rain beating against the thick old glass. "I was napping and hadn't noticed how beastly the storm is. That must be why Emmy didn't come." She dropped the curtain and turned to her visitors. "Of course you and your husband can stay."

Philip asked, "May I put my horses in your shed?"

"By all means. It's no night to be traveling." After Philip went outside, the woman turned to Nicole and smiled apologetically. "You must think me a poor hostess. I'm Mrs. Turner. Let me take your cloak, my dear."

"I am Nicole Chambord," Nicole said as she handed over the mantle. Even soggy, it caused Mrs. Turner to raise an eyebrow, but the older woman made no comment as she hung the garment on a peg by the door.

Nicole continued, "My companion is Sir Philip Selbourne. He is not my husband, but"—she hesitated fractionally—"my cousin. We were on our way to his home, Winstead Hall."

Mrs. Turner's eyes brightened with interest. "So he's the squire of Winstead. I know of the family, of course, they're important folk hereabouts. His father died last winter, didn't he?" She gave an appreciative smile. "I didn't know Sir Philip was so young. He's a handsome lad, isn't he?"

Nicole nodded agreement. Sir Philip *was* handsome, not with the flamboyant, Byronic dash of Lord Masterson, but he had a pleasing aspect that was more appealing every time she looked at him.

Knowing it was not her place to say any such thing, she asked, "May I let my cat out? Poor Merkle has had a difficult day." She lifted the lid of the basket.

Pushed beyond the limits of patience, Merkle instantly scrambled out and jumped to the floor, then swung her head back and forth as she suspiciously examined her new surroundings.

Before the little calico could take a step, a menacing feline growl

sounded from a shadowy corner by the wood box. The growl was followed by a large, bristling tabby who slunk into the center of the room
with flattened ears and a dangerous gleam in its green eyes.

Judging discretion to be the better part of valor, Merkle raced across
the flagged floor and darted under a low chest of drawers, the tabby flying
in hot pursuit. "Oh, dear!" Nicole said unhappily. She took a step toward
the cats, but Mrs. Turner put her hand up.

"Don't worry," the older woman said. "Moggy won't hurt your puss.
She just wants to make it clear whose house this is."

Sure enough, Moggy didn't follow the smaller cat under the chest.
Instead, the tabby crouched down, tail flicking, in a waiting position that
effectively trapped the calico under the furniture, but offered no real
threat.

With crisis turned to stalemate, Mrs. Turner said, "I'll make you and
Sir Philip a nice cup of tea. You must be freezing."

As the older woman hung a kettle on the hob so that the water could
be brought to the boil, Nicole drew her chilled self closer to the hearth.
"Forgive me, madame, for this is none of my business, but who is the
Emmy you were expecting? A member of your family who has been
caught away from home by the storm?"

"No, she's a girl from Blisworth, the nearest village. She helps out
sometimes," Mrs. Turner explained. "My son is coming for Christmas
tomorrow and bringing his new wife, Georgette. Robert is a solicitor in
London and doing very well for himself."

She gave a rueful smile. "Vanity doesn't diminish with age, child. I
wasn't well enough to go to the wedding so I've never met my daughter-
in-law, but I do know that she's the daughter of a judge, and my cottage
will appear poor to her. Still, I wanted everything to be as nice as possible.
Emmy was going to help me with the baking and decorating, but she must
have decided to stay home because of the weather." Mrs. Turner sighed
and spread her hands, which were twisted with arthritis. "So much for
vanity. I can't manage everything myself, so Georgette will just have to
accept me the way I am."

"It is not vanity to wish to put one's best foot forward." After a
moment's hesitation, Nicole offered shyly, "Will you allow me to help
you? With a whole evening in front of us, together we can accomplish
most of what you wish."

Mrs. Turner gave her guest a shocked glance. "It wouldn't be fitting for you to do such humble work. You're gentry."

Thank heaven her, kind hostess didn't know what Nicole had been just the night before! "Preparing a home for Christmas is not work, but great pleasure."

While the older woman debated, Philip returned, accompanied by a gust of damp, icy air. He was carrying the baggage. As he hastily closed the door, Nicole said gaily, "We are in luck, Philip. Mrs. Turner is planning her Christmas preparations, and if we are very, very good, perhaps she will let us help her."

Mrs. Turner chuckled. "You're a clever minx. Very well, I'd be delighted to have your help, but first, you both need some tea and bread and soup. Take your coat and hat off, Sir Philip, and come warm yourself by the fire."

"You're very kind, Mrs. Turner." Holding his chilled hands toward the flames, he continued, "My sister and I are very grateful."

The older woman gave him a sharp look. "I thought you and Miss Chambord are cousins."

Without missing a beat, Philip said, "We are, but Nicole is so much a member of the family that I think of her as another little sister."

Nicole watched with admiration. If this was a sample of his skill at dissembling, he should have no trouble convincing his mother that the scandalous female he'd brought home was actually a respectable poor relation of Lord Masterson's.

Her levity faded as she perched on the oak settle and accepted a teacup from Mrs. Turner. Even if Sir Philip could lie like Lucifer, it simply wouldn't do. Nicole had done considerable thinking on the long drive from London and had reached the miserable conclusion that she must tell Lady Selbourne the truth, for it would be impossible to work for the woman under false pretenses. If Lady Selbourne was as tolerant as her son, perhaps she would not mind Nicole's appalling lapse from grace . . . but more likely she would be outraged and refuse to have such a doxy under her roof.

Nicole knew she should tell the baronet of her determination to confess all, but he would try to change her mind and it would be difficult to resist his arguments. With a sigh, she stirred sugar and milk into her tea. At least when Lady Selbourne ordered her out of the house, Sir Philip probably wouldn't allow Nicole to be tossed into a snowbank. Likely he would consider it his duty to buy her a coach ticket back to London. She would be no worse off than she had been yesterday.

She gave Sir Philip a surreptitious glance from the corner of her eye. He was standing, his head almost touching the smoke-darkened beams of the ceiling as he smiled and chatted with their hostess. He seemed too large and energetic for such a small cottage. And as Mrs. Turner said, he was a handsome lad.

No, not a lad, a man, one who was kind and considerate and wonderfully solid. Returning her gaze to her tea, Nicole felt a small, dangerous twist deep inside her. As an émigrée separated from her own class by poverty, she had resolved to build a life as an independent, respected businesswoman. There was no husband in that picture, for Nicole had never met a man for whom she could feel more than liking.

But it would be easy—so, so easy—to fall in love with Sir Philip Selbourne. He was very close to the dream husband she had imagined for herself when she was a child, before she realized that the Revolution had made it impossible for her to meet such a man as an equal.

Appalled at the thought, she swallowed a huge mouthful of tea, scorching her tongue in the process. *Mon Dieu!* What a fool she was; her situation was quite difficult enough without developing a hopeless *tendre* for a man she could never have.

The baronet thought of her as a waif, a hapless female who reminded him of his sister. From kindness he was helping her, but that was all there would ever be between them. When he was ready to marry, he would choose a wife of his own class who could bring him a dowry and an impeccable reputation; the sort of honorable female who would starve rather than sell her virtue.

As Nicole sipped more cautiously at her tea, she realized with a bitter pang that she might have been better off braving the hazards of the London streets. Instead, by impulsively accepting Sir Philip's offer, she was risking her heart.

WORKING gingerly to keep from being stabbed by the needlepointed leaves, Philip used a length of dark thread to attach the last silver-paper ornament to the last branch of holly. Then he got to his feet and arranged the brightly decorated sprays of holly, pine, and ivy along the narrow ledge of an oak beam that ran across the wall a foot above the fireplace mantel.

After all of the greens had been tacked to the beam, he took a length of shining scarlet ribbon and twined it through the boughs, working from the left end to the right, then back again. When he was done, he stepped back and surveyed his efforts with great satisfaction. Mrs. Turner's new daughter-in-law would have to be very hard to please not to enjoy the results, for the mass of fragrant, brightly decorated greenery turned the whole cottage into a festive bower. "What do you think—should I use more ribbon?"

Mrs. Turner sniffed the pine-scented air with delight and touched a silver paper star that hung from a spray of holly. "No, it's perfect just the way it is. I only hope your mother won't mind that you gave away the ribbon and silver paper she ordered."

"There's still ample left for Winstead Hall." With an elaborate show of casualness, Philip sidled over to the table where Nicole was assembling the last batch of mince pies. "Can I have one?" he asked hopefully.

Nicole looked up just in time to swat his hand before he could snatch one of the three-inch-wide tarts cooling on the end of the table. Laughing, she said, "You are exactly like an impatient six-year-old, Sir Philip."

"In my family it's traditional to try to wheedle sweets from the cook." He made another attempt to steal one of the tarts, this time successfully eluding Nicole's not-very-determined effort to stop him. The warm, crumbly shortcrust pastry disappeared in two bites. "Mmm, delicious."

The same could be said of Nicole, he noticed as she slid the last tray of mince pies into the oven built into the wall by the fireplace. With a towel tied around her waist and a dab of flour on her nose, she was adorable. More than that, her bright good nature created happiness all around her.

Mrs. Turner chuckled as she watched her young guests. "Now that you're finished, Nicole, it's time for us to relax and enjoy the results of all our hard work. Besides, I want you to sample a Turner family tradition."

Their hostess lifted a poker that had heated to red-hot in the fire, then plunged it into a wide-mouthed jug of spiced cider. The cider hissed and bubbled around the glowing metal, releasing the rich scent of apples and nutmeg.

After Mrs. Turner had poured them each a mug of mulled cider,

Nicole brought over a platter of baked tarts and they all took seats by the fire. Moggy, who had long since given up watching Merkle in favor of the more fascinating study of food preparation, promptly leaped onto Mrs. Turner's knees and raised her nose for a sniff of pastry.

Not to be outdone, Merkle slunk out from under the chest of drawers, darted across the rag rug, and hopped onto Nicole's lap, where she turned in a circle three times before settling down.

Outside, the freezing rain still fell, but in the old cottage, all was warmth and good fellowship. As they chatted back and forth, Philip had trouble remembering that he had known Nicole less than a day, Mrs. Turner for only four hours. The chance that had brought them together and the time spent cooking, cleaning, and laughing had made them almost a family.

Halfway through her second mug of mulled cider, Mrs. Turner said, "All we need now is Christmas music. Do you both sing?"

"Willingly, but not well," Philip replied. Then he remembered the music box in his baggage. "But I have something that will get us started properly."

It took only a moment to retrieve the music box from his luggage and wind the key. As he carried the box across the room, the bright notes chimed through the cottage, easily rising above the sounds of crackling fire and spattering rain.

After the mechanism had slowed to a halt, Mrs. Turner reached out and touched the delicate porcelain angel, her lined face glowing with pleasure.

"Such a lovely thing." She glanced at her guests. "Shall we sing along with it?"

Philip wound the music box again, and together they sang "The First Noel." From there they moved into other carols. While none of them had an outstanding voice, all could carry a tune, and together they made a very decent set of carolers.

Eventually Mrs. Turner yawned, covering her mouth with one thin hand. Then she removed Moggy from her lap and got to her feet. "Gracious, but I'm tired. You'll find that when you reach my age, sleepiness comes on you very quickly. You young people can stay up late if you like, but I'm going to bed."

"Not quite yet." Philip stood and picked up the sprig of mistletoe that he had earlier tied with a loop of ribbon. It took only a moment to hang it from a hook on a beam in the center of the ceiling. With a smile, he said, "I'll not let you go without a Christmas kiss."

Mrs. Turner laughed and joined him under the sprig. "You'll turn my head, Sir Philip. I can't remember the last time a handsome young man tried to lure me under the mistletoe."

When Philip started to give her a light kiss on the cheek, she firmly grasped his shoulders and pulled his face down for a solid buss. "I'm not going to waste this opportunity," she declared. Then she scooped up Moggy and retired to the tiny bedroom behind the main chamber.

Nicole followed Mrs. Turner with a hot brick for the older woman's bed, then returned to the main room. "I'm tired, too. It's been a long day."

"Stay until we've finished the mulled cider." Philip divided what was left into their two mugs. Then they took seats on opposite sides of the hearth.

After a few minutes of companionable silence, Philip mused, "I never would have guessed that I'd spend such a fine evening with two females I'd not even met twenty-four hours ago."

Nicole smiled. Curled up in Mrs. Turner's cushioned Windsor chair, she and Merkle were a picture of domestic bliss. "Moments like these are gifts, as lovely as they are fleeting."

"A pity that we can't stop time when we're happy, but life changes so suddenly and unexpectedly," Philip said. "A year ago at Christmas my father was alive and seemed in the best of health. Then he died, and nothing will ever be the same again." Perhaps it was the result of the alcoholic kick of the cider, but he found himself adding, "And change begets more changes. A year from now, my mother will probably have remarried."

Nicole's brows drew together. "She is planning to take another husband?"

"Not yet, but I think she will. The estate next to ours is owned by the Sloanes, who have been family friends forever. John Sloane was my father's best friend, just as Emily was my mother's. The children of both families grew up together. Emily died three years ago, and now my father is gone too."

Philip swallowed the last of his drink. "Just before I went to London, John Sloane spoke to me in my capacity as head of the family. He wanted to let me know his intentions for when Mother is out of mourning. He and she have always been very fond of each other. Now he hopes that in time she'll marry him." Philip smiled humorlessly. "It's an odd experience when a man who has been like an uncle asks one's blessing to marry one's mother."

"I can see where it would be," Nicole said gently. "How did you feel about it?"

Philip grimaced. "I felt a brief desire to hit him. Then I shook his hand and said that if Mother accepted his proposal, I would wish them both happy."

"Well done." She gave him a warm smile. "But I think you still feel some guilt and resentment?"

"I'm afraid so. Not very admirable on my part. Yet I honestly want my mother to be happy and I'm sure she will be with John Sloane." He smiled with self-deprecating humor. "When I told my sister what John Sloane had said, Marguerite raised her brows and said that of course they would marry—that if John and my mother had died, my father would probably have married Emily after a decent interval had passed. Apparently my understanding is not very powerful."

"No, it's merely that women take a deeper interest in things like love and marriage." Nicole cocked her head to one side thoughtfully. "Will it help if I say that being possessive of your mother was a perfectly natural first impulse? I would have felt the same way if my mother surprised me with the announcement that she intended to take another husband. It's common for families to oppose the remarriage of a widowed parent. But your second impulse was generous, and that's the one you obeyed."

Philip let out a slow breath. "It does help to hear you say that. Though I don't quite understand why I've confessed such unworthy thoughts to someone I hardly know."

"It is precisely because we are almost strangers," Nicole said with a trace of sadness. "I am a safe repository of unworthy thoughts because I am transitory in your life."

"But if you become my mother's companion, you will be part of the household." At least, until his mother remarried. Then she would no longer need a companion, and Nicole would need a new position, Philip realized. Still, she would be safe at Winstead for at least a few months.

Nicole muffled a yawn. "Time I went to bed. If you wish to stay up longer, I'll take the bed in the loft and you can sleep down here."

Philip got to his feet. "No, I'll take the loft. It's drafty up there, and I wouldn't want you to take a chill." He smiled. "If I haven't given you lung fever yet today, I don't want to do it now."

Nicole picked up the empty mugs and placed them on the kitchen table. As she crossed the room toward the quilts that Mrs. Turner had provided, she passed under the mistletoe, an opportunity that Philip was not about to pass up.

Intercepting her under the sprig, he took her shoulders and said, laughing, "Happy Christmas, Nicole."

She looked up at him, lips parted and brown eyes wide, her delicate features framed in dusky curls. "Happy Christmas, Sir Philip," she replied in a husky whisper.

He bent his head and kissed her. Nicole melted against him, her arms sliding around his neck, her soft mouth spicy with apple and cloves. She felt as delicious as she had the night before in his bed, but this time she did not simply yield. Instead, she welcomed him, and what began as a Christmas kiss rapidly developed into an embrace for all seasons. It was a moment of fire and sweetness that Philip wanted to last forever.

With a shock, he realized that once again tears were running down Nicole's cheeks. He ended the embrace, using his hands to support her when she swayed. "Why are you crying?" he asked in bafflement. She had not been unwilling, he was absolutely certain of that. "This is not like last night."

"No," she whispered as she brushed the back of her hand across her eyes. "That's why I'm crying."

He looked at her a little helplessly. "I don't understand."

"It's better that you don't." She closed her eyes for a moment, then opened them again, her manner matter-of-fact. "If I am going to be your mother's companion, we really mustn't kiss like that. It's . . . it's distracting. It lacks propriety."

Perhaps, but it didn't lack anything else. In fact, Philip very much wanted to kiss her again, so that he could savor the nuances more fully, but clearly the moment had passed.

More than a little confused, he lifted one of the lamps. "Good night,

Nicole. I'll see you in the morning." The ladder to the loft was in a corner of the room, and he lost no time climbing up, taking off his outer clothing, and crawling into the narrow bed that had once been used by Mrs. Turner's son.

However, in spite of a tiring day, it took Philip a long time to fall asleep. He kept wondering just what it was that he was better off not understanding.

CHRISTMAS Eve morning dawned clear and bright. Outside, ice sparkled on every surface and coated leaves and twigs with crystal brilliance, but the magical conditions were short-lived. By the time the inhabitants of the cottage had finished a breakfast of bacon, eggs, and apple muffins, most of the ice was gone and traveling conditions were safe again.

Nicole was grateful when Sir Philip left to go into Blisworth to make arrangements for repairing the curricle. She had made an absolute fool of herself last night, and this morning she could not look him in the eye. Thank heaven the dear, foolish man didn't understand how the female mind worked, or he'd realize how silly she was.

He had been quite right that last night's kiss was different from the one the night before. When she'd been hired to warm his bed, she had been frightened and stoic, but under the mistletoe she had been eager. She loved his touch, loved his taste, and wanted with all her heart to follow the kisses to their natural conclusion.

Sadly, her heart was the only one engaged. Perhaps Sir Philip did not think of her quite as a sister, but he had made it clear that he was not the least bit interested in acquiring a wife. And nothing less would do; Nicole had been willing to sell her virtue rather than starve, but she wasn't going to give it away to a man who didn't love her.

Years from now, when Philip was ready to marry, he would choose a bride whose family and fortune were similar to his own. It was ironic, really. Nicole was too wellborn to be Philip's mistress, but too poor, too déclassé, to be his wife.

It was a depressing train of thought, so Nicole determinedly started decorating an old vine wreath that Philip had found in the shed. The addition of sprigs of holly, fragrant crab apples, and a flamboyant red bow made the wreath perfect for the outside of the front door. After it had been hung and admired, Mrs. Turner said, "You have a gift for making things pretty."

"Thank you." Nicole closed the door again. "I'm sure that Georgette will have a fine time here."

"I hope so." Mrs. Turner rubbed absently at one of her gnarled knuckles. "Robert keeps asking me to come live with him in London, but it will never do if his wife and I don't get on."

"I see," Nicole said softly. "That's why you are so particularly concerned about this visit."

"I'm just a country woman of yeoman stock. I'm afraid Georgette will be ashamed to have someone like me in her house. To make it worse, her own mother died when she was a child, so likely she's used to having things her own way. She won't want me around."

Nicole wished there was some comfort she could offer, but any words would sound hollow, for there was a very real chance that the judge's daughter would not wish for too much intimacy with her husband's rustic mother. "If Miss Georgette doesn't appreciate you, it will be her loss."

Mrs. Turner sighed and changed the subject. "Your feelings for Sir Philip aren't sisterly, or even cousinly, are they?"

At the unexpected comment, Nicole's face flooded with hot color. "Am I that obvious?"

"Only to someone who notices such things," the older woman said. "I doubt that he does. Most men don't notice love until it hits them over the head. You'll just have to be persistent. In a discreet sort of way, of course."

Attaching Philip's interest would take more than persistence, and it was far too late for discretion. Not wanting to explain, Nicole said, "Is there anything else you'd like me to do? It will surely be hours before the carriage is repaired."

As Nicole's mother had often said, work was the best antidote for the dismals.

IT was early afternoon when Sir Philip drove up in the repaired curricle. Nicole came out to greet him. "I was in luck," he said cheerfully. "The wheelwright wasn't too busy. Are you ready to go? We can be home in an hour."

"Splendid," Nicole said, her voice a little hollow. If they were at Winstead in an hour, in two hours she would be on her own again. Briefly she considered postponing her confession for two days, until Boxing Day was over, but that would be too dishonest. She gave Philip a false, blinding smile. "I'll put Merkle in her basket and get my cloak."

After Philip had loaded cat and baggage into the carriage, Mrs. Turner came out to say farewell. Philip took her hand. "You saved our lives, Mrs. T., and gave us a splendid evening as well. Will you allow me to compensate you for your trouble?"

She shook her head. "Taking you in was the Christian thing to do, and I'll not accept money. Besides, I had a fine time, too. Perhaps sometime when you and Nicole are driving by, you'll stop for a cup of tea."

Philip wished he could do more, but accepted her comment at face value. Then he straightened up and saw Nicole's gaze go very deliberately from him, to Mrs. Turner, to the leather portmanteau that held the presents, then back to him.

For a moment he didn't understand. Then he smiled. Of course; why hadn't he thought of that? He unpacked the music box and offered it to his hostess. "I understand why you don't want money, but will you accept this, as a reminder of a special evening?"

Mrs. Turner took the music box with reverent hands. "You've found my weakness, young man. Thank you—this is the prettiest thing I've ever owned in my life."

She opened the box, and they all listened with pleasure as the carol chimed through the crisp winter air. Nicole knew that never again would she hear "The First Noel" without thinking of Sir Philip and Mrs. Turner, and these brief, happy hours when their paths had crossed.

The music was just ending when the rattle of a carriage could be heard coming up the lane. Mrs. Turner's expression became tense. "That must be Robert and Georgette."

Philip went to hold his horses' heads while Nicole took the music box from the older woman. "I'll put this inside for you." Under her breath she added, "Courage! I'm sure Georgette will love you."

Nicole set the music box on the kitchen table and was stepping through the front door when a chaise entered the yard, passing by Philip's curricle, which was drawn over to the side. As soon as the chaise stopped, a stocky, dark-haired young man tumbled out and swept Mrs. Turner into his arms.

"Happy Christmas, Mother," he said exuberantly. Clearly the young solicitor was not ashamed of his countrified parent.

Then Robert turned to the chaise to help his wife down. As Nicole watched, Mrs. Turner touched her hair nervously.

Then came the Christmas miracle. The girl who climbed from the carriage was not the haughty judge's daughter whom Mrs. Turner had feared. Instead, she was a golden-haired elf whose huge blue eyes mirrored Mrs. Turner's own nervousness. As the two women came face-to-face, Robert said proudly, "Mother, this is Georgette. Isn't she everything I said?"

Mrs. Turner smiled. "Welcome to my home, Georgette. You're even lovelier than Robert said."

The elf blushed. "I've been looking forward so much to meeting you. Robert speaks often about you and growing up in the country—the way you and he and Mr. Turner worked and read and laughed together. It sounds like the most wonderful childhood imaginable." Wistfulness showed in the depths of her wide blue eyes. "May . . . may I call you 'Mother'? I've never had a mother of my own, and I've always wanted one."

Her face transformed by joy, Mrs. Turner said, "Nothing would make me happier, my dear." She stepped forward and hugged her new daughter.

Nicole was edging her way toward Philip when the newcomers belatedly realized that there were strangers present. After introductions and handshakes all around, Nicole and Philip drove off down the lane. Nicole's last glance over her shoulder showed the Turners going into the cottage, Robert in the middle with one arm around his mother and the other around his wife.

Nicole felt a prickle of bittersweet tears. She did so love a happy ending. There wouldn't be one for her, but she didn't doubt that the three Turners would be happy.

PHILIP was silent during the seven-mile drive to Winstead Hall, but not because the familiar road required all of his attention. Instead he found himself thinking of the young woman sitting quietly by his side. In the day and a half he'd known her, he had seen her many different ways: as a pretty little tart, as a gallant waif, as an uncomplaining traveler, as a young woman with warmth and kindness for everyone. She was lovely, desirable, intelligent, and agreeable; everything, in fact, that a man would want in a wife. No dowry, of course, but he could afford to marry for love.

But he didn't want a wife! Moreover, he couldn't possibly be in love with a girl he'd just met. Could he?

The more Philip thought, the more confused he became. He'd never been in love, apart from one or two infatuations when he was younger, and even at his most infatuated he'd known that what he felt was passing madness, not true love. But his feelings for Nicole were different from anything he'd experienced before. He liked the idea of having her around all the time, day and night. Definitely at night, but equally definitely during the day. He liked talking with her, and listening to her, and he couldn't imagine ever growing tired of having her around. Was that love?

He had not reached any conclusions when they arrived at Winstead. As they drove up the sweeping entrance road, Nicole drew her breath in sharply. Her reaction made Philip see his home as if for the first time. Winstead Hall was only a few decades old, built for comfort rather than defense. It was also quite beautiful, a triumph of the Palladian style. As Philip drew the curricle to a halt in front of the portico, he tried to visualize Nicole coming down the stairs as mistress of Winstead. It was surprisingly easy to conjure the image up.

A manservant came to take the reins of the curricle, and Philip helped Nicole down. She was very silent as she accepted the cat basket and accompanied him up the stairs and into the hall. She had the same nervous expression that Mrs. Turner and Georgette had worn when they met, and for the same reason. Philip gave his guest a reassuring smile, knowing that his mother would quickly put her at her ease.

Even as the thought crossed his mind, Lady Selbourne came floating down the stairs. She was a remarkably youthful-looking woman, with dark hair and a face marked by a lifetime of laughter.

She did raise her brows at the sight of the appalling scarlet cloak, but made no comment. She'd always been hard to perturb, even the time Philip had led his pony into the vestibule with the intention of having it to tea. Giving her unexpected visitor a friendly smile, Lady Selbourne said, "Philip, I'm so glad to see you. I was beginning to fear that you might not be back in time for Christmas. Did the weather cause you trouble?"

"A bit. We had a minor accident near Blisworth and had to spend the night, but it was nothing serious." After kissing his mother's smooth cheek, Philip ushered the two women into the drawing room. "Mother, this is Miss Nicole Chambord."

Her dark eyes bright with curiosity, her ladyship said, "I'm pleased to meet you, Miss Chambord. Let me ring for some tea. You must both be chilled from the drive."

Philip's gaze went to Nicole. Her hands were clenched around the handle of the cat basket, and she looked as if she were riding in the tumbril to the guillotine. Yet her head was high, and she had a grave dignity that touched him in ways he couldn't explain. Wanting to relieve her anxiety, he said, "Miss Chambord is a distant relation of Masterson's and in need of a situation. I thought we had a position here that would suit her."

Lady Selbourne nodded with understanding. "I see. You were thinking she could be a companion for me?"

"Perhaps." Philip looked into Nicole's enchanting, expressive brown eyes, and pure madness struck him. "Or if she's interested, there's another position available. As my wife."

A bomb thrown into the drawing room couldn't have struck with greater impact. Both women stared at him with identical expressions of shock, and Nicole almost dropped Merkle's basket. Philip hastily took it and released the cat.

As he did, the silence was broken by his mother going into gales of laughter as she looked first at her son, then at the young woman she had just met. "Oh, Philip, my only and adored son," her ladyship gasped when she could speak again. "Have you learned nothing of French savoir faire from me? This is *not* the way to offer a young lady a proposal of marriage!"

Face scarlet, Nicole blurted out, "The situation is much worse than that, Lady Selbourne, for I am not a young lady. My only relationship to Lord Masterson was that he hired me to spend the night with your son as a . . . a Christmas present." She blinked hard. "If Sir Philip really meant what he said, it is only because he wants to save me from ruination."

Lady Selbourne's laughter ceased, and she plumped down on a velvet-covered chair rather quickly. After a long, alarming silence broken only by the ticking of the mantel clock, she said, "It sounds as if you are already ruined." Aiming a gimlet gaze at her son, she said in a dangerously reasonable tone, "I have trouble believing that you would bring a doxy to Winstead. Am I wrong, Philip?"

Philip winced, realizing that he couldn't have handled the matter more badly if he had tried. "I did meet Nicole in an irregular manner," he admitted, "but she's not a doxy. As an orphaned émigrée, she was forced to earn her living as a seamstress. Several days ago she was unjustly discharged, so she accepted Masterson's offer because she was penniless and totally without prospects. When I realized that she was gently bred, of course I couldn't take advantage of her situation. So I brought her here." After a moment, he added stiffly, "I assure you, nothing improper occurred."

"God forbid that I should consider her turning up in your bed as improper," Lady Selbourne said dryly. Her shrewd gaze went back to Nicole. "Is what Philip says true, Miss Chambord?"

Nicole nodded miserably.

Her fingers drumming on the right arm of her chair, Lady Selbourne studied her potential daughter-in-law. At length she said, "Well, you've a practical mind, and that's no bad thing." Switching to French, she said, "Tell me about your family."

Seeing that Nicole was speechless, Philip said helpfully, "Her mother is related to a count."

"Which one?"

Finding her tongue, Nicole said in French, "The Count du Vaille, but the connection is remote."

Lady Selbourne bit her lip absently. "The Count du Vaille? He's also a distant relative of mine, so you and I are in some way related. Where in France did you live?"

Still in French, Nicole sketched in her background and the story of how her family had been forced to flee to England. After listening intently, Lady Selbourne thought for a moment, then began tapping one dainty foot. "*Très bien*. With the du Vaille connection, the world can be told that you are a cousin to whom we offered a home. After a few months of proximity, no one will be surprised if there is a happy announcement."

Nicole gaped at Lady Selbourne. "You mean that you would approve of such a match?"

Philip's mother gave her son an affectionate glance. "I have been doing my best to find my son a suitable bride, and you are the only girl who has caught his fancy. Philip is very like his father—an easygoing English-man, but once he makes his mind up, nothing will shake him from his path. While I would certainly not approve of him marrying a courtesan, I have heard nothing about your past that disqualifies you from becoming his wife."

Voice choked, Nicole exclaimed, "But he can't possibly marry an unknown female with no reputation! He knows nothing of me."

"I know that you're honest and lovely and brave and kind, and enchantingly unexpected," Philip said. "What more do I need to know?"

"But . . . but I could be lying about everything," she said helplessly.

"You are the most ruthlessly honest female I've ever met," he retorted. "I may not have much savoir faire, or a deep understanding of the female mind, but I do know that."

Lady Shelbourne gave a low chuckle. "Resign yourself, Miss Chambord. If Philip has decided that he wants to marry you, you had best accept it. Granted, his proposal was cabbage-headed in the extreme, but I've always found his judgment to be sound."

She got to her feet. "I think it's time to leave you young people to sort this out." Leaning over, she scooped up Merkle, who was sniffing inquir-ingly about her slippers. "You're a pretty little puss. Would you like a Christmas ribbon around your neck? Not red, that would clash with the orange in your fur. Green would be better." She floated out of the room, the calico cat draped across her shoulder.

Nicole stared after her until the door closed. "I've never met anyone quite like your mother."

"She is rather remarkable. You remind me of her a bit." Philip caught Nicole's hand and drew her over to sit beside him on the sofa. "Now, *ma petite,* shall we discuss our future?"

"How can we have a future?" she protested as she settled next to him. "We hardly know each other." She swallowed hard, determined to keep her head. "Why do you want to marry me?"

He smiled. "I rather think I'm in love with you. Isn't that the best of reasons?"

She gave him a level look. " 'Rather think' isn't enough. I don't want to be one of your broken-winged birds or injured hedgehogs that you take in from pity."

Philip's laughing face sobered. "I might try to help a waif because of pity, but I'm not foolish enough to marry for such a reason. I enjoy your company, I admire you, and I desire you. If you turn me down, it's myself I'll pity, not you, for I've never met another woman with whom I could imagine spending my life." His hand tightened on hers. "But just as you don't want me to propose from pity, I don't want you to accept from gratitude or desperation."

"I wouldn't," Nicole assured him. "I've seen what love should be like between man and wife, and I won't settle for a marriage that is merely convenient."

He caught her gaze with his. "Do you think that someday you might be able to love me?"

Philip's nearness and the warmth of his eyes were rapidly disabling her logic. Looking away from his face, she whispered, "Last night I realized that I was falling in love with you, but it never occurred to me that you might reciprocate. You made it very clear that you didn't want a wife."

"I didn't. I still don't want 'a wife.' What I want is you, *ma petite,* for now and always. I've never thought of marrying before. Now that I've met you, I can think of nothing else." He gently brushed a curl from her temple. "I know this is very sudden. There's no need to rush to a decision—since this is a house of mourning, it will be several months before a betrothal could be announced. That will give us time to become sure of our feelings. As my mother said, you can be a distant cousin come to keep her company. No one will question that."

"I don't really need more time," Nicole said shyly, looking at him from under her dark lashes. "You make my heart sing with happiness. I think it must be love, for I can't imagine anything better or more right."

"Neither can I." With a burst of exuberance, Philip scooped her up in his arms and whirled her around, not caring if she thought him a Bedlamite. Setting his laughing lady back on her feet, he said, "Shall we seal our agreement with a kiss?"

Not waiting for a reply, he drew her into an embrace. Nicole received him eagerly, her pliant body molding to him with the sweet enthusiasm of a playful kitten. And she was a quick learner; her kissing had improved since the night before.

That being the case, it was a distinct shock for Philip to realize that Nicole was weeping. Lifting his head, he said wryly, "My dearest Christmas tart, why are you crying this time?"

She smiled and ducked her head against his chest. "Because I'm so happy. I'm sorry, Philip, I'm just a watering pot." She looked up with sudden anxiety. "Perhaps you should reconsider."

"I suppose I'll become accustomed to tears, as long as they are mostly of the happy variety," he said philosophically as he pulled her back into his arms. "Besides, if I cried off, I'd never again see you sitting on the bed with a red ribbon tied around your neck." He grinned. "The best Christmas present I ever had."

"With you, *mon coeur,* every day will be Christmas." Then Nicole laughed mischievously. "I shall have to think up something very special for Guy Fawkes Day."

This time when they kissed, she didn't shed a single tear.

The Black Beast of Belleterre

To Binnie, who has more Beauties and Beasties than anyone I know.

HE was ugly, very ugly. He hadn't known that when he was young and had a mother who loved him in spite of his face. When people had looked at him oddly, he had assumed it was because he was the son of a lord. Since there were a few children who were willing to be friends with him, he thought no more about it.

It was only later, when his mother had died and accident had augmented his natural ugliness, that James Markland realized how different he was. People stared, or if they were polite, quickly looked away.

His own father would not look directly at him on the rare occasions when they met. The sixth Baron Falconer had been a very handsome man; James didn't blame him for despising a son who was so clearly unworthy of the ancient, noble name they both bore.

Nonetheless, James *was* the heir, so Lord Falconer had handled the distasteful matter with consummate, aristocratic grace: he installed the boy at a small, remote estate, seen that competent tutors were hired, and thought no more about him.

The chief tutor, Mr. Grice, was a harsh and pious man, generous both with beatings and with lectures on the inescapable evil of human nature. On his more jovial days, Mr. Grice would tell his student how fortunate the boy was to be beastly in a way that all the world could see; most men carried their ugliness in their souls, where they could too easily forget their basic wickedness. James should feel grateful that he had been granted such a signal opportunity to be humble.

James was not grateful, but he was resigned. His life could have been worse; the servants were paid enough to tolerate the boy they served, and one of the grooms was even friendly. So James had a friend, a library, and a horse. He was content, most of the time.

When the sixth lord died—in a gentlemanly fashion, while playing whist—James had become the seventh Baron Falconer. In the twenty-one years of his life, he had spent a total of perhaps ten nights under the same roof as his late father.

He had felt very little at his father's death—not grief, not triumph, not guilt. Perhaps there had been regret, but only a little. It was hard to regret not being better acquainted with a man who had chosen to be a stranger to his only son.

As soon as his father died, James had taken two trusted servants and flown into a wider world, like the soaring bird of the family crest. Egypt, Africa, India, Australia; he had seen them all during his years of travel.

He discovered that the life of an eccentric English lord suited him, and developed habits that enabled him to keep the world at a safe distance. Seeing the monks in a monastery in Cyprus had given him the idea of wearing a heavily cowled robe that would conceal him from casual curiosity. Ever after, he wore a similar robe or hood when he had to go among strangers.

Because he was young and unable to repress his shameful lusts, he had also taken advantage of his wealth and distance from home to educate himself about the sins of the flesh. For the right price, it was easy to engage deft, experienced women who would not only lie with him, but would even pretend they didn't care how he looked.

One or two, the best actresses of the lot, had been almost convincing when they claimed to enjoy his company, and his touch. He did not resent their lies; the world was a hard place, and if lying might earn a girl more money, one couldn't expect her to tell the truth. Nonetheless, his pleasure was tainted by the bitter awareness that only his wealth made him acceptable.

He returned to England at the age of twenty-six, stronger for having seen the world beyond the borders of his homeland; strong enough to accept the limits of his life. He would never have a wife, for no gently bred girl would marry him if she had a choice, and hence he would never have a child.

Nor would he have a mistress, no matter how much his body yearned for the brief, joyous forgetting that only a woman could provide. Though he was philosophical by nature and had decided very early that he would not allow self-pity, there were limits to philosophy. The only reasons why a woman would submit to his embraces were for money or from pity. Neither reason was endurable; though he could bear his ugliness and isolation, he could not have borne the knowledge that he was pathetic.

Rather than dwell in bitterness, he was grateful for the wealth that buffered him from the world. Unlike ugly men who were poor, Falconer was in a position to create his own world, and he did.

What made his life worth living was the fact that when he returned to England, he had fallen in love. Not with a person, of course, but with a place. Belleterre, in the lush southeastern county of Kent, was the principal Markland family estate. As a boy James had never gone there, for his father had not wished to see him. Instead, James had been raised at a small family property in the industrial Midlands. He had not minded, for it was the only home he had ever known and not without its own austere charm.

Yet when he returned from his tour of the world after his father's death and first saw Belleterre, for a brief moment he had hated his father for keeping him away from his heritage. *Belleterre* meant "beautiful land," and never was a name more appropriate. The rich fields and woods, the ancient, castlelike stone manor house, were a worthy object for the love he yearned to express. It became his life's work to see that Belleterre was cared for as tenderly as a child.

Ten years had passed since he had come to Belleterre, and he had the satisfaction of seeing the land and people prosper under his stewardship. If he was lonely, it was no more than he expected. Books had been invented to salve human loneliness, and they were friends without peer, friends who never sneered or flinched or laughed behind a man's back. Books revealed their treasures to all who took the effort to seek.

Belleterre, books, and his animals—he needed nothing more.

Spring

Sometimes, regrettably, it was necessary for Falconer to leave Belleterre, and today was such a day. The air was warm and full of the scents and songs of spring. He enjoyed the ten-mile ride, though he was not looking forward to the interview that would take place when he reached his destination.

He frowned when he reined in his horse at the main gate of Gardsley Manor, for the ironwork was rusty and the mortar crumbling between the bricks of the pillars that bracketed the entrance. When he rang the bell to summon the gatekeeper, five minutes passed before a sullen, badly dressed man appeared.

Crisply he said, "I'm Falconer. Sir Edwin is expecting me."

The gatekeeper stiffened and quickly opened the gate, keeping his gaze away from the cloaked figure that rode past. Falconer was unsurprised by the man's reaction; doubtless the country folk told many stories about the mysterious hooded lord of Belleterre. What kind of stories, Falconer neither knew nor cared.

Before meeting Sir Edwin, Falconer knew that he must ascertain the condition of the property; it was the reason he had chosen to visit Gardsley in person rather than summon the baronet to Belleterre. Once he was out of sight of the gatekeeper, he turned from the main road onto a track that swung west, roughly paralleling the edge of the estate.

On the side of a beech-crowned hill, he tethered his mount and pulled a pair of field glasses from his saddlebag, then climbed to the summit. Since there was no one in sight, he pushed his hood back, enjoying the feel of the balmy spring breeze against his face and head.

As he had hoped, the hill gave a clear view of the rolling Kentish countryside. In the distance he could even see steam from a Dover-bound train. But what he saw closer did not please him. The field glasses showed Gardsley in regrettable detail, from crumbling fences to overgrown fields to poor-quality stock. The more he saw, the more his mouth tightened, for the property had clearly been neglected for years.

Five years earlier, Sir Edwin Hawthorne had come to Falconer and asked for a loan to help him improve his estate. Though Falconer had not much liked the baronet, he had been impressed and amused by the man's sheer audacity in asking a complete stranger for money.

Probably Hawthorne had been inspired by stories of Falconer's generosity to charity and had decided that he had nothing to lose by requesting a loan. Sir Edwin had been very eloquent, speaking emotionally of his wife's expensive illness and recent death, of his only daughter, and how the property that had been in his family for generations desperately needed investment to become prosperous again.

Though Falconer had known he was being foolish, he had given in to impulse and lent the baronet the ten thousand pounds that had been requested. It was a sizable fortune, but Falconer could well afford it, and if Hawthorne really cared that much about his estate, he deserved an opportunity to save it.

But wherever the ten thousand pounds had gone, it hadn't been into Gardsley. The loan had come due a year earlier, and Falconer had granted a twelve-month extension. Now that grace period was over, the money had not been repaid, and Falconer must decide what to do.

If there had been any sign that the baronet cared for his land, Falconer would have been willing to extend the loan indefinitely. But this . . . ! Hawthorne deserved to be flogged and turned out on the road as a beggar for his neglect of his responsibilities.

Falconer was about to descend to his horse when he caught a flash of blue on the opposite side of the hill. Thinking it might be a kingfisher, he raised his field glasses again and scanned the lower slope until he found the color he was seeking.

He caught his breath when he saw that it was not a kingfisher but a girl. She sat cross-legged beneath a flowering apple tree and sketched with charcoal on a tablet laid across her lap. As he watched, she made a face and ripped away her current drawing. Then she crumpled the paper and dropped it on a pile of similarly rejected work.

His first impression was that she was a child, for she was small and her silver-gilt tresses spilled loosely over her shoulders rather than being pinned up. But when he adjusted the focus of the field glasses, the increased clarity showed that her figure and face were those of a woman, albeit a young one. She was eighteen, perhaps twenty at the outside, and graceful even when seated on the ground.

In spite of the simplicity of her blue dress, she must be Hawthorne's daughter, for she was no farm girl. But she did not resemble her florid father; instead, she had a quality of bright sweetness that riveted Falconer's attention. His view was from the side and her pure profile reminded him of the image of a goddess on a Greek coin. If his old tutor, Mr. Grice, could have seen this girl under the apple tree, even that old curmudgeon might have wondered if all humans were inherently sinful.

She was so lovely that Falconer's heart hurt. He did not know if his pain was derived from sadness that he would never know her, or joy that such beauty could exist in the world. Both emotions, perhaps.

Unconsciously he raised one hand and pulled the dark hood over his head, so that if by chance she looked his way, she would be unable to see him. He would rather die than cause that sweet face to show fear or disgust.

When he had made his plea for money five years earlier, Sir Edwin had mentioned his daughter's name. It was something fanciful that had made Falconer think her mother must have loved Shakespeare. Titania, the fairy queen? No, not that. Ophelia or Desdemona? No, neither of those.

Ariel—her name was Ariel. Now that Falconer saw the girl, he realized that her name was perfect, for she seemed not quite mortal, a creature of air and sunshine.

Though he knew it was wrong to spy on her, he could not bring himself to look away. From the way her glance went up and down, he saw she was sketching the old oak tree in front of her. She had the deft quickness of hand of a true artist who races time to capture a private vision of the world. He was sure that she saw more deeply than mere bark and spring leaves.

A puff of breeze blew across the hillside, lifting strands of her bright hair, driving one of her crumpled drawings across the grass, and loosening blossoms from the tree. Pink, sun-struck petals showered over the girl as if even nature felt compelled to celebrate her beauty. As the scent of apples drifted up the hill, Falconer knew he would never forget the image that she made, gilded by sunshine and haunted by flowers.

He was about to turn away when the girl stood and brushed the petals from her gown. After gathering her discarded drawings, she turned and walked down the opposite side of the hill, away from him. Her strides were as graceful as he had known they would be and her hair was a shimmering, silver-gilt mantle. But she had overlooked the drawing that had blown away.

After the girl was gone from view, Falconer went down and retrieved the crumpled sheet from the tuft of cow-parsley where it had lodged. Then he flattened the paper, careful not to smudge the charcoal.

As he had guessed, the girl's drawing of the gnarled oak went far beyond mere illustration. In a handful of strong, spare lines, she implied harsh winters and fertile, acorn-rich summers; sun and rain and drought; the long history of a tree that had first sprouted generations before the girl was born and should survive for centuries more. That slight, golden child was a true artist.

Since she had not wanted the drawing, surely there was no harm in keeping it. Knowing himself for a sentimental fool, he also plucked a few strands of the grass that had been crushed beneath her when she worked.

He watched for the girl as he completed his ride to the manor house, but without success. If not for the evidence of the drawing in his saddle-bag, he might have wondered if he had imagined her.

Sir Edwin Hawthorne greeted his guest nervously, gushing welcomes and excuses. He had been a handsome man, but lines of dissolution marred his face and sweat shone on his brow.

As Falconer expected, the baronet was unable to repay the loan. "The last two years have been difficult, my lord," he said, his eyes darting around the room, anything to avoid looking at the cowled figure who sat motionless in his study. "Lazy tenants, disease among the sheep. You know how hard it is to make a profit on farming."

Falconer knew no such thing; his own estate was amazingly prof-itable, for it flourished under loving hands. Not just the hands of its mas-ter, but those of all his tenants and employees, for he would have no one at Belleterre who did not love the land. Quietly he said, "I've already given you a year beyond the term of the original loan. Can you make par-tial payment?"

"Not today, my lord, but very soon," Sir Edwin said. "Within the next month or two, I should be in a position to repay at least half the sum."

Under his concealing hood, Falconer's mouth twisted. "Are you a gamester, Sir Edwin? The turn of a card or the speed of a horse is unlikely to save you from ruin."

The baronet twitched at his guest's comment, but it was the shock of guilt, not surprise. "All gentlemen gamble a bit, of course, but I'm no gamester. I assure you, if you will give me just a little more time . . ."

Falconer remembered the neglected fields, the shabby laborers' cottages, and almost refused. Then he thought of the girl. What would become of Ariel if her father's property was sold to pay his debts? She should be in London now, fluttering through the Season with the rest of the bright, wellborn butterflies. She should have a husband who would cherish her and give her children.

But a London debut was expensive, and likely any money her father managed to beg or borrow went on his own vices. In spite of the isolation of his life, Falconer was not naive about his fellow man. He was surely not Hawthorne's only creditor. The man had probably borrowed money in every direction and had debts that could not be repaid even if Gardsley was sold.

Falconer felt a surge of anger. A man who would neglect his land would also neglect his family, and a girl who should have been garbed in silks and adored by the noblest men in the land was wearing cotton and sitting alone in a field. Not that she had looked unhappy; he guessed that she had the gift of being happy anywhere. But she deserved so much more.

If Falconer insisted on payment now, her father would be ruined, and the girl would probably end up a poor relation in someone else's house. Unable to bear the thought, Falconer found himself saying, "I'll give you three more months. If you can repay half of the principal by then, I'll rene-gotiate the balance. But if you can't pay . . ." It was unnecessary to complete the sentence.

Babbling with relief, Sir Edwin said, "Splendid, splendid. I assure you I'll have your five thousand pounds three months from now. Likely I'll be able to repay the whole amount then."

Falconer looked at the baronet and despised him. He was a weak, shallow man, unable to see beyond the fact that he had been spared the consequences of his actions for a little longer. "I'll be back three months from today."

But as he rode home to Belleterre, he was haunted by one thought. What would happen to the girl?

ARIEL returned to the house for lunch, pleased that she had done several sketches worth keeping. Her satisfaction died when she found that her father had taken the train down from London that morning. As soon as the butler told her, Ariel put one hand to her untidy hair, then darted up the back stairs to her room.

As she brushed the snarls from her hair, she wondered how long Sir Edwin would stay at Gardsley this time. Life was always pleasanter when he was away, which was most of the time. But while he was here, she must tread warily and keep out of his sight. Alas, she could not escape her daughterly duty to dine with him every night. He would criticize her unladylike appearance; he always did. He would also be quite specific about the many ways in which she was a disappointment to him.

Once or twice Ariel had considered pointing out that he didn't allow her enough money to be fashionably dressed even if she had been so inclined, but caution always curbed her tongue. Though not a truly vicious man, Sir Edwin was capable of lashing out when he had been drinking, or when he was particularly frustrated with his circumstances.

Still brushing her hair, she wandered to her window and looked out. She loved this particular view. The clouds were dramatic this afternoon; perhaps she could go up on the roof and try to capture the sunset in watercolors. But no, that wouldn't be possible tonight, since she would have to dine with her father.

She was regretfully turning away from the window when a strange figure came down the front steps. It was a tall man wearing a swirling black robe with a deep, cowled hood that totally obscured his face. Since Gardsley was said to have a ghost or two, Ariel wondered if one of them was making an appearance. But the man who moved so lithely down the steps seemed quite real. Certainly the horse and the Gardsley footman who brought it were not phantoms.

Abruptly she realized that the figure could only be the mysterious, reclusive Lord Falconer, sometimes called the Black Beast of Belleterre. He was a legend in Kent, and the maids often talked about him in hushed, deliciously scandalized whispers.

Ariel had heard him described as both saint and devil, sometimes in the same breath. It was said that he gave much to charity and had endowed a hospital for paupers in nearby Maidstone; it was also said that he held wild, midnight orgies on his estate. Ariel had looked up the word *orgy,* but the definition had been so vague that she hadn't been able to puzzle out what was involved. Still, it had sounded alarming.

Stripped of rumors and titillated guesses, the gossip about him boiled down to three facts: he had grown up in the Midlands, he was so hideously deformed that his own father had been unable to bear the sight of him, and he now concealed himself from the gazes of all but a handful of trusted servants, none of whom would say a word about him. Whether their silence was a product of fear or devotion was a source of much speculation.

As Ariel watched him swing effortlessly onto his horse, she decided that his deformity could not be of the body, for he was tall and broad-shouldered and he moved like an athlete. She wondered what made so unwilling to show his face to the world.

Even more, she wondered why Lord Falconer was at Gardsley. He must have had business with her father. That would explain why Sir Edwin had unexpectedly returned from London.

Ariel had just reached that conclusion when Lord Falconer glanced up at the facade of the house. His gaze seemed to go right to her, though it was hard to be sure since his face was shadowed. Instinctively she stepped back, not wanting to be caught in the act of staring. Although, she thought with a hint of acerbity, a man who dressed like a medieval monk had to expect to attract attention.

Dropping his gaze, he turned his horse and cantered away. He rode beautifully, so much in tune with his mount that it seemed to move without the use of reins or knees. Stepping forward again, Ariel watched him disappear from sight.

The Black Beast of Belleterre. There was a larger-than-life quality about the man that was as romantic as it was tragic. She began considering different ways to portray him. Not watercolor, that wasn't strong enough. It would have to be either the starkness of pen and ink or the voluptuous richness of oils.

She stood by the window for quite some time, lost in contemplation, until her attention was caught by another figure coming down the steps. This time it was her father, followed by his valet. As she watched, the carriage came around from the stables. After the two men had climbed in, she heard her father order the driver to take him to the station. So he was going back to London without even asking to see her.

Silly of her to feel hurt when their meetings were so uncomfortable for both of them. Besides, now she would be free to go up on the roof and paint the sunset. But Ariel found that unexpectedly thin comfort. A sunset no longer seemed as interesting; not when she had just seen the enigmatic Lord Falconer.

Yes, pen and ink would be best for him.

Summer

Falconer returned to Gardsley exactly three months after his first visit. The day was another fine one, so, despising himself for his weakness, he took the same detour across the estate that he had taken before. The land was in no better shape and the hay would be ruined if it wasn't cut immediately, but he did not care for that. His real purpose was a wistful hope that he might catch a glimpse of the girl. But she was not sketching on the hill today. The blossoms were long gone from the tree and now small, hard green apples hung from the branches.

Regretfully he turned his horse and rode to the house. He had had his solicitor make inquiries about Sir Edwin Hawthorne and the results had confirmed all of Falconer's suspicions. The baronet was a gambler and a notorious seducer of other men's wives. He was away from Gardsley for months on end, and had been hovering on the brink of financial disaster for years.

The solicitor's report had gone on to say that Sir Edwin's only daughter, Ariel, was twenty years old. She had had a governess until she was eighteen. Since then, she had apparently lived alone at Gardsley with only servants for company. On the rare occasions when she was invited into county society, she was much admired for her beauty and modesty, but her father's reputation and her own lack of dowry must have barred her from receiving any eligible marriage offers.

Falconer had trouble believing that part of the report. Surely the men of Kent could not be so blind, so greedy, as to overlook such a jewel simply because she had no fortune.

The butler admitted Falconer and left him in a drawing room at the front of the house, saying that Sir Edwin would be with his guest in a moment. Falconer smiled mirthlessly. If the baronet had the money, he would have been waiting with a bank draft in hand. Now he was probably in his study trying desperately to think of a way to save his profligate hide.

Falconer was pacing the drawing room when he heard the sound of raised voices, the baronet's nervous tenor clashing with the lighter tones of a woman. The drawing room had double doors that led to another reception room behind, so Falconer went through. The voices were much louder now, and he saw that another set of double doors led into Sir Edwin's study, where the quarrel was taking place. The baronet was saying, "You'll marry him because I say so! It's the only way to save us from ruin."

Though Falconer had never heard Ariel's voice, he knew instantly that the sweet, light tones belonged to her. "You mean it will save *you* from ruin, at the cost of ruining me! Even I have heard of Gordstone—the man is notorious. I will not marry him."

Falconer felt as if he had been struck in the stomach. Gordstone was indeed notorious—a pox-ridden lecher who had driven three young wives to their graves. Not only did he have an evil reputation, but he must be over forty years older than Ariel. Surely Sir Edwin could not be so vile as to offer his only daughter to such a man. Yet Gordstone was wealthy and Ariel's father needed money.

In a transparent attempt to sound reassuring, Sir Edwin said, "You shouldn't listen to backstairs gossip. Lord Gordstone is a wealthy, distinguished man. As his wife, you'll have a position in London's most amusing society."

"I don't want to be part of London society," his daughter retorted. "All I want is to be left alone here at Gardsley. Is that so much to ask?"

"Yes, dammit, it is!" the baronet barked. "A girl with your beauty could be a great asset to me. Instead, you hide here and play with pencils and paints. In spite of your lack of cooperation I've managed to arrange a splendid marriage for you, and by God, you'll behave as a proper daughter and obey me."

Voice quavering but defiant, Ariel said, "I won't! I'll be twenty-one soon. You can't make me."

She was stronger than she looked, that delicate, golden girl. But even as the admiring thought passed through Falconer's mind, he heard the flat, sharp sound of flesh slapping flesh, and Ariel cried out.

Sir Edwin had struck his daughter. Nearly blinded by rage, Falconer put his hand on the knob to the study. He was about to fling the door open when he heard Ariel speak again. "You won't change my mind this way, Papa."

Though he could hear tears in her voice, she did not speak as if she had been seriously injured, so Falconer paused, his hand still on the doorknob. What happened between Sir Edwin and his daughter was none of Falconer's business, and if he intervened, the baronet would surely punish the girl for it later, when her champion was not around.

"Don't worry—I'll find a way that will change your mind," Sir Edwin snapped. "If you don't marry Gordstone, you won't have a roof over your head, for Gardsley will have to be sold. Then what will you do, missy? Go to your room and think about that while I talk with that ugly brute in the drawing room. If I can't persuade him to give me another extension of my loan, I'll be a pauper, and so will you."

Falconer turned and retreated noiselessly to the drawing room at the front of the house. He was standing there, looking out the window, hands linked behind his back, when the baronet entered the room.

"Good day, my lord," Sir Edwin said in a voice of forced amiability. "You've come just in time to hear good news. My daughter is about to contract an advantageous alliance, and I will be able to repay you out of the settlement money. You need only wait a few weeks longer, for the bridegroom is anxious for an early wedding."

Falconer turned and stared at his host. As the silence stretched, Sir Edwin became increasingly nervous. Falconer knew that his stillness disturbed people. Once, behind his back, someone had said that it was like being watched by the angel of death.

When he could bear the silence no longer, the baronet said, "Are you unwell, my lord?"

After another ominous pause, Falconer said, "I've already extended the loan twice. Since Gardsley is your collateral, I can have you evicted from here tomorrow if I choose."

Sir Edwin paled. "But you can't ruin me now, not when a solution is so close at hand! I swear that within a month—"

Falconer cut the other off with a sharp motion of his hand. "I can indeed ruin you, and by God, perhaps I will, for you deserve to be ruined."

Almost weeping, the baronet said, "Is there nothing I can do to persuade you to reconsider? Surely it is the duty of a Christian to show mercy." He stopped a moment, groping for other arguments. "And my daughter . . . will you destroy her life as well? This is the only home she has ever known."

His daughter, whom the villain proposed to sell to Gordstone. Falconer's hands curled into fists when he thought of that golden child defiled by such a loathsome creature. He could not allow the girl to marry Gordstone. *He could not.* But how could he prevent it?

An outrageous idea occurred to him. To even consider it was wrong, blasphemous. Yet by committing a wrong, he could prevent a greater wrong. When he was sure his voice would be even, Falconer said, "There's one thing that would change my mind."

Eagerly Sir Edwin said, "What is it? I swear I'll do anything you wish."

"The girl." Falconer's voice broke. "I'll take the girl."

HALF an hour after Ariel was sent to her bedroom, her father came up after her. She steeled herself when, he entered, praying that she would be strong enough to resist his threats and blandishments. She was still shaken by what he had revealed earlier. Though Sir Edwin had never spent money on his estate or on her, she had always assumed that he had a decent private income or he could not have afforded to live in London. But today he had informed her that his entire fortune was gone and she must marry the despicable Lord Gordstone.

Yet she couldn't possibly marry Gordstone. A fortnight earlier her father had brought the man to Kent for the weekend. In retrospect it was obvious that the real purpose of the visit had been for the old satyr to look Ariel over. Once he had caught her alone and pounced on her like a dog discovering a meaty bone. His foul breath and pawing hands had been disgusting. After escaping his embrace, she had spent the days in distant fields and had barred her door at night until he left.

Without preamble her father said, "You didn't want to marry Gordstone, and now you don't have to. Another candidate for your hand has appeared. Sight unseen, Lord Falconer wants you."

"Lord Falconer?" Ariel gasped, her mind going to the dark, enigmatic figure she had so briefly seen. "How can he want to marry a female he has never even met?"

"Ask him yourself," Sir Edwin replied. "He's in the drawing room and wants to speak with you." Mockingly he stepped back and gestured her to go ahead of him. "It appears that you'll be the salvation of me in spite of yourself. You can't say I haven't done well by you, missy—you have your choice of two wealthy, titled husbands! Most girls would cut off their right arms to be in your position."

Ariel doubted that many girls would sacrifice a limb for the privilege of being forced to choose between a revolting old lecher and a faceless man known as the Black Beast, but she kept her chin high when she walked past her father.

She gave a fleeting thought to her loose hair, but there was no time to tidy herself. In this her father was right; if she behaved like a young lady, sipping tea instead of roaming the fields, she would be prepared for such a momentous interview. Surely if she were dressed properly, she would be less afraid.

She entered the drawing room with her father's heavy hand on her arm. The Black Beast of Belleterre stood in front of the unlit fireplace, tall and dark and so still that the folds of his robe might have been carved from stone. Trying to conceal the trembling of her hands, Ariel linked them together behind her.

"Here's the girl," Sir Edwin boomed. "So excited by the prospect of receiving your addresses that she rushed right down. Ariel, make a curtsy to his lordship."

As she obediently dipped down, the hooded man said, "Leave us, Sir Edwin."

"That wouldn't be proper." Though the baronet's tone was virtuous, his hard glance at his daughter showed that he didn't trust her to say the right thing without him there.

Sharply Falconer repeated, "Leave us! I will speak with Miss Hawthorne privately."

Ariel surreptitiously wiped her damp palms on her skirt as her father reluctantly left the room. In spite of what he had said and done earlier, she watched him go with regret, for he was a known quantity, unlike the frightening man by the fireplace. Even without the hood, he would have been hard to see clearly, for he had chosen to stand in the darkest part of the room.

Falconer turned to her. "Your father told you why I wish to speak with you?"

Not trusting her voice, she nodded.

His voice was the deepest she'd ever heard, but the commanding tone he had used to address her father was gone. In fact he sounded almost shy when he said, "Don't be afraid of me, Ariel. I asked your father to leave so we could speak freely. I know you're in a difficult position and I want to help. Unfortunately the only way I can do so is by marrying you."

Startled, she said, "You know about Gordstone?"

"While I was waiting to speak to your father, I overheard the discussion between you."

Unconsciously Ariel raised one hand to her cheek where a bruise was forming. When she did, the folds of Falconer's robe quivered slightly and the atmosphere changed, as if a thundercloud had entered the room.

Her face colored and she dropped her hand, embarrassed that this stranger had heard what had passed between her and her father. It explained a great deal; apparently the Black Beast of Belleterre was enough of a gentleman that he had been upset by her father's bullying.

But that didn't answer a more basic question. Thinking of those ill-defined orgies, she asked, "Why are you offering marriage to someone you've never met?"

"No young lady should be forced to wed Gordstone. I had not intended ever to marry, so offering you the protection of my name will not deprive me of anything." His tone became intense. "And that is exactly what I am offering—a home and the protection of my name. I will not require . . . marital intimacy of you."

Her blush returned, this time burningly hot. The maids always lowered their voices when they spoke of the marriage bed, or of the nonmarital haystack. Ariel guessed that the subject might be related to orgies, but that told her nothing worthwhile. Haltingly she said, "Do you mean that it will be a . . . a marriage in name only?"

He grasped at the phrase with relief. "Exactly. You told your father that you wished to be left alone at Gardsley. I can't give you that, for it's just a matter of time until he loses the estate, but if you like the country, you'll be happy at Belleterre. You'll be free to draw or paint, or do anything else you desire. I promise not to interfere with you in any way."

Her eyes widened. How could he know about her art and how important it was to her? Vainly she tried to see Falconer's face within the shadows of the cowl, but without success. There was something uncanny about the man; no wonder he had such an alarming reputation. "Your offer is very generous, but what benefit will you derive from such a marriage?"

"The warm glow that comes from knowledge of a deed well done," he said with unmistakable irony. Seeing her expression, he said more quietly, "It will please me if you are happy."

She began twisting a lock of hair that fell over her shoulder. He seemed kind, but what did she know of him? She wasn't sure she trusted disinterested generosity. If she became his wife, she would be his property, to do with as he wished.

Guessing her thoughts, he said, "Are you wondering if you can trust the Black Beast of Belleterre to keep his word?"

So he knew his nickname. This time when she blushed, it was for her fellow man, for inventing such a cruel title. "I'm confused," she said honestly. "An hour ago, I scarcely knew you existed. Now I'm considering an offer of marriage from you. There's something very medieval about it."

He gave an unexpected rumble of laughter. "If we were in the Middle Ages, you would have no choice at all, and the man offering for you wouldn't be wearing a monk's robe."

So he had a sense of humor. For some reason that surprised her, for he was such a dark, melodramatic figure. She sank down into a chair and linked her hands in her lap while she considered her choices. Marrying Gordstone she dismissed instantly; she'd become a beggar first.

Perhaps she could stay at Gardsley for a while, but sadly she accepted that her days at the only home she had ever known were numbered. Even if her father received some unexpected financial windfall, he would soon squander it. He cared only for London society and placed no value on his estate beyond the fact that being Hawthorne of Gardsley gave him position.

She could look for work. Wistfully she thought of Anna McCall, who had been her governess and friend for six years. Anna had been discharged on Ariel's eighteenth birthday because Sir Edwin had not wanted to continue paying her modest salary.

Anna had gone to a fine position with a family near London. Perhaps she could help Ariel find a situation, for the two women still corresponded. But Anna was older and much more clever, while Ariel was young and vague and had no skills except drawing. No one would want her for a governess or teacher.

If she wouldn't marry Gordstone, couldn't stay at Gardsley, and was incapable of supporting herself, she had only one other choice—accepting Falconer's proposal. Of the paths open to her, it was the hardest to evaluate. Yet even if the man was lying and he wanted to use her to slake his mysterious male needs, he couldn't be worse than Gordstone, and if he genuinely wanted no more than to offer her a home, she might be happy at Belleterre.

Lifting her head, Ariel gazed at the dark stranger who waited patiently for her answer. She wished she could see his face; no matter how misshapen his visage was, it would be less alarming than the hood. Nonetheless, she said steadily, "If you truly wish it, Lord Falconer, I will marry you."

Humor again lurking in his voice, he said, "You've decided that I'm the best of a bad lot?"

"Exactly." Her lips curved up involuntarily. "Apparently I inherited some of my father's gambling blood."

"Very well then, Ariel," he said, his deep voice making music of her name. "We shall marry. I guarantee that your life at Belleterre will be no worse than your life here, and if it is within my power, I shall see that it is better."

She could hardly ask fairer than that. Nonetheless, that night in her bed, she cried herself to sleep.

THEY were married three and a half weeks later, after the crying of the banns. Ariel's father had insisted that she must have a fashionable wedding gown, and he had taken her to a London dressmaker.

As always, she had hated the noise and the crowds of people. Even more, she hated the white silk gown, with its bustle and train and elaborate flounces that made her feel like an overdecorated cake. Most of all, she had hated the corset and steel hoops she must wear to make the dress fit properly.

Just before they left the dressmaker's salon, she heard Sir Edwin tell the proprietor to send the bill to Lord Falconer of Belleterre. So her father would not spend his own money even for his daughter's wedding gown. Any sentimental regrets she had about leaving her home vanished then.

She slept badly during the weeks between her betrothal and her marriage, and she went to the church on her wedding day with dark circles under her eyes. She wouldn't have been surprised if the groom had taken one look at her and changed his mind, but he didn't. She suspected that he was as nervous as she, though she wasn't sure how she knew that when he was completely invisible under his cowled robe.

For a moment she had the hysterical thought that she might not be marrying Lord Falconer, for anyone could hide under a robe. She reminded herself sharply that his face might be hidden, but his height and smooth, powerful movements were proof of his identity.

It was a very small wedding, with only Ariel and her father, the vicar and his wife, and an elderly man who stood up with Lord Falconer. Based on a faint but unmistakable scent, Ariel surmised the elderly man was a groom. Ariel had invited Anna McCall, but her friend had been unable to come, for the interesting reason that she herself was getting married the same day.

Though the ceremony went quickly, there were several surprises—the first when the vicar referred to the bridegroom as "James Philip." Ariel knew that his family name was Markland, but with a small jolt she realized that she hadn't known his given name. He was a stranger, a complete stranger, and she had agreed to marry him without knowing either his name or what he looked like. She glanced up at his face, but the church was old and shadowy, and the cowl effectively prevented her from seeing anything even though she stood right next to him.

The service progressed. The next surprise came when Falconer lifted her icy hand so that he could slide the ring on her finger. He used both hands to hold hers, and she found his warm touch comforting.

Then she glanced down. She hadn't seen his hands closely before, for he tended to hold them so they were not readily visible. Now she saw that his left hand was so heavily scarred that the two smallest fingers must be almost useless. She could not help but stare.

He saw her reaction and dropped his hands as soon as the ring was on her finger. The sleeve of his robe fell over his wrist, and once more the damage was invisible.

She wanted to tell him that her reaction had been simple surprise, not repulsion, but she couldn't do that now, in the middle of the wedding ceremony. She bit her lip as the vicar concluded the ritual, declared them man and wife, and said with strained joviality that it was time to kiss the bride. Ariel had wondered what would happen at this point. Would her new husband abstain, or would he actually kiss her and she might learn something of what he looked like?

Once again, he surprised her by lifting her right hand and kissing it, very gently. His lips were warm and smooth and firm, just the way lips should be. She wanted to weep, and didn't know why.

They turned and left the church, married. No wedding breakfast had been planned, for Ariel had guessed that Lord Falconer would be uncomfortable at such an event. Nor would there be a honeymoon; they would go directly to Belleterre where her possessions should have already been delivered.

Just before stepping outside, she saw Falconer give an envelope to her father, but she said nothing until she and her new husband were alone in their carriage. As she disposed her billowing skirts, she asked, "How much did it cost you to buy me?"

He shifted uneasily on the leather seat, but didn't avoid the question. "I canceled a loan of ten thousand pounds and gave your father ten thousand pounds beyond that. He's supposed to use it to settle other debts, though I doubt that he will."

She inhaled the spicy sweet scent of her bouquet of white rosebuds and pale pink carnations. "That's a very high price to pay for a good deed. You could have endowed another hospital for twenty thousand pounds."

"I suppose so," he said uncomfortably, "but I consider it money well spent."

Ariel was looking straight ahead, her eyes on the velvet lining of the carriage. He took advantage of that to study her profile again, this time from much closer than on the occasion when he'd first seen her. But today she wasn't that carefree girl under the apple tree. Beneath the veil her flaxen hair was drawn up in a complicated style of coils and ringlets, and her gown made her look terrifyingly fashionable.

Her beauty and sophistication alarmed him. Where had he ever found the audacity to offer for such a paragon? It was tragic that because of her father's fecklessness, she was now tied to a man wholly unworthy of her. "A pity that you never had a London Season. There you could have found a husband to your taste instead of being forced to choose between two unpalatable alternatives."

To his surprise she smiled humorlessly. "I did go to London for a Season when I was eighteen."

He frowned. "Then why aren't you married? You must have been a stunning success."

She began plucking the ribbons that trailed from her bouquet. "Oh, yes, I was a success—proclaimed a Beauty, in fact. And there were several proposals of marriage. Fortunately they were improperly made to me rather than my father, so I was able to decline without him learning about them."

"Why did you refuse? Were they all men like Gordstone?"

She twined a ribbon around one slender figure. "None were so dreadful as he, but neither did they want to marry *me*. They just wanted to win the latest Beauty. And win is the right word. Courtship was a sport, and I was one of the Season's best trophies. None of the men who proposed marriage knew anything about me, or cared about the things I cared about." She glanced up at him, her blue eyes stark. "To be a Beauty is to be a thing, not a person. Perhaps you, more than most men, can understand that."

Her words struck him with the impact of a blow. For the first time he realized just how much more she was than the beautiful child he had seen on the hillside. After taking a deep, slow breath, he said, "Yes, I understand what it is to be a thing, not a person. I don't blame you for resenting that. But even so, you would have been better off married to one of those men, someone who would have given you a real marriage and a position in society."

"I'm not sure I would have been better off. I was telling my father the truth when I said that I preferred a quiet life in the country. He can't bear quiet; I suppose that's one reason we've never understood each very well." Visibly shaking off her mood, she said, "I don't believe I've properly thanked you for saving me from Gordstone. I really do appreciate what you've done." After a slight hesitation, she added, "James."

Startled, he said, "No one calls me that."

"Would you rather I didn't?"

"No, please, suit yourself," he said, his voice constricted. He was deeply moved to hear her use his name; no woman had done so since his mother had died.

Thinking of his mother's death, he dropped his left hand from sight behind his thigh. Ariel had viewed the scars with distaste when he had put the ring on her finger; that was to be expected, since she was without flaw herself. But she had the good manners of natural refinement and had done her best not to show her revulsion.

For the rest of the journey to Belleterre neither of them spoke, but the silence was less awkward than he had expected. When the carriage pulled up in front of his home, he helped her out, then said lightly, as if the matter was unimportant, "After this moment, you need never endure my touch again."

He started to remove his right hand from hers, but she clung to it. Softly, her great blue eyes staring up at him, she said, "James, you mustn't think that you repel me. We are almost strangers, but you have been kind to me, and now we are married. Surely we will have some kind of relationship with each other. I hope it will not be a strained one."

He pulled his hand from her clasp, knowing that if he felt the touch of her slim fingers any longer, he would want to do more than just hold her hand. "It won't be strained. In fact, you will scarcely see me, except by chance around the estate."

She frowned. "It sounds like a very lonely life. Can't we at least be friends, perhaps sometimes keep each other company?"

It would be very hard to be friends with her, but obediently he said, "If that is your wish. How much company do you want?"

She bit her lower lip, looking enchantingly earnest. "Perhaps . . . perhaps we might dine together every night. If you don't mind?"

"No, I won't mind." He reminded himself that her request stemmed from the basic need for human interaction rather than any special liking for him, but even so, joy swirled through him at the knowledge that she had actually requested his company on a regular basis.

She took his arm as they began walking up the steps, surprising him again. She was a brave child, and an honorable one, willing to do her duty. Solemnly he promised himself that he would not take advantage of that willingness.

The servants were lined up inside the house to meet the new mistress. Ariel knew that she would never remember all the names until she knew them better, but she was impressed by the general air of well-being. If orgies were held at Belleterre, they didn't seem to distress the servants.

Nonetheless, she sensed deep reserve among them, as if they were doubtful about her. She supposed it was only natural for them to be wary about a new mistress. Once they discovered that she didn't intend to make sweeping changes, they would relax.

Introductions over, Falconer turned her over to the housekeeper to be shown to her rooms. Mrs. Wilcox was remote but polite as she took her new mistress upstairs. As she passed through room and halls, Ariel observed that her new home was furnished in excellent, if rather austere, taste. It was also well kept, with floors and furniture gleaming with wax and not a speck of dust anywhere.

On reaching their destination, the housekeeper opened the door and said, "Your belongings were delivered and the maids have unpacked them, your ladyship. If there is anything that you want, or if you wish to make changes, you have only to ask."

Ariel's first impression was that she had stepped into a garden, for every available surface was covered with vases of welcoming flowers. She drifted through the scented rooms, awed by the size and luxury of her accommodations. Not only was there a well-furnished bedroom and sitting room, but another large chamber that was almost empty.

It took a moment for her to realize that the room was a studio, for there was a north light and an easel in the corner. Her eyes stung. Had he known what this would mean to her? He must have guessed; though he was a stranger, he understood her better than her own father had.

Behind her a soft Kentish voice said, "I'm Fanny, your ladyship, and I'm to be your personal maid. Do you wish to take off your gown and rest before dinner?"

Gratefully Ariel accepted the girl's suggestion, for the stress of the day had left her exhausted. She slept well and woke refreshed. Fanny appeared again and helped her dress. In one of the surprises that was starting to become commonplace, Ariel discovered an armoire full of new clothing. Apparently the dressmaker in London had been commissioned to make her a whole wardrobe as well as the wedding gown.

Her husband had judged her taste well, for most of the dresses were loosely cut tea gowns. They would be perfect for daytime in the country, particularly for painting and walking. The colors chosen were clear, delicate pastels that suited her fair hair and complexion. Ariel was beginning to suspect that the Black Beast had the eye of an artist.

When she went down to dinner, she found her husband waiting in the morning room. He greeted her gravely and inquired if everything was to her taste. She assured him that her rooms were lovely, especially the studio. Then they went together into the family dining room. He tensed when she took his arm, and she wondered if he found her touch distasteful.

The family dining room was still very large, and one end of the room was quite dark even though the summer sun had not yet set. Ariel had thought that when her husband ate he might put his hood back, but he didn't. Since his chair was in the dark end of the room and she was a dozen feet away, at the far end of the polished table, she saw nothing of his face.

The dinner was a quiet one until the end, when bowls of fruit had been served. After the footman had left the room, Ariel said, "Do you always sit or stand in the shadows?"

He paused in the act of peeling a peach. "Always."

"Is that necessary?"

"To me it is." Slowly he began slicing away a spiral of peach skin, his long fingers deft. In the shadows it was impossible to see the scars on his left hand. "I have said that you can do whatever you wish at Belleterre. In return, Ariel, I ask that you respect my wishes in this matter."

She bit her lip. "Of course, James."

The rest of the meal passed in silence. When they were done, they rose and went into the hall. Ariel had thought that perhaps they would sit together after dinner, but instead her husband said, "Good night, my dear. If you wish to read, the library is through that door on the left. The selection of books is wide, and of course you are welcome to add anything you want to the collection."

She realized that he had been quite serious when he had said they would see little of each other. Well, she had wanted a quiet life, and it appeared that her wish would be granted. She was just saying good night when a scrabble of claws sounded on the polished marble floor.

Ariel looked up to see a dog trotting eagerly down the hall. It was the ugliest dog she'd ever seen, rawboned and splotchy and of very dubious parentage. But its shaggy face glowed with canine bliss as it reached its master, then reared up and balanced on its haunches.

Falconer scratched the dog's head, and a pink tongue lolled out of its panting mouth. "Did you come to meet your new mistress, Cerberus?"

Amused at the name, Ariel said, "Cerberus has no interest in me. Clearly it's you he adores with his whole canine heart."

Falconer's robe quivered, as if in a slight breeze. "It doesn't take much to win a dog's heart."

Ariel was beginning to realize that she could read the movements of the fabric to determine her husband's moods; very useful, since his face was concealed. Though she was new to the skill of robe reading, she guessed that he was uncomfortable with her comment about being adored. Poor man, did he feel unworthy of even a dog's devotion?

With sudden ferocity, she wanted to know more about the stranger she had married. She wanted to know what had made him what he was. In time, surely, she would. After all, they were living under the same roof.

From the corner of her eye, Ariel caught more motion. Turning her head, she saw a black-and-white cat entering the hall. It moved very strangely, and she realized that it was missing one foreleg. Still, it seemed to have no trouble getting around. Ariel knelt and rubbed her fingers together, hoping the creature would come to her.

"That's Tripod," Falconer said. "Her leg was accidentally cut off by a scythe."

After a disdainful look at Cerberus, the cat hopped over to Ariel and rubbed against her outstretched fingers. She smiled. "Thank you for condescending to meet me, Tripod."

Jealously the dog trotted over to ask for some attention. As Ariel ruffled the droopy ears, she murmured, "What a funny-looking fellow you are. You remind me of a picture of a musk ox that I once saw."

In a low voice her husband said, "Any ugly creature is assured of a home here."

Ariel froze for a moment, feeling that she had committed some dreadful faux pas. Then she rose to her feet and said calmly, "You are a very kind man, James, to take in waifs and strays. After all, I am one of them. Good night."

Then she went upstairs to the charming rooms where she would spend her wedding night alone.

THOUGH he had seen her with his own eyes, conversed with her over dinner, Falconer had trouble believing that she was under his own roof. In his mind he never used the name Ariel; to him his wife was *she,* as if she were the only woman in the world.

What he had not expected was how tormenting her presence would be. It had been ten years since he had lain with a woman, and he had become reasonably comfortable with his monkish life. But no more; though he still wore the robes of a monk, he ached with yearning. He wanted to touch his wife's blossom-smooth skin, bury his hands in her silky hair, inhale her sweet female scent. He wanted more than that, though he would not allow himself to put words to his base thoughts.

After she had gone to bed, he went outside and walked from one end of Belleterre to the other as dusk became night. Cerberus trotted obediently behind, ready to defend his master from the lethal attacks of rabbits and pheasants.

As soon as it was dark enough, Falconer pushed back his hood, welcoming the cool night air, for he burned. He despised himself for his body's weakness, for it was unthinkable that a monster such as he could lie with the angel he had married. At least, unlike Gordstone, he knew that he was a monster. But in his heart he was no better than the other man, for he could not stop himself from desiring her.

It was very late when he returned to the house. To his surprise, when he went upstairs a light showed under his wife's bedroom door. Was she also having trouble sleeping? Perhaps he should go and talk with her, reassure her about her new life.

Though he knew he was lying to himself about his motives, he literally could not prevent himself from going down the hall and tapping on her door. When there was no answer, he turned the knob and eased the door open, then crossed the room to the bed.

She had fallen asleep while reading, and she lay with her head turned to one side, her pale blond hair spilling luxuriantly over the pillow. She wore a delicately tucked and laced nightgown, and she was the most beautiful being he had ever seen.

He picked up the book that she had laid on the coverlet. It was one of his own volumes of William Blake, the mystical poet and artist. A good choice for a girl who was also an artist. He set the volume on the table by a vase of roses, turned out the lamp, and ordered himself to leave the room.

But he allowed himself one last look. The bedroom curtains hadn't been drawn, and in the moonlight she was a figure spun of ivory and silver. He drank in the sight, knowing that he could never permit himself to do this again, for he could not trust himself so close to her.

When he had memorized her image well enough to last a lifetime, he turned to go. He was halfway to the door when his resolve broke and he went back again. Against his will his hand lifted, began reaching out to her.

With a violence that was all the more intense for being subdued, he turned to the vase of roses and gripped the stems with his left hand. Ignoring the thorns stabbing into his fingers, he stripped the blossoms away with his right hand. Then he slowly scattered the fragile scarlet petals over her like a pagan worshiping his goddess. They looked like black velvet as they drifted down the moonbeams.

One petal touched her cheek and slid over the soft curve, coming to rest on her throat, exactly the way he longed to touch her. As the intoxicating scent of roses filled the air around him, more petals spangled her gilt hair and delicate muslin gown, rising and falling with the slow rhythm of her breath.

When his hand was emptied, he took a shuddering breath. Then he turned and left her room forever.

Autumn

Ariel added a little more yellow paint to the mixture, stroked a brushful across her test paper, then critically examined the result. Yes, that should do for the base shade of the leaves, which were at the height of their autumn color. In the next two hours, she made several watercolor sketches of the woods, more interested in creating an impression of the vibrant scene than in drawing an exact copy. As James said, now that photographers were able to reproduce precise images, artists had more freedom to experiment, to be more abstract.

The work absorbed her entire attention, for watercolor was in many ways the most difficult and volatile medium. When she finally had a painting that satisfied her, she began packing her equipment into the special saddlebags that one of the Belleterre grooms had made to carry her supplies around the estate. The glade was deeply peaceful. Above her head tall, tall elm trees rustled in the wind like a sky-borne river.

It had not taken long for her life to fall into an easy routine. As her husband had promised, she had quiet, freedom, and anything else that money could buy. The size of the allowance he gave her was staggering, and it had been exciting to order the finest papers and canvases, the most expensive brushes and pigments, and never have to consider the cost.

It also proved educational to have such wealth at her disposal. She found that after she had bought her art supplies, there was little else to spend the money on. She scarcely even needed to buy books, for the Belleterre library was the finest she had ever seen. Nor did she have to buy clothing, for she had the wardrobe her husband had given her when they married.

He had also given her an exquisite, beautifully mannered gray mare. Foxglove was the prettiest horse on the estate, for the rest of the beasts were an odd-looking lot. Though quite capable of doing their jobs, they tended to have knobby knees, lop-ears, and coats that were rough even after the most thorough grooming. The pairs and teams didn't match at all. She suspected that, like Cerberus and Tripod, the horses had been given a home because they hadn't been appreciated by a world that valued appearance over capability.

Ariel found the mismatched horses endearing and almost resented the fact that her husband had bought Foxglove for her. Did he think she was incapable of appreciating anything that wasn't perfect? Apparently. Yet because his intention had been to please her, she could hardly complain.

Yes, James had given her exactly the life of peace and freedom that he had promised. She could draw and paint to her heart's content, for she no longer had to spend most of her time trying vainly to oversee her father's neglected estate. Her work was improving, and some of the credit for that must go to her husband, for they often discussed art over dinner. His knowledge of painting was remarkable and his insights very helpful, for her abilities were more intuitive than analytical.

Yet instead of mounting to ride back to the house, Ariel put her arms around Foxglove's neck and buried her face against the mare's glossy, horse-scented hide. She was a very lucky young woman. That being the case, why was she so miserable?

"Oh, Foxy," she said in a choked voice. "I'm so lonely—lonelier than I've ever been in my life. Sometimes it seems as if you're my only friend." Though it sounded perilously like self-pity, the statement was true. If she hadn't asked that her husband dine with her, days on end would have passed without her seeing him.

She looked forward all day to those meals, for he was the pleasantest of companions, well-read and amusing, able to discuss any subject. In spite of her youth and frequent ignorance, he was never rude or disdainful of her opinion. In fact, the discussions were making her much more knowledgeable, and she enjoyed them enormously.

Yet no matter how pleasant the meal, as soon as it was over James would bid her a polite good night and withdraw. She would not see him again until the next evening, except perhaps by chance in the distance as he rode about the estate.

The Belleterre servants were a surprisingly reserved group. Ariel had been on easy terms with everyone at Gardsley, but Falconer's people were as distant now as they had been the day she arrived, four months earlier. The one exception was Patterson, the old, half-blind groom who had been her husband's best man at the wedding. He at least was always friendly, though not very forthcoming. Patterson, Foxglove, Cerberus, and Tripod were almost the whole of Ariel's social life. Even her friend Anna hadn't written in months, presumably because she was absorbed in her new family.

With a sigh Ariel mounted and turned Foxglove toward home. She had always been able to live quite happily in her own world. She had never been lonely until she came to Belleterre. Now she reckoned it a good night when Tripod deigned to sleep on her bed.

She had changed, and the blame could be laid at her husband's door. Solitude was no longer enough because she loved being with him—loved hearing his deep, kind voice, loved laughing at his dry sense of humor. She would have been happy to trail around after him like Cerberus. But she couldn't, for she knew James wouldn't like that. She was just a young and not very interesting female. Though he was willing to share one meal a day with her, more of her company would probably bore him to tears. She didn't dare jeopardize what she had by asking for more than he was willing to give.

As she reined in Foxglove in front of the stables, Patterson ambled out to help her dismount. When her feet were safely on the ground, Ariel impulsively asked a question inspired by her earlier thoughts. "Patterson, why are all of the servants so reserved with me? Is it something I've done?"

The old man paused in the act of unpacking her painting materials. "No, milady. Everyone considers you very proper."

"Then why do I feel as if I'm being judged and found wanting?" Ariel said, then immediately felt foolish.

The groom took her words in good part. " 'Tisn't that, milady. You're much admired," he said. " 'Tis just that folks are afraid you might hurt the master."

She stared at him. "Hurt him? Why would I do that?" A horrible thought occurred to her. "Surely no one thinks I would poison him so that I could be a wealthy widow!"

"Not that, my lady," he said quickly. " 'Tisn't that sort of hurt that folks are worried about." He heaved the saddlebags from the mare. Without looking at Ariel, he said, "Don't need a knife or gun or poison to break a man's heart."

"His lordship scarcely knows I'm alive," she said, unable to believe the implication. "I'm just one more unfortunate creature that he brought to Belleterre because I needed a home."

"Nay, milady. You're not like any of the others." In spite of the cloudiness of his eyes, Patterson's gaze seemed to bore right through her. "I've known that boy most of his life, and he never brought home anyone like you."

Ariel's mind unaccountably went to the morning after her wedding. There had been blood red rose petals all over the bed when she woke. She had been surprised and a little uneasy, until she decided that some of the flowers had fallen apart and been blown by the wind. But they had fallen very strangely if it was the wind. She had a mental image of James scattering her with rose petals, and an odd, deep shiver went through her.

Was it possible that he cared for her, as a man cared for a woman? She rejected the idea. He didn't want her for a wife; from all appearances, his nature was as monkish as his clothing.

As she hesitated, caught in her thoughts, Patterson said, "I think he's in the aviary, milady. If you like, I can take your pictures up to the house."

As a hint, there was nothing subtle about it. "Please do that, Patterson. And thank you."

Ariel's steps were slow as she walked through the gardens to the aviary. If she understood the old groom correctly, James did care about her, at least enough that she had the potential to hurt him. Not that she would ever do so, but the opposite side of that potential was that she might be capable of making him happy. She often felt deep sadness radiating from her husband, and the possibility that she might be able to reduce that was tantalizing.

Her steps became even slower when she came within sight of the aviary. It was an enormous enclosure made of elaborately molded, white-painted cast iron. Not only was it large enough to include several small trees and a little pool, but there was a shed where the birds could shelter during bad weather.

The aviary was home to dozens of birds, most of them foreign species that Ariel didn't recognize. She often came by to watch them fly and chatter and play. In particular she enjoyed coaxing the large green parrot into conversation. Several times she had done sketches of the aviary's residents, trying to capture the quick, bright movements.

Today her gaze went immediately to her husband, who was inside the enclosure. Instead of his usual calf-length robe, he was garbed in a dark coat and trousers such as any gentleman might wear for a day's estate management. However, his head and shoulders were swathed in a cowled hood that concealed his face as effectively as the longer robe.

Ariel had occasionally seen him dressed this way, but always in the distance. Close up, he was a fine figure of a man, tall and strong and masculine. His black coat displayed the breadth of his shoulders. His movements fascinated her—the turn of his powerful wrist when he stretched out his hand so that a small brown bird could jump onto it, his gentleness as he stroked the small creature's head with one forefinger, his warm chuckle when the parrot swooped down and landed on his shoulder with a great thrashing of wings.

The birds loved him, not caring what his face was like. The same was true of all the creatures who lived at Belleterre, and all the humans, too, including Ariel.

Or perhaps what she felt for her husband wasn't quite love, but it could be, if given a chance. She yearned for his company, for his touch. In her limited life she had never known anyone like him—not just for the obvious reason of how he dressed, but for his kindness and knowledge. It no longer mattered that she didn't know what he looked like; she was so accustomed to his hood that it had in effect become his face.

But how could an ignorant young woman tell a mature, educated man that she yearned to be more to him? Praying that inspiration would come,

Ariel unlatched the door and entered the aviary. Cerberus, who had been lying outside, lurched to his feet and tried to enter with her, but she firmly held him back.

As the door clinked shut behind her, James turned. Surprise in his voice, he said, "I thought you were painting, Ariel."

"I was, but the light changed, so I decided to stop after I did a picture that I was somewhat satisfied with."

A smile in his voice, he said, "Is an artist ever wholly satisfied with her own work?"

She smiled ruefully. "I doubt it. I know that I never am."

While she tried to think what to say next, the parrot flew to a branch and crooned, "Ar-r-riel. Ar-r-riel."

Surprised, she said, "When did he learn that?"

James shrugged. "Just now, I imagine. He's a contrary creature. Once I spent hours unsuccessfully trying to teach him to say 'God save the Queen.' The only thing he learned that day was the phrase 'Deuce take it,' which I said just before I gave up in exasperation."

The bird obligingly squawked, "Devil take it! Devil take it!"

Ariel laughed. "Are you sure that 'deuce take it' is what he learned that day?"

Her husband joined her laughter. "It appears that my bad language has been exposed. Sorry."

"James . . ." Not sure how to say what she wanted, she took several steps toward her husband.

To her dismay, he moved away. "Have you ever seen one of these parakeets close up?" He laid a hand on a branch and a bird hopped on. "Lovely little creatures." It was neatly done, as if he was not retreating but had merely seen something that caught his attention.

Ariel felt tears stinging in her eyes. Patterson must be wrong; if James cared for her in a special way, he would not flee whenever she approached. She was struggling to maintain her composure when the blue-breasted parakeet suddenly skipped up her husband's arm and disappeared into the folds of the hood where it wrapped around his throat.

For Ariel it was the last straw. Even that silly little bird, which wouldn't make two bites for Tripod, was permitted to get closer to James than she was. Her loneliness and yearning welled up, and with them her tears. Humiliated, she turned to leave the aviary, wanting to get away before her husband noticed.

But he noticed everything. "Ariel, what's wrong?"

She shook her head and fumbled with the door, but the latch on this side was stiff. As she struggled with it, her husband came up behind her and hesitantly touched her elbow. "Has your father tried to reach you, or upset you in some way?"

It was the most natural thing in the world for her to turn to him, and for him to put his arms around her. She was crying harder than she ever had in her life, even when her mother died. But dear God, how wonderful it felt to be in his embrace! He was so strong, so warm, so safe.

Tall as well—the top of her head didn't quite reach his chin, which put his shoulder at a convenient height. Trying to stop her tears, she gulped for breath, pressing her face into the smooth dark wool of his coat.

"Ariel, my dear girl," he said, rocking her a little. "Is there anything I can do? Or . . . or are you crying because you're married to me?"

"Oh, no, no, that's not the problem." She slipped her arms around his waist, wanting to be as close as she could. "It's just . . . I'm so lonely here. Would it be possible for us to spend more time together? Perhaps in the evenings, after dinner. I won't disturb you if you want to work or read, but I'd like to be with you."

It was as close as she could come to putting her heart in his hands. He didn't answer for a long time, so long that she thought she might suffocate because she couldn't seem to breathe normally. One hand stroked down her back, slowly, as if he were gentling a horse. Finally he said, "Of course we could, if that's what you want."

"But will you mind?" she asked, needing to know if he was willing or simply indulging.

She felt a faint brush against her hair, from his hand or perhaps his lips. "No, I won't mind," he said softly. "It will be my pleasure."

She was so happy that her tears began to flow again. It gave her an excuse to stay just where she was, in his arms. She would never tire of his embrace, for she felt as if she had come home. Besides happiness, she felt deeper stirrings that she didn't recognize. They frightened her a little, but at the same time she knew that she wanted to explore them further, for they had something to do with James.

She became aware how much tension there was in her husband. Reluctantly she stepped away, for she didn't want to wear out her welcome. "It's getting late." Suddenly aware of the untidiness of her hair and the stains on her painting clothes, she said, "I must go and change for dinner."

"This evening, if you like, we can sit in the library," he said hesitantly. "I've some letters to write, but if you don't think you'll be bored . . ."

"I won't be." She was almost embarrassed at the transparent happiness in her voice. "I'll see you at dinner." This evening would be the first step, and eventually there would be others. She wasn't sure exactly where the path would lead, but she knew that it was one she must follow.

THE meal was the most lighthearted they had yet shared. Falconer wondered if his wife was looking forward to spending the evening together as much as he was, then decided that was impossible. Still, she was happier than he had ever seen her.

Though he hadn't realized until now, when the difference was obvious, she had been growing increasingly quiet, her characteristic glow muted. He reminded himself that even self-contained young women who enjoyed solitude needed some companionship, and for Ariel, he was what was available. He would not take her desire to see more of him too personally—but that didn't mean that he couldn't enjoy it.

They went into the library for coffee, still talking, tangible warmth between them. Falconer was careful not to strain that fragile web of feeling, for he wanted it to grow stronger.

She took a chair and gracefully poured coffee from a silver pot. Garbed in a blue silk gown, she looked especially lovely tonight, her delicate coloring as fresh as spring flowers. As she handed him his cup, she said, "Today I got a letter from my former governess, Anna. Have I ever told you about her?"

When he answered in the negative, Ariel continued, "After leaving Gardsley, she found a position teaching the two daughters of a widower who lives in Hampstead, just north of London."

He stirred milk into his coffee. "Is the man intellectual or artistic, like so many of those who live in Hampstead?"

"So he is. Mr. Talbott designs fabrics and furniture for industrial manufacture and is quite successful with it. He also has the good sense to appreciate Anna. In fact, they married on the same day we did. They went to Italy for a honeymoon and have only just returned. Anna apologized for not writing but said that she's been so busy and happy that she didn't quite realize how much time had gone by. She has invited us to visit her in Hampstead—the house is very large." Ariel looked shyly over her coffee cup. "Would you be willing to do that sometime? You'll like Anna, and Mr. Talbott sounds like a wonderful man."

Falconer frowned, but he didn't want to spoil the mood of the evening. "Perhaps someday."

Ariel regarded him thoughtfully, then changed the subject. They talked of other things until the coffee was gone. Then she stood. Falconer feared that she had changed her mind and was going to go upstairs until she said, "I'll read while you do your letter writing." She gave him a bright, slightly nervous smile. "I don't want to distract you from your work."

When she was this close, it was hard to think of letters, but obediently he went to his desk and started writing. He had a large and varied correspondence, for letters were a way to be involved with people without having to meet them face-to-face.

Cerberus was pleasantly befuddled by having them both in the room and wandered back and forth, flopping first by Falconer, then ambling to the chair where Ariel was reading. Tripod was lazier and simply curled up on the desk on top of a pile of notepaper. Falconer could not remember when he had been happier. The library, with its deep, leather-upholstered furniture, had always been his favorite room, and having Ariel's presence made paradise itself seem inferior.

But the evening became even better. Hearing a sound beside him, he absently put his left hand down to ruffle the dog's ears. Instead, he touched silken hair. Glancing down, he saw his wife curled up against his chair. "Ariel?" he said, startled.

She glanced up, both teasing and apologetic. "Cerberus enjoys having his head scratched, so I thought I'd try it." Her smile faded. "I'm sorry, I shouldn't have disturbed you."

"No need to apologize." He turned his head away so that she couldn't see under the cowl. "I'm ready for a break." As if they had a life of their own, his fingers twined through her shining tresses. He had thought his scarred fingers had little sensation, but now he would swear that he could feel each gossamer strand separately.

With a soft, pleased sigh she relaxed against the side of his chair. For perhaps a quarter of an hour they stayed like that while he stroked her head, slender neck, and delicate ears. As he did, joy bubbled through him like a fountain of light, and his mind rang with the words of Elizabeth Barrett Browning's famous sonnet. *How do I love thee? Let me count the ways. . . .*

For he did love this exquisite girl who was his wife. On their wedding day, when she had expressed her dislike of being courted solely for her beauty, he had felt ashamed, for he could not help but be bewitched by her loveliness. Yet even that first moment, when the sight of her had been like an arrow in his heart, he had sensed that her beauty was even more of the spirit than of the body.

The idyll ended when Tripod, deciding that she needed attention, jumped down into Ariel's lap. Ariel laughed and straightened up. Falconer started to withdraw his hand, but before he could, she caught his fingers. Then she very deliberately laid her cheek against the back of his hand.

Her skin was porcelain smooth against the coarse scars that crippled his two smallest fingers and made the rest of his hand hideous. Yet she did not flinch. He began to tremble as waves of sensation pulsed through him, beginning in his fingers and spreading until every cell of his body vibrated. For the first time he wondered if it might be possible for them to have a real marriage. She did not seem repulsed by the scars on his hand; was there a chance that she might be able to tolerate the rest of him?

The thought was as frightening as it was exhilarating. His emotions too chaotic to control, he got to his feet, then raised her to hers. Hoarsely he said, "It's time for bed. But perhaps in the morning, you might join me for a ride?"

Her smile was breathtaking. "I'd like that."

He turned out the lights, then escorted her upstairs to her room, the animals trailing along behind. At her door she turned to him. "Good night, James. Sleep well."

In the faint light of the hall, she looked eager and accessible, her lips slightly parted, her hair delectably disheveled from his earlier petting. Instinct told him that she would welcome a kiss, and perhaps more. But she was so beautiful that he couldn't bring himself to touch her.

"Good night, Ariel." He turned and walked away, feeling so brittle that a touch might shatter him. The idea that they might build a real marriage was too new, too frightening, to act on. He might be misinterpreting her willingness. Or, unspeakable thought, she might believe herself willing but change her mind when she saw him. One thing he knew: if she rejected him after he had begun to hope, he would be unable to endure it.

ARIEL went to bed in a state of jubilation. He had been happy to have her with him, she knew it. He hadn't even minded when she had foolishly succumbed to her desire to come closer. Best of all, he wanted her to ride with him. Perhaps they might spend all day together. And perhaps even the night . . . ?

The idea filled her with blushing excitement. She was unclear what happened in a marriage bed, but knew that holding and kissing were involved. She definitely liked those things; she still tingled from the gentle fire of his touch.

If intimacy began with a kiss, in what exciting place might it end?

Her fevered emotions made it impossible for her to sleep. Finally her tossing and turning elicited a growl of protest from Tripod, who needed her twenty hours of sleep every day. Ariel surrendered and got out of bed. As she lit the lamp on her desk, she decided that the best use of her high spirits was to answer Anna's letter, for she was now in the same elevated mood that her friend had been.

Her stationery drawer contained only two sheets of notepaper, which wouldn't be enough. She must get more from the library. Humming softly, she donned her robe, then took the lamp and went downstairs. The shifting shadows made her think of ghosts, but if there were any about, they would surely be benevolent ones. She must ask James about Belleterre's ghosts; any building so old must have at least three or four.

With ghosts on her mind Ariel opened the library door, then blinked with surprise. In the far corner of the room, framed by dark shelves of books, floated an object that looked horribly like a skull. She gave a sharp, shocked cry.

A flurry of sounds and movements occurred, too quick and confusing for Ariel to follow. The object whirled away, accompanied by a soft, anguished exclamation. Almost simultaneously there came a thump, a swish of fabric, then a resounding slam of the door at the far end of the library.

Shaken and alone, Ariel knew with a certainty beyond reason that something catastrophic had just occurred. She raggedly expelled the breath she had been holding, then walked to the far corner of the room. A low lamp burned on a table; that was how she had seen . . . whatever it was that she had seen. A book lay open on the floor, and she knelt to pick it up—Elizabeth Barrett Browning's *Sonnets from the Portuguese*.

Dear God, the other occupant of the library must have been James with his hood down. She tried to recall the fleeting image that had met her eyes when she had entered the room, but try as she might, she could remember no details. The floating object had been the right height for his head; the skull-like whiteness must have been his hair, pale blond like hers, or perhaps prematurely white. Covered by his dark robe, the rest of his body had been invisible in the dark, which had made the sight of him so uncanny.

With sick horror she guessed that he had dropped the book and fled because of her shocked exclamation. She leaned dizzily against the bookcase, the volume of poetry clutched to her chest. He must have thought she was reacting to his appearance with disgust.

But she hadn't even really seen him! She had simply had ghosts on the mind, then been disconcerted when she saw something ghostly. But to James, who was so profoundly ashamed of his appearance, it must have seemed as if she had found him repulsive. He would not have fled like that, without a word, if he hadn't been deeply wounded.

Anguished, she realized that this was what the servants had feared. She had the power to hurt her husband, and unintentionally she had done so. He must ache all the more because they had been starting to draw closer together; certainly that fact magnified her own pain.

Determined to explain to him that it had all been a ghastly mistake, she turned out the light he had left, then lifted her own lamp and went upstairs to his rooms. She hesitated outside the door, for she had never been inside and to enter uninvited was an invasion of the privacy that he wrapped around himself as securely as his cowl. But she couldn't allow the misunderstanding to go uncorrected. The pain in her heart was well-nigh unbearable, and he must hurt even more.

She turned the knob to his sitting room, and the door swung smoothly inward, but there was no one inside. Swiftly she searched the sitting room and the bedroom next door. Nothing but solid, masculine furniture and richly colored fabrics. She opened the last door and found herself in his dressing room, but he was not there, either. She was about to leave when her eye was caught by a small, framed picture.

She was startled to see that it was one of her own drawings, but not one she had done since coming to Belleterre. Frowning, she examined it more closely. It was a sketch of her favorite oak tree at Gardsley, and it had been done in springtime. The paper had been crumpled, then flattened, and some of the charcoal lines were blurred.

Realizing that it was a drawing that she had discarded, she cast her mind back to when she must have sketched this particular subject. It had been the day that she had first seen James, when he had visited her father. He must have found the drawing then.

She touched the elaborate gilded frame, which was far more costly than the sketch deserved. No one would frame such a drawing for its own sake, so it must have been for the sake of the artist. She felt incipient tears behind her eyes. Yes, he must care for her, little though she deserved such regard.

Swallowing hard, she withdrew and quietly searched the public areas of the house, stopping when she discovered that the French doors in the drawing room were unlatched. The housekeeper would never have permitted such laxity, so James must have gone outside this way.

He could be anywhere. She refused to believe that he would harm himself—the incident in the library couldn't have been that upsetting—so soon he would come home. Determined to wait up for him, she returned to his rooms and curled up on the sofa with a knee rug around her. But in spite of her intention to stay awake, eventually fatigue overcame her.

She was awakened by his return, even though he made no sound. Her head jerked up from the sofa, and she stared at her husband. His hood was firmly in place, and he was so still that she could tell nothing of his mood. Her lamp was guttering, but outside the sky was starting to lighten.

Quietly he said, "You should be in bed, Ariel."

She drew a shaky breath and went straight to the heart of the matter. "James, what happened in the library—*nothing* happened. I didn't see you, just unexpected movement. That's why I was surprised."

She was still fumbling for words when he raised one hand, cutting her off with his gesture. "Of course nothing happened," he agreed in an utterly dispassionate voice. "It occurred to me that since you've been lonely, perhaps you should visit your friend Anna for a few weeks."

Ariel rose from the sofa, the knee rug clutched around her. "Don't send me away, James," she begged. "You don't understand."

As if she hadn't spoken, he said, "You'll like Hampstead—close enough to London to be interesting, far enough away to be quiet. Send Mrs. Talbott a note today and see if it's convenient for you to come."

He stepped to one side, holding the door open in an unmistakable invitation to leave. "You might as well go. With winter coming there's much to be done around the estate and I won't have much time for you. I don't want you to be bored, so it will be best if you visit your friend."

She repeated desperately, "James, you don't understand!"

"What is there to understand?" he asked, still in that soft, implacable voice.

Defeated, she walked to the door. She paused a moment when she was closest to him, wondering if she should take his hand, if touch might convince him where words couldn't.

Sharply, as if reading her mind, he said, "Don't."

A moment later she was in the hall outside and his door had been firmly shut behind her. Numbly she pulled the knee rug around her shivering body and walked down the long passage to her own rooms.

Perhaps she should do what he suggested. Not only would she benefit from Anna's warm good sense, but if she was gone for a fortnight or so, it would give her husband time to recover from the unintentional hurt she had inflicted. When she returned, he would be more open to her explanation. Then they could begin again. After all, the incident had been so trivial.

She refused to believe that he might not recover from it.

Talbott House, Hampstead
October 20th
Dear James,

Just a note to tell you that I've arrived safely. It's wonderful to see Anna again, she is positively blooming. Mr. Talbott is a broad, merry elf who is everything hospitable. He makes wonderful toys for the children. I had wondered if his daughters might resent the fact that Anna went from being their governess to their mother, but they adore her. Apparently their own mother died when they were very young.

I'll finish this now so that it can go out in the next post, but I'll write a longer letter tonight.

Your loving wife,
Ariel

Talbott House, Hampstead
November 10th
Dear James,

You were certainly right about Hampstead. It's a charming place, full of interesting people. Not at all like the ghastly society sorts that I met during my Season.

Remember the letter I wrote where I wondered who owned Hampstead Heath? I've since been told that the gentleman who held the manorial rights to the heath recently sold them to the Metropolitan Board of Works so that the area will be preserved for public use forever. I was glad to learn that, for people need places like the heath. Walking there reminds me a bit of Belleterre, though of course not so quiet and lovely.

Last night we dined with a young literary gentlemen, a Mr. Glades. He is something of a radical, for he teased me about being Lady Falconer. He's very clever—almost as much so as you—but his mind is less open, I think.

I know you must be terribly busy, but if you found time to scribble a note to tell me how you are, I would much appreciate it. Of course, soon I'll be home myself, so you needn't go to any special bother.

Your loving wife,
Ariel

Belleterre
November 20th
My dear Ariel,

No need to rush back. I'm very busy doing a survey of improvements needed on the tenant farms. My regards to your amiable host and hostess.

Falconer

Talbott House, Hampstead
December 1st
Dear James,

Last week, to amuse the girls, I made some sketches illustrating the story of Dick Whittington's cat. Without my knowing, Mr. Talbott showed them to a publisher friend of his, a Mr. Howard, and now the fellow wants me to illustrate a children's book for him! He says my drawings are "magical," which sounds very nice, though I don't know quite what he means by it. While I'm flattered by his offer, I don't know whether I should accept. Would you object to having your wife involved in a commercial venture? If you don't like the idea, of course I shan't do it.

Almost time for tea—I'll add to this later tonight.

I miss you very much.

Your loving wife,
Ariel

Belleterre
December 3rd
My dear Ariel,

Of course I don't object to you selling your work. Very proper of Mr. Howard to appreciate your talent.

In fact, perhaps you should purchase a house in Hampstead since you've made so many friends there. It will be convenient if you decide to illustrate more children's books. Find a house you really like—cost is no object.

Falconer

Talbott House, Hampstead
December 4th
Dear James,

While I like Hampstead, I'm not sure we need a second house, and I certainly can't buy one unless you see it. We can discuss the matter when I come home.

Also, I want to ask your opinion of the financial arrangements Mr. Howard has suggested. I don't particularly care about the money, for your generosity gives me far more than I need, but I don't want to be silly about it, either. Later this evening I'll copy out the details of his proposal, then post this letter in the morning. I look forward to your reply.

> Your loving wife,
> Ariel

Belleterre
December 6th
My dear Ariel,

Mr. Howard's contract seems fair. However, I can't recommend that you return to Kent just now, for the weather has been very gray and dismal. Far better to stay with your friends, since Hampstead and London will be more amusing than the country. Besides, from what you've said, I gather that all of the Talbotts grieve when you talk about leaving. And what of the literary Mr. Glades? You said he claims you are his muse— surely you don't want to leave the chap inspirationless.

> Falconer

Talbott House, Hampstead
December 7th
Dear James,

When I mentioned your letter to Anna, she suggested that you might like to come to Hampstead, and we could spend Christmas with the Talbotts. She says there is much jolliness and celebration. Perhaps too much—*I'm not sure that it would be the sort of thing you'd like. Also, as much as I love Anna and her family, I would rather my first Christmas with you was a quiet one, just the two of us. And Cerberus and Tripod, of course. Has Tripod forgiven me for going away? Cats being what they are, she has probably expunged me from her memory for my desertion.*

Eagerly awaiting your reply,

Your loving wife,
Ariel

P.S. The only inspiration Mr. Glades cares for or needs is the sound of his own voice.

Falconer finished the letter, then closed his eyes in pain. He could hear her voice in every line, see her vibrant image in his mind. It was torture to read her letters, and she wrote faithfully every day, with only rare, faint reproaches for his almost total lack of response.

Yet what could he write back? *I am dying for love of you, beloved, come home, come home.* Not the sort of letter one could write to a woman who had been horrified to see his face.

Drearily he got to his feet and stared out the library window. The fitful weather had produced a brief bit of sunshine, but it was winter in his heart. Loyal child that she was, Ariel would come home if he let her, but to what? Her life in Hampstead was full and happy. What would she have at Belleterre but disgust and loneliness? He could not allow her to return.

Mr. Glades, the literary gentleman, figured regularly in her letters. Clearly the man was besotted with her, though she never said as much. Perhaps, in her innocence, Ariel did not realize the fact.

Falconer had had the man investigated and discovered that the Honorable William Glades was handsome, wealthy, and talented, part of a glittering literary circle. He was also considered an honorable young man. A bit full of himself, like clever young chaps often were, but otherwise he was exactly the sort of man Ariel should have married.

Falconer leaned heavily against the window frame. He'd once read of savages who could will their own deaths. Though he'd been skeptical at the time, now he believed that it was possible to do such a thing. In fact, it would be easy to die. . . .

He wrapped his arms around himself, trying to numb his despairing grief. The heart of his spirit was dead, and it would only be a matter of time until his physical heart also stopped.

The sunshine was gone and the sky had darkened so quickly that he could see his own face faintly reflected in the window glass. He shuddered at the sight, then returned to his desk and lifted his pen.

> *Belleterre*
> *December 8th*
> *My dear Ariel,*
>
> *I never celebrate Christmas; it's a foolish combination of sentimentality, exaggerated piety, and paganism. Still, I don't want to deprive you of the festivities, so I think you should stay with the Talbotts for the holidays.*
>
> *Falconer*

After reading her husband's latest letter, Ariel lay down on her bed and curled up like a hurt child. She did not cry, for in the previous two months she had shed so many tears that now she had none left to mourn this ultimate rejection. Though James was too courteous to say so outright, it was obvious that he didn't want her ever to come back to Belleterre. She still believed that he had once cared for her, at least a little, but plainly his feelings had died that night in the library.

She forced herself to face her future. Though she loved her husband, he would never love her; he couldn't even bear to have her under his roof. Therefore she might as well take his suggestion and buy a house in Hampstead. There was a charming old cottage for sale only five minutes' walk from the Talbotts. It had a lovely view over Hampstead Heath and was just the right size for a woman and a servant. Though James would have to pay for it, she vowed to work hard at illustration so that eventually she would no longer need his money to survive.

Supporting herself now seemed possible. It would be far harder to make the rest of her life worth living.

Christmas

"Did you have a nice walk?" Anna called.

"Splendid." Ariel knelt and helped little Jane Talbott from her cocoon of coat, bonnet, scarf, and muff. "Even in winter the heath is full of wonderful, subtle colors. I never tire of it."

The older girl, Libby, said, "Hurry, Janie, for we can't help decorate the tree until we've had tea."

Anna, a tall woman with nut brown hair, entered the front hall. "Thank you for taking the girls for a walk to wear down their high spirits." She smiled indulgently as the children scampered off to the nursery. "They're so excited that I'm afraid they'll vibrate to pieces between now and Christmas. And if they don't, I will!"

"Courage—only two more days to go." Ariel removed her own coat and bonnet. "Did anything come in the post for me?"

"This package arrived from Mr. Howard." Anna lifted it from the hall table and handed it over.

"Nothing from Belleterre?"

"No, dear," Anna said quietly.

Ariel glanced up and made herself smile. "Don't look so sorry for me, Anna. I daresay this is all for the best."

Her friend's eyes were compassionate, but she was too wise to offer sympathy when Ariel's emotions were so fragile. Instead she said, "Certainly everyone in Talbott House will be in raptures if you buy Dove Cottage. You'll never get Jane and Libby out from under your feet."

"I love having them around," Ariel said. "And Libby has real drawing talent. It's a pleasure to teach her." Glancing at the package from the publisher, she continued, "If you'll excuse me, I'll go up to my room. Mr. Howard said he was going to send another story for me to consider."

As Ariel climbed the stairs, she gave thanks for Anna's understanding. All of the Talbotts had been wonderful; Ariel did not know how she would have survived the last two months without their warmth and liveliness.

As a Christmas present to the family, she had done an oil painting of the four of them together. It was one of the best pieces of work she'd ever done; sorrow seemed to be honing her artistic skills.

As she expected, the package contained the project that Mr. Howard wanted her to do next. He had been so pleased with *Puss in Boots* that he was now talking of doing an entire series of classic fairy tales, all to be illustrated by Ariel.

With a stir of interest she saw that he had sent her two different *Beauty and the Beast* books. Oddly enough, though Ariel had a vague knowledge of the story, she had never read one of the many versions of the old folk tale. Lifting the larger of the volumes, she began to read and soon discovered that it was a much more powerful story than *Puss in Boots*. Moreover, the visual possibilities were enticing.

Ariel was halfway through when the back of her neck began to prickle. In an odd way the tale resembled her own life, though reality was sadder and more sordid. At the end it was a relief to learn that Beauty and her Beast lived happily ever after. Ariel supposed that was why people read such fanciful tales: because real life couldn't be trusted to end as well. But as she set the story aside, she was haunted by the image of the Beast, who had almost died of sorrow when Beauty left him.

The rest of the day was taken up with festivities. She helped the Talbotts decorate the tree. After the girls were sent giggling to bed, the adults went to a nearby house where they shared hot mulled wine and conversation with a dozen other neighbors. The small party helped distract Ariel from her misery. As she went to bed, she gave thanks that the next few days would be so busy. By the beginning of the New Year, she might be prepared to face her new life.

But the old life was not done with her, for she fell asleep and dreamed of *Beauty and the Beast*. She herself was Beauty, young and confused, first fearing the Beast who held her captive, then learning to love him. What turned the dream into nightmare was the fact that her captor was not a leonine monster but James. He was a haunted, noble creature who was dying for lack of love, and as life ebbed from him, he called out to her.

She awoke with an agonized cry. How could she have left him? How could she have let him send her away? Even awake, she heard his voice in her mind, the deep, desolate tones echoing across the miles that separated them. She slid out of her bed, determined to leave instantly for Belleterre.

As soon as her feet hit the icy floor, she realized the foolishness of her impulse. It was three in the morning and she couldn't leave for hours yet.

Still, she could pack her belongings so that she would be ready first thing. She threw herself into the task with frantic haste and was done in half an hour.

The thought of the hours still to wait made her want to shriek with frustration. Then inspiration struck. She settled down at her desk with drawing paper, pen, and ink.

Feeling as if another hand guided her own, she drew a series of pictures with feverish, slashing strokes. She had not bought a Christmas gift for her husband since he had been so firmly opposed to celebrating the holiday. Now she was creating a gift so vivid that it might as well have been drawn with her heart's blood rather than India ink.

As she wept over the last drawing, she prayed that he would accept it in the spirit offered.

THE footman opened the front door of Belleterre and blinked in surprise. "Lady Falconer?"

"None other," Ariel said crisply as she swept past him into the front hall. "Is my husband in the house?"

"No, my lady. I believe he intended to be out on the estate all day."

"Very well." She surveyed her surroundings, unsurprised to see that there wasn't a trace of holiday decoration. "Please ask Mrs. Wilcox to join me in the morning room immediately. Then have my things taken to my room. Be particularly careful of the drawing portfolio."

As the footman hastened to obey, Ariel went to the morning room, which was the smallest and friendliest of the public rooms. While she waited for the housekeeper, Tripod came skipping into the room. The cat was halfway to Ariel before she remembered her grievance. With ostentatious disdain, Tripod sat down, her back turned to the mistress of the house who had dared to go away for so long. Only the twitching tip of her tail betrayed her mood.

"We'll have none of that, Tripod." Ariel scooped the cat into her arms and began scratching around the feline ears. Within a minute, the cat began to purr and stretch out her neck so that her chin could be scratched. Ariel hoped wryly that her husband would be as easy to bring around.

Soon Mrs. Wilcox joined her. Always dignified, today the housekeeper was positively arctic. In a voice that was only just within the bounds of politeness, she said, "Since your arrival was unexpected, your ladyship, it will take a few minutes to freshen your rooms."

Ignoring the comment, Ariel said, "How is my husband?" When the housekeeper hesitated, Ariel prompted, "Speak freely."

Mrs. Wilcox needed no more encouragement. "Very poorly, my lady, and it's all your fault! The master looks as if he's aged a hundred years since you left. How could you go away for so long, after all he's done for you?"

How bad was "very poorly"? Though she ached, Ariel kept her voice even. She was mistress of Belleterre, and she intended to fill the position properly. "I left because he sent me away," she said calmly. "It was very bad of me to obey him. It shan't happen again."

She set down the cat and stripped off her gloves. "I want every servant in the house put to work decorating Belleterre for the holidays. Greens, ribbons, wreaths, candles . . . everything. Send a man to cut a tree for the morning room, and have the cook prepare a Christmas Eve feast. I realize that time is limited, but I'm sure Cook will do a fine job with what is available. Oh, whenever the table is set in the future, always put my place next to my husband's rather than at the far end."

Mrs. Wilcox's jaw dropped. Ariel added, "And when doing the decorating and cooking, don't stint on the servants' quarters. I want this to be a holiday Belleterre will never forget. Now off with you—there's much to be done."

"Yes, my lady," the housekeeper said, her eyes beginning to shine. She paused just before leaving the room. "You won't leave again, will you? He needs you something fierce."

"Wild horses won't get me away unless he comes, too," Ariel promised. She needed her husband something fierce herself.

CHRISTMAS Eve—the thought of going back to the empty house was almost more than Falconer could bear.

He was so weary in spirit that he didn't notice how brightly lit the house was, but when he entered the front hall he was struck by the scent of pine and holly.

He stopped, blinking at the sight that met his eyes. The hall was wreathed in garlands of greenery accented by scarlet berries and bows, and a footman stood on a ladder, tucking shiny holly leaves behind a pier glass for the final decorative touch.

Falconer demanded, "By whose order was this done?"

As the nervous footman fumbled for a reply, a clear, light voice said, "Mine, James."

He would recognize her voice anywhere, yet it was so unexpected that he couldn't believe she was really here. Even when he turned and saw his wife walking down the hall toward him, he was sure he must be hallucinating. Exquisite in a scarlet-trimmed gown, her flaxen tresses tied back simply with a black velvet bow, she had to be an illusion born of his despairing dreams.

But she certainly looked real. Stopping in front of him, Ariel said, "Come and see the tree before you go up to bathe and change for dinner."

Bemused, he followed her into the morning room, which was scented by tangy evergreens and sweet-burning applewood logs. Ariel gestured at the tall fir that had been set up in one corner. "Patterson chose the tree. Lovely, isn't it?"

Hoarsely he said, "Ariel, why did you come back?"

"I am your wife and Belleterre is my home," she said mildly. "Where else would I be at Christmas?"

"I told you to spend the holiday with your friends."

She linked her fingers together in front of her, the knuckles showing white. "When we married, you offered me a home. Are you withdrawing that offer?"

"You don't belong here." Anguish lanced through him, as if a knife was being turned in his heart. He had thought that she understood and accepted that their lives should lie apart, but apparently not. Now he must go through the agony of saying the words out loud; he must send her away again. "You mustn't blight your life through misplaced loyalty, Ariel. Our marriage is one of convenience only. I'm almost twice your age—you're scarcely more than a child."

"I'm old enough to be your wife," she retorted.

He edged toward the shadowed end of the room, trying desperately to keep his defenses from crumbling. "I never wanted a wife."

"But you have one," she said softly. "Why do you run from me, James? I know I'm not clever, but I love you. Is it so unthinkable that we be truly married?"

"Love?" he said, unable to suppress his bitterness. "How could a beautiful girl like you possibly love a man like me?"

His words acted like a spark on tinder. "How dare you!" she said furiously, looking like a spun sugar angel on the verge of explosion. "Because men think me beautiful, do you think I have no heart? Do you think I am so superficial, so blinded by my own reflection in the mirror, that I cannot see your strength and kindness and wit? You insult me, my lord."

Helplessly he said, "I meant no insult, Ariel, but how can you love a man whose face you have never seen?"

Her blues eyes narrowed. "If I were blind and could see nothing, would you think me incapable of love?"

"Of course not, but this is different."

"It's *not* different!" Her voice softened. "I fell in love with you because of your words and deeds, James. Compared to them, appearance is of no great importance."

When the black folds of his robe quivered she knew that he was deeply affected, but not yet convinced. She knelt by the tree and pulled out the portfolio of drawings she had done for him. "If you want to know how I see you, look at these."

Hesitantly he took the portfolio and laid it on a table. Ariel stood next to him as he paged through the loose drawings. If any of her work had magic, it was this, for the drawings came straight from her heart and soul. The images made up a modern *Beauty and the Beast* and showed exactly how she had seen her husband, from her first glimpse of him at Gardsley to the present. Under each picture she had written a few spare words to carry the story.

James was the focus of every picture, forceful, mysterious, larger than life. Though his face was never shown, he was so compelling that the eye could not look elsewhere. He was the enigmatic Black Beast of Belleterre, his dark robes billowing about him like thunderclouds. He was the compassionate, patient Lord Falconer, caring for everyone and everything around him. And he was James, surrounded by adoring birds and beasts, for every creature who knew him could not help but love him.

Then he sent Ariel away. The last drawing showed him lying in the Belleterre woods on the point of death, his powerful body drained of strength and his great heart broken. Ariel wept beside him, her pale hair falling about them like a mourning veil. The legend below read, "I heard your voice on the wind."

He turned to the last sheet and found a blank page. "How does the story end?" he asked, his voice shaking.

"I don't know," she whispered. "The ending hasn't been written yet. The only thing I know is that I love you."

He spun away, his swift steps taking him into the shadows at the far end of the room. There he stood motionless for an endless interval, his rigid back to Ariel, before he turned to face her. "I was ugly even as a child. My mother used to say what a pity it was that I took after my maternal grandfather. But that was normal ugliness and would not have mattered greatly. What you will see now is a result of what happened when I was eight."

She heard his ragged inhalation, saw the tremor in his hands as he raised them to his hood, then slowly pulled the folds of fabric down to his shoulders. Her eyes widened when she saw that he was entirely bald. Of course; it explained why she had had the fleeting impression of a skull when she'd seen him in the library.

Yet the effect, though startling, was not unattractive, for his head was well shaped and he had dark, well-defined brows and lashes. He might have modeled for an Asiatic warlord in a painting by one of the great Romantic artists.

Voice taut, he continued, "My mother was taking me to Eton for my first term, and we spent the night at Falconer House in London. That night there was a gas explosion in her bedroom. I woke and tried to help her, but she was already dead."

He raised his damaged left hand so Ariel could see it clearly. "This happened when I pulled her body from the burning room. The smaller scars on my scalp and neck were made by hot embers that fell on me." He touched his bare head. "Afterward I was struck with brain fever and was delirious for weeks. They thought I would die. Obviously I didn't, but my hair fell out and never grew back. I was never sent to school, either—it was considered 'unsuitable.' Instead my father installed me at a minor estate in the Midlands, so he wouldn't have to think about me."

James closed his eyes for a moment, his expression stark. "Can you be as accepting in the particular as you were in the abstract?"

Ariel walked toward him, and for the first time their gazes met. His eyes were a deep, haunted gray-green, capable of seeing things most men never dreamed of. Coming to a stop directly in front of him, she said honestly, "You have the most beautiful eyes I've ever seen."

His mouth twisted. "And the rest of me? My father refused to look at me, my tutor often told me how lucky I was to have my hideousness visible rather than concealing it as most men do."

She smiled and shook her head. "You're a fraud, my love. I'm almost disappointed. I'd expected much worse."

His expression shuttered. "Surely you're not going to lie and call me handsome."

"No, you're not handsome." She raised her hands and skimmed her artist's fingers over the planes of his face, feeling the subtle irregularity of long-healed scars, the masculine prickle of end-of-the day whiskers.

"You have strong, craggy bones—too strong for the face of a child. Even without the effects of fire and fever, it would have taken years to grow into these features. Did you ever see a picture of Mr. Lincoln, the American president who was shot a few years ago? He had a similar kind of face. No one would ever call it handsome, but he was greatly loved and deeply mourned."

"As I recall, the gentleman did have a good head of hair," James said wryly.

Ariel shrugged. "A bald child would be startling, almost shocking. Yet now that you are a man, the effect is not unpleasant—rather dramatic and interesting, actually."

She stood on her tiptoes and slid her arms around his neck, then pressed her cheek to his. As tension sizzled between them, she murmured, "Now that you have nothing to hide, will you promise not to send me away again? For I love you so much that I don't think I could survive another separation."

His arms came around her with crushing force. She was slim but strong, and so beautiful that he could scarcely bear it. "Unlike the Beast in your story, I can't turn into a handsome prince," he said intensely, "but I loved you from the first moment I saw you, wife of my heart, and I swear I will never stop loving you."

Her laughter rang like silver bells. "To be honest, in both the books Mr. Howard sent me, the handsome prince at the end was quite insipid. Your face has character—it's been molded by suffering and compassion and will never be boring." She tilted her head back, her shining gilt hair spilling over his wrists. Suddenly shy, she said, "Did you notice what's above your head?"

He glanced up and saw mistletoe affixed to the chandelier, then looked back at her yearning face. Curbing his fierce hunger so that he wouldn't overwhelm her, he bent his head and touched his lips to hers. It was a kiss of sweetness and wonder, a promise of things to come. His heart beat with such force that he wondered if he could survive such happiness.

Instinct made him end the kiss, for they risked being consumed by the flames of their own emotions. Far better to go slowly, to savor every moment of the miracle they had been granted.

Understanding without words, Ariel said breathlessly, "It's time we changed for dinner, for it's going to take some time to decorate the tree. I brought some lovely, new ornaments from London. I hope you'll like them."

He kissed her hands, then released her. "I'll adore them."

Christmas Eve became a magical courtship. He discarded his robe. Then they dined close enough to touch knees and fingers rather than being separated by a dozen feet of polished mahogany. Laughing and talking, they turned the tree into a shining, candlelit fantasy. And the whole time, they were spinning a web of pure enchantment between them. Every brush of their fingertips, every shy glance, every shared laugh at the antics of Cerberus and Tripod, intensified their mutual desire.

When they went upstairs, he hesitated at her door, still not quite able to believe. Wordlessly she drew him into her room and went into his arms. As they kissed, he discovered an unexpected aptitude for freeing her from her complicated evening gown.

Her slim, curving body was perfect, as he had known it would be. With lips and tongue and hands, he worshiped her, as enraptured by her response as by the feel of her silken skin under his mouth. She was light and sweetness, the essence of woman that all men craved, yet at the same time uniquely Ariel.

She gave herself to him with absolute trust, and the gift healed the dark places inside of him. He could actually feel blackness crumbling until his heart was free of a lifetime of hurt and loneliness. Such vulnerability should have terrified him, but her trust called forth equal trust from him.

Already he could scarcely remember the haunted man who had been unable to believe in love.

In return for her trust, he gave her passion, using all of his skill, all of his sensitivity, all of his tenderness. Their bodies came together as if they were two halves of the same whole that had finally been joined, and when she cried out in joyous wonder, it was the sweetest sound he'd ever heard.

After passion had been satisfied for the first time, they lay tranquil in each other's arms. He had never known such rapture, or such humility.

In the distance, church bells began to toll. "Midnight," he murmured. "The parish church rings the changes to celebrate the beginning of Christmas Day."

Ariel stretched luxuriously, then settled against him again. "Christmas—a time of miracles and new beginnings. What could be more appropriate?"

"Indeed." He brushed his fingers through her hair, marveling at the spun-silk texture. "I'm sorry, my love, I didn't get you a present."

She laughed softly. "You gave me yourself, James. What greater gift could I possibly want?"